The House of the Bright-Eyed Wolf

Michael Hayward

Also by Michael Hayward

Fiction
Fortuna's Favour

Poetry
Rosa's Last Ride
Reproductions
A Victorian Artist at Home
Fire on the Mountain
The Metamorphic Technique

For further details please contact:
mhayward57@yahoo.com

Copyright © Michael Hayward 2024
All rights reserved
ISBN: 9798346143741

The cover illustration is taken from the genealogical
roll of the kings of England (modified)

To the past and present members of the Blue Room writing group

Contents

1. The Funeral 1
2. Aclea 36
3. Growing Pains 70
4. Journey to Rome 109
5. Borderlands 149
6. A Time for Giving 188
7. Pilgrims' Goal 227
8. Hospitality 259
9. Homecoming 286
10. Mercia 311
11. The Bride 349
12. The Followers of Guernir 382
13. The Flux 414

Unknown — Aethelwulf — Osburh

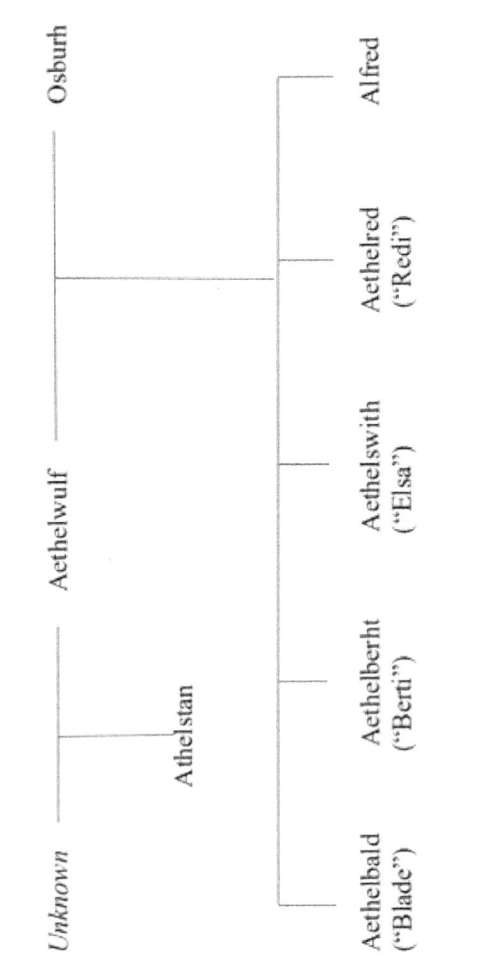

Athelstan

Aethelbald ("Blade")
Aethelberht ("Berti")
Aethelswith ("Elsa")
Aethelred ("Redi")
Alfred

The Royal House of Wessex 850 AD

1. The Funeral

King Aethelwulf stood on the beach at Reculver, looking down at the body of his son. It was a grey, cold day with a light drizzle in the air. The sort of day when spring seems more hopeless than winter. He stared across the beach at the great North Sea breaking sullenly against the rocks guarding the harbour. He had always feared this sea. Even at the time of his greatest success, when he'd swept into this land from the west as great Mercia crumbled. Even then, the sea had been what it was now – a bringer of death, and the instruments of death.

He looked back down at his son. They had put him in a rock pool to preserve the body for his father's viewing. A large stone had been placed over his chest to prevent him floating to the surface. Athelstan – noble stone. He had not thought of this when he had named him so. The young man's lips were pale, as was his face. There was a bruise on his temple which would have come from a blow while he was still alive. Someone had strapped up his jaw to prevent that terrible yawn of death. His features were beginning to swell a little. But, even so, he almost looked as though he might pull himself up from beneath the stone, emerge spluttering into the air, and be what he had been before. A bit of a nuisance, touchy, headstrong, brave as a lion. He sensed the bitterness of his loss, but from a distance somehow. No doubt it would come to him later, with the smart of memories and hopes unfulfilled.

Aethelwulf sighed and turned away. Ealdorman Elchere, who had been watching him closely, came forward.

'Is my lord the king satisfied that this is his son, King Athelstan?'

'Yes, it's him,' Aethelwulf replied. 'Tell me how it happened.'

'The king knows that we received news from fishermen that large numbers of pagan ships were heading here. We fought them away last autumn, but they came back onto the island when the storms came. We cleared them away again only a month past but they were coming back. My lord Athelstan was determined that this time they would not be able to land.'

'I know,' said Aethelwulf. Elchere was not usually so long in getting to the point. A stubborn, doughty fighter, but normally one of few words. He must be nervous. Perhaps he thinks I'll hold him responsible? A king's son, himself a king, does not die every day.

'My lord Athelstan sent me with some boats to Richborough to guard his rear. The pagans often attack the channel at both ends.'

Aethelwulf nodded. It was a problem he was familiar with. This channel of water at the far end of his realm, protected from storms by the bulk of the Isle of Thanet, had been a weakness since time began. Once in the channel, St Augustine's Canterbury, soul of the nation, was but an easy sail away.

'And did any pagan ships show at Richborough/'

'Yes, my lord,' Elchere replied eagerly. 'Ten ships, but we beat them away.'

'And in the north?'

Elchere's face fell. 'Hundreds, my lord. An invasion fleet. Witnesses talk of the whole sea being covered with ships.'

'And how many did Athelstan have?"

'Eighty.'

'*Eighty?* And he set out to do battle with hundreds?'

'It wasn't like that, my lord. To begin with, there were only about eighty pagan ships. The numbers were even. And we had been successful against them many times. The other ships were waiting until my lord Athelstan was committed to the fight. Only then did they appear.'

'But surely someone must have seen them? Do you have no system of lookouts?'

'We do, my lord, but the fishermen had all taken flight at the appearance of the first ships.'

'What about lookouts on the shore?'

'The ships were far out to sea, my lord. By the time they were seen from the shore, it was too late.'

Aethelwulf sighed again. He had no right to judge. Athelstan had held this vulnerable eastern land for him since little more than a boy. It was a heavy responsibility he had given him. And he had done so well. So well that he'd started to take him for granted? He felt a stirring of guilt, which he beat back down. He could not afford self-accusations with the sea wolves at loose on the land once more. 'How many survived?'

'We lost eighteen boats. Many of them managed to escape to the west as the pagans sailed down the channel. Of those we lost, some of the crew made it to shore.'

'Did anyone survive from my son's boat?'

'Yes, my lord.'

'The captain?'

'Yes.'

'Is he here?'

If Ealdorman Elchere was nervous facing the king, the Friesian captain was terrified. Visibly shaking and stammering. 'My lord king, my lord king,' he threw himself at Aethelwulf's feet. 'If only it had been me!'

'Get up,' said Aethelwulf quietly.

The captain got slowly to his feet, his gaze fixed on the ground.

'I want to know what happened,' Aethelwulf said simply. 'I know that you sailed out to battle, thinking you were facing a similar number, and that many more pagan ships then arrived. I have seen my son's body. He has a bruise on his temple but it doesn't look to be a death wound. I believe he must have drowned.'

'Yes, my lord king.' The Friesian was calmer now, although he kept his eyes averted. They were good sailors, the Friesians. And this captain, Aethelwulf knew, was one of the best.

'So, did you engage the pagans?'

'We spent a long time getting into position beside them, my lord. It's a difficult stretch of water – there are rocks and shallows. And a north-easterly was blowing, which helped the pagans and hindered us. They had planned the attack for when a north-easterly was blowing, of course. They were trying to go round us and we had to work flat out to stop them.'

'And were you successful?'

'We caught the first ship.' This time the captain raised his eyes and Aethelwulf could see a hint of pride in them. 'We got the irons on it and boarded it. My lord Athelstan was the first to board.'

'And then?'

'Then I saw the other pagan ships massing in the distance. And our own boats starting to fly before them. But we couldn't move. We were tied to another ship and there was a battle going on. I couldn't disengage with my lord Athelstan and most of our men fighting there. By the time they had overcome the enemy and we were in a position to cut ourselves free, the whole pagan fleet was almost upon us.'

'And what did my lord Athelstan tell you to do?'

'To make for the west as fast as I could. He went to man an oar himself. But we were a long way behind most of the others.'

'Did the pagans catch you?'

'No, my lord king,' the captain replied gloomily. "But they had ships on either side of us, and they drove us onto The Devil's Rock.' And with these words, his composure left him. 'I'm so sorry!' he cried, and fell to his knees once more.

Aethelwulf had seen boats drive onto rocks before and knew the terror of the collision, the rending boat, the roaring sea, and jeering sea wolves on every side. The memory enough to break this seasoned captain. Once again, he felt the sharpness of Athelstan's loss. They would bury him as a king in Canterbury.

But first, the captain at his feet. He must have faced death many times on the sea, but seemed completely unmanned by the thought of it at his hands. Or was it the disgrace he feared? Certainly, he would never sail a ship again in this country. But Aethelwulf felt no desire for another death.

'You must leave this land,' he said. 'You and your crew. Go home, and do not come here again. You are not welcome in Wessex any more. Any of you found here in three days' time will be put to death.'

The captain looked up at him, got to his feet and bowed. 'Thank you, my lord king. I will tell of your mercy.'

Aethelwulf turned back to a group of his companions, dismissing the captain from his thoughts. 'Diarmait,' he called out.

An elderly man, more shabbily dressed than the others, came forward.

'Sire?' he said in a pleasantly soft Irish voice.

'This is Athelstan,' Aethelwulf said, indicating the body in the pool. 'My eldest son. I don't think you ever met. Athelstan died defending this land from pagan invaders. He went out with fifty boats, overcame one of the pagan ships and was then surrounded by so many of the enemy that the sea barely had room to hold them all. They surrounded my son to cut him down but the home of the winds took him before they could do so. And now she gives him back to us.'

Diarmait looked down sympathetically at the body. 'He almost looks as though he could rise again.'

'Only Our Lord could rise again,' Aethelwulf responded. 'But he can live again. In your words. I want you to add him to our family's tale.'

'Certainly, Sire. When will you hear it?'

'Tomorrow night. After the funeral.'

Diarmait bowed and remained where he was, staring at the face of the young man in the pool.

Aethelwulf motioned Elchere to follow him and they walked a little way along the beach.

'Is Canterbury safe?'

'Yes, my lord king. It took two days, but we fought them off.'

'How much is damaged?'

'The abbey badly. Being outside the walls, it had to be abandoned. The pagans took it over. And burnt it when they left.'

'The abbot?'

'Is safe, as are the monks. They had plenty of warning this time and made it into the town. With the relics and treasures.'

'The cathedral?'

'Some minor damage around the gates and outbuildings. We stopped them taking it. They tried to start fires but we put them out.'

'The town?'

'Some areas bad. Mostly in the south. We had to pull back from there to defend the cathedral and the archbishop. A number of fires and,' Elchere made a face, 'the usual.'

The usual. Women violated. Some driven mad. Children with their skulls smashed as a barbaric game. Men tortured to please savage gods, or to assuage the anger of devils denied treasure and an easy victory. What sort of judgement on them was this horror let loose from the bowels of hell?

'How did you get rid of them?'

'Sent a force upriver. Ships. are the only things they really care about – they'd rather lose half a crew than a ship.' Elchere shrugged. 'Maybe there was easier prey elsewhere.'

'And they've gone west?'

Elchere nodded. 'They landed at Rochester. We fought them off again. They've moved on to London.'

'It's more than just a raid, then?'

'They must have close to two hundred ships. They want more than gold this time. They want land.'

Aethelwulf fought down a feeling of revulsion at the thought of such people as neighbours. 'If they want land, they'll have to fight for it,' he said thoughtfully. 'And on our terms, not theirs. Away from their ships.'

'Yes.'

'You think it will come to that?'

'I'm certain of it, my lord. These people have no homes any more, only their ships. They tried to take the Franks' land. The Franks beat them off, and so they've come here to take ours.'

'And meanwhile they're in Mercia. How long do you think the Mercians will hold them?'

'They have to fight. King Beorthwulf cannot afford to lose London.'

Aethelwulf nodded. Elchere knew more than how to fight. Mercia was riven with factions. Beorthwulf had seized power ten years ago but his hold on the crown had never been secure. There were plenty of contenders ready to take his place should he prove unequal to defending the great port.

'So, London should keep them busy for a few weeks at least?'

'Yes, my lord.'

'Long enough to bury my son,' said Aethelwulf bleakly.

*

The nave of the cavernous cathedral was cold and gloomy, in contrast to the chancel, where hundreds of candles cast a brilliant light. Within this haven of light, the three officiating priests, in white robes edged with black, intoned the Latin Mass of the Dead. The coffin of Athelstan, king of Kent and Sussex, rested on a low table before them. Swinging censers dispatched the heavy sweetness of frankincense into the borders between light and gloom, resting above the congregation in a haze. At regular intervals in the mass, monks from behind a screen would sing, as though from another world, of sorrow and consolation.

King Aethelwulf, in the front row of the nave, close both to the coffin and the light, felt his heart and spirit rising with the smoke coils of frankincense and the monks' angelic singing into a better, more spacious world. How he envied those monks! What wouldn't he give to live with their assurance of deliverance? But then, only a few days ago, they had been fleeing in terror from the pagans. None of us, it seems, can escape this dark world for more than a few transcendent moments. Except through death. He looked at his son's coffin, the polished wood shining in the candle light. No, he did not envy Athelstan. Poor boy. To be taken so young and unawares. Unready perhaps? The thought troubled him and he crossed himself automatically and muttered a prayer for his son's soul. Who knew what lay beyond for any of us? On the screen, from behind which the monks were singing so sweetly, was painted a Day of Judgment, with those on the Saviour's left hand tumbling or being pulled down by demons into the fires of hell. Maybe this is what is happening to us already? Maybe these are the final days of which the Saviour spoke?

He thought back a few hours to his entrance into Canterbury. The blackened gates and ruined buildings, the haggard faces looking up at him, some with no hope in their eyes. No one cheered, but there were a few curses hurled at him from the outskirts of the crowd. And he saw a few demonic, mocking smiles. Either from those driven crazy, or something worse. Satan lingering in those he had touched.

His mind went back to happier times, a quarter of a century ago, when his father had defeated great Mercia and he himself had swept through Sussex and Kent as their acclaimed new king. The crowds had cheered him then. And later, after his father's death, when he had returned west to rule the Wessex heartland, sending Athelstan to rule Sussex and Kent in his place. Then it had seemed that the future of their house was secure. He had made a pledge to go to Rome as a pilgrim to give thanks to God and offerings for continued protection. And he had not done so. Were these vicious pagans with their hellish cruelty a reminder of what he had promised and left undone? And was their house that secure? Athelstan had left no children, and although Aethelwulf had four other sons, who knew in these dangerous times if they would survive? If God was angry with him, it would not take much for their lives to be extinguished. Athelstan's fate showed that.

At Aethelwulf's side, his wife Osburh had thoughts of her own. She too was thinking back over the years to when her father had first presented her, a shy and blushing girl of fourteen, to the man who would become her husband. There had been no thought of marriage back then. Ten years older than her, he was already married with a son, Athelstan, now lying in his coffin before them. No thought of it? Well, maybe that wasn't strictly true. She had thought of it – the look in his brown eyes had kept her awake many sleepless nights – but only in the way young girls do think the impossible, and have to learn to put it behind them.

But then King Aethelwulf's wife had died in childbirth and, after a sufficient period of mourning had passed, a new wife was needed. And somehow she and her father had managed it. Her father, in charge of the king's household, had plenty of opportunity to ensure that his pretty daughter, coming into full bloom, was in the king's presence more often than potential rivals. And she? Well, at sixteen she knew how to make herself agreeable to a man. Aethelwulf was a good man, still was a good man, she thought. He didn't take her for granted, which he might have done, given his rank was so much higher than hers. When he fell in love with her, there was no question but that he would marry her, despite the strong opposition of his father, the stern warrior King Egbert. He had made it clear to her that she brought nothing to the House of Wessex.

It had helped that Aethelwulf had been set up as king of Sussex and Kent by then and was less dependent on his father. Even so, it had taken Aethelwulf a long time to persuade him that her kinship links with the old royal families of Sussex and Kent would help him in establishing his rule in these newly acquired domains.

Her thoughts returned to the coffin before her. She had tried to love Athelstan. She had wanted to take his mother's place, particularly in the early years of her marriage, when a series of still births had made her despair of ever having children of her own. But somehow he had never let her. Maybe the age gap between them was not big enough, maybe he had too many memories of his own mother, or maybe, like his grandfather, he just didn't think she was good enough. Whatever the reason, it was a secret relief to her, when, in the joy of having given birth to a healthy baby son at last, was told that King Egbert had decided that the ten year old Athelstan would move to his court and be trained for the role of a future ruler there. She didn't see much of Athelstan after that, and when she did, they met almost as strangers, with careful courtesies on both sides.

And so now, at his funeral, she did not feel the overwhelming grief she might otherwise have done. She was sad for Aethelwulf – it was a hard blow for him. But she had given him other sons to take Athelstan's place. Still young it was true, but Athelstan had only been sixteen when he became king. Aethelbald was already seventeen and everyone said he would be a mighty fighter. Maybe this death would delay Aethelwulf carrying out his threat of going to Rome. Her heart always sank at the thought of that. When kings of Wessex went to Rome, they didn't come back.

She considered the scene before her. It didn't speak to her soul in the way that she knew it did to Aethelwulf's. To her, this stark contrast between dark and light, the heavy sweetness of frankincense, the frigid singing and the robed men speaking in a foreign tongue offered no consolation or future promise. It was just odd. Foreign. She had been a Christian all her life, and her father before her. When the kings converted, everyone else had to. It had been necessary and not difficult to pay lip service. But as for an inner conviction, that was different. The old religion had flowed in the blood of her ancestors for hundreds of years, keeping them company and explaining every step along the way of life. There were gods for men and gods for women, gods for fighting and gods for childbirth, gods for death and gods for life. But this strange, eastern religion, with its one god, who was also somehow three, with its cult of worshipping a death on a cross and ceremony of eating god – what could that mean? How could that relate to our lives here? And despite preaching peace and love, it demanded obedience and killed those who disagreed.

Many years ago, a Christian king of Wessex, Caedwalla, had invaded her island homeland and converted her ancestors to his religion by killing one third of the population. And then he'd gone to Rome to be baptised and have his sins washed away. Even as loyal servants of Caedwalla's successors, it was not something her family had forgotten.

But there, men killed each other even without religions to spur them on. And she could see that his belief – however strange it might seem to her – had helped make her husband into a good man. It was his belief that had made him treat her as an equal and determined to marry her against his father's opposition. There were plenty of others who would have used her for their enjoyment and then moved on to a more advantageous marriage. But Jesus Christ did not permit such behaviour amongst his followers, and so he deserved her respect for that.

She looked at the three priests getting ready to celebrate the ceremony of Holy Communion. What a curious mixture they were. Only Christianity would put them all together and say that they were holy men. Ceolnoth, the archbishop of Canterbury, had a shrewd, slightly humorous face. He looked as though he was enjoying a secret joke, which perhaps he was. A Mercian who had found favour and preferment in Wessex needed great political skills, and Ceolnoth had those in abundance. It was always hard to know what he was thinking.

Towering over the archbishop was the fierce figure of Ealhstan, bishop of Sherborne. The man was a great warrior, veteran of a hundred battles against the British in the west, the Mercians in the north, and pagans everywhere. Her husband's most trusted military adviser and a distant relation, what on earth was he doing in a priest's robes? The hand raised in blessing above the chalice which the archbishop had now placed on the altar was scarred with countless wounds. No one knew how many men he had killed.

The third figure, keeping himself slightly back from the two bishops, was much more in accordance with Osburh's views of what a Christian priest should be. But then she knew him much better than the other two. Swithun of Winchester had been her husband's tutor and was now his confessor and mass priest. As such, he was always with them at court. But unlike many courtiers, who became puffed up with a sense of their own importance, Swithun didn't seem to have a sense of himself at all. He remained the same whoever he was talking to – always courteous, always interested. And there was a deep joy in his eyes when he looked on you, which was totally impersonal and came from beyond this world. A child of God rejoicing in the sight of another divine creation. It was a look which made Osburh feel that there must be something in the Christian religion after all.

Beside his mother, sitting and standing when the adults did, a frown of concentration on his face, was Aethelred, her second youngest son. Known to the family as Redi. He was pleased that his elder brothers and sister weren't there, enabling him to have the place of honour next to his mother and father. He had only seen Athelstan once or twice and barely remembered him, but he had persuaded his father to let him look into the coffin and see the white, dead face. He stared sternly down at it and was pleased to turn away without a tear. He saw his father look at him with a wondering eye.

Next to Redi was his tutor Colman, a minor annoyance to him as it was a reminder of his infant status. Part of the reason for his frown of concentration was to discourage whispered explanations from Colman as to the meaning of the liturgy.

A greater annoyance to Redi was the presence of his younger brother, Alfred, whom he called Little Elf, sitting on the other side of Colman. Alfred, he had argued with his mother, was far too young to be attending so serious and solemn occasion as a funeral. He wouldn't understand what was going on, he'd probably start talking or misbehaving at an important part of the service and, worst of all, he'd have to have his nurse with him. But Osburh wasn't to be persuaded. 'Athelstan was Alfred's brother as well as yours, Redi. And even if he doesn't fully understand what's going on, it's important for him to be there. He'll remember it later.'

So, Alfred was there. With his nurse. Redi tried to ignore them. At least, Alfred was quiet. The few times Redi glanced at him, he was staring up in wonder at the smoke coils of frankincense rising up into the dark air.

*

Aethelwulf sat by the fire in a private room of the royal manor outside Canterbury. The funeral had gone as well as could be expected. The only mar had been when Athelstan's widow, Gleda, had collapsed as the coffin of her husband was lifted up to be transported through the town for burial amid the blackened buildings of St Augustine's abbey. The kings of Kent were buried at the abbey; pagan desecration would not stop that tradition.

Gleda had been supported and comforted as the mourners followed the coffin in a solemn procession. The sombre dignity of the occasion imparted itself to the crowd lining the route and there was no repetition of the curses or mockery hurled at Aethelwulf on his arrival.

After the burial and blessings, he had spent an hour talking to the most important clerics and townsmen. He confirmed Elchere in his position of military commander and overlord of Kent until such time as a royal successor to Athelstan was determined. He agreed with the archbishop and abbot the sum to be paid the church for the perpetual prayers to be made for his son's soul. And then he listened to the immediate concerns of the townsmen and arranged for money to be paid them to help in rebuilding their town and providing for those left bereaved or destitute by the pagans' attack.

Then at last he was free to ride off with his attendants away from the stricken town and into the sweet Kent countryside where he had spent some of the happiest days of his life. He had stayed in this manor many times with Osburh when they were a young couple basking in love and sunshine. Death seemed far away back then. He had sat in this very chair, waiting for her to come in and tell him that Athelstan was asleep at last. The fingers of his right hand traced the remembered scroll of the chair's decoration.

A soft knock on the door, as though twenty-five years had slipped away.

'Come in.'

And here she was again. A few more lines on her face, but still recognisable as Oslac's young girl, whose timid look had stayed in his mind's eye. Her figure a little fuller, but still desirable after eight confinements. How on earth had she managed to avoid the heaviness of mothers ten years her junior? Not through prayers to Our Lord, he knew that much. Some pagan, feminine magic.

He motioned for her to sit on his lap, which she did with a little smile. He buried his face in the curve between her neck and shoulder, breathing deeply the scent of her hair and skin.

'My Wulf,' she said fondly, running a hand through his hair. 'How hard it is for you.'

He said nothing but let the sense of her fill his nostrils and charge his skin. The grimness of the past few days, the grimness yet to come, he let it all slip from him in the accustomed warmth of his wife's body.

They were silent for several moments, gently holding, caressing and drawing comfort from one another until Osburh gave voice to a thought which had been troubling her.

'It's such a shame about Gleda.'

'She'll be all right,' said Aethelwulf, reluctant to move his head away from her. 'They'll give her a draught to help her sleep. I thought it was fitting – don't you think a woman should be upset at her husband's funeral?'

'Oh, not that. But going into a convent. It seems such a waste. She's still young.'

This time Aethelwulf did pull his head away from his wife's neck. 'You think nuns should only be old, do you?'

'Not if they have a vocation, no. But I don't think Gleda has one. She's grieving. How can she make a decision about the rest of her life in such a state?'

'She's not. Nuns don't take final vows for a number of years.'

'Yes, but once she's in a convent, what else is she going to do? She's not going to meet anyone, is she? Apart from other nuns. They have to sit behind a screen even for family visits. It's inhuman.'

'Is there anything about the religion in which you were baptised that you approve of?'

'I just don't see why women have to be locked away from the world. Particularly members of the royal family. Our family. She is our daughter-in-law, after all.'

'She has a sister,' Aethelwulf said shortly.

'That's cruel.'

'Not at all. It's much better for us that she is in a convent than married to some ambitious ealdorman. We've only been lords here a short time. The old house of Kent still commands strong loyalties.'

'There, I knew you'd had a hand in it. You could have found her someone to marry who wouldn't have been a threat.'

'You never know who will be a threat, especially when they marry into the royal family. It would have to be someone whose status was so far below hers that it would be an indignity for her to marry him. She's made the best choice.'

'Or been made to make the best choice,' said Osburh bitterly.

'I didn't make her. It was her decision," Aethelwulf replied.

'It's such a hard life the novices lead. She'll have to scrub floors, empty chamber pots and get up in the middle of the night in the freezing cold. And she's not used to it. Do you know how many novices die or go mad? Gleda's so gentle. How will she survive?'

'By trusting in the Lord.'

'That's your answer to everything unpleasant.'

'How did you survive your confinements?' Aethelwulf asked.

It was a dangerous question, which Osburh had no intention of answering. After three still births, she had stopped calling on the Christian god and his virgin mother when her time came, and gone back to prayers and offerings to Frige, the old goddess of childbirth. And had healthy children ever since. But Aethelwulf didn't know that. And never would if she could help it, whatever he might suspect.

'That's different,' she said quietly.

'Why?'

'Every woman is prepared to face death to bring new life into the world. To have children.'

'And to serve the Lord, to be His spouse, to grow in love for Him, to pray for all His creation, including us as we face invaders come straight from the jaws of hell – you think that is less important?'

Osburh recognised that they had strayed onto hazardous territory. He'd be talking about going to Rome soon if she wasn't careful.

'I don't know,' she said mournfully. 'I'm just a foolish woman. But I'm fond of Gleda. I shall miss her.'

'We didn't see her that much.'

'No, but she was good for Athelstan. I was so hoping they'd have children.' As she said it, she realised the pointlessness of such a hope now and the finality of Athelstan's loss hit her for the first time. She suddenly burst into tears, a mixture of grief and shame, burying her face into Aethelwulf's chest.

It was his turn now to hold her tight and run his hand through her hair. We make an odd couple, he thought. But somehow they worked together – their differences complementing each other. His first wife, Athelstan's mother, had been much more conventionally pious and dutiful, but he'd never felt for her what he felt for Osburh. He'd taken no risks for her, maybe that was it.

Osburh's crying ceased and she looked across at him, a tentative smile through tears. He kissed her lips slowly and luxuriantly.

'Is everything ready for this evening?' he asked.

'We're getting there,' she replied. 'Ealhstan and Swithun have both insisted on sleeping in the great hall with the men. For very different reasons.'

Aethelwulf didn't need telling what the reasons were. Ealhstan, Bishop of Sherborne, would want to be with the men he commanded in battle. Swithun would just want to cause the least trouble.

'And the archbishop?' Aethelwulf asked.

'He's asked to be excused. He's hosting a feast for those made destitute by the pagans. Not a very good reason – I'm sure someone could have taken his place. But I didn't press him.'

'You were right not to. Tonight will be about the House of Wessex. A Mercian would feel out of place. What about Ealdorman Elchere?'

'I've put him in the bur next to ours. I think he's had enough of being with his soldiers for a while.'

'Make sure he is given every attention. We will be relying on him to hold this land for us over the next few years.'

'Are you not going to appoint Blade to be king here?'

'He's still young. And untried. Athelstan had fought many battles by his age. But Blade will have his opportunity soon, I fear, to do some fighting.' It was a thought he did not want to dwell on this evening. 'And the boys?'

'Redi is with Colman, who's teaching him the poem Diarmait composed for him to recite this evening. And Alfred is wandering all over the place as usual, with Yetta in heavy pursuit. The last time I saw him, he was in the great hall, watching Diarmait.'

'He shouldn't be disturbing him. Diarmait has important work to do.'

'Alfred doesn't disturb him. He just sits and listens with his eyes wide open. He told me he wants to be a poet when he grows up.'

'I think we'll be more in need of his prayers than his poems, the way things are going,' Aethelwulf responded sombrely.

Osburh made no reply. That was a battle for another day.

*

After the burial of their brother, while their parents met with the chief mourners and discussed whatever it was that grown-ups discussed on such occasions, Redi and Alfred were allowed to leave the gloomy occasion early. Osburh decided that they had had more than enough solemnity for one day and should be allowed some time to play before it got dark. Redi had mixed feelings about this. Part of him would have liked to have gone around the people with his father, looking stern and important. But then there might be weeping women. He'd been rather shaken by Gleda's noisy collapse at the cathedral. The thought of having to meet her and other similarly distressed women was a little unnerving. So he didn't make much protest at Osburh's decision, particularly when she told him that he would be allowed to stay up for the early part of the funeral feast that night, whereas Alfred wouldn't, because he was too small.

'You're too small, Little Elf,' Redi explained to Alfred, as they rode together in a wagon to the royal manor outside Canterbury with Colman and Alfred's nurse, Yetta. 'You wouldn't understand.'

Alfred looked at his brother blankly, uncertain what he was talking about. His head was still full of images from the funeral service. He had been particularly impressed by one of the acolytes, whose job had been to swing the censer from which the clouds of sweet frankincense had issued. He would like to do that. He decided to get some practice in.

When they arrived at the manor, they were allowed out into a meadow at the back of the great hall.

'I'll be Daddy and you can be a pagan invader!' Redi cried, sensing that the vanquishing of a pagan Little Elf would be the best way of coming to terms with what had happened to Athelstan, and somehow putting it right.

Alfred wasn't very keen on being a pagan invader, even when Redi started to pelt him with clumps of earth to rouse his fighting spirit. His ambition remained to be an acolyte swinging a censer. Amidst the grass of the meadow, he found a discarded falconry glove with a training line still attached. If he held the line quite close to the glove and let the rest of it trail over his shoulder, he could swing the glove with it backwards and forwards. It wasn't quite the same as a censer and obviously no sweet smoke came out of it, but it was good enough to be getting on with. He began to pace slowly up and down the meadow, chanting mysterious words to himself whilst swinging the glove.

A well-aimed clump of earth with a stone embedded in it hit him on the left ear, causing him to drop the glove and give a howl of pain, which brought both Colman and Yetta running.

'He hit me with a stone!'

'I didn't,' said Redi defensively. He knew he was going to get the worst of it. The adults always took Alfred's side, just because he was younger. 'It was a piece of earth.'

Colman picked up the offending clump and looked at it sternly, 'You shouldn't throw things like this at your younger brother.'

'He was meant to be attacking me.'

'He was just playing with a glove. He wasn't doing you any harm.'

'He was *meant* to be doing me harm,' said Redi exasperatedly. It was no good – he wouldn't get a monk and a woman to understand. 'How's he going to learn about fighting if each time he gets the tiniest blow, you cosset him as if he was still a baby?' He glowered at Yetta, into whose broad arms Alfred was seeking refuge.

'He's still very young,' Colman said. 'There's plenty of time for him to learn about fighting.'

'Really? With pagans attacking us now? Killing my brother!'

'I don't want to play your silly game,' Alfred cried from the safety of Yetta's arms. 'You wanted me to be a pagan.'

'Well, someone's got to be.'

'Not necessarily,' said a soft voice behind them. It was Swithun, drawn from his prayers by the noise in the meadow. 'You could both be Christians. Fighting together. We may well need you to do that.'

'How can we fight together when there's no-one to fight?' Redi asked, but more quietly. His father treated Swithun as someone important.

'You could teach him," said Swithun. 'He'll learn more from you teaching him than from you hitting him. Particularly as you're twice his size,' he added mildly.

Redi looked a little shamefaced. 'I wouldn't have hurt him,' he said. 'It was only a game.'

'You did hurt me,' said Alfred accusingly.

'What's this?" said Swithun, spying Alfred's discarded glove on the ground.

'He was swinging it up and down,' said Redi. 'Acting stupid.'

'Like a sling?' asked Swithun. 'David facing Goliath?'

Alfred smiled. He didn't know who David was, but he knew that he was someone that churchmen liked a lot. When they compared you with David, they were approving of you.

'He's not David,' Redi said, annoyed again. David had been the youngest son who had surpassed all his brothers. Not a good comparison. He preferred the story of Joseph, the second youngest son, who was far more important that Benjamin, the youngest.

'All right, Joseph,' said Swithun with a smile, reading his thoughts. 'But you were nice to your younger brother, weren't you?'

'Only after teaching him a lesson.'

Swithun laughed, a rare occurrence, which bemused the still slightly hostile Redi. 'Good for you,' he said.

'You know the story well. We shall have to find you some boys of your own age to fight with. You're right – we do need fighters. And you will need to learn how to lead them.'

'Excuse me, father,' said Colman. 'But I should be going inside with Prince Aethelred now. The king wished me to teach him the poem he is to read tonight.'

Redi's good humour was fully restored. Not only had the important Swithun looked kindly on him, which meant he was unlikely to get into trouble for hitting Alfred, but he was also reminded of his forthcoming attendance at a feast for the first time that night.

'You can't come, Little Elf,' he reminded Alfred, now venturing away from Yetta's arms. 'You're too small.'

With that parting shot, he allowed himself to be led away by Colman to tackle the poem.

'I don't want to go with him anyway,' Alfred said to Swithun. 'He always ruins things.'

'Stay and play a while longer then, Alfred,' said Swithun. 'You don't need anyone else to play with, do you? Not with that powerful imagination of yours.' He glanced at Yetta. 'You'll keep an eye on him?'

'Yes, father. We'll come in when the horn sounds."

'Good.' Swithun gave a general smile encompassing them both, before following Redi and Colman back towards the manor buildings.

Freed from his brother's interference, Alfred picked up the falconry glove with a view to resuming his censer swinging and chanting. But before he had taken more than a few steps, he heard the sound of real music issuing forth from the great hall. The notes of a harp being plucked by expert fingers overrode his thoughts of solemn mysteries with the promise of a sweeter enchantment. Diarmait must be practising for the evening. He dropped the glove and ran towards the great hall, with Yetta following at a more sedate pace.

*

It was evening and the hall was full. King Aethelwulf sat at the centre of the high table with his wife, Osburh, at his right hand side and Bishop Ealhstan at his left. Also seated with him at the high table were Ealdorman Elchere and other high-ranking Kentish nobles. At the long tables below them sat the fighting men – the king's companions intermingled with the thanes and freemen of Kent, many of whom had taken part in the recent battles against the pagans. Apart from some female slaves bringing in food and drink from time to time, Osburh was the only woman in the room. That was no discomfort for her. She had been to many of these male warrior feasts before and relished the tang of battles past and to come – the boasts, the songs, the drunken laughter, the sudden confrontations and tearful embraces which usually followed. It was the old way for the tribe to renew its bonds of loyalty, to mourn its losses, to celebrate its history and prepare to fight once more. As a way of saying goodbye to Athelstan, it made more sense to her than those cold services in the cathedral and abbey.

But she felt the lingering effect of those services. The mood in the hall was subdued. It was right for a funeral feast to start solemnly. But the mood would have to change sometime. There needed to be a progress from sorrow to acceptance. Otherwise, what was the point of having a feast at all? As the king's wife (the men of Wessex would not call her queen), she had a role in encouraging the change of mood, but she could not initiate it. Only the king could do that. The attention of every man was, in varying degrees, fixed on the king, waiting for him to give a sign. But Aethelwulf was lost in thought and seemed unaware, even of her at his side, let alone the men before him. Diarmait could help, but he too needed a sign from the king. Without it, he would go on playing the same sombre tunes he had been playing since the beginning. The feast had been going on for almost two hours. Hunger was satisfied, men were looking around. Something needed to happen. If the king didn't take the lead, someone else would. And who knew what would happen then?

She looked around the hall and saw Redi sitting at a table near the front with Swithun on one side of him and Colman on the other. She'd forgotten about Redi; he ought to be in bed.

'Shall we ask Redi to recite his poem, my dear? He shouldn't stay up much longer.'

No reply. She might just as well not be there; the feast might just as well not be happening. Aethelwulf stared fixedly at the cup of wine in front of him. She looked over at Swithun. He was an intelligent man, despite being a priest. He read the direction in her eyes and turned and spoke to Redi. Through the smoke of the hall, Osburh could see the panic in Redi's eyes, as though he was next to her. Poor Redi, she thought, her heart softening in sympathy. You weren't expecting to be the first, were you? But you're the only one I can call on to wake your father up and get this feast moving. So help your mother now and make her proud of you.

Swithun was on his feet, pulling a reluctant Redi with him.

'Listen!' Swithun cried in the time-honoured manner, his voice resounding through the hall and silencing conversation. 'Prince Aethelred will now pay tribute to his brother, the great King Athelstan!'

Osburh thanked him with her eyes. If there were more priests like Swithun, she might even become a Christian. A proper Christian, that is. The man had no fear. And unlike many priests, he knew the value of the old ways as well. But now her thoughts were caught up in anxiety for Redi. After such a splendid introduction, he had to get through his poem, however badly. The hall would be with him – he didn't need to do much, but a little he did.

'Athelstan, the king, captain of men,' Redi's treble voice was shaky, but clear. Osburh could hardly breathe, concentrating with her whole being on willing him further.

'Ring-giver to warriors – my brother
For eleven winters you ruled this land,
Defender of hearth and maiden,
The first into battle always,
Sinker of the nailed ships, the sea-wolves' bane –
They fled before your ash wood spear.
None of them would boast of your blood
When fate unwound its skein for you.
Only the whale-road, which no man rules,
Was big enough to take you.'

Osburh felt a mounting sense of exhilaration as Redi negotiated the poem's difficulties, becoming more assured as he neared the end. There was something captivating about the contrast between the child's voice and the adult words it was speaking. She sensed the attention of everyone in the hall, including Aethelwulf, focusing on the little boy at the front with the same intensity as she was. And when he had finished, there was silence for a moment, before a roar of approval broke out around him, with men pounding their fists on the tables in front of them. Osburh could see no more as her eyes flooded with tears, but she heard her husband rise up beside her.

'Well spoken, Prince Aethelred, my son.'

Redi blushed with pleasure. He looked around him in some confusion at the reaction his recital had provoked. A man was even presenting him with a gold coin from his father. What was he meant to do now? He was saved from further embarrassment by Swithun's hand gently pulling him down.

'Well done, young prince,' Swithun smiled his approval. 'Now you need to keep very quiet, because if you do, your mother might forget that she was about to send you to bed and you'll be able to stay for Diarmait's recital.'

Redi kept his eyes fixed on the table in front of him to avoid catching his mother's eye. He tried to make himself look as small as possible. He very much wanted to hear Diarmait. There would be so much to tell Little Elf about!

Aethelwulf, roused from his thoughts, gave the sign for Diarmait to begin the great poem of Wessex. Redi kept his eyes down until Diarmait had struck up the first notes on his harp and it was too late for his mother to interrupt. Then he looked up towards the old poet, determined to remember everything.

'The royal house of Cerdic is my tale,
scion of Woden, Godwulf and Hathra,
of Scaef, the son of Noah, ark-born,
Methusaleh, Enoch who did not die,

*Seth, Adam and Christ, the father of all.
Who has not heard of the mighty Cerdic,
like Abraham leaving his native land
in answer to God's call? How after years
of breaking foam furrow in the homeless whale-road,
he sailed up the double tide river
with five ships of feeding wolves and his son,
Cynric the fearless and undefeated.
And how they fought for this Promised Land,
watering the fields with their battle-sweat,
year upon year growing ever stronger,
no longer to be numbered by men,
as the Lord blessed their valour and daring,
extending their rule to the setting sun.'*

Most of the men in the hall had heard the poem many times before but, even so, it was always an occasion when a master poet sang it. And, for the attentive, it was never quite the same. There were always variations, depending upon the mood of the times, the audience and the poet. No one knew who had first composed it, but every poet who had ever recited it had added a little of themselves to it, so that like a river, its course might look the same, but it was always changing, always new. The most obvious change, working out over hundreds of years, was the infiltration of Christianity and biblical references into an originally totally pagan construct. But there were smaller, more fleeting changes too, which were there sometimes, other times not, prompted by unspoken desires or needs. A good poet was one who knew how to answer the unspoken from the mass of material at his command. Diarmait, not Wessex-born, from a land far beyond the setting sun, with no blood loyalty, had only his skill and heart wisdom, learnt over long years in foreign courts, to tell him where to go. But Aethelwulf trusted him; he had got it right before. It was not necessary to say that this feast was a solemn occasion; the death of the king's son was sufficient for that. Diarmait kept the image of that submerged face before him as he sang. Nor was it necessary to say that the great majority of the men in the hall had been fighting for their lives and land, or would be soon. And so this recital must needs be sombre and serious, but proud also – giving sufficient reasons for fighting again.

Would the men of Kent feel the same way about a poem in praise of Wessex? Probably not. They had their own poems, their own traditions. But they needed to know that Wessex was strong and confident, able to defend both it and them. Diarmait paid little attention to the audience before him when he started his recitation. The mood – something indefinable, invisible – was what was important. If he kept his inner eyes on that, concentrated on that alone, then all would be well.

'Ceawlin the mighty, son of Cynric,
scourge of the Britons for thirty winters,
ruler of twice his fathers' land,
victor at Dyrham, where three kings died,
and the western lands fell to us,
voyager with Cutha, his brother,
beyond the Great River to Fethanleag,
and the wood where Cutha died,
cut down by a traitor's hand.
Days of disaster followed then
as godless men fought one another
and Ceawlin the mighty was overthrown.
But at the darkest time, the dawn is near –
the light of Christ shone in the east.

*Pope Gregory sent St Augustine
and the Good News began to make its way.
Ceolwulf, son of Cutha, rightful ruler,
won back the throne and many victories –
under him, the land grew fat again.
A greater gift by far was given us
by Cyngelis, nephew of Ceolwulf,
when he welcomed Birinius
to preach God among us, leading the way,
accepting the waters of faith at his hand.'*

Osburh frowned to herself. This poem was becoming more and more Christian. If Diarmait continued in this vein, there was a danger the men of Wessex would start to think they could defeat the pagans by praying rather than fighting. She recognised Aethelwulf's influence. But her husband was a warrior as well as a Christian. Even now, he'd be formulating a plan of campaign against the pagans in his mind. He'd probably start discussions with Ealhstan tomorrow. She sneaked a glance over at the old warrior bishop. His face was impassive. She suspected that he might prefer a bit more fighting in the poem as well. But now the kings were becoming Christian, they'd be fighting for the faith, and so maybe Diarmait would spend more time on their battles. He'd be getting to Caedwalla soon. Her blood turned a little cold, as it always did at the thought of that Christian murderer of her ancestors.

*'Caedwalla, the warrior of the Lord,
bringer of faith to the heathen folk,
conqueror of the land beyond the sea.
Who has not heard of Caedwalla?
His victories like comets in the sky,*

*the death wound he bore to his Master in Rome,
washing it clean in baptismal waters,
bound in white cloth, he went home to the Lord.
And Ine, his successor, the lawgiver
and builder, founder of churches,
for forty winters he gave us peace
before he too was called by the Lord
to exchange the passing glories of this world
for a pilgrim's staff and eternal favour,
creator of our church in Rome,
next to the tomb of St Peter himself.'*

Diarmait was nearing the end of the poem. Although almost eighty winters separated the abdication of King Ine and the return from exile of King Egbert, Osburh's grim father-in-law, these were the years of Mercian ascendancy, when its great kings Aethelbald and Offa had dominated southern England and beyond, reducing Wessex to little more than a dependency. With his inner eye fixed on what was needed, Diarmait glided over this time of weakness and betrayal to land triumphantly on King Egbert's return and the great victory over Mercia at Ellendun, followed by the despatch of his son Aethelwulf and Bishop Ealhstan into Sussex and Kent. Throughout Diarmait's recital, there had been a deepening silence in the hall as people gradually became caught up in his tale, which coming through the mists of the centuries gained ever clearer focus. From traditions of the long past, he was now singing of events which many in the hall had witnessed. And the heroes he was now extolling were the men seated at the high table in front of them.

'Great King Aethelwulf with Ealhstan his bishop

ruled here among us for fifteen winters,
dispenser of the flames of the falcon's field,
upholder of proud traditions, shield for all –
who does not remember that glorious time?
And when the death of great King Egbert
called him west to rule the heartland,
he sent Athelstan, his peerless son,
bright with the promise of golden youth
to take his place as anointed king.
We saw the son's strength and wisdom grow,
sending down roots, binding together
our great nations ever closer.
Husband of royal Gleda,
they ruled in concord and justice.
And when the sea wolves came, our king
Athelstan the brave was first to the fight,
attacking the pagans' cruel ships
with never a thought for his safety,
sending those devils back down to hell.
The fate which rules over all decreed
he was to be taken from us young
as so many of the brave have been.
He is in glory now with his forebears –
Cerdic, Cynric, Cealwin,
Cutha, Ceolwulf and Cyngelis,
Caedwalla, Ine and Cynewulf,
King Egbert, the great restorer –
they are looking down on all of us
to see if we will prove worthy
of the kingdom they bequeathed us
to follow their kinsman and our lord,
Aethelwulf the undefeated,
in exacting the blood price for his son.
Only the death of every pagan

who has dared to profane this holy land
will be sufficient to pay that price.
And so my song ends for now
and it ends upon a question:
when my song begins again
of whose deeds will I be singing?'

Diarmait stepped back and lowered his harp, his recital over. There was a deep silence as men pondered the challenge which had been set them. And then King Aethelwulf started to clap slowly. Others joined in but in their own time so that the sound swelled over a minute or so until it became a mighty wave of noise, with everyone in the hall clapping, banging the table in front of them, stamping their feet and shouting approval. The moment of fear which Diarmait always felt in the silence after a recital passed. He felt young again, his work done. He walked forwards, smiling happily, bowing and bathing in the warmth of the applause, which filled the Great Hall and seemed to go on forever.

2. Aclea

The fighting in London lasted longer than Aethelwulf had anticipated. Various agents and refugees kept him informed of its progress. The Mercians were fighting for their land, and many of the pagans were unused to fighting in the dense, narrow streets which lined the waterfront. A young ealdorman called Burgred led a successful raid which destroyed half the pagan ships and set fire to their camp. Aethelwulf even began to wonder if the Mercians might prove successful in defending their town.

It was a fine day in early summer when a solitary horseman rode into Winchester asking to see the king. It was rare enough for anyone to travel alone in these troubled days, although this man was armed and looked as though he could take care of himself. What was even rarer was that he had a small boy on the horse with him. Aethelwulf received him in his great hall, along with Bishop Ealhstan and other counsellors.

'What is your name, stranger?'

'Cynehelm, lord king.'

Aethelwulf looked closely at the man before him. Dusty from travel and fatigue. But his sword and armour were of good quality and he bore himself proudly. A noble. The name was familiar, as was the face. He searched his memory.

'I believe I knew your father.'

'You did, sire.'

Aethelwulf nodded. He had him now. A counsellor of Wigmund, the ill-fated Mercian king overthrown by Beorthwulf ten years ago. Of royal descent himself.

Mercia had many royal families. Too many. And this was his son.

'You come from London?'

'I do.'

'And how go things there?'

'Badly.'

'In what way?'

The man looked at the ground, weighing his words before speaking. A careful man. 'Our king has started talks with the pagans.'

'To surrender the town?'

'It's hardly worth surrendering. It's smoke and ashes. Hardly a building left standing.' He looked at the ground again, as though remembering horrors.

'Buildings can be rebuilt,' Ealhstan's harsh voice cut in.

Cynehelm looked over at him. 'Indeed, lord bishop.'

'If not to surrender the city, then to pay them off and persuade them to go elsewhere?' Aethelwulf asked.

'Yes, sire.'

'You were present at these talks?'

'I was.'

'And?'

'To begin with, they laughed at us and said they could take our silver without our help. But then they started to argue amongst themselves. The leaders want land, but they have to reward their men. And London won't support them now – it's a wasteland. They have to move on and they know it.'

'So, why have talks with them?' Ealhstan cut in again.

'The king needs the fighting to stop. The army is beginning to desert. His authority is crumbling. And he needs to ensure that when the pagans move, they move south, not west or north.'

'Has anything been decided?'

'The pagans have said they will take ten thousand pounds of silver and London in return for moving south.'

'*And* London?'

'Yes.'

'And the king?'

'The king is considering it.'

'He's considering giving them London?' To abandon London was one thing, to give it quite another.

'He's desperate, sire.'

'Is he asking the pagans to help him?' Ealhstan again. 'Against people like you?'

Cynehelm flushed. 'I have no power.'

'Are you here on behalf of the king?' Ealhstan continued.

'No.'

'Does he know you're here?'

'No.'

'That's why you've come without a guard, isn't it? People talk. Why come here?'

Cynehelm looked for help to Aethelwulf for a respite from his bishop's questions.

'You are of royal lineage,' Aethelwulf observed mildly.

'My family is weak,' Cynehelm said. 'We have been prominent in the past, it is true. If there is fighting for the crown of Mercia then we will not be contenders. But we will be targets. I have come seeking protection from the king of Wessex, particularly for my son.' He indicated the boy, who had been standing quietly by his side. 'His mother is dead and there is no-one to whom I can entrust him. His name is Ceolwulf.'

Aethelwulf looked at the boy. About Redi's age, maybe a little younger.

'And what do you offer in return for our protection?'

'My service.'

'You have land in Mercia, no doubt? And men?'

'I do.'

'For those to be pledged to the king of Wessex could be seen as treachery in Mercia.'

Cynehelm was silent again, considering. 'I am no traitor,' he said finally. 'I have fought for King Beorthwulf. But I do not know what will happen in these dangerous times for Mercia, when it appears fighting is not enough. I do not believe it is treachery to seek protection in these circumstances.'

'Who will be king of Mercia in a year's time?' Ealhstan interjected again.

'I don't know.'

'Who do you think?'

'Ealdorman Burgred is the one people are turning to.'

'But not you?'

'He is a kinsman of Beorthwulf. No friend to my family.'

Aethelwulf had made up his mind. 'Will you go back to Mercia for us? If we look after your son?'

'If that is what you wish, sire.'

'It would be an act of friendship,' Aethelwulf said. 'I think that is a better way of looking at our relationship than service. I have no designs on Mercia, you know. But our great nations should be friends, particularly in view of the common threat which faces us both.'

'What do you want me to do?'

'To be a friend, as I say. To keep me informed of how things are going in Mercia. No, not a spy,' he added as he saw Cynehelm's face fall. 'I'll make it clear that you have my friendship. The fact that your son is at my court will be reason enough for people to know where your sympathies lie. But there may be Mercians who will want to speak to Wessex, but not be able to travel here as you have. They can speak to you instead.'

'Very well,' said Cynehelm. 'But it will be difficult at the moment. And dangerous.'

'Stay a while with us, then. Let's see how things develop in Mercia first. You will want to see your son settled in any event. And I would like to hear more about these pagans from you. It sounds as though we may be meeting them soon.'

*

Three weeks later, King Aethelwulf stood on the summit of Leith Hill, looking north towards London. Below him, in the woods on the slope of the hill, was gathered a sizeable portion of the fyrd of Surrey – men who knew this land, whose home it was. In the valley clearing ran the old Roman road. In winter, when the rains came, this was the only secure way through the valley's mud. Even now, in summer, it was the most obvious route for an invading army coming south.

There were various places along the road where an attack could be made. Most obvious was at the river crossing. But, although the pagans would be vulnerable crossing the river, the ground there was broken and difficult. Even if an attack was successful, it was unlikely to be conclusive. Most of the pagans would probably escape with their route back to London relatively clear. No, they needed to be attacked beyond the river crossing, in land they were less likely to have scouted, where an escape back to London would be more difficult. And where more open ground would enable a greater concentration of men to be massed.

He had decided on Aclea. The broad valley had been mostly cleared of trees but the slopes of Leith Hill were still wooded and could hide a large number of men. The woods were some distance from the road but the men in them would not be the first to attack. Just after Aclea, the road dipped down, starting its descent off the chalk downs. And so, although it looked open with good visibility, the descent meant that for a couple of miles the pagan army heading south would not be able to see very far ahead at all. Half of Aethelwulf's army – the fyrds of Hampshire and Sussex – were currently gathering about a mile below Aclea. When the signal was given, they would march north up the road, appearing suddenly before the pagans and engaging their shield walls with them. Only when the two forces were fully engaged would the men from the Surrey fyrd move from the woods on Leith Hill to attack the pagans in the rear. At the same time, the remainder of Aethelwulf's army – the Berkshire fyrd and some independent warriors – would be marching from the east to spring the trap and surround the pagans, blocking any escape route.

The plan depended upon over-confident pagans, willing to march all their forces into unfamiliar territory, without an advanced guard to spy out any dangers. Aethelwulf was hopeful this condition might be met. From Cynehelm, he had learnt a little about the pagan leaders. They were young – that was the most important thing. The old leaders, veterans of the Frankish wars, were not there. Where they had gone, no one knew – Ireland perhaps, or maybe back to Denmark. The pagan armies were always fluid, with men joining and leaving for mysterious reasons of their own. But the lack of veterans, who would be alive to the risk of ambushes, was helpful. According to Cynehelm, the most prominent pagan was a young man called Sigurd, strikingly handsome, but vain – absurdly conscious of his luxuriant, yellow hair. 'During the talks we had with them in London, he always had a polished shield near him,' Cynehelm had reported with a wry smile. 'So he could sneak a glance at himself now and then.'

There were other leaders as well but they all appeared to be as young and untried as Sigurd. Maybe this was part of a pagan plan to test new blood and see how they fared? Certainly, from what Cynehelm had said, they all seemed anxious to prove themselves as soon as possible. An opponent in a hurry is a gift from God. The more Aethelwulf heard about the pagans, the calmer he became. He recognised God's hand. Athelstan would be avenged. And then he would go to Rome, as he had promised.

But for now, there was little to do but wait. He narrowed his eyes and looked north. The views from up here were tremendous. But his eyes weren't. After only a few miles, the road vanished into a haze. He would have to leave it to younger eyes to spot the first sight of the pagans' approach.

'Where's Swithun?' he asked those around him.

'Here I am, my lord.' Calm and smiling before him.

'I would talk with you a while.' He turned to the guards around him. 'Keep a close watch. Call to me immediately you see them.'

'Yes, sire,' they replied.

Aethelwulf walked with Swithun to a fallen tree trunk. 'Let's sit here.'

They did so. Aethelwulf remained silent for a few moments. 'Is everything taken care of?' he asked eventually. 'The men?'

'Masses have been said,' Swithun replied. 'Confessions made. The mood is good.'

Aethelwulf nodded. He'd made his own confession and heard mass an hour ago.

'Something still troubles you, my lord?'

'The old problem. A feeling of disobedience. An unkept promise.'

'Your promise is not unkept. You have just not been able to fulfil it yet. A king has many demands upon him. For him to leave his country is no small matter.'

'It's not meant to be a small matter. The greater the sacrifice, the greater God's glory.'

'If it's a sacrifice called for by God. Otherwise, it's just misguided pride.'

'What do you mean?'

'If Abraham had decided to sacrifice Isaac because he thought it might please God, he would have been guilty of a great sin. The followers of Baal are condemned for just such sacrifices of children. It was only because God *did* call Abraham to sacrifice his son, that his response was one of faith.'

'I don't understand.'

'Why did you make this promise to go to Rome? And at a time when you had just been entrusted with the rule of a kingdom? Didn't you think your people would need you?'

'Kings of Wessex have gone to Rome before.'

'Caedwalla was dying. And Ine was an old man. Neither expected to return. And neither did. Do you expect to return if you go?'

Aethelwulf looked at the ground. 'You think the promise was a sin, then?'

'I don't know what it was. But I suspect that what it once was, and what it now is, are two different things.'

'In what way?'

'I suspect that when it was first made, it was an exuberant declaration of gratitude by a young man, for whom things were going very well. Now I suspect you see it as some form of escape from a world you've grown tired of.'

Aethelwulf gave a tight smile. 'You know me too well, my friend. But doesn't every pilgrim want to escape this world? Are they all wrong? Should everyone be staying where God has placed him? Have you told the Irish?'

'If you mean the great missionaries, they didn't travel to escape, but to proclaim God's word. They *knew* they were being called by God.'

'Well, Ine, then?'

'I don't know. He did some good things in Rome. He built a church, he founded the Saxon quarter. He forged links for us with the Holy See, which have slipped in recent years. But I don't think his going was good for Wessex. The country declined after he left. Until your noble father restored it.'

'An earthly kingdom.'

'Entrusted to him, and to you, by God. You know the parable of the talents.'

Aethelwulf frowned. 'Has my wife been talking to you?'

'No more than usual.'

'So, you think I ought to remain a prisoner here?'

'We are all prisoners in this world. St Paul rejoiced in being a prisoner of the Lord.'

'St Paul went to Rome.'

'That was his calling.'

'And mine is to stay here?'

'You are doing tremendous things here, my lord. As, God willing, we are about to see.'

'And my promise?'

'Pray to God. He will show you how to fulfil it. And it will be His way, not yours. That is what is important.'

Aethelwulf nodded. 'That is good advice, Father. Will you pray with me now?' He rose from the tree trunk and knelt on the bracken before it.

'Of course,' Swithun smiled and dropped to his knees beside him. They remained there in silent prayer together, until a call from the guards alerted Aethelwulf to the approach of the pagan army, sighted in the distance.

*

Prince Aethelbald, eldest son of King Aethelwulf and Osburh, commonly known by friends and family as Blade, due to his fascination since childhood with swords, was preparing for his first serious combat. He had been on some raids in the west before, carefully looked after by his father's men, but this he knew would be different. This would be a full-scale battle against trained warriors intent on taking the kingdom. He was well aware that Ealhstan would have been told to keep him away from the front line, from that murderous clash of shield walls. But who knew what would happen in the heat of battle? He pulled out his sword Bloodthirst from its scabbard, marvelling as so often before at its clean, deadly line. How many times had he been warned by women with flushed faces and raised voices that real swords weren't playthings, they could end the lives of those foolish enough to touch them? Well, he had handled a real sword now for many years and it had done him no harm. Maybe today would be the day when it fulfilled the purpose for which it had been forged.

His father had wanted him to stay with the Surrey fyrd in the woods on the slope of Leith Hill. They had the easier task, attacking the pagans in their rear after the initial clash. Blade knew that his father had no high opinion of him. Athelstan had been the favoured one. But then Athelstan didn't have to live with the old man and endure his pious sermons. It was easy for Athelstan to keep on his right side. And now Athelstan was dead, his father made little secret of his preference for Berti, Blade's younger brother. But Berti was weak, always suffering from one illness or another. Less of a threat to the old man, no doubt, but hardly a king in waiting.

Blade had decided long ago that he couldn't depend on his father for any favours. Very well, he was willing to make his own good fortune. He was still the king's son and the only one now capable of succeeding him. Berti was too weak, and Redi and Alfred too young. So the king had to show him outward respect. And if he could win the people's respect as well, the king would have to treat with him. Athelstan's throne remained waiting to be filled.

This battle was the perfect opportunity for Blade to step out from his father's shadow, but he wouldn't do so by staying in the woods with the Surrey fyrd. He needed to be where the battle was fiercest, with the fyrds of Hampshire and Sussex. That was where any glory would be won today. And so at the war council, to which his father had to invite him as his heir, Blade had objected to being assigned to Ealdorman Huda and the Surrey fyrd, and said he would fight with the men of Hampshire, whose fyrd he had helped to raise. His father, taken by surprise, could not object outwardly to his son requesting a place of more danger, particularly when Wulfstan, the Ealdorman of Hampshire, and Bishop Ealhstan, who had overall command of the fyrds approaching from the south, were agreeable to having him with them. Aethelwulf would have told Ealhstan to keep him out of danger. In addition, Blade had his own band of companions. He had no objection to being looked after in the battle's heart. What was important was that he was there.

Still mounted on his horse, Blade looked over at the fyrds assembling in their battle order, listening to the shouts of command and the cursing of the clumsy or slow. He watched Ealhstan exchanging a few words with the leaders, bellowing out encouragement to the men in his battlefield voice. That was a fighter for you. How many battles had he fought? Too many to count. He looked twenty years younger, in his element, with a fierce smile of anticipation on his face as he wheeled his horse between the various groups. Blade felt a stirring of anticipation within himself also. A heightening of his senses. Fear? If so, it was not unpleasant. Today he would discover who he really was.

'We'll be moving soon,' Leofgar said with a smile. Leofgar was his best friend and closest companion. His parents had been killed in a pagan raid and he had been brought up at court. Despite his difficult start in life, he had a cheerful disposition. Blade, who had a tendency to brood on injustices, particularly his father's attitude to him, valued his friend's ability to laugh such things off as minor irritations. 'Life's too short,' was a favourite saying. Even so, Blade sensed a certain steel in Leofgar's smile today. He never talked about his parents.

'Time to dismount,' Ealhstan had ridden up beside them. 'Leave your horses with the grooms over there. We'll go up in the second wave. You stick with me. You're observing this fight, my lord prince, you're not joining it. When you and your companions have got rid of your horses, you join Wilfrid over there.' He pointed out a dark middle-aged man. 'He has orders to keep an eye on you and stop you doing anything foolish.'

'Are the pagans. . . ?' Leofgar began.

'Yes,' Ealhstan interrupted. 'Five miles up the road. Beyond Aclea. They've probably spotted us by now as well. So we have to move. Quick!'

He wheeled his horse and was gone to another group of men. Blade wondered if he would ever be like Ealhstan, marshalling his forces, confident of unquestioning obedience. He rode over with Leofgar and the others to the grooms and dismounted.

There was something serious about getting off one's horse. This wasn't a hunt or a raid. He could tell they all felt it. Everyone was quiet, sorting shields, checking weapons. The world was different with your feet on the ground – slower, more considered. People were different, too – more formidable, less easy to dismiss. It was a descent of sorts and yet it was important – an entrance into a harder, darker world, which is where all battles were decided. Blade was conscious of appraising stares being directed at himself and his companions as they walked over to join Wilfrid's group. He was conscious also of the size of some of these men in their heavy battle armour, the long spears and distant looks of those getting ready to lead the advance. His treasured Bloodthirst suddenly felt small beside him.

'Good, my lord prince,' Wilfrid greeted him gravely. 'The men will appreciate having the king's son amongst them. But they do not expect you to lead them. They have good leaders, as you see. And they will protect you. There is no shame in that. There will come a time when you will be leading them, but this is not that time. You need to learn what it is like in the battle's heart first. Everyone here understands that. Do you?'

'Yes,' said Blade.

'My job is to keep you safe. If you die, I die. And like most soldiers, I don't want to die. So, you do what I say and when I say it. If you don't, then I will hit you over the head with this,' he pulled out a club from his belt. 'It will do you some damage, but it won't kill you. And when you come to, you'll need to explain to your father why you disobeyed orders. Do we understand one another?'

'Yes,' Blade muttered. This was his father at work. Keeping him dependent, reminding him through this underling that he was still worth nothing. Well, words weren't important. He'd heard longer lectures in his time. What mattered was action. This insolent Wilfrid knew no more than anyone else what would happen in the next few hours. Blade turned away from him and rolled his eyes at Leofgar, who smiled. Still with that steely look.

A general murmur, some shouts and they were off up the Roman road, clanking gradually uphill. When they reached the top of the rise, the pagans might be in sight. At least to someone. Off his horse, Blade could see little more than the backs of those in front of him. He saw Ealhstan ride up to the top of the rise with Ealdorman Wulfstan, but then they both rode back, dismounted and joined their respective men.

'Why can't we stay on our horses?' Blade asked Wilfrid. 'We'd see more.'

'What do you want to see?'

'The pagans, of course.'

'You'll see them soon enough.'

'But we could go quicker on horses.'

'We don't need to go quicker. A man on a horse is too tempting a target, my lord prince. Some bowman would fancy his chances in bringing you down. And horses bolt when the fighting starts. Horsemen would be all over the place in no time. The pagans could just march straight through us. The only way to stop them is with a solid line. And that can only be held by men on foot.'

They had reached the top of the hill but, to his annoyance, Blade could see no more than when he had been walking up the hill. A mass of backs and heads. 'Can you see them?' he muttered to Leofgar. He had no desire for further conversation with Wilfrid.

'I smell them,' said Leofgar through gritted teeth. Sure enough, his nostrils flared. He was definitely different today. It was as though he had been taken over by some dark spirit. The cheerful, easy-going Leofgar was far away now. Blade had heard of battle fury taking over a man. Is that what had happened to his friend? To those around him? Why didn't he feel it? He felt the same as he always did. Was he taking this all too lightly as some sort of game? He felt a sudden chill in his heart. He could die today. And soon. Was he ready for that? Did he even know what it meant?

As these new thoughts and questions flooded into him, Blade's desire to see the enemy disappeared. Leofgar was right – sight was not that important. There were other senses which could be used. No longer concentrating on trying to observe, Blade fell silent, aware of the silence around him, broken only by the steady trudge of feet and clank of metal.

And then they stopped. He saw no more than he had before, but he knew that the pagans must now be in sight to those at the front. He felt the ripple of fear and anticipation passing though everyone. He was glad he had stopped talking in time. He was as ready now as he ever would be.

Or so he thought. The roar which suddenly erupted from all around him almost took his head off. And then ahead of them came an answering roar, only slightly less loud. So, they were that close.

Moving forward again, this time with every nerve taut. He smelt them now. Or maybe it was his own sweat he smelt. Leofgar was pushing ahead on his left, head down like a bull. He felt a hand grasp his right shoulder. It was Wilfrid. 'Not so fast,' he said. 'We stay back. You need a cool head now.'

Blade slowed his pace and tugged at Leofgar, who looked at him with uncomprehending eyes. 'Easy, Lief,' he said. 'You parents will be avenged today anyway. I want you alive to see that happen.'

The mask of Leofgar's face showed little recognition, but the distraction caused by Blade's tug slowed him anyway and another line of men passed them to support the front.

Blade heard the clash of the shield walls in front of him as the armies smashed into one another head on. Wilfrid had a hand on him again, but he felt no desire to keep going forwards. He couldn't anyway. The forward momentum which had caught them all up was checked, and like a river hitting an obstacle, the currents of men around him were confused, circling. The clang of metal, the shouts and curses were very close. Blade heard a horrible scream, which didn't sound like it came from a man. Maybe it was an outraged spirit, forced from a body.

He sensed he was being sucked in; the forward movement had begun again. Wilfrid was shouting at men to move from around them but Blade felt curiously detached from the surge on either side of him. It was as though he was being taken to a different place. He had a sudden memory of being swept up into his father's arms as a young child and being borne through the air and placed down somewhere completely different.

And then he saw them for the first time. The pagan shields, the raven banner overhead. Pushing their own men back. Maybe he hadn't been going forwards at all; it was just that all round him were going back. The noise seethed around him, pushing him even deeper into himself. Someone collapsed in the wall ahead of them, and he caught sight for a moment of a triumphant enemy face flushed with the battle's heat before a man ran up to fill the gap, treading on the dead man in his haste.

The Blade drew Bloodthirst for the first time. His hands were sweating. The wall was buckling in front of them in several places. Men were running from everywhere to shore it up but he sensed that the pagans were prevailing. The stench of pagan breath was almost upon him.

'What the bloody hell are you doing here?'

It was Ealhstan. Enormous and blood red. Glowering down at him. 'Wilfrid!'

'I've been trying to keep him back!' Wilfrid shouted.

'Get out now! This wall is about to go.'

Even as Ealhstan spoke, a pagan surge forced its way through the wall ahead of them, cutting down men on either side and scything their way forward with exultant cries. Ealhstan turned in fury, smashing his mace down on those of the pagans within his reach. Blade suddenly saw a man heading directly for him with axe held high. This was the moment. He took two steps forward, smashed his own shield into the other's and swung Bloodthirst across the man's unprotected neck. He saw blood gush out from the wound, bubbles appear at the man's mouth and a look of surprise in his light blue eyes. But then there was another man almost upon him with a sword about to thrust. But before he could do so, Wilfrid had hit him from the side, knocking him to the ground. Stopping only to thrust his sword into the twitching body, Wilfrid pulled Blade away from the pagans' attack.

'Where's Leofgar?' panted Blade when Wilfrid allowed a pause, several lines of men now separating them from the fighting around the broken wall.

'With the Devil for all I care!' Wilfrid growled, still smarting from Ealhstan's rebuke.

Blade looked down at Bloodthirst, now christened. They'd killed a man.

*

King Aethelwulf had remained at the top of Leith Hill a long time, watching the pagan army marching down the Roman road. They looked relaxed and unwary. He even spotted the leader called Sigurd. Riding on a fine horse and unhelmeted, his yellow hair shining in the sun. Never had an opportunity like this presented itself to

Aethelwulf. The pagans were normally as elusive as the wind. Truly, God was delivering them into his hands.

'We kill them all,' he said to Ealdorman Huda. 'Not one prisoner. They are to be wiped from the earth. That's the only way this pestilence can be defeated.'

Huda nodded. 'The men are aware. They won't need persuading. Everyone has lost someone or something to the pagans.'

'The signal has been given to Ealhstan?'

'Yes, you can see them starting to assemble.'

Aethelwulf could. From his lofty vantage point, he could see the whole battlefield spread out before him. On the lower ground to the south, the fyrds looked to him like swarms of ants, expanding and contracting with purposeful activity as they drew themselves up into battle order and started to advance. He saw Ealhstan on his horse riding back and forth, organising the whole. And further up the road, still unaware, the pagans marched confidently on. The scouts they had were pitiful, only a few hundred yards ahead of the main body. Aethelwulf watched intently, waiting for the moment of recognition. On the hillside, a few hundred yards away, Swithun was still praying. This was a sort of prayer also, thought Aethelwulf. But it was different. He sensed the battle excitement rising in his gut. The pagans could still bolt when they saw the force ahead of them. It was like a hunt – trying to encircle a deer, which could at any moment change course and dart through the softly advancing men. Should he have ordered the Surry fyrd to advance earlier out of the woods? No, if the pagans saw them, they would definitely bolt. They could only move out from their cover once battle had been joined. There was nothing he could do until then but watch.

The most critical moment was approaching. If there was a wise head among the pagan leaders, he would realise what a dangerous position they were in when he saw the force marching towards them. It wasn't wise to go riding at the head of an army with no helmet on because of your fine yellow hair. But who knew if Sigurd and the others were as careless as had been suggested to him? Surely, someone must appreciate the danger of flank attacks from an enemy given time to prepare? He shouldn't have made that comment to Huda about killing them all. It was tempting fate. Joshua in the Bible had said it, but Joshua had definite instructions from God. Did he? He sneaked another glance over at Swithun. That was a good man. His prayers would be heard.

Now they'd seen them! The scouts had passed through a deserted Aclea and reached the spot where the road began its descent. And, less than a mile away seen the Hampshire and Surrey fyrds marching up the road. Aethelwulf watched them swing their horses around and go galloping back to Sigurd. Surely, he'd have to fight? The fyrds were too close for him to turn his back on them now. Unless he retreated a little way and then turned and fought. But he'd need to be organised and prepared to do that. And what sort of signal would it give to his men if he turned away at the first sight of the enemy?

Aethelwulf strained his eyes, trying to distinguish more of the exchange. Sigurd was signalling to others to join the consultation.

'What do you think he'll do?' Aethelwulf couldn't resist muttering to Huda.

Huda didn't reply. He knew better than to make a guess, which a few moments might prove wrong.

Aethelwulf was praying under his breath. Was it right to pray for the death of others? The pagans had no doubt done so to their bloody gods. Swithun would be praying for something different. Peace. But there could be no peace with these people. He watched Sigurd and those around him, willing them to make the decision which would deliver them into his hands.

And then they did. He felt a spurt of triumph as he saw Sigurd gesture forwards. The other leaders galloped back to their posts and dismounted as the pagans assumed battle formation. Aethelwulf stared with a certain savage satisfaction at the figure of Sigurd getting off his own horse and handing it to an attendant. He was positively fond of the man now. He looked over to Huda and grinned, 'At least he's putting on his helmet.'

'We'll spot him nonetheless,' said Huda grimly. 'Do you want him alive?'

Aethelwulf shrugged. 'We'd only have to kill him later. I don't think a person like that can tell us anything worth knowing. He'd just spit venom. It's not worth risking a life for that. Let him go to his gods fighting.'

Huda nodded. 'I'll go down then.'

'Yes. You know what to do. Wait until they're engaged and then move as quickly as you can.'

Huda left to join his men and lead the advance of the Surrey fyrd out of the woods. Aethelwulf watched him moving purposefully off the hill's brow, with attendants clustering around him.

'Move as quickly as you can,' he repeated to Huda's back and to himself. 'The risk is that they break through Ealhstan's men before you can get there.'

At least Ealhstan knew what it was like to face a pagan assault. He'd been doing so for the past thirty years. And been successful more often than not.

Remaining on the hill's summit, even with his guard around him, Aethelwulf suddenly felt very lonely. Part of him would have liked to have been going down with Huda to join the battle now. In the excitement and heat of conflict, everything else was forgotten. The past and future became irrelevant. Only the present mattered, and in the present one could truly live. But there was still his third force, the Berkshire fyrd in the east, to activate before the trap was sprung. Without the woodland protecting the Surrey fyrd, they had to move later. He needed to wait to give them their signal to advance, which would be the raising of the king's dragon banner on the hill beside him. Only then would he be able to leave this lonely vantage point. In the meantime, he would have to watch as an impotent spectator. If the pagans broke through Ealhstan's men, then it would all be over anyway, and his carefully-laid plans would amount to nothing.

*

The wall was beginning to buckle again. Blade, kept back a hundred yards from the murderous front line by a vigilant Wilfrid, could nevertheless feel the strain and desperation of those in front of him as if they were his own. In a way they were. Every nerve in his body was stretched tight. If the wall gave way, the distance between him and beserker pagans breaking through would be little enough defence.

A similar thought must have occurred to Wilfrid. 'Go back and find your horse,' he muttered.

'I'm not running away.'

'Don't be stupid. Your responsibility is to survive this.'

'I tell you, I'm not running away. You'll have to use that club of yours. And risk Bloodthirst's bite. If I go back, why shouldn't everyone else?'

Ealhstan was back amongst them. This time too preoccupied with holding the line to pay attention to the prince in his midst.

'Forward!' he shouted, directing a number of Blade's companions towards the wall with sweeping motions of his enormous arms. Blade, seeing his opportunity, ran forwards after them before Wilfrid could do anything. In the dense mass of bodies pushing towards the wall, there was no way he could be held back. He was safe. Well, maybe not safe, he thought with a burst of exultant humour. But safe from Wilfrid at least.

'Don't push so hard.' A voice to his right. An older man, not someone he recognised. 'We support the wall, we don't push it over.'

So. More waiting. But this time expecting a gap to open ahead at any moment and the conflict claim him. There was no rank here. He had put himself into a position where anyone and everyone was sword fodder, waiting to be claimed. One of his companions to his left darted forward as an axe crashed down onto the head of someone in the wall, knocking them to the ground. Blade cursed himself for being too slow and then watched as his companion, in too much haste to fill the gap, stumbled over the fallen body and was immediately cut down by the advancing pagan.

'Force *and* cunning,' Blade said to himself, drawing Bloodthirst and advancing slowly towards the man. Let him stumble over the bodies this time.

The man, flushed with two kills in quick succession, gave a roar as he saw Blade advancing towards him. Blade hesitated – through fear or design? It was enough for the man to rush forwards with his axe held high once more. Blade lifted his shield to parry the axe's blow and then stepped forwards himself, scything Bloodthirst across the man's unprotected neck. He heard the scream, felt the jar through his arm and body as Bloodthirst half-took the axe wielder's head off. No time to look back or think. Time only to negotiate the mound of three bodies and lock shields with his companions. He was in the shield wall now.

He noticed Leofgar on his left, but there was no time to speak, even had he wished to. Another pagan was upon him, thrusting a spear towards his head.. He ducked behind the shelter of his shield, glanced at Leofgar, who nodded. They pushed their shields outwards and the spear twisted out of the pagan's hand and fell to the ground. But he recovered swiftly, took a step backwards and met their thrust with his own shield. Then, with a full-throated shout, he advanced once more, smashing his shield against Blade's and almost knocking it out of his hands. Blade clung desperately on to his shield and managed to parry the pagan's sword thrust.

By now he had lost all sense of time. He could not say if it was a matter of moments or hours that he stayed locked in the shield wall, parrying the pagan's blows and trying to find an opening to attack. He had a feeling of being caught up in a tremendous force, bristling at every point with potential agony, requiring a huge amount of concentration to resist. The effort was more mental than physical – a locking of wills with the man in front of him. Something intensely personal. He knew this man now, although he'd only caught a glimpse of him in a moment of terror when he'd knocked his shield out of position. He knew that he was older than him, much more experienced. A good fighter, not a beserker. Someone whose blows were calculated, who had a fall back position.

Blade decided that he couldn't beat such a man on his own. He stopped looking for openings to make an attack himself and concentrated all his efforts on survival. Something deep inside him noticed a pattern in the man's attacks – how he would always push forward on the left and sweep low with his sword to the right. After the third time of parrying this attempted attack, Blade felt a spurt of confidence within his fear. He was aware of a strange delight bubbling within him. *This is what fighting is. And I can do it!'*

*

Up on the hill, King Aethelwulf was watching anxiously the clash of shield walls below him. To begin with, the force of the pagan attack had pushed the fyrds back. He felt the impact physically – his breath caught in his throat and a nauseous taste rose in his throat. They would break through! In his lust for total victory, he'd not allowed enough men to take the initial blow. Man for man, the pagans were better fighters. They were bound to be – it was all they lived for. You needed at least two farmers to counter one pagan warrior. That was basic, the first thing his father had taught him. Men lost their hunger and ferocity with families and land to occupy them. He had been so intent on surrounding the pagans that he'd ignored that basic lesson. By the time the Surrey and Berkshire fyrds reached the fighting, it would be too late.

The rallying of the fyrds' shield walls gave Aethelwulf some respite. He recognised Ealhstan's hand. And, after all, it wasn't as if the fyrds were all farmers – they had experienced warriors in their ranks as well, whom Ealhstan would know how to use. They'd lost some ground but the wall was still intact and that was all that mattered.

Even so, it was agonising to watch the shield walls rippling back and forth and hear the far off cries and clashes reaching him through the bright summer air. The pagans were still going forwards. The centre, in which unbeknownst to Aethelwulf, his eldest son was now locked in mortal combat, was holding its own, but either side was slowly being pushed back. If the sides gave way, then the pagans could surround them before being surrounded themselves.

Where was the Surrey fyrd? Surely, Huda should have started out by now? He looked down to where the Surrey fyrd should have been emerging from the woods, but a spur of the hill blocked his view. He wouldn't see them until they were halfway to the fighting. Should he start the Berkshire fyrd now? No, they were even further away. They wouldn't make any difference to the conflict now raging. They were there to shut off any escape. He could have used them otherwise but it was too late to do so now. How over-confident he had been to leave men to block an escape rather than fight a battle!

'Can you see the Surrey fyrd at all?' Aethelwulf muttered to one of his guards.

'No, sire.'

'Do we have someone further down the hill watching for them?'

The man looked uncertain. If they had, it wasn't something he knew about. Surely, that was something the king would have arranged?

'Well, keep your eyes fixed down there. And let me know as soon as you see anything. And tell everyone else to do so. And you,' he signalled to another guard. 'Go down the hill to that spur over there. As soon as you see our men coming out from the woods then signal back here. Wave your hands. I need to know as soon as they are on their way.'

'Yes, sire.' The man hurried off on his mission. Probably pointless. He might well not be able to see any more down there than they could up here. But it gave the impression of action, of doing something, rather than being at the mercy of events now beyond his control. He paced restlessly along the hilltop, glancing occasionally at the battle below, occasionally at Swithun, still on his knees praying. Waiting was terrible, but he had to wait. 'Have a little faith,' he told himself. 'The wall is being held. Not long now.'

And then a shout from the guards. He hurried over to them.

'You see them?'

'Yes, sire. Down there.' The man pointed to a ridge coming up from a hollow, some distance from the wood's edge. Aethelwulf saw a brown blur, which could be anything. Curse his eyes!

'You see them, too?' he asked another guard.

'Yes, sire.'

The man down on the spur was waving as well. They must be there.

'Good,' said Aethelwulf. 'Raise the banner.'

The dragon banner of Wessex was lifted high. Hopefully, someone in the Berkshire fyrd had better eyes than he did. More waiting. It would be some time before the fyrd came into view of even the sharpest eyes. In the meantime, Aethelwulf looked below. Yes, even he could now see the Surrey fyrd streaming up the shallow hill towards the Roman road. Only a few minutes more and they would be behind the pagans. Some of the pagans had seen them. Some of the pagans had seen the dragon banner as well. Well, they'd have difficulty getting away with the shield walls now fully engaged.

'Can anyone see the Berkshire fyrd?' Aethelwulf called out, anxious to be on his way.

An answering cry from the far side of the hilltop. Aethelwulf hurried over.

'There, sire.'

He squinted where the man was pointing. Yes, there was movement in the eastern distance. That must be them.

'Let's go, then,' he ordered. 'The pagans are surrounded. We'll finish them off.'

The men gave a cheer.

'Do we take the priest?' someone asked, gesturing towards a still kneeling Swithun.

Aethelwulf felt a stab of conscience, as though aware of Swithun's gaze resting upon him.

'No,' he said gruffly. 'It will be no place for a priest.'

*

Something had changed. The fact registered itself on Blade's mind without his knowing quite what. The man in front of him was hesitating, no longer pressing forwards. Some noise, different from battle cries, sounding up ahead. Concern, confusion – put into words by a triumphant Leofgar on his left. 'The Surrey boys!' he shouted with a fierce grin, lunging at the pagan before him. Drawing blood. Blade smelt fear, uncertainty. He pushed forward with his shield, looking for an opening once more.

'Easy.' A voice in his ear. Wilfrid had found him again. 'He'll give way now. You mustn't follow him. The wall has to go forward together."

Sure enough, the man was giving way, along with the whole pagan wall. But in a line still. Not broken yet.

'Keep the line!' Ealhstan's voice bellowing behind. 'Anyone who breaks it is a dead man. Advance three now!'

Blade lined his shield up against Leofgar's on his left and Wilfrid's on his right. Together they pushed forwards, advancing three paces.

'Wait!' Ealhstan again, taking control of the wall.

'They'll come back at us,' Wilfrid said. 'They have to. There's nowhere else for them to go. They're being attacked from behind now. The only way they can survive is by breaking through. They'll throw everything at us soon.'

'You hear that, Lief?' Blade turned to his friend. "They're going to come back at us. They're not broken yet.'

Leofgar turned glazed eyes upon him. He had a gash running down his cheek. He looked in a dangerous, unheeding mood.

'Stay in line,' Blade muttered. 'That's an order.'

'Advance three now.'

They pushed forward again. The wounded pagan in front of Leofgar stumbled backwards. With a cry,

Leofgar swung his sword down past his flailing shield, cutting him down to the ground.

'For God's sake, get back, Lief!'

'The bastards are running!'

From the corner of his eye, Blade could see that some of the pagans were indeed running away. But the mass of men in front of them still looked solid. The gap in the pagan wall caused by Leofgar's kill was quickly filled.

'It's not over yet,' he cried to Leofgar. 'Get back in line!'

Lefogar reluctantly obeyed.

'I know that bastard,' Leofgar panted.

'Which one?'

'The pretty one with the yellow hair, trying to organise them. He was there when they killed my parents.'

'Lief, that was years ago. He would have been a child.'

'There was a child there,' Leofgar snapped. 'He was underneath the tree I was hiding in. I had plenty of time to look. It's him, I tell you.'

'A boy and a man look different.'

'He's the image of his father. He was a pretty man, too. I remember watching him preen himself before slitting my father's throat.'

'You can't be sure,' Blade muttered.

'The bastard's wearing my father's helmet!'

Blade gave up. There was no arguing with Lief in this mood. He'd be seeing his parents' killers everywhere. Who knows, maybe he was right? If not the killers of his parents, then certainly the killers of other people's.

'Advance three now.'

And then they came. A desperate surge as the pagan wall threw itself against them, spitting blood curses and calling on their gods. Blade, caught off balance, was knocked to the ground by the force of an axe smashing into his shield. He looked up to see a pagan sword raised to plunge down into him and tensed himself to receive the blow. But Wilfrid, eyes on his charge, was there, thrusting his sword under the pagan's raised guard, bringing him down in a welter of blood.

Blade scrambled to his feet. Another man was upon him. Frantically, he parried the blows descending upon his shield. The axe which had knocked him down was still lodged in it.

The pagan surge was spending itself. Blade felt the desperate attack of his opponent falter. From behind his shield, he caught a glimpse of the man, his shield dangling loosely by his side. Someone's spear had found its mark. It was easy now to push forward and thrust Bloodthirst into the man's unresisting body. As though he was waiting for death.

'Advance three now.'

Now the pagans in front of them were melting away. Blade could see the dragon banner in the distance. If his father was here, it must be close to the end. He just needed to keep his concentration.

The blond leader in front of them had found a horse and was hurriedly mounting it.

'Lief, no!'

No effect. With a cry, Leofgar leapt forward, running full pelt towards the man to prevent his escape. The man looked up, missed his footing in the stirrup and fell to the ground. Blade watched helplessly as Leofgar's furious charge was cut short by a spear through the throat from one of the remaining pagans.

'Who was that bloody fool?' Ealhstan again. The man seemed everywhere.

Blade lurched forward to follow his friend. Only then was he conscious of a tight grip on the back of his tunic. Wilfrid.

'Don't be a fool as well! The pagan's dead anyway – he won't get away on a horse.'

'But Lief!'

'He's dead, too. That was his fate. You could see in his eyes that he was marked for death.'

Sure enough, as the wall advanced and reached the spot where Leofgar had fallen, Blade could see that his life had fled.

'Take his body back for burial,' Wilfrid suggested. 'That would be a service for him. You've fought bravely today, my lord prince. It is all but over now. Just the slaughter to come.'

But Blade, staring at Leofgar's prone body, his face still with a snarl of rage upon it, was in the mood for the slaughter. He would see this through. Finish the job for his friend. 'The women can bury him,' he said.

Ahead, he could see the Surrey fyrd hacking into the rear of the pagans, who were twisting and turning, like fish caught in a net. And there was his father, motionless on a white horse by the dragon banner, watching the completion of his plan.

Over to the east, fleeing pagans were being cut down by the advancing Berkshire fyrd.

'Advance in a line and engage!' Ealhstan's roar. No need to limit the advance to three paces now. The pagan will to resist was broken. With nowhere to go, surrounded on all sides, they could do nothing but die. Blade, in a cold fury, lost count of the men he killed then. Like pig-sticking, he thought to himself, thrusting Bloodthirst into another pagan body, watching the lifeblood spurt out, hearing the death cry once more before moving on to another kill. At one point, Wilfrid touched his right hand and pointed to a mass of corpses, including that of the blond leader Leofgar had pursued. Someone had no doubt claimed his horse. Horses were valuable.

Such a waste, Lief, such a waste, Blade thought, before turning back in his cold emptiness to kill another pagan.

Some time later, he didn't know how long, there were no more pagans to kill. Just mounds and mounds of their corpses. He felt sick, choked down the bile rising in his throat. What do you do when there are no more pagans left to kill?

'Well done, my lord prince!' Ealhstan huge, bloody and jubilant. 'You fought like ten men today! Let us go to your father.'

He shouldered a way for them through the crowd surrounding the king, still motionless on his white horse.

'My lord king!' Ealhstan exclaimed. 'My congratulations! You have a lion of a son. No one fought braver than he at the battle's heart. He is truly a leader of men. The future is bright for your glorious house.'

Aethelwulf looked down from his horse. His gaze was distant. Blade could see no triumph or affection in it.

'Well done, my son,' he said levelly. 'You have made your father very proud.' He unbuckled his sword, which had remained sheathed throughout the battle, and handed it down. 'I know your fondness for swords. So have mine as a token of my increased esteem.'

There was a cheer from those around him as Blade took the sword. He unsheathed it. There was intricate carving on the blade. A finer sword than Bloodthirst, no doubt of it. But was he to abandon Bloodthirst now after what they had just been through together? No. This was a ceremonial sword. It had not been drawn in anger. And was that a mocking look in his father's eyes? *I know your fondness for swords.* Somehow he knew that, whatever he might say, his father's view of him remained the same. Old men don't change their minds unless forced to. Well, what did he expect? Whatever the king might think, others had certainly been impressed with him this day. He handed the sword to a companion, keeping Bloodthirst with him.

'The king does me great honour,' he responded coolly. 'We are indebted to his wisdom for this great victory.'

'To God, my son,' Aethelwulf corrected him.

To God. That would explain his distant look. He's been praying. Trying to reconcile this slaughter with his God.

3. Growing Pains

'How is he?' Osburh demanded anxiously.

Yetta tried to reply but could not. Her helpless wide-eyed look was answer enough. Osburh pushed past her into the small room where Alfred lay. Alive! Thank you, my lady Frige. His breathing still shallow and irregular, his brow still burning, but alive. Osburh felt a wave of relief that Yetta's look had not meant what she'd feared.

'All right, Yetta,' she said. 'Go and get some sleep. I'll take over now.'

'You need to sleep yourself, my lady.'

'I'll sleep when he's well,' she replied. *And if he doesn't get well, I'll never sleep again.* She banished the thought angrily. He will live. Merciful Frige, you gave me this child and have kept death from him before. You cannot mean to take him now. I named him as one of your acolytes, despite my husband's opposition. You told me he would become a great man. His life has only just begun and yet he has already pierced my heart more than any of my other children. No, you will not take him. You will send Eir, your beautiful companion, to wipe this fever from his brow.

At this thought, she dipped a cloth into a bowl of water beside the bed and gently wiped Alfred's face. Still burning. He moaned a little, his eyelids flickering.

'Alfred,' she whispered. 'Be strong. I'm here with you. I'm always with you.'

Not quite true that, she thought with a stab of guilt. Since Alfred had fallen ill two days ago, complaining of a pain in his stomach, she had been beside him most of the time. But she had been forced to leave his side for a few hours to greet Burgred, the new king of Mercia, arrived on an official visit to the House of Wessex and, it was understood, to pay court to her only daughter, Aethelswith. They had been preparing for Burgred's visit for weeks. An alliance with Mercia had always formed part of Aethelwulf's plans, and for her not to greet its new king would have been a grave affront. So she had had to leave Alfred in Yetta's care for a few torturous hours, put on her finest garments and try to smile graciously at her important guest. He was a short, wiry man. Not so very old. Polite, but then so he should be if he had come a-wooing. In normal times, she would have enjoyed this meeting, had indeed been looking forward to it. But these were not normal times and she'd had difficulty in concentrating on anything the man was saying. Eventually, she'd had to apologise for failing to reply to a question.

'I'm so sorry, my lord. It's my youngest son. He's fallen very ill . . .'

Aethelwulf had frowned at that. Private affairs should not intrude on matters of state, but she was damned if she was going to pretend that everything was all right just to please some king of Mercia. If she did, she'd be expected to attend the banquet in his honour that evening and she certainly wasn't going to do that with Alfred's life hanging in the balance. After her revelation, Burgred had had little option but to insist that she return to Alfred's side. Rushing back, she had feared the worst. Frige had been known to punish neglectful mothers, who spent the rest of their lives in agonies of guilt. But no, he was alive. Wild horses or a declaration of war by Mercia would not drag her away from his side now.

She held one of his little hands. Hot and sweaty. But was the pulse becoming a little calmer, stronger? She breathed in deeply, trying to fill her mind with the sweetest and gentlest of thoughts, as if she could draw the fever out through his hand and breathe health and happiness back in.

How long she remained there, she did not know. Time had lost its meaning. Everything focused on this little boy, willing his breathing to deepen, some sign that the worst was over. It was dark now, she noticed. They would have started the banquet by now. At least no-one had come for her.

The door opened at that thought.

'Mother?'

Aethelswith. She turned her head slightly, reluctant to let any of her attention leave Alfred, even for a moment.

'What is it, my child?'

'The doctor's outside. He wants to see Alfred.'

'No.'

'He says that father . . .'

'I don't care what your father may have said to him. He's not coming in. Tell him if he's needed, I'll send for him.'

Doctors were all right in their place. When you were well. But not when you were ill. She'd seen too many illnesses get worse under doctors' ministrations to trust Alfred to one at this critical moment. He'd start questioning the wise woman's remedies she was using to combat the fever. He'd probably want to bleed the boy because of something a Greek had written hundreds of years ago. She was not going to waste her energies arguing with a doctor when she needed them all to focus on Alfred's every breath, ensure him of her presence. That is what would cure him. And if it didn't, then she would die as well and go and join him in the afterworld.

'Mother?' Aethelswith again.

'Have you sent the doctor away?'

'Yes, He wasn't very happy.'

'No, he wouldn't be.'

'Mother, can I come and sit with you and Alfred? I'm frightened.'

'The spinning, child!' Osburh exclaimed, suddenly remembering. 'Who's spinning? It mustn't stop – you know that.'

'Yetta came and asked to take over. She said that she couldn't sleep and it was the next best thing to sitting with Alfred.'

Osburh felt a spurt of annoyance at Aethelswith for giving up such an important task to a slave. But then Yetta was no ordinary slave. She loved Alfred more than anyone, except herself. Certainly more than Aethelswith did. But there, she was being unfair. The girl was only young, and surrounded by brothers. It wasn't easy for her, and she'd been spinning for hours. She was probably tired.

'Come and join me then,' she said. 'There's a seat here. But we must be quiet and concentrate on Alfred. He's still very ill.'

Aethelswith sat herself down beside her mother and snuggled close to her.

'Alfred, Elsa's here,' said Osburh, using the name which Alfred, who struggled to pronounce Aethelswith, called his sister, and which the family had adopted as a pet name for her.

'Hello, Alfred,' said Elsa, leaning forwards. 'We're all waiting for you to get better. Diarmait has composed a special song for you.'

'Tell him you love him,' breathed Osburh.

It was quite dark in the room but, even so, Osburh thought she could see a hurt look cross her daughter's face.

'Of course I love you,' Elsa said with a note of complaint in her voice. 'You know that, don't you, Alfred?'

'I'm sorry,' whispered Osburh. 'I'm just so worried for him. I don't know what I'm saying half the time.'

'You're just tired, mummy. We all are. We'll watch together and help one another.'

Osburh felt sudden tears prick her eyes. Elsa could be irritable and peevish but she had a good heart. She'd never really given her credit for that, never loved her in the way she loved the boys. And maybe it was too late to do much about that now if Aethelwulf decided that an alliance with Mercia was worth the investment of his daughter.

'Thank you,' she said, running a hand over Elsa's hair. Her father's thick hair. 'You're right. I do need you. I'm glad you're here.'

Together they watched in silence, and it was easier than watching alone. Her fear had been that Alfred would resent his sister's presence as being a rival claim on her attention. But he showed no signs of increased restlessness as they were talking to one another. It was easier talking to Elsa, dealing with her known concerns, than the one-sided conversation with Alfred, anxiously scanning his face for some sign of a response. And their known voices should be a comfort to him. So when Elsa broke the silence with a question, she decided it would not be wrong to respond.

'Mummy, why is it so important that we should continue spinning while Alfred is ill?'

Osburh dipped the cloth in the bowl again and wiped Alfred's brow. Still burning. The wise woman had said that the heat would continue rising until the crisis was reached. If the fever broke, then he would start to sweat profusely and the danger was over. If it didn't break . . . no, that was not a possibility which she would entertain. He did seem calmer, tossing and turning less often.

Elsa knew the answer to her question. As did Alfred. It was something she had told them many times. But it would be good to tell them again. In honour of Frige. To show that their thoughts and prayers were still with her, even if Yetta was doing the spinning.

'Frige holds the destiny of us all in her hands, Elsa. She spins each thread of life and then weaves it into the world's wyrd. If a thread snaps then a life is lost. So, we are spinning the thread of Alfred's life to make sure that it is strong and does not snap. And making sure that Mother Frige is aware of our prayers to her for his coming through this night.'

'Is it the same as what the monks are doing?'

Ever since Alfred had fallen ill, Swithun had arranged for perpetual prayers to be said for his recovery.

Osburh considered. It was an intelligent question. And whatever she thought about his religion, she knew that Swithun was a good man. His praying for Alfred's recovery could only help.

'I don't know,' she replied at last. 'I suppose we can all only do what seems right to us. Mother Frige has been good to me and I trust her. No doubt the monks feel the same about Jesus Christ.'

'But you're a Christian, aren't you?' Elsa persisted. 'You come to church with us.'

At some other time, Osburh might have temporised, as she had had to do so often in matters of religion. But this was not some other time. And this was her daughter, who might soon be having to make her own decisions in life.

'We women must adapt ourselves to our menfolk, Elsa. If they hold strong beliefs, then we must hold them too. Outwardly.'

'And inwardly?'

'Inwardly, I follow the old religion. I always have.'

Elsa was silent, considering.

'What does Mother Frige think about you going to church?' she asked eventually.

The girl was definitely intelligent. How had she underrated her all these years?

'I don't know,' Osburh admitted. 'I can only hope that, being a woman herself, she will understand. And shield me from her husband's wrath.'

'I believe in Jesus,' said Elsa.

Osburh suddenly felt old and very lonely. 'That's probably just as well,' she said quietly. *My lady, forgive me. What can I do?*

Elsa slipped her hand into her mother's. 'And I love you, mummy. Thank you for talking to me as a grown up.'

Osburh smiled sadly. She would miss Elsa. They were just getting to know one another. 'You are a grown up,' she said. 'Almost.'

She had no doubt that Elsa would be well aware of the main reason for King Burgred's visit. She was far too intelligent not to have worked that out, even though nothing had been said to anyone. And nothing was said now. She sensed Elsa's reluctance to hear about the man sitting in the hall with her father, maybe even now discussing her future.

Osburh shared her reluctance. There was little enough time for them to be together. And this small room, which had been a place of dread for her only an hour or so ago, now seemed like some sort of haven against the world outside. How much was Alfred and how much Elsa, how much Mother Frige and how much Jesus Christ, she did not know. Only that love held them all and was a healing force. She leant against her daughter and started to cry.

Elsa put her arm around her and drew her closer. 'It's all right, mummy. You can sleep now. You're exhausted. You've been up for two days and nights. Don't worry. Alfred will come through this. Yetta is spinning and I am watching.'

*

'I am sorry my wife is unable to join us this evening,' Aethelwulf said. 'Our boy Alfred is still very ill. She insists on watching over him.'

'I quite understand,' Burgred replied. 'I'm only sorry that my visit should have come at such a difficult time for you all.'

'We are concerned, although the doctor does not think that the illness is life-threatening.' It would help if my wife would let him see his patient, Aethelwulf thought but did not say. 'Prayers are being said in the chapel.'

'I'm sure that everything which can be done is being done,' said Burgred. 'Ultimately, all our lives are in God's hands.'

He's a smooth character, thought Aethelwulf. Very different from Beorthwulf, his cousin and predecessor, who had been something of a bully, holding Mercia's feuding factions together through a combination of force and fear. It was the only way, he thought, to rule such an impossible country – so many different tribes and traditions, hatreds and rivalries. Only a strong man could rule them all. And Mercia's kings had always been strong men. The successful ones, that is. The weak ones soon perished. But this Burgred seemed a very different proposition – small, polite, even-tempered. He'd not flickered an eyelid at the presence of Cynehelm at Aethelwulf's table. He'd bowed gravely on being introduced and said calmly, 'We are acquainted.'

Aethelwulf had been impressed. A man should be able to control his emotions, a king most of all. He believed this man capable of diplomacy, of playing off one quarrelsome family against another, which was an essential kingly attribute. But did he have the strength to back up his diplomacy? He had led the most successful attack against the pagans in the battle over London. And to overthrow another king implied a certain amount of strength and ability to use force. Had Beorthwulf been overthrown? He had died conveniently enough in a small village in the north of the country, some distance from Burgred's ancestral lands. No one seemed to know the precise circumstances of his death. That could be seen as fortunate. Mercia had more than enough blood feuds already. But Aethelwulf suspected that the one person who almost certainly did know how Beorthwulf had died was sitting beside him now, with a look of polite concern for the health of his little boy.

'My congratulations, brother king,' he said, 'on your recent elevation.'

'Thank you,' Burgred replied. 'The congratulations of the king of Wessex are a treasure indeed. My poor country has suffered much in recent years, but your goodwill is wealth.'

Yes, definitely smooth. Aethelwulf saw no profit in continuing to exchange compliments with him – the man would no doubt be able to keep that going all night. He decided to instil a little realism into the conversation.

'It's no secret that our kingdoms have had their differences over the years,' he said. 'I have fought your forebears, brother king.'

'Indeed,' Burgred replied. 'In different times.'

'In different times, as you say. We have no quarrel now, as far as I am concerned. Our borders are fixed. I am content that it is so. And I have long held the view that a strong England needs a strong Mercia.'

Burgred bowed his head slightly. 'I am delighted to hear that from your lips, brother king. Everyone knows how much the whole of England owes to the valour of Wessex, particularly your magnificent victory over the pagans at Aclea.'

Aethelwulf allowed the compliment. Aclea had certainly been magnificent – the entire pagan invading force wiped out in a day. It would be no bad thing for Mercia to always remember it. 'We have rid ourselves of the pagans for now. But I am not so foolish as to think that another swarm will not be infesting our shores before long. We must remain strong, alert and united.'

'That is my greatest wish also,' said Burgred solemnly.

Aethelwulf's mind was almost made up. Only the Lord could see directly into the heart of another. And with a man like this one, he doubted whether, even if he were to remain with them for weeks, he would be any clearer as to the man's essential worth. He said the right things, reports of his valour were good, he conducted himself well and had been unanimously acclaimed king without rival of a country whose alliance he needed. What more could he ask for? Only Elsa would find out in time who he really was. And if the truth was not good, it would be too late to do anything about it. But that was the wager one always made in these matters; and women's destiny as the weavers of peace held its own risks. Sometimes one got a beautiful cloth, other times a cracked loom.

But Beorthwulf's death troubled him. He had not liked the man, and Mercia was undoubtedly better off without him. But if Burgred had ordered his death, could he entrust his only daughter to a murderer? Even a murderer with very good reasons? *My lord Jesus*, he prayed, *send your Spirit to guide me now*.

'My brother king,' he said hesitantly, 'I am a Christian. As is my family.'

'I am a Christian, too,' said Burgred, puzzled. 'As is all of Mercia. Is not every civilised person a Christian?'

'It is my dearest wish to go on pilgrimage to Rome before I die.'

'A very worthy wish. Many kings have done so before you.'

'Yes. And before the Lord, a king is no different from any other pilgrim. Just as, when we come to be judged, we will not be treated differently from those who are our subjects in this world.'

'I'm afraid that I do not understand why you mention this now,' said Burgred.

'I am troubled by the death of King Beorthwulf.'

Burgred became very still. His gaze was piercing. 'Why so, brother king?' he asked softly.

'He was a hard man. I believe that he had blood on his hands. It is difficult for kings not to have blood on their hands, particularly if they win the crown through their own efforts, rather than inheriting it from a strong father.'

'Mercia has suffered much since great King Offa's line died out,' said Burgred. 'We have not had Wessex's good fortune of stable rule in recent years. I aim to put that right.'

'I wish you well in your task. But I am concerned for King Beorthwulf. Facing the Lord unshriven.'

'That is a risk which every Christian faces in this world of violence. Not everyone has the good fortune to have a priest on hand when they die. And who knows? Maybe Beorthwulf confessed his sins before he died. He must have known his life was in danger.'

'Why do you say that?'

'Because there was a rebellion against him. And yes, I was one of the leaders of that rebellion. Because he had let our country down and concluded a shameful peace with the pagans. A king can only rule in Mercia with the consent of his lords. Beorthwulf had lost that consent.'

'I don't question that,' said Aethelwulf. 'Neither do I question your right to rule, having been acclaimed by your lords. My concern is a more private one – the death of Beorthwulf. Does anyone know how he died?'

'I am told he had taken refuge in a village in the forest of Sherwood, north of Nottingham. His men had deserted him and he was trying to recruit the villagers to his service. They refused and a dispute arose. I am told that Beorthwulf drew his sword and was struck down. Nobody knows by whom. It may have been more than one villager.'

'Has there been any trial?'

'No. Every villager swears that they do not know who killed him and I am not going to kill a whole village when it may very well have been self-defence. As I am sure you will appreciate, that is not the way for a new ruler to endear himself to his people. But I swear to you, as a Christian and on peril of my soul, that the villagers did not kill him on my orders. I will not pretend that it was not convenient that he died when he did, as far as our country is concerned. His death almost certainly saved us further bloodshed. But I did not order it.'

'Thank you,' said Aethelwulf. 'I am sorry to have had to question you on such a sensitive matter, but it was important for me to know. Your frank explanation does you credit, brother king. I hope that our friendship and association will be long and fruitful for both our countries.'

'Amen to that,' said Burgred.

There was some movement in the doorway and Swithun entered the hall. Aethelwulf turned to him sharply. 'Do you bring me news, Father?'

'Good news, thanks be to God,' Swithun replied. 'Prince Alfred's fever has broken. The doctor is with him and says he is out of danger. He is weak, but he will live.'

Aethelwulf bowed his head. 'Thanks be to God, indeed. And thank you for your prayers, Father. Please keep them up for him to regain his full strength.'

'We will all do that, sire.'

'How is my wife?' Aethelwulf asked.

'Exhausted, sire. The doctor has ordered her to take some rest.'

'Is she?'

'She has retired to bed, yes.'

Obeying the doctor, thought Aethelwulf. She must be tired.

'Is anyone with the boy now, apart from the doctor?'

'Princess Aethelswith, sire. She has been with her mother these past hours, tending to Alfred. A great support to them both. A veritable angel of compassion.'

Aethelwulf smiled to himself. If Swithun wasn't such a holy man, he'd make an excellent courtier. He was ahead of them all in praising Elsa to her potential suitor.

'I'll go to them,' Aethelwulf said. He turned to Burgred, 'Brother king, will you accompany me?'

'Gladly.'

They made their way out of the hall and up to the room where Alfred lay, watched over by Elsa and the doctor, both of whom were startled by the sudden arrival of the two kings.

Aethelwulf sat down on a stool beside Alfred's head and stared intently down at him.

'He's sweating very heavily.'

'That is a good sign, sire. It is the fever leaving him,' said the doctor.

Elsa wiped Alfred's brow with the damp cloth., trying to ignore the presence of the stranger standing beside Swithun, feeling her own cheeks beginning to burn. Why had her father brought him here now, when she was barely dressed?

'This is my daughter, Aethelswith,' she heard her father say. 'King Burgred of Mercia.'

She raised her eyes reluctantly and looked at him. He wasn't tall, but what did that matter? Not so very old – maybe in his thirties. Her fear had been someone her father's age, with a bulging belly and hair growing out of his ears. Dark. A self-contained air. But he was looking at her with respect. His eyes a little averted as well. Not staring. Aware of her nervousness. Who knows, maybe a little nervous himself? He would hide that well, she decided. Something within her stirred – maybe relief, but also amusement at catching herself attributing qualities to a man she'd only just met.

*

Alfred's recovery was slow. To begin with, it was quite agreeable lying in bed with a dreamy feeling, listening to people talking or reading him stories. But after a few days, he was bored of that and wanted to get up. It was a nasty shock when he tried to do so. His legs shook beneath him and he felt a stabbing pain in his stomach. He fell to the floor and Osburh scolded him back to bed. After that, it was not so agreeable being an invalid. He began to worry that he'd never be allowed out of bed again. The doctor looked concerned and conferred regularly with Osburh, even bringing in another doctor to examine him at one stage. The man looked down at him unsympathetically, prodded him sharply in various places and asked him lots of brusque questions, hardly listening to his replies. Alfred was aware of some battle going on between his mother and the doctors – he heard raised voices outside his door and saw them glowering at one another when they were with him. The doctors made him drink a lot of foul-tasting medicine. And when they had gone, his mother gave him some more, equally unpleasant.

Uncertain of what was happening to him, but acutely aware of the hostile atmosphere all around, Alfred longed to escape, to at least go outside, into the sunshine which tantalised him from his window. But one thing his mother and the doctors were agreed upon was that he had to stay where he was, while they argued around him.

His nurse, Yetta, was a calming influence, sitting beside him for hours on end with her spindle, saying little. But Alfred realised that Yetta, comforting presence though she was, wouldn't have any say in what was going to happen to him. Swithun, when he looked in, nearly always managed to cheer Alfred up with some encouraging words, but he was too busy to be able to stay for long. Diarmait bought his lyre up to the sick room and played some tunes, but this resulted in Alfred getting so excited and distressed when he had to leave that further visits were prohibited.

He obtained little comfort from most of the family members who came and kept him company. His mother, perhaps because of her battles with the doctors, often seemed exhausted and emotional when she was with him. She would stare at him with a fixity which made Alfred feel uncomfortable. Once, when he was awaking from a sleep, he was aware of his mother looking down at him and heard her say, softly but intensely, 'I will not let them bleed you, my darling boy.' He knew it was something he was not meant to hear and so he didn't ask her what bleeding was. It seemed to be another threat hanging over him.

Elsa, when she came to sit with him, was bossy as usual, but less inclined to talk than she normally was. She was lost in thoughts of her own. Alfred had heard the slaves talking about her in connection with a visiting Mercian. Something was going on which was absorbing her attention. Alfred had never felt very comfortable with his sister and so was not anxious for her to talk to him. If she was talking to him, she'd probably be telling him off for something or other. But her remoteness, so different from the Elsa he knew, was another slightly unsettling mystery.

His father visited him rarely and stayed only briefly. He talked of God, and of accepting everything because it all came from Him and had a purpose. Alfred didn't understand what he was talking about and was not unhappy when he left.

He was even happier when Redi left. Redi was the worst visitor of all. He was delighted that Little Elf was confined to bed for an indefinite period. He breezed into the sick room with tales of life outside in the glorious sunny weather. He told Alfred of being taken hunting, of watching the hawks fly after their prey, and the progress he was making in riding, glowing with outdoor health and humour. Alfred buried his head in his pillow and, after making a number of scenes, eventually succeeded in getting Redi banned from visiting him.

There was only one family member whose visits Alfred looked forward to – his elder brother Aethelbert, or Berti, as he was known. Bertti had suffered from long illnesses in the past and knew what it was like to have to stay in bed while others were active around him. He didn't preach at Alfred, or try to persuade him that he was better than he was. Instead, he regarded him with an invalid's confederacy.

'It's not easy,' he said in answer to Alfred's questioning as to how he had endured staying in bed for so long and, more importantly, how he had managed to get out eventually. 'You have to listen to your body. Other people will give you all sorts of advice, but if you listen to your body, it will tell you what to do and when to do it.'

'Mummy says I get upset too easily.'

'Then practise not getting upset. When you find yourself getting upset, start thinking about other things. It's very useful learning how not to get upset. Some people never do. There are lots of useful things you can learn lying in bed. It needn't be wasted time.'

With Berti to encourage him, Alfred started to think of all the things he could do, rather than those he couldn't. He started lessons with Colman, who was under-employed now that Redi was spending most of his time hunting. Stories from the Bible took him away into a strange land of deserts and lions, of cruel kings and brave holy men. Of a terrifying God who thundered in smoke on the top of a mountain and a gentle God who walked on water and died on a cross. He was the one they worshipped in church, Alfred knew, although it wasn't easy to connect what went on in church, with the stories he discussed with Colman. On the whole, he preferred David, who fought battles and played on a harp like Diarmait, although Colman told him that David wasn't as good as Jesus and did some bad things, for which God punished him. But as Colman refused to say what the bad things were, Alfred felt that they couldn't be that bad and needn't stop him liking David, particularly as Colman admitted that, on the whole, he was very good.

The lessons with Colman went on longer and longer as Alfred, in the first flush of enthusiasm, kept on asking questions. The doctors grumbled that he would tire himself out but Aethelwulf was not about to restrict his son in learning scripture.

'If his health is in danger, as you say,' he retorted to the doctors, 'then what is more important than his learning to love God?'

He was rather proud of Alfred's enthusiasm for the Bible. He was aware that none of his other sons shared his religious convictions. At least he had one boy who might follow him on the most important journey of all.

'Colman says he's one of the most intelligent boys he's ever taught, particularly given his young age,' Swithun reported.

'Do you think he'll make a priest?' Aethelwulf asked.

Swithun hesitated. 'He's very young,' he said finally. 'He has a sharp mind, he's curious and has a strong imagination. All good things, but they could lead him in many different directions. To be a priest is a calling – a calling to self-sacrifice. It's too soon to tell whether Alfred has that.'

'He's not strong, though, is he?' said Aethelwulf. 'To rule in this world, one must fight. If he's too weak to fight, then . . .' He was about to say, 'being a priest is the next best thing' but realised it might not be a tactful thing to say to Swithun, and not exactly what he thought, either. 'He could help in other ways,' he concluded instead.

'You don't know that he's too weak to fight,' Swithun replied. 'It's too soon for that sort of judgement as well. Many great kings and leaders have suffered illnesses when young. Early suffering can make one stronger. And rulers need wisdom more than strength.'

Aethelwulf nodded. Yes, it was too soon. But he'd always thought of Alfred as a priest. Berti as well, perhaps, although Berti had never shown Alfred's enthusiasm for the Bible. If Berti became a priest, he'd be a politician like the Archbishop of Canterbury. Alfred might actually believe.

'I'd like to encourage him,' he said. 'But not too much. What do you think I should do?'

'Give him a psalter. It's a bit early but he's shown enthusiasm for David, and the psalter is David's work above all else.'

'It's in Latin.'

'Yes,' said Swithun with a smile. 'Colman can start teaching him Latin using it. If Alfred learns Latin to understand the word of God, then it may be a sign he is being called to become a priest.'

Alfred's enthusiasm at being given a book of his own was a little tempered by the fact that it was in a foreign language. He struggled to pick out words in English with Colman's help. How was he going to manage in Latin? Still, it was a book, and it was his. Redi didn't have a book. Next time he came and taunted him, he'd tell him to go away as he was reading his book. He fingered the soft leather covering and the gold studs which held it in place, turned over the creamy thick pages in a sort of wonder. The regular thick black letters fascinated him as some deep mystery. But it was a mystery he couldn't penetrate and he spent most of his time looking at the bright illustrations contained within the capital letters at the beginning of each psalm. These he could understand, the black writing he couldn't, was rather frightened of it. Even when Colman began to take him through the first psalm, explaining what the words meant, he couldn't really connect the labyrinthine explanations with the mysterious writing.

Osburh, suspicious of the monks' influence on her son, did not find it difficult to draw his attention away from the psalter with a book of English poems full of battles, dragon-slaying and large, vibrant pictures. Alfred turned to this eagerly. He had heard many of the poems before but to have them within his hands, to look at the pictures and relate them to the stories he knew, to listen to familiar words in rhythms which set his heart pounding – that was something special. Even King David was overshadowed. Colman complained to Swithun that the boy had less persistence than he'd given him credit for.

'He's young,' Swithun replied, unconcerned. 'It's not unnatural. The main thing is that he's growing stronger.'

And he was. Whether it was through listening to his body, through lessons and books (or the desire to escape them) or simply the passage of time, Alfred was slowly managing to leave his bed for longer and longer periods. His shaky feet regained their strength, the pain in his stomach died down to a background ache, and every day he ventured further away from his room. The doctors retreated to the background, and Osburh silently congratulated herself for seeing her boy though his danger.

*

Aethelwulf knew he had seen the face before. It was not a face to be forgotten easily – gaunt and severe with eyes that flashed a dark light. A priest from another world.

'Do you remember me, my lord king?'

'Yes,' Aethelwulf said thickly. There was ice around his heart.

'And you remember the tale I told you?'

'Yes.'

The priest's lips formed into the shape of a ghastly smile. Aethelwulf's teeth ached as he forced them into a returning grimace.

'Come,' said the priest, beckoning him forward. 'You are to see what I told you yourself.'

'Jesus Christ, protect me,' Aethelwulf muttered, following the beckoning finger.

And there it was, just as the priest had told him before – a stone city with noble buildings. And, towering above them all, an enormous church. Aethelwulf followed his guide through a door which seemed to stretch up into the sky. Inside, was a strange blue light, streaming in through coloured windows. And, as the priest had said, the church was full of row upon row of desks, with a child at each one, reading a book.

'Look closer,' said the priest, still with that awful smile.

'I believe you,' said Aethelwulf. 'I never said that I didn't.'

But his reluctance was not strong enough to counter whatever had led him here and he found himself, definitely shaking now, behind a boy, looking over his shoulder at the book he was reading.

The priest had appeared to him many years before and told him of being taken to this church by another guide, who showed him the children reading books. When he looked closer, he saw that in each of the books they were reading, underneath each line of black writing was a line written in blood. When he had asked his guide what it meant, he had been told that the lines of blood were the sins of the Christian people, polluting their sacred books. And the children were the souls of saints who read, grieved and prayed for repentance before it was too late. Before the lines of blood completely flowed over the precepts of God.

And Aethelwulf, looking over the boy's shoulder, saw what he had feared he would. Except this time there were two lines of blood for every line of black and as he looked, appalled, the blood seemed to be expanding before his eyes and forming into the shape of his children.

'I must look away,' he gasped to himself. But the vision held him in its grip. He realised that there was something familiar in the head of the boy over whose shoulder he was looking. The boy was turning his head. In a moment, he'd be looking into his eyes . . .

He woke with a shout, kicking out at the blankets in his haste to get away.

'What is it?' Osburh was beside him, pulling the blankets back over his shaking limbs. He looked at her uncomprehendingly, his eyes wild.

'What is it?' she repeated, concerned. 'Don't worry. Whatever it was, it was only a dream. You're safe here with me.' She passed her hand gently over his brow. Ice cold.

He closed his eyes and sighed deeply.

'It wasn't just a dream,' he said at length. 'It was *the* dream.'

'I don't understand.'

'The dream I've had before – the priest, the church and the children reading. Except this time it wasn't just the priest telling me – I saw it myself with my own eyes. And the lines of blood were getting bigger.'

Yes, she remembered that dream. And she knew what was coming next. She steeled herself to resist.

'It's still just a dream,' she said. 'Whether you saw it or the priest saw it. It makes no difference'

'It's not just a dream,' he said quietly. 'It's a warning.'

'Of what?' she asked, wishing he would open his eyes and look at her. He needed warmth. She lay down on his chest and hugged him to her. 'You're a good man, Wulf. And your people are good, too. But they have suffered, we all have – that's where the blood comes from. It's not your fault.'

This time, he did open his eyes and look at her. But his eyes were cold.

'The lines of blood weren't suffering, they were sins – that's what the priest said.'

'That's what priests always say,' said Osburh, exasperated beyond her usual caution. 'They're obsessed with sins. Sins are what give them their power. If there were no sins, there'd be no need for priests.'

Aethelwulf pushed her off him, sat up and glared down at her. 'You're talking like a devil.'

Osburh sighed. She had gone too far. She would get nowhere attacking his religion. 'I'm sorry,' she said. "I know we're all in need of God's mercy; me, most of all. But what are you doing that's so wrong? You've beaten the pagans. No one's had so splendid a victory over them as you. Isn't that a sign that God approves of you?'

'We were permitted to win this time. Next time,' he shrugged. 'Who knows? They may not have such foolish leaders. We can't expect them to keep on walking blindly into traps. And if it comes to an even fight. . .' he paused – it was getting light outside already. 'They may very well beat us. It wouldn't take much. This country is worm-eaten. There is no virtue any more. The smallest of victories would start people defecting to the pagans if they thought it worth their while.'

Osburh sat up and put an arm tentatively around him. 'Not with you as their king,' she said. 'You've fought for them so many times. They will fight for you.'

Aethelwulf gave a bitter smile. 'You think too well of people, my dear. That's where your religion lets you down. It takes no account of sin.'

She sensed his weariness as they sat there together in the pre-dawn light. Weary of fighting. Sick to death of constant battles, which changed nothing, apart from brutalising the country more. Not the first king of Wessex to have thought that way; and seen Rome as a personal solution.

'You remember when I last had this dream?'

'You said you'd go to Rome,' she said, deciding to tackle it head on.

'And you persuaded me not to.'

'We had young children, Wulf. We still have young children. Who will protect them with you gone? And do you plan to return.? If so, who will hold the kingdom for you? You're worried that people won't fight for you? They're much less likely to do so with you on the other side of the world.'

She could feel his exasperation rising. She was only telling him things he already knew. He would have raised these objections with himself hundreds of times before. But that was no reason for her not to raise them again.

'Blade is old enough now,' he replied.

'You said you didn't trust him.'

'He can rule in the east with Elchere. Elchere tells me that he is doing quite well over there. And he showed he could fight at Aclea. I have to give him his chance soon anyway. Otherwise, he'll try and take it from me. But I don't want to give him the main kingdom to rule.'

'Who would rule here?'

'Berti.'

'Berti? He's never fought a battle in his life.'

'Ealhstan can do the fighting for him. He would do so anyway.. Berti is clever. And loyal. I trust him. That's more important than being able to fight.'

'But does he have enough authority?'

'He only has to hold the kingdom for me for a year or so. He can do that, with Ealhstan by his side.'

'If you trust Ealhstan.'

'Ealhstan has served our family for fifty years. I see you're determined to keep on raising objections. There is never an ideal time for a king to leave his kingdom. But this is as good a time as any. It will take the pagans some time to recover from Aclea. And I'm not getting any younger. The dream returning is a warning. Telling me I must go now before it's too late. It is not a selfish desire, as you seem to think. It is for the kingdom. And our family. The blood I saw started to form itself into images of our children, Osburh. We could be under a curse. Athelstan's death may just be the beginning.'

Osburh felt an icy chill in her heart. She believed in the power of curses. She couldn't see what they might have done to deserve one, but then what had her ancestors done to deserve Caedwalla?

'And you think your visit will lift a curse, if there is one?' she asked.

'It's a pilgrimage, not a visit. The fulfilment of a vow.'

She didn't like vows. They only led to trouble. But if an unfulfilled vow threatened her children, then it had best be fulfilled. Her resistance was weakening.

'Why would your pilgrimage be important for the kingdom?' she asked. 'Do you think it is under a curse as well?'

Aethelwulf considered. 'We have become cut off from Rome,' he said. 'It is the source of our virtue. It is something beyond the mere struggle to survive. It is the greater world, and the world beyond the greater world. If I go, if the king goes, as a pilgrim, then the link will be re-established. Virtue and knowledge can flow into this country once more. And saints can again show us that there is more to this life than our own selfish concerns.'

'That's hoping for a lot,' said Osburh quietly.

'Yes,' Aethelwulf agreed, watching the watery sun. 'And we can learn to hope again as well.'

*

King Burgred stayed at the court of Wessex for two weeks. When he left, he did so betrothed to Princess Aethelswith. Elsa was pleased that he had at least stayed for two weeks. She had always feared being sent off to marry a complete stranger. As to what she felt. . . she did not examine that too closely. Other women had told her of love and she had seen its effect on some of her friends. The inner absorption, sense of disorientation, sudden swings between delight, despair and back again. . . no, she didn't really feel any of that. Maybe the absorption a little, but not in him. The change in her life, her status, what her future would be – these were the considerations which occupied her. She sometimes had to remind herself of the man who was going to effect all this change.

Not that she was hostile to him, or to the idea of becoming his wife. He seemed pleasant enough. His face and figure didn't set her heart a-flutter, but neither did they repel her. And he was very polite, not oppressive. She found a lot of men at her father's court oppressive. Even without meaning to, even without any physical movement, their greedy male presences seemed to reach out towards her. He was not like that. In fact, he seemed quite good at minimising the effect of his presence. Maybe that was why she found it quite easy to forget him and didn't have to struggle with powerful impressions, good or bad. His eyes when they looked at her did not have that acquisitive glint she saw in so many of her father's men. They were thoughtful, a little sad and. . . unreadable.

She did wonder how a man who appeared so unforceful had managed to become king. She remembered the previous king of Mercia. He'd been like a wild boar. God, if she'd had to marry *him*! Her body shrank at the thought. But Burgred – she said the name to herself, trying to get used to it – well, he was a mystery, she supposed. And good at remaining so – maybe that was how he had become king?

He had called on her every day. They had gone riding together or sat in the bur with her companions making conversation. One of the pleasantest aspects of the courtship for Elsa was seeing the immediate increased importance it gave her at court. The only daughter amongst five sons, she was used to being overlooked and missing out on activities designed for the boys, having to content herself with women's work – spinning, weaving, nursing, cooking – little more than a servant at times. But now she'd suddenly become important, with her own companions, whose duty it was to look after her and make her appear attractive. She need never have to do any more cooking in her life, and didn't intend to.

The courtship with Burgred was a little stilted. They agreed about the saving grace of Christianity and the cruelty of pagans. He asked about her life, which she tried to make sound more interesting than it was. She asked about Mercia, to which he gave only vague answers. Only on the last day did he open up a little, explaining why he must leave her.

'The Welsh have come down the Severn. They're attacking Shrewsbury.'

'Is it serious?'

'It's always serious,' he replied. 'But not critical. We have been fighting the Welsh for hundreds of years. When they think we're weak, they attack us. When we think they're weak, we attack them. That's how it is with the Welsh, I'm afraid. We make treaties with them from time to time, but they never last.'

'And are you weak now?' Elsa asked, wanting to make the most of this moment of openness.

He looked at her with his hooded gaze. 'No,' he replied evenly. 'But whenever there's a new king, the Welsh will always test him out to see if they can gain any advantage from the change. So I must go and prove to them that they can't, by driving them back to their mountains.'

Aethelwulf meanwhile was discussing his dream and renewed plans to go to Rome with Swithun, the man he trusted above all others.

'There will be opposition,' said Swithun. 'And not only from your wife.'

'But the dream!'

'Dreams do not always mean what we think they do.'

'Anyone would think you were a man of the world,' Aethelwulf grumbled. 'The last time I had this dream was when I promised to go to Rome. Do you not want our country's link with the Holy Father and the seat of the apostles to be re-established?'

'With all my heart. But that can be done without your going. Why not send a delegation? The Holy Father will understand why you can't go in person. Rome itself is being attacked by infidels. And the journey is a dangerous one – there are pagans and bandits everywhere.'

'Death on pilgrimage guarantees entry into heaven.'

'It is not you I am worried about – it is what you leave behind.'

'That's why I have to go now. It will take the pagans at least a couple of years to recover from the defeat we gave them at Aclea. I'm not foolish enough to think that they won't be back. But Aclea was a victory from God and I need to go and give thanks for that. There is more to fighting the pagans than defeating them in battle. Surely, you above all people should know that?'

Swithun looked at the ground a few moments before replying. 'We are blessed to have you as king, sire. My arguing with you is due to my fear as to what will happen here if we lose your guiding hand.'

'It's only for a year or two. I've been waiting to do this my whole life. And the dream tells me that now is the time. We all need faith; and I have faith in you, Father. Your prayers and wisdom, along with Ealhstan's strong right arm will keep my kingdom safe, and my sons in order.'

'God grant that it be so.'

But despite the dream and his firm intention, Aethelwulf did not leave for Rome. King Burgred's prediction to Elsa that he would drive the Welsh back into their mountains proved over-optimistic. The Mercians were defeated outside Shrewsbury and driven back before the triumphant Welsh. Aethelwulf's doubts about Burgred's strength and ability to hold his kingdom together increased. But he'd made his commitment to him. Mercia could not be allowed to fail. But unless the Welsh were drive back, it would descend into civil war again. He could not send his daughter to a country in the process of tearing itself apart. And so when Burgred and his witan appealed to him for help against the Welsh, he knew that he must give it, and remain to do so. Something as important to the country's well-being as this could not be left to his untried sons.

Having made his decision, and despatched an advance guard of his household troops to bolster the Mercian defences while an army was being raised, he summoned Swithun to him once more.

'So, Father, it seems you were right. Not for the first time.'

'It gives me no pleasure, sire.'

'I cannot go. But I'm not ignoring the dream. I will send a delegation, as you suggested. You will head the delegation.'

Swithun bowed. 'It will be my honour to represent you to the Holy Father, sire.'

'Or I should say, you'll head the delegation in practice. Someone else will represent me to the Holy Father.'

'May I ask who, sire?'

'My son, Alfred.'

'Alfred!'

'I've given it much thought,' said Aethelwulf. 'And prayer. Do you not approve?'

'He's very young. And the journey is a long one.'

'The journey is a long one. But if that was to be the conclusive argument every time, no one would ever go. Alfred being young, I don't see as a problem. He will be well looked after. You and I will see to that. And for the young, everything is a journey anyway. It will be a lasting experience for him, something he can draw upon in the future. Of all my sons, Alfred is the one who would most benefit from going to Rome.'

'All you say is true,' Swithun acknowledged. 'My concern is if he is strong enough for the journey.'

'He has recovered from his illness. That is another reason for him to go. People who have recovered from a serious illness should go on pilgrimage to give thanks for their deliverance if they are able. What better pilgrimage could Alfred make than to the shrines of the holy apostles themselves?'

*

Osburh was appalled when she heard of her husband's decision. She went to confront him immediately.

'You can't do this,' she told him abruptly. 'Go to Rome yourself, if you must, but don't send a little boy in your place. My little boy.'

Aethelwulf glowered at her. 'It is not your place to tell the king what he can and cannot do.'

'It's a thousand miles! Through dangerous foreign lands, full of people who wish us ill. He's a weak boy. He almost died recently! He'll never survive it.'

'You think I'm sending him alone? There will be an army of people to look after him. King Charles and the emperor have both guaranteed him safe passage through their lands. There will be guides and fighting men to scare away any bandits. He is going in my place and will receive the respect due to a king. You should be pleased for him.'

'But he's so young! It's cruel to send him away like this.'

'I was two years old when my father left me at the emperor's court to return to this country and regain his throne. I didn't see him or my mother for another four years.'

'But you were safe!' Osburh almost howled. 'That's why your father didn't take you with him. Whereas you're deliberately exposing Alfred to all sorts of dangers.'

'Nothing in this world is safe!' Aethelwulf snapped. 'I would have thought even a woman would have realised that by now. As you say, Alfred almost died recently. And that was with all you women fussing over him. What difference did that make?'

'A great deal. Without it, he'd be dead.'

'You think you saved him? You flatter yourself, my dear. The Lord saved him. And the Lord will keep him safe on his journey, because he will be doing the Lord's business.'

Osburh hated her husband at that moment. She saw the gap between them widening to a chasm. The way he used his God to justify all manner of cruelty. Another Caedwalla. She couldn't attack his religious arguments without exposing her lack of belief in them. He knew that, of course. She could see an almost mocking look in his eyes, daring her to say something that would condemn her to the status of a pagan traitor.

'Is there not someone else you can send in his place?' she asked dully, knowing as she did so that it was close to an admission of defeat. 'What can Alfred say to the pope? Berti would be a better ambassador for you.'

'Berti is needed here. I'm taking him with me on the Welsh expedition. I'll make a soldier of him yet.'

'Redi then!' said Osburh desperately.

'You'd prefer Redi to go than Alfred?'

'At least he's older. And stronger – he hasn't almost just died.'

'No. Alfred is the one. There are all sorts of reasons why.'

'Let me go with him, then.' She was aware of sounding weaker and weaker. Beseeching. A dull pain extending its grip on her heart.

'You want to leave me?'

Oh God, yes, she thought but didn't say.

'And Redi? What about Redi?' he continued.

'You're forcing me to choose between them anyway, aren't you?'

'Alfred will be gone less than a year. I've told you he'll be well looked after. It will be an adventure for him. Why do you want to deprive him of that?'

She was beaten. Completely and utterly beaten. He knew that as well as she did. That's why his tone had softened and he was looking at her more gently. She was no longer a threat to his precious plans. She wasn't sure of herself any more. Even his sly insinuation that she was being selfish in trying to keep Alfred for herself. . . maybe he was right? She no longer knew. Her head was spinning. She was conscious of a pain deep within, and weariness. Such weariness. Maybe this long fight over Rome had been what had kept her going and now that it was lost, it no longer seemed possible to fight for anything else. Or worth it.

He was looking at her with some concern now. 'Are you all right, my dear? You don't look well.'

Alfred received the news that he was to go to Rome with some bewilderment. Swithun said that it was a great honour and proof that his father loved him. Redi said that it was because he was going to become a priest. He was being sent with a lot of other priests to meet the chief priest, while the people who were going to be warriors, like Redi himself, stayed to fight. Alfred wasn't sure that he wanted to become a priest. He tried to ask his mother about it, but she got upset whenever he did, and there was a look in her eyes which frightened him, and so he stopped trying. He turned to Berti again.

'Treat it as an adventure,' Berti counselled. 'You'll see lots of new places and people. I envy you, Alfred.'

'I don't want to leave mummy, and Yetta, and you, Berti.'

'We'll all be here when you get back. And you'll have so many things to tell us.'

'I'll be lonely.'

'You'll have Swithun with you.'

'Swithun's nice, but it won't be the same. He's always talking about God. It will be like being in church the whole time. Redi says it's because I'm going to be made a priest.'

'Redi's jealous, Alfred. It's hard for him, seeing his younger brother being given an opportunity over him. You need to understand that and make allowances for his feelings.'

'It's not something I wanted.'

'No,' Berti agreed. 'But sometimes princes are given things we don't want and have to accept them anyway. Father wants you to be the one to go. You want to please him, don't you? Show him you're someone he can rely upon?'

'Yes.'

'It's an important job he's given you, Alfred. You're representing our country to the Holy Father himself.'

'I won't know what to say to him.'

'You won't need to say anything. Swithun will do all the talking. You just need to be there, that's all.'

Even with Berti's reassurances, Alfred felt uncomfortable at the thought of his important journey. It all seemed unreal – he didn't know what it meant. People were starting to look at him differently, as though he was some kind of stranger. But there didn't seem to be anything he could do about it. Back from a successful initial expedition against the Welsh, Aethelwulf had thrown himself into preparing for the expedition he had long dreamed of with a fervour that could hardly have been greater had he been going himself. The court hummed with activity as the king assembled a force of fighting men to escort the expedition, consulted with churchmen, wrote letters and issued directions. Months passed. Autumn subsided into winter, and winter gave way to spring. The March gales blew and subsided. Easter came, the ceremonies charged with a new immediacy for Alfred by the thought that he would soon be travelling to their source.

And then one fine late April morning, the feast of St Mark, everything was ready and Alfred was told they would be leaving the following day. There was a feast that evening to mark the departure of the expedition to Rome. It was held in the same royal manor outside

Canterbury as had been the funeral feast for King Athelstan some two years before. This should have been a happier occasion. King Aethelwulf himself was jubilant at the thought of his at last beginning to address the promise he had made so long ago. But there were other feelings than the king's abroad that night, sensed if not completely understood by Alfred, which made his father's high spirits seem a little unnatural. His mother had been ill for weeks and remained in her room. He knew that something was wrong between his parents. His mother was changing, becoming more emotional. When he went to see her in her room, she would clasp him to her with a tightness which wasn't like the gentle hugs and caresses she used to give him before. And the look in her eyes, both intense and frightened, made him uncomfortable. She would tell him strange things, insist that he never forget old gods he had hardly heard of. Or that he was named after the elves and should always honour them. He longed for his mother, but the old mother, not this new, troubling one. There were times when he was secretly relieved to leave her, and that was a horrible feeling.

Redi had been hostile to him for months, his hostility growing stronger as the preparations for the expedition's departure increased. Alfred tried to bear in mind what Berti had said and not respond to Redi's taunts and jibes, even beatings on occasion. It wasn't easy. But Redi had found a new friend in Ceolwulf, son of Cynehelm. Redi went around with Ceolwulf and made it clear that Alfred wasn't welcome with them. Alfred felt the pain of exclusion, but on the whole it was better than being with Redi in his current mood of resentment.

Sat at the high table, near his father and Redi, Alfred did not enjoy the farewell feast, even though it was the first time he'd been allowed to stay up for a feast and sit at the high table. He could sense the hostility from Redi, sitting two places away, emanating towards him. Fortunately, Swithun sat between them. Alfred was grateful for the shield of his presence. He decided now, listening to Diarmait singing a strange song about a dying king travelling to Rome to wash his wounds in the waters of baptism, that he was pleased to be leaving. Home and his family had become too unsettling; he would be safer with Swithun. At least he knew where he was with him.

They left the next morning. Alfred did not want to say any more goodbyes to the small group gathered to see them off. He just wanted to be gone. And then he saw his mother walking towards him. She had risen from her sickbed to see him one more time. She was holding a book in her hand. Overcome by an impulse of longing, he ran towards her and hugged her as she bent down towards him. She was shaking and her skin was hot.

'Mummy,' he said. 'I don't want to go.'

She burst into tears and then with an effort lifted him up onto her hip as she used to. She kissed him on his lips and tried to blink away her tears and force a smile.

'You must go, Alfred,' she said, smoothing his hair with her hand. 'You're going to make us all very proud. Particularly your mummy.'

'Can't you come with me? I'll miss you.'

'I'll miss you, too. But it won't be for long. Look I've brought you the book of poems. It's yours now, Alfred. My gift to you.'

Alfred looked at the book she was giving him. It was a beautiful book, but he would have preferred to have her going with him.

'Now I'm going to have to put you down,' said Osburh, still with that tight smile. 'You've become a big boy now. And I'm not as strong as I used to be.'

She lowered him back down to the ground. They both stood looking at one another, neither wanting to be the first to turn away. The moment of indecision was resolved by Swithun placing his hand softly on Alfred's shoulder.

'We have to go now, Alfred. Say goodbye to your mother.'

'Goodbye, mummy.'

'I'll pray for you, Alfred,' she said hurriedly. 'Please pray for me.'

He turned and followed Swithun. Something made him turn back to look at her one more time. Her hand shot up in a wave. Still that tight, fixed smile. Oh well. Maybe things would be different when he got back.

Osburh watched them depart, her body rigid, her eyes staring fixedly ahead. Only when she was certain that they were out of sight, did she relax her grip on herself. She breathed out with a long sigh, closed her eyes, and fainted.

4. Journey to Rome

From Canterbury, the expedition made its way southeast to the Channel coast at Dover, where a fleet of boats was waiting to transport them to the West Frankish kingdom. Peasants working in the fields stared fearfully at the grand men on horses and the warriors marching behind them. It could only be an army, and when armies marched out in the bright spring sunshine, starvation and death were often the harvest.

The expedition itself had no such fears. Men who had grown tired of hanging around the king's court for weeks on end were pleased to be on the move, happy to be heading over the sea on an adventure, a mission of peace and pilgrimage to foreign lands. Some sang as they marched along, while others who had been overseas before told tales of what lay ahead to wide-eyed believers and good-humoured sceptics alike.

Alfred, riding some of the way on a small colt of his own, soon forgot the departure from his mother and sadness at home in the excitement of the journey, which seemed to have infected all of them. Even Swithun, persuaded to ride a horse himself by the importance of his position, had a smile on his face, enjoying the sunshine and sensation of movement.

The first sight of the sea was greeted with a cheer. Alfred looked out at the wide expanse of water. He had seen the sea before, but always as a barrier, beyond which one could not go, something which Yetta warned him about. The idea of going over it made him feel a bit funny. He would have been nervous, but everyone was so cheerful and the weather was so fine that any nervousness lost itself in the general mood of anticipation.

Arriving at Dover, a different world awaited them. A world of ships and foreign-looking men, who spoke of tides, channels, weights and rocks. Alfred learned that seamen on land talked a lot. Innumerable conversations and consultations about the embarkation seemed necessary. As they were clearly not going to be going anywhere that day, Swithun directed Colman to take Alfred to the house which had been reserved for them to rest after their journey.

But Alfred was far too excited to rest and after they had unloaded their baggage and eaten, he persuaded his tutor that it was too sunny to rest indoors and they could do so just as well by the seashore.

'Have you ever been over the sea, Colman?' he asked as they were sitting on a stony beach, looking over the water to the bustle of men around the waiting boats.

'I was born over the sea,' Colman replied with a hint of pride.

'Really? I didn't know that. Where were you born?'

'At Rheims.'

'Are you a Frank?'

'My mother is; my father was Irish.'

'Like Diarmait?'

'Yes. The Irish are great travellers, Alfred. And those who travel for God are the greatest travellers of all.'

'Did your father travel for God?'

'He did.' Colman looked at the stones of the beach with a slightly sad, reflective smile. 'But then he met my mother, I was born, and he stopped travelling. He became a carpenter – towns like Rheims always need carpenters. But I was always destined for the church.'

'How did you come to England?'

'I was a monk at St Bertin, which is an abbey not far from where we will land. Your father was looking for a tutor for his children. I'm told no one suitable could be found in England. My lord Swithun knows our monastery well. He came to our abbot with your father's request. Our abbot chose me and I went back with my lord Swithun to your father's court and have been there ever since.'

'Do you miss your monastery?'

'A monk should not cling to things of this world, Alfred. He goes where he is told to, or where the Spirit wills him. As the Bible says, no man who, having put his hand to the plough, looks back is fit for the kingdom of God.'

'I miss my mummy already.'

'Pray for her. That's what she asked you to do, isn't it? If you pray for her, it will bring her closer to you.'

Alfred frowned. It didn't seem half as easy as Colman was suggesting. Maybe he wasn't good enough.

They set sail early the next morning. The sunshine of the day before had gone. It was a grey, windy day. The songs and good humour of the day before had gone too. Everyone seemed nervous and in a hurry. Alfred found himself bundled onto a boat and left while men walked back and forth between the boats or shouted across at one another. At last they were on their way. He felt a moment of terror at thinking he was on the boat alone, surrounded by strangers, but then he saw Swithun and Colman at the far end. It was better being on the water. The men were calmer, knowing what they had to do. Alfred watched fascinated as they shipped their oars a hundred yards or so from land and hoisted a large tan sail. The sail flapped weakly a few times before being pulled into line with the wind. There was a moment when it caught, a cracking sound as it filled out and tugged its sheets tight. The boat, which had been drifting, sprang to attention and they were off once more, carving a way through the waters. Alfred watched the same transformation taking place on the boats around him. He looked back at the chalk cliffs of England receding into the distance.

'A following wind,' Swithun sat down beside him. 'If it stays in this direction, we'll be in St Judoc before nightfall.'

'Is that where we're going? St Judoc?'

'For the first few days, yes. We have a present for the abbot. You see those two boats there?' He pointed over to two large vessels riding low in the water. 'They're full of lead.'

'Lead?'

'For the abbey roof at Ferrières. The abbot wrote to your father asking for it. When you pass over someone's land, Alfred, it's a good idea to give them a present. Particularly if you happen to know it's a present they want.'

'Are we taking a present to the Holy Father?'

'Of course. The richest present of all.'

Alfred was silent, looking back.

'Are you enjoying your first sea journey?'

'Yes. We're going so fast, aren't we?'

'The wind isn't always as favourable as this.'

The wind remained favourable and the fleet of boats arrived at St Judoc in the late afternoon. A crowd of people had gathered on the shore to greet them. Abbot Lupus himself was there, smiling at the safe arrival of his cargo. The activity of Dover was redoubled as the

Franks assisted in unloading the boats and transferring the lead to wagons. Lupus greeted Swithun as an old friend and then walked over to Alfred, who was standing on the beach with his bags, a little lost again in the midst of all the activity.

'Welcome to Francia, my lord prince,' Lupus smiled encouragingly down at him. 'You do us great honour.'

He spoke with an accent but Alfred could understand him.

'You speak English,' he said.

'There is not so much difference between our languages. Particularly here in the north. We are used to having English people amongst us. It is our pleasure to make them welcome. I hope that you will find your stay with us very comfortable, my lord prince.'

Berti had told him that people would be more polite to him than they were at home. It was because he was representing the king. What was it he had been told to say in reply?

'My father, the king, sends his greetings, my lord abbot. He wishes me to assure you of his very best wishes.'

Lupus's smile broadened. 'I am delighted to hear it, my lord prince.'

They left the men loading the wagons on the beach and Lupus escorted them into St Judoc, Alfred riding on the front of Swithun's horse.

'Who told you to say that to Lupus?' Swithun asked as they were riding along.

'Berti. Was it wrong?'

'No. It was very good. The Franks love formal compliments.'

'I'm not sure what it meant.'

'Nothing really, but that doesn't matter. They still like having them. Lupus will be telling everyone how polite you are. . . for an Englishman.'

Alfred realised that even if people spoke English, it didn't mean he was not in a foreign country. He suddenly felt very tired and did not object when Colman told him that they would not be eating with the abbot. Swithun had decided that he needed an early night after the sea-crossing. Alfred did not disagree. With a jumble of impressions in his head, he didn't want to see anyone for a while. He and Colman ate in silence soon after arriving at the hostel run by the monks. It was still light when Alfred went into the room prepared for him. He said his prayers, remembered his mother, climbed into bed and was asleep.

*

Swithun sat late that evening with Abbot Lupus. The abbot was in an expansive mood, still pleased about his delivery of lead.

'It's so difficult to obtain any significant amount in this country,' he complained. 'The pagans have disrupted all normal trade. They grow bolder every year. Their terrible boats are swarming up and down the Seine. The king, may God bless him, does what he can. The emperor even came last year to help in the fight against them. But they are like the flies in summer – however many you kill, there are always more.'

'I'm sorry to hear that,' said Swithun.

'We rejoiced at your magnificent victory over them at Aclea. We still do rejoice at it, even though it means they attack us now instead of you.'

'They still attack us. No-one is free from them.'

'That's true enough,' Lupus agreed. 'What have we done to deserve them? I suppose the answer to that is clear enough. Not kept the faith. Like the Israelites, we're being punished for our sins. It's the time of Jeremiah come again.'

'That book you asked me for,' aid Swithun, sensing where Lupus was heading.

'Oh yes!' Lupus's eyes brightened with a scholar's gleam. His requests for the loan of books were notorious throughout Christendom. 'Jerome's commentary on Jeremiah. Did you have any success?'

'I'm sorry. I made enquiries of all our monasteries. In Mercia and East Anglia as well as Wessex. I don't think there's a copy in the whole of England. At least, southern England. I don't know about the north.'

'I wrote to Ealdsige in York last year. I thought the city of Alcuin might still have a good library. But I've had no reply from there so far.'

'I'm afraid there's been a sad falling off since the days when the emperor sent to England for his scholars. We need help from you now. Francia overtook us in the fields of learning long ago.'

'We do what we can,' said Lupus, not averse to the compliment. 'But it's hard to find the eternal in this world of ours.'

'Have you tried the Irish? Heaven knows what they still have hidden away in their monasteries. Has anyone yet managed to work out how John of Erin managed to learn Greek?'

'The general consensus is that only he and the Devil will ever know the answer to that,' Lupus replied with a chuckle. John of Erin was a brilliant scholar who had arrived in Francia some years ago and rapidly established himself as a favourite at the court of King Charles. 'I did ask John, but I don't think he has ever had much influence over his fellow countrymen. That may be why he decided to try his luck with us.'

'Which monastery did he come from?' asked Swithun, who was one of many churchmen intrigued by this flamboyant figure.

'I think he was at Clonmacnoise for some time. Wasn't every Irish scholar? But he doesn't speak much of his past, and we don't ask. We're just grateful to have his present. He's transformed the palace school and is producing scholars at a rate not seen since Alcuin. If our reputation for learning has improved, which you're kind enough to suggest, he's one of the main reasons why. The king thinks the world of him.'

'But Archbishop Hincmar doesn't, I'm told,' said Swithun, a little mischievously. Lupus in an expansive mood was his best chance of gathering the latest information about the relations between Francia's great characters. Of particular importance as they would be travelling on from St Judoc in a few days to Rheims, see of the formidable Hincmar.

'Well, it's this wretched Gottschalk business,' said Lupus gloomily. 'I can see both sides and so I try to keep my mouth shut as best I can. But the man writes to me. He writes to everyone. That's part of the problem. If he just kept quiet then the thing would blow over in time. But he's temperamentally incapable of keeping quiet.'

'Should he keep quiet? On a matter of such importance? If he believes that what he says comes from God and St Augustine, doesn't he have a duty to proclaim it at every opportunity?'

Lupus frowned. 'That's what he would say. But the Church has ways of raising these issues, and he is not following those ways.'

'Because they tell him to keep quiet. If he has a message from God, if he is a prophet, then would it not be a mortal sin for him to keep quiet?'

'*If* he has a message from God,' Lupus rejoined. 'Who is to decide that? Him? If everyone who thought they had a message from God was allowed to speak then we wouldn't be able to hear ourselves think. The Tower of Babel would be nothing in comparison.'

'And yet you say you can see both sides.'

Lupus stared at him. 'Are you playing devil's advocate, my friend? Or trying to trap me?'

'I would like to understand the issues. We hear so little in England. And what we do hear is distorted. My king will want to know. And I'm meeting Archbishop Hincmar in a few days. I understand he's holding another council about Gottschalk.'

'Yes.'

'To condemn him?'

'He's already been condemned. The council will set out the Church's position on predestination. As drafted by Hincmar. He asked John of Erin to help him with the declaration. But when you ask philosophers to express an opinion, you're never quite sure what you'll get. Hincmar didn't find John's contribution helpful.'

'He agreed with Gottschalk?'

'No. But as far as Hincmar was concerned, he completely missed the point. Ever since the great St Augustine explained to us that God has predestined the souls that are to be saved, the question has remained, has he also predestined those that are to be damned? Augustine left that question unanswered, some would say with very good reason. Gottschalk answers it with an emphatic yes. One can see his logic – if God chooses the saved then surely by doing so, he must also choose those who are not to be saved. Even if that's just by denying them the grace that will take them out of their sins. But where does that leave the God of love who has counted every hair of our heads? And what incentive is there for anyone to try to be good if their fate has already been decided? The same objection Augustine faced, but in an even stronger form.'

'What did John of Erin say?'

'He denied there was such a thing as predestination at all.'

'Disagreeing with St Augustine? Isn't that dangerous?'

'It was more a philosophical sleight of hand. He said that for God everything is an eternal present – that's Boethius, of course. And so, there can be no predestination because that implies a before and after, which doesn't exist in eternity. Philosophically very clever, but of no help to Hincmar. God may exist in an eternal present, but the Church has to deal with us sinful mortals, who exist in time. And we need hope more than circuitous logic, especially in these dark times. You know I love the ancients as much as anyone, but they didn't have Christ and they didn't have faith, and the Church is right to put those above clever logic.'

'It sounds as though you agree with Hincmar.'

'I do. It's a hard job he has. And he's no mean intellect himself. He accepts that there needs to be room for scholars to question past assumptions. If they are stifled, then knowledge stagnates. There has to be room for John of Erin, just as there would have been room for Gottschalk, had he not been so determined to make a stand. Scholars in love with their own ideas make bad leaders – they don't consider anything else.'

'So, what is the Church's position on predestination? What will the council decide?'

'Are you suggesting I can see into the future?' Lupus responded with a smile.

'I'm sure Hincmar would have consulted you as well. As one of the great intellects in the kingdom.'

'Please don't flatter me, my friend – you know how dangerous it is.'

'I'm sorry. But I'm sure you know. I expect you had a hand in drafting the declaration.'

'No, it's Hincmar's work. But I don't disagree with it. It may be less philosophically consistent than John of Erin would like, but there is more of faith, hope and charity in it.'

'Does it accept predestination?'

'Of course. For the blessed.'

'But not for the damned?'

'God knows everything before it has happened. So, there must be foreknowledge – Boethius again. But that is not the same as predestination. God's will is that everyone be saved. Free will does exist, as does grace, which is available to all. The fact that some do not receive grace, and the reasons why not, are mysteries of God, which we cannot understand. But, as St Augustine taught, our very striving to be good and live a Christian life is a sign of grace working within us.'

'I like that,' said Swithun.

'Good,' said Lupus with another smile. 'Do tell Hincmar. I'm sure he'll be pleased.'

'Will Gottschalk accept it?'

'Alas, no.' Lupus's face darkened. 'I'm afraid Gottschalk is beyond redemption. In this world, at least.

It is a tragedy – a great mind, but one which refuses to accept any authority but its own.' His eyes were troubled as he looked at Swithun. 'I did try, my friend. I did try as hard as I could with him to accept the compromise being offered. None of us can say we know the will of God. But he was adamant that he was right, and now that he has suffered for his belief, he will be even more adamant.'

'What will happen to him?'

'Nothing more. He's been whipped and his writings burned. He's confined to his monastery and not allowed to write or lecture. That will continue. This isn't about him any more, although he'd be mortified to hear that. It's about someone far greater – St Augustine himself.'

'I can see that Gottschalk pressed too hard,' said Swithun. 'And that action had to be taken against him. But the idea. . .'

'The idea resonates,' Lupus agreed. 'Particularly in these days when we are being attacked by barbarous men of appalling cruelty, whom it's tempting to think must be predestined to hell. But where does it lead? Christ told us to love our enemies, not to gloat over them going down to hell. John of Erin says that there is no difference between philosophy and religion. I disagree. In philosophy, you can just consider an idea for its own sake, but in religion you have to look at where that idea is leading you. And if it is leading you down and away from the faith, then the Church is entitled to question it on that ground alone.'

*

Abbot Lupus decided that he would escort the English party as far as Rheims. Partly to show honour to the

House of Wessex, but also because he enjoyed talking to Swithun. Alfred, riding behind the distinguished churchmen with Colman, struggled to understand what they were talking about so cheerfully. No easy task as they kept on slipping into Latin, which he was still at the beginner's stage of learning with Colman. He ought to have paid more attention to the psalter his father had given him.

'What are they talking about?' he asked Colman.

Colman looked up nervously. He didn't like to eavesdrop on his superiors. And the Frankish abbot talked in explosive bursts, which weren't always that easy to follow, even with his knowledge of Latin. But the king's son must be answered. He listened intently for a few moments, hoping Swithun wouldn't turn round.

'A Roman called Cicero,' he said eventually to Alfred.

'A Roman? Are we going to meet him?'

'No, he died a long, long time ago. Before even Our Lord was born.'

Alfred tried to assimilate the information. He knew that there had been a great Roman kingdom a long time ago and that they had even ruled in England. But before Our Lord was born? How was that possible?

'So, before Cerdic?' he asked hesitantly.

'About as long before Cerdic as Cerdic is before us. Maybe longer.'

Alfred thought back to the great poem of Wessex he had heard Diarmait recite. How far away Cerdic seemed from them, separated by name after name, generation after generation. A shadowy figure lost in the mists of time. And this Roman, whom Swithun and the Frankish abbot were chatting cheerfully about, was twice as old as Cerdic.

'How do they know anything about him?'

'Cicero? Cicero is famous, Alfred. Anyone who reads Latin knows of Cicero. He wrote a lot of books.'

'What about?'

'About everything. About how to rule, how to persuade people to do what you want them to, what to believe, how to grow old, how to keep your friends.'

'He knew all that?'

'He learnt it. And we learn from him.'

'Where did he learn it from?'

'There were Greek scholars before the Romans, Alfred.'

Before the Romans? How far back did the world go?

'What about King David? When did he live?'

'Oh, a long time before the Greeks.'

Alfred felt slightly giddy. He didn't know what to think. The vast swathe of time stretching back before him made him feel very small and insignificant. But the memory of some people persisted despite the passing of ages.

'Books make you live forever, don't they?' he said wonderingly.

'Not all books,' corrected Colman. 'Only the Word of God is eternal. But other books. . . yes, they can keep your memory alive for a long, long time. If they are good, and if they survive. Books can be destroyed even more easily than men, Alfred. They need people to care for them.'

*

After days of riding through the flat north Frankish countryside, stopping at monasteries for the night, they arrived at Rheims. Colman fell quiet on approaching his native city. Alfred respected his need for silence. He suddenly felt a stab of homesickness himself. He concentrated on the sight of the city before him to try and dispel the feeling. The buildings were bigger than they were at home and many were of stone. Above everything loomed the mighty cathedral. Alfred had been told that this was the holiest city in Francia – it was where the Frankish king, at the head of three thousand warriors, had been baptised a Christian and sworn to worship and defend what he had once burned and destroyed. The Holy Spirit in the form of a dove had come down from heaven with a flask of sacred chrism in its beak for the king's anointing. The Archbishop of Rheims was the greatest churchman in the whole of Francia – keeper of mysteries and arbiter of faith.

Alfred had heard much talk of the great Archbishop Hincmar on the journey. He was nervous of meeting him, imagining a towering figure like Ealhstan, but holier. So he was disappointed when he did meet him to see that he was a short, slight man, considerably smaller than Swithun, or even Abbot Lupus. But he had a stern, ascetic face and a gaze which seemed to go straight through you. Alfred bowed to him in some confusion, not knowing what else to do.

'We are very pleased to welcome you, my lord prince.' A deep, strong voice. And the gaze had softened a little, looking down at him and sensing his confusion. 'The news of your journey to the holy city of Rome on behalf of your pious and noble father fills us with great joy. The resources of Francia will be mobilised to ensure your safe and speedy passage on so sacred a mission. And when you reach the borders of our kingdom, the emperor himself has pledged an escort for you.'

'You are very kind, my lord archbishop,' Alfred managed to reply. He felt no impulse to ask the archbishop how he could speak English so well. It seemed natural that he would be able to do anything he set his mind to. There was something overpowering about the man, despite his small size.

'Our noble King Charles sends his warmest greetings also. Affairs of state compel his attendance elsewhere in the kingdom and so he cannot meet you himself, which he would like to have done. But although the king cannot be with us, it happens by chance that the queen and Princess Judith are staying with us for a few days and they I know will be delighted to meet you.'

Alfred understood this to mean that he'd be allowed to stay up for dinner. The audience with the archbishop was over and he was shown to a room where he could change and rest before the meal. Swithun had given Colman the evening off to go into the city and try and track down any relatives or old friends. Alfred lay on the softest bed he had ever known and looked up at a carved stone ceiling, wondering what the queen and Princess Judith would be like.

There was a knock on his door, which was immediately swung open by a girl not waiting for a reply. She stepped quickly into the room and closed the door behind her. Alfred stumbled to his feet at the unexpected intrusion.

'Oh, sit down,' she said. She was only a little bigger than him but her bright, bold face and manner told him that she was a number of years older. She surveyed him critically. 'You're very small, aren't you?'

This must be the Princess Judith. He ought to be polite. 'Would you like to sit down?'

'No, thank you. I prefer to stand. I may need to leave suddenly. My mother thinks I am having a lesson with John of Erin. When she realises that the lesson ended ten minutes ago, she will be wondering where I am. You haven't seen me, is that understood?'

She spoke authoritatively, expecting to be obeyed.

'Yes.' He could no more think of disobeying her than he could Swithun. 'You speak English very well.' Everyone in Francia seemed to speak perfect English. It made him feel inferior.

'I speak five languages,' the girl said in a matter-of-fact tone. 'My father keeps changing his mind as to whom I'm to marry. It won't be anyone in Francia. It might be Wessex, so English is one of my languages.' She looked again at him critically. 'I don't think I'll be marrying you, though. You're much too small. You have some elder brothers, don't you?'

'Three.'

'Are any of them married?'

'No.'

'What are their names?'

'Aethelbald, Aethelberht and Aethelred.'

She wrinkled her nose. 'They all sound the same. You English have no imagination. Tell me about them.'

'Aethelbald fought at Aclea with my father. And now he's ruling in the eastern kingdom. He's not been made king there yet, though.' Alfred didn't know what else to say. Blade had always been a distant figure who'd had little time for him. But it seemed to be enough for Princess Judith. For the first time since entering the room, she looked quite impressed.

'What about Aethelberht?' she asked.

'Oh, Berti's wonderful,' Alfred replied enthusiastically. 'He's so kind and clever. He thinks of other people so much.'

'Is he a fighter?'

'Well, he's been ill a lot in the past. But he's recovered now and is fighting with my father in Wales.'

'And Aethelred?'

Redi? Alfred tried to think of something positive to say about Redi. No, it was impossible. 'Redi's awful.'

She smiled. 'He's not much older than you, is he?'

'No, and he's a bully.'

'Well, I'm the eldest, so you'll get little sympathy from me. You could try my father – he has older brothers. My father and I disagree on a lot of things.'

There was a noise of voices some distance away.

'I have to go now,' said Judith. 'That's my mother on the warpath. Nice not to have met you, Alfred. I look forward to meeting you for the first time this evening.'

She gave another bright smile, swung open the door, and was gone as swiftly as she had come.

Dinner that evening was a strange affair. Alfred was aware of various tensions around the table, although he didn't know their causes. He was introduced to the queen who, somewhat to his surprise, didn't speak English. The queen, small and plump, talked a great deal but Alfred could only understand what she was saying if her clerical attendant, a tall, red-haired Irishman, translated for her. This man was introduced to him by Hincmar, a little wearily, as John of Erin. Alfred understood that he was Princess Judith's tutor, but also that he had other positions of importance at the Frankish court. He talked to the queen and Hincmar as an equal. The queen paid a lot of attention to what he said and asked him questions even when he wasn't translating for her. Hincmar seemed less impressed by him and maintained a moody silence throughout much of the meal. Swithun and Lupus also said little, perhaps taking their lead from their host. Princess Judith, on being introduced to Alfred, had greeted him very formally in more stilted English than she'd used earlier, allowing herself to be corrected by John of Erin. Apart from that, she kept silent, her eyes fixed demurely on the table in front of her. The queen and John of Erin chattered happily away, unconcerned by the silence of the others around them. Alfred, out of his depth and wishing Colman was there to explain matters to him later, concentrated on his food and hoped the meal would soon be over.

'Young prince, the queen would like to know what are your impressions of Francia?'

The sound of English startled him. He looked up to see John of Erin staring directly at him. Even worse, Princess Judith had raised her eyes from her plate and was also looking at him.

'Er,' Alfred struggled to think of a reply. 'I like it very much. You're all so clever.'

That caused a laugh around the table and even a faint smile from Hincmar. Alfred hoped that would be the end of his questioning, but the queen, on having his reply translated to her, immediately spoke some more to John of Erin and Alfred learned his ordeal was not yet over.

'Is there anything else you'd like to ask about our country? Anything you don't understand about it?'

Alfred turned to Swithun for assistance but was answered by a slight shake of the head. He did have a question, however. One that Colman had been unable to answer.

'When did your country first start to believe in Our Lord?'

'That's an interesting question,' said John of Erin, suddenly sounding more serious. 'What makes you ask that?'

'Well, I've been told that your king became a Christian in the cathedral here.'

'That's true.'

'But there were other Christians here before that time.'

'Yes.'

'That's what I don't understand. In our country, no one became a Christian before the king.'

John of Erin turned and translated for the queen. He then asked Hincmar something, to which Hincmar only shrugged. Alfred wondered whether he should have kept quiet.

'This country heard the good news of Our Lord earlier than yours,' John of Erin explained. 'But the land was less united. There were many kings – some believed and some didn't, just as even now there are kings in the northern lands who do not believe. A great king emerged from the east. When he became a Christian in this cathedral, it was very important. But he wasn't the first in this land to believe.'

'Who was?' Alfred asked.

'It was long ago. No one can say for sure. But St Denis established the first church in Paris, and if he was the Athenian convert of St Paul mentioned in the Bible, then he must have been one of the first.'

'*If* he was the Athenian convert of St Paul,' growled Hincmar.

'It is a disputed point,' John of Erin conceded calmly. 'Although many distinguished people, including the great Hilduin of St Denis, have been convinced that he was.'

This drew an angry snort from Hincmar, which John of Erin ignored, turning back to translate for the queen.

'Personally, I think it would be an honour for Francia if its founding saint was St Paul's convert,' he continued, having finished his translation. 'Denis the Areopagite is a remarkable writer.'

'Whether he is a remarkable writer or not isn't the issue,' said Hincmar. 'A serious Christian doesn't believe something just because he'd like it to be true.'

'I agree,' John of Erin replied, unconcerned by the implied rebuke. 'Opinion is divided, as I have said. Clearly, the archbishop does not believe that our St Denis was St Paul's convert. Others of almost equal distinction believe that he was.'

'And what do you believe?' asked Hincmar.

'Me? I don't know. I keep an open mind. I agree it's not been proved either way. But I think it's an interesting idea.'

The meal broke up soon afterwards.

'Was I wrong to ask my question?' Alfred asked Swithun when they were alone.

'I don't think it did much harm,' Swithun replied. 'I suspect they would have argued anyway – I'm told that they usually do. But as a general rule, Alfred, it's a good idea not to ask questions of people you don't know. Unless you happen to know the answer already.'

'Who is Hilduin of St Denis?'

Swithun's lips twitched into an almost smile. 'He was Archbishop Hincmar's mentor and teacher. I can see why Hincmar finds John of Erin exasperating – he's too clever by half.'

Alfred was pleased when they left Rheims. His first impression of Frankish royalty and high clergy had been rather unsettling. He'd had the impression of being continually examined and found wanting. Particularly by Princess Judith. That meeting with her rankled. Why did she think she was so superior to him? Just because she was older? Like Redi.

Colman, too, had found his visit to Rheims difficult. He'd discovered that his mother had died two years previously (his father having died long before). The friends of his childhood and the family which still remained had treated him as a stranger.

'I can understand that,' he said to Alfred on a rare occasion when he had wanted to talk about it. 'I would be a stranger to them. They hadn't seen me for over twenty years. When we enter the service of the Lord, we don't go back unless the Spirit leads us. Not even when our mothers die.' But he sounded sadder than he had on the beach at Dover. When they weren't having lessons, he and Alfred spent long periods riding together in silence.

*

Travelling south, the days settled into a routine. With the heat growing stronger, they started early – a hurried breakfast before dawn, usually in some abbey or hostel, with monks or slaves flitting around in the background like so many bats. The muffled curses or grumbles of sleepy soldiers, the clink of weapons, the clatter of hooves and they were away as the first rays of the sun climbed over the horizon. To begin with, they rode in silence, each coming to terms with another day. Then as the sun established itself, men would start to talk and joke, the coolness of the early morning giving way to warmth and other people.

While travelling, Alfred's lessons continued, with Colman speaking Latin and him struggling to understand. In Rome, there would be a reception with the Holy Father and he was anxious to understand as much as possible, and to at least say a few words in response. As they left northern Francia behind, he could understand less of what their hosts were saying.

At midday, they would stop, sometimes at a hostel, but more often outdoors in whatever shade could be found. They would eat and rest until the worst of the sun's heat had passed, and then continue their journey to wherever they were staying the night.

In such fashion, the days passed, until it felt to Alfred as though he had always lived this travelling life. They crossed a large river and left King Charles' domain, entering that of his brother, Emperor Lothair. An imperial guard was waiting for them on the other side of the river. Alfred heard strange accents in the long discussions which followed. Eventually, they were on the move again, the guard riding with them.

'Is everything all right?' he asked Swithun when he had the chance.

'Yes, but crossing the mountains is not always easy. There can be snowfalls. So the emperor has provided us with this escort of local men, who know the mountains, to see us over them and into Italy. It's a kindness.'

Snowfalls? In this heat. What had changed since they crossed the river? The land still looked the same.

But as they travelled on, they started to climb over hills, down steep valleys, and back up again. The baking plains were left behind. The air grew cooler and the skies were more often cloudy. And then one morning, after they'd been climbing gradually for a couple of hours, the men ahead stopped on a small ridge and fell silent.

'Come here, Alfred,' Swithun beckoned him forward. 'Take his horse, someone. Now, Alfred. Climb up onto my horse.'

He did so and Swithun manoeuvred his horse through the silent mass of men.

'Lord have mercy on us,' he heard one of the Wessex men say as Swithun stopped his horse on the edge of the ridge.

And there, in the distance, was another world. A surge of rock rearing up into the sky and above, at a height which seemed impossible, pinnacle upon pinnacle of deathly white. Alfred felt a chill in his heart and, from the faces of the men around him, he could see he wasn't the only one.

'We're not going over that,' he said. 'We can't.'

'We can and we will,' Swithun replied, loud enough for the others to hear. 'Thousands make the journey every year. Anything is possible for those with faith.'

Prayers were more noticeable amongst the company as they made their way down off the ridge and along a long valley beside a great lake, the mountains getting ever closer. Two days after leaving the lake, they were in the foothills, other men coming to help show them the safest way up. The track was well-worn but one afternoon, rumours of bandits gathered in ambush up ahead made their guards lead them up a much smaller, steeper track to bypass the danger. They had to dismount from their horses and lead the increasingly jittery animals, shivering in their summer coats, up after them. They were now in the heart of the mountains, walls of rock and snow closing in around them. The chill in Alfred's heart spread to his face and fingers.

Suddenly a deep booming sounded. Swithun's hand shot out and clasped Alfred's arm.

'What is it?' Alfred gasped.

'Avalanche.'

The whole of the mountain to their right looked to be coming down. A cascade of white boiling down into the valley far below with a mighty roar.

'Don't worry. It's miles away. Don't look – keep your eyes on the ground.'

It was hard not to look at it. There was something beautiful as well as terrible in the sight. One of the horses, spooked beyond endurance, started to whinny and rear. The man leading her cursed as tried to keep her on the track.

'Let her go!' someone shouted. 'She'll pull you off.'

The man let go of the reins with a start and the horse, bucking wildly and blindly, raced off the track, over the edge and into open air. They watched it fall, legs still kicking. No resistance any more.

Alfred's head dropped. Swithun said the Our Father, the avalanche exhausted itself and they continued upwards in silence. They spent the night, cold and cheerless, in bare huts. Alfred slept little, his head full of the mountain's roar, the boiling snow and falling horse. But the next day, the ground levelled out and they reached the pass, the southern lands stretching away below on the other side. Everyone cheered, looking forward to the end of their ordeal. But as they made their way down, a guide came back with news that the bandits they had avoided on the way up were waiting in a valley below. This time there was no alternative route to take.

The soldiers surrounded them, their weapons ready. For hours, they proceeded down like that, nerves taut, awaiting an attack. But none came. They passed the valley where the guide had seen the bandits. They must have melted away, deterred by the size of the force coming down. But there was no certainty that they might not come back, or try and attack them in the rear. So they continued as they were, ears pricked and eyes straining for the sound or sight of any hostile movement.

Eventually, they left the dangers of the mountains behind and were travelling along the banks of a great river as the countryside grew gentler and the heat began to return. The roads were busier now. They came across other pilgrims bound for Rome. Alfred looked around curiously at a land so different from his own. So old and dry – a land where books and empires came from. How far they had travelled.

They stopped and rested at the great pilgrim hostel of Pavia, recovering from the journey before embarking on the final leg to Rome. Alfred was glad to understand snatches of the conversations going on around him. The hostel's guest master, a jovial monk, was pleased to have a prince from Wessex staying.

'A famous queen from your country is buried here,' he told Alfred one day. 'Would you like to come and see her grave?'

Alfred looked at Swithun, who seemed surprised, but nodded. They followed the guest master out to the church attached to the hostel. He led the way to a dark corner of the church and a small black stone, set into the wall, which had a few words inscribed on it in Latin. '*Eadburh, Queen of Wessex, Abbess'*, he translated slowly to himself.

Such a small memorial for a queen,' the guest master observed. 'But then she was a servant of God for many years after her husband's death, and such servants do not seek the grandeurs of this world. Even so, it is a little surprising,' he said, with a sideways glance at Swithun, 'that her country does not seek to honour her with a more fitting memorial. Her father, King Offa, was a great king, and she knew an even greater, the Emperor Charles himself.'

Her father was indeed a great king,' Swithun responded drily. "But of Mercia, not Wessex. Wessex does not remember Queen Eadburh with fondness, brother. Indeed, we have had no queen in Wessex since her time. I rejoice to hear that she found God after this prince's grandfather exiled her from our country. I hope that your prayers are helping her soul's journey, but I'm afraid that you will never receive alms from Wessex to honour a woman whom we remember as a cruel oppressor. If the great emperor regarded her differently then perhaps you should ask his successor? Or the House of Mercia? Although I have to tell you that much has changed in that kingdom since the time of King Offa.'

The guest master spread his hands out in an apologetic gesture. 'We see so few people from England these days. And those we do see. . .' he paused, choosing his words carefully. 'It is not always wise to pay too much attention to what they say. We must cater for all. That is why it is such a pleasure to have truly distinguished visitors from England. I hope that where the royal prince and you, my lord bishop, lead, many others will follow.'

'I hope so, too,' Swithun replied. 'It is one of the reasons for our journey. And when others do follow,' he added with a slight smile, 'you now know it may not be a good idea to show them this tomb. That is, if they come from Wessex. Mercians, possibly.'

Once away from the guest master, Alfred had lots of questions. Why had he not heard of Queen Eadburh before? What had she done that was so terrible?

Swithun looked uncomfortable. 'There are many stories about her. It was not a good time in our history.'

'What are the stories?' Alfred insisted.

'Eadburh did have a powerful father. King Offa was the great king in England in her day. Far more powerful than the king of Wessex to whom she was given in marriage. She exiled your grandfather, Alfred, and would have killed him if she could. Rumours have it that she killed her husband instead, although that was never proved. She would have ruled over us all, but not according to custom, simply her own fancy. It was only when your grandfather returned victorious after King Offa's death that we were delivered from Eadburh's tyranny. That is why there are no queens in Wessex any more, Alfred. That is why your mother is not a queen. The men of Wessex will not accept a woman having that much power over them again.'

*

At last, the end of the journey was at hand. Waking on the day when they were to ride into Rome, Alfred felt a fluttering in his stomach. So many times had he heard the name of Rome, so many longings were directed towards it. What on earth would the real place be like?

His first impression was of an enormous pile of shattered stones rising up from the plain. He had seen the remains of Roman buildings at home, heard tell that the men who built them must have been giants to have built and lived in such houses. But nothing to compare with this – the whole horizon filled with rubble, pierced at intervals by towering columns, pedestals and lintels. A great people must have lived here once but they were long gone, and their creations in an advanced stage of decay.

'It has been attacked many times,' Swithun explained, noticing the look on Alfred's face. 'It is still being attacked. The Holy Father has only finished building some new walls to protect the city from the Saracens. These things,' he indicated the scene before them with a sweep of his arm, 'are creations of men, and like all the creations of men, they only last a certain time before returning to the earth. The old Rome was a great city, Alfred, but we do not value Rome because of what it once was, but rather because of what was planted here. A seed which falls and dies, but rises up once more a hundredfold. That is what is important about Rome, not these buildings.'

Even so, it was hard to ignore the buildings. But as they drew closer, they saw people engaged in familiar tasks – ploughing fields around the stone remains, washing clothes in the river, minding children who stared up at them with large, dark eyes. Sights which softened the sense of fear and desolation which the first sight of Rome had caused in Alfred. Life went on here the same as anywhere else. And closer too, he saw that the ancient stone was being put to use with shelters and houses fashioned from it. Some of the old buildings even survived, massive and patched against the passing of time.

Deeper into the city and the buildings closed in upon them. Alfred had never seen such a concentration of wrought stone, of smooth pillars glowing with a lustrous sheen, veined in red and green. And gigantic statues of men on horses. Churches everywhere – a golden glitter of angels and saints looking down on them from pediments, bells chiming all around, and often the sound of chanting from deep within dark interiors. Mixed with the shouting heat of crowded streets, blinding bright one moment and then plunged in shadow the next. Unfamiliar smells reached up around him. He felt giddy and confused by the assault on his senses. Hard to distinguish one from the other any more.

They crossed the river through a walled gatehouse and saw sights more familiar – wooden houses, although many with charred timbers. Space once more, but the space of destruction. It was clear that a mighty fire must have swept through this area of wooden buildings some time ago, punching wide gaps in its warren of streets, black scorch-marks showing the flames' lethal passage. Some rebuilding was going on, but on a small scale. It would take years to fill in the blackened gaps at that rate. It was much more subdued than over the river, as if the air of tragedy still hung over it.

'This is our place,' Swithun informed him. 'Ever since the time of your ancestor, King Ine, it has been set aside for English pilgrims. It's a great honour, Alfred. We are near the tomb of the prince of the apostles, the great St Peter himself, who holds the keys to heaven for all.'

Alfred looked around him. He tried to feel proud and told himself that buildings didn't matter.

'It looks sad,' he couldn't help but say.

'Well, there's been a big fire, as you can see. And the Saracens have attacked it as well. The Holy Father can only do so much. He's built these wonderful new walls, which should protect from the Saracens. It's for us to rebuild – it's our place. If we want St Peter to look after us, if we want our pilgrims to find favour here, then we must bring this place back to what it once was. We need to show ourselves worthy of what we've been given.'

'What can we do?' Alfred looked around again at the scene of devastation.

'Gold and silver usually help in cases like these,' Swithun replied with a small smile. 'Just as we brought lead to Abbot Lupus for his monastery's roof, so we're bringing gold and silver to the Holy Father. And skilled men. There are always things kings and princes can do to help further the cause of the Lord. And even aside from the gold and silver, our coming here will be a cause for celebration and new hope for those of our people living on here. It shows them they are not forgotten, that your father has them all in his thoughts and prayers.'

They turned a corner and there, soaring up from amidst the low, burnt buildings, was by far the largest church which Alfred had ever seen. Rectangular and massive against the sky, streaked with black, it looked as though it might have dropped down from heaven itself. They stood and looked at what was a suitable ending for their journey.

'Is that where the Holy Father lives?' Alfred asked eventually.

'He lives there sometimes,' Swithun replied. "But, more importantly, it's where St Peter is buried. It houses the seed which is eternal. Only Jerusalem houses a greater.'

They were lodged in a stone house next to St Peter's and went to pray that evening at the apostle's tomb to give thanks for their safe arrival. Alfred, kneeling in the dark crypt, trying to understand the muttered Latin around him, started to shiver. A sharp pain was rising in his stomach. 'I'm not going to be ill again,' he told himself. 'The holy apostle will keep me well.'

But the illness was upon him. He was both hot and cold at the same time and his thoughts were beginning to float away in a jumble. His stomach felt as though it was on fire. He clutched at the sleeve of Swithun, kneeling beside him.

'What is it?' An annoyed whisper.

'I. . . I. . . don't feel well.'

After that, he didn't remember much. He may have fallen to the floor because there seemed to be people crowding in above him. The external world seemed to have gone, eaten up by the pain in his stomach. He wondered vaguely if this is what it had been like for the houses outside when the fire seared its way through them. Impossible to ignore the pain. If he tried to do so, it became worse, insisting on his complete attention. If he watched it with all his might, breathed it in and let it fill him completely, then it was bearable. Just.

How many days passed like that, he did not know. He became aware from time to time that he was in a large, light room with a view of St Peter's. Strangers would come in and look at him. Swithun and Colman were there sometimes. If they spoke to him, he didn't hear.

He was withdrawn from the world, wrapped up in a blanket of pain.

And then, one day, he knew it was passing. His stomach was calmer, his breathing easier, the pain receding. He was able to respond to Swithun when he came in, and told him that he was feeling better.

'Praise be to God!' Swithun exclaimed. 'Our prayers have been answered.'

Alfred was aware for the first time of how old his guardian looked, the deep lines on his face. He'd not been aware of prayers, although maybe his staring at the pain was a form of prayer. And why did he fall ill when they were praying to St Peter himself? Wasn't the whole point that the saints were meant to make you feel better? It wasn't easy to understand.

He had to stay in bed for another week, getting steadily more restless. He dreaded the long convalescence he'd had to endure before but was delighted to find that this time he recovered more quickly. Once up, he was able to stay up. He was still a little light-headed, but he kept quiet about that to avoid further attention from doctors.

Eventually, he was allowed out to walk along the top of the new city walls with Colman, looking down at the city spread out below them and the plains beyond. He noticed that the area outside the walls to the south also had large blackened areas.

'They've had a fire there as well,' he observed.

'Pagans,' Colman replied shortly. 'No place is free from them, not even the Eternal City.'

One morning, they made an expedition through the suburbs to another massive church, this one housing the tomb of St Paul.

'We are to pray here and give thanks for your recovery to the great St Paul,' Colman informed him.

Alfred was nervous. He'd fallen ill when praying to St Peter. And St Paul was meant to be an even fiercer saint than St Peter. What would he do to him? At the front of the church was a large statue of the saint. Alfred kept his head down and crossed himself hurriedly, certain that the saint would be glowering at him. Once inside, he did not look around at the dark, looming space but kept close to Colman. He stared at the floor, trying to concentrate his thoughts on feeling sorry for how bad he was. At the tomb of the apostle was the chain with which he had been manacled in prison. Alfred tried to imagine being chained in a dark prison and accused himself of it all being his fault. 'I'm so sorry,' he kept repeating to himself. If he accused himself of everything and tried to share in the suffering, then maybe the saint would relent and not strike him down, guilty though he was.

It seemed to work. Though he was concentrating so hard in an attempt to block out everything else, the pain would have been able to cut through his concentration had it been coming back. Outside in the sunshine, feeling the same as he had before going into the church, he gasped with relief. 'Thank you, St Paul,' he muttered. 'Thank you for sparing me.'

Swithun was waiting for them on their return. 'Tomorrow is an important day,' he announced. 'You are to be anointed by the Holy Father himself.'

*

It was the first time that Alfred would be back inside St Peter's since the evening of their arrival and he was terrified. Praying at the apostle's tomb had almost killed him, and now he was to meet the apostle's living successor. He fully expected to drop dead on the spot.

Swithun tried to reassure him. 'The Holy Father is a kind old man. You've nothing to fear from him. The anointing is a great honour. It will make you a spiritual son of the Holy Father and the Holy See.'

He would definitely die. As soon as the Holy Father looked into his eyes and saw how bad he was, how unworthy he was to be anyone's spiritual son, then, kind old man or not, his anger would blaze out and reduce him to a pile of smoking ashes.

But there was no getting out of it. Swithun made that much clear. 'This is why we have come all this way, Alfred. This is why your father sent you.'

'But I'll die!' Alfred howled.

'Then you'll die as a prince of Wessex,' snapped Swithun in exasperation. 'Doing your father's will.'

At that, he became calmer. He was still sure that he would die, but if it was doing his father's will, then at least there was a purpose to it. And it wasn't so much about him any more, but rather what he represented – the country of Wessex, of England even.

'You're doing it for all of us,' said Swithun, as though reading his mind. 'You want your father to be proud of you, don't you? Your mother?'

His mother. A sudden overpowering memory of saying goodbye to her in Canterbury – her hot skin and fixed smile – flashed through him, leaving a sense of intense sadness. How to deal with such sadness? Maybe it wouldn't be so bad to die, after all.

Even so, he was shaking the following morning, as he dressed in the crisp white tunic laid out for him. All his clothing was new. A better quality than he had ever known. A dark blue cloak, a gold ring of intricate design. A lamb without spot or blemish. On the outside at least.

The evening before had been taken up with Swithun and Colman rehearsing him as to what to say and do when presented to the Holy Father. A papal official had even arrived to discuss the ceremony. He looked at Alfred with expressionless eyes.

They were to fast in preparation. Alfred lay awake into the night, cold and empty. Only when rising and putting on the unfamiliar, ceremonial clothes did his fear return, causing him to shake against his will.

Swithun, entering the room and seeing his shaking charge, frowned. 'Remember,' he said, 'you're representing your country.'

Outside in the sunshine, it was better. The soldiers gathered around him. They had shed their arms for the ceremony, but even so, the vigour of their presence was a source of support. With their strong bodies lining up behind him, Alfred felt better able to face whatever lay ahead in the darkness. They waited silently in the sunshine for an hour or so as clergy scuttled in and out of St Peter's. Alfred tried to remember what he had to do. He had stopped shaking but his mind was blank. Eventually, after some final discussions between Swithun and one of the Roman clergy, they were ushered forward to enter the towering main door of the basilica church.

They walked through the door, which closed with a crash behind them. The darkness seemed total. Alfred wondered if he had died already. But then he was conscious of a hand tugging him down. It was Swithun. Of course, they had to kneel at the entrance. The soldiers behind him were already on their knees. He dropped down to join them. He felt less noticeable. Could anyone see him in the darkness?

As he stayed kneeling on the cold stone floor, his eyes adjusted to the darkness and began to distinguish shapes. He could see enormous pillars on both sides, one after the other, reaching forwards through the gloom. Following the lines of pillars, there were pools of light at the far end of the church. In the largest pool of light was a gold throne, on which a man was sitting. Alfred realised that the man was looking straight towards them and, if his gaze was as sharp as he was sure the Holy Father's was, he would have seen him be the last to drop to his knees. He felt the gaze upon him and the comforting presence of those around him drop away. He lowered his head and stared at a stone paving slab in front of him, frightened and miserable. And then someone touched him on the shoulder. He looked up. It was the official with the expressionless eyes who had visited them last evening. He was motioning for him to stand up. Alfred looked around. Everyone else remained kneeling; only he was being told to rise. He hesitated, but then Swithun placed a hand under his elbow and pushed upwards. He clambered reluctantly to his feet. At least Swithun was getting up as well.

The official led the way down through the lines of pillars. Alfred followed, his heart pounding as the light strengthened and the man on the throne grew closer. If only Swithun was walking beside him, but he was keeping resolutely a few paces behind. There was to be no shield between himself and the Holy Father.

They stopped just before the throne. The light was dazzling now. Alfred dropped to his knees unbidden.

"Surge, puer mi."

He understood that much from his lessons with Colman. He stood up. The man was looking down at him from the throne. He was dressed all in red with a long cloak. He beckoned Alfred forward.

"Propius accede."

Alfred's legs started to shake again. This would be the moment when the Holy Father would see how sinful he was and strike him down. But Swithun was behind him and there was nowhere else for him to go. He slowly mounted the steps of the throne, keeping his eyes lowered. If the Holy Father couldn't see his eyes then maybe he wouldn't be able to see how bad he was.

No use. As he drew close, the pope bent down, cupped a hand under his chin, and gently raised his head up. Before Alfred realised, a pair of twinkling, light blue eyes were staring straight into his. He shut his eyes automatically, tensing in readiness for an explosion of anger and pain.

It didn't come. When he opened his eyes again, the pope was still looking at him with that twinkling gaze.

'I no bite,' he said in English with a smile.

Alfred didn't know what to think. He had been so sure that he would be dead by now and on his way down to hell, that to still be alive and smiled upon by an old man with a friendly face was confusing in the extreme.

'Welcome a Roma,' the pope continued slowly. 'English always welcome a Roma.'

Now was the time for him to say something in Latin in reply, to repeat what Swithun and Colman had drilled into him last night. But he couldn't say anything. His tongue stuck to the roof of his mouth and all he could do was stare at this man, who had for some unknown reason decided not to kill him.

The pope seemed willing enough to conclude the audience and move on to the ceremony. Alfred was aware of two acolytes approaching either side of the throne. The pope indicated for him to stay where he was and started to recite a prayer in Latin, the rhythmic phrases reaching out from the past to the present. He was calling down the Holy Spirit. Alfred's legs began to shake once more. This is when it would happen. This is when he would be rejected. The Holy Spirit knows everything. Suddenly the pope's hand descended onto his head. He felt a bolt of energy and light pass through him and was no longer afraid.

'Spiritum sapientiae et intellectus.'

From behind him, he knew not how far away, Alfred heard people saying Amen.

'Spiritum consilii et fortidudiniis.'

'Amen.'

'Spiritum scientiae et pietatis.'

'Amen.'

'Spiritum timoris Dei.'

'Amen.'

The seven gifts of the Holy Spirit. An acolyte was now approaching with a phial of oil. The pope dipped his thumb into the oil and made the sign of the Cross on Alfred's forehead.

'Confirmo te chrismate, in nomine Patris et Filii et Spiritus Sancti.'

'Amen,' Alfred managed to breathe.

The pope patted him on the cheek. 'Now you are soldier for Christ,' he said in English. 'And my son.'

At that, a choir began to sing in joyous tones. Alfred looked around in a daze. Swithun helped him down from the throne and the two acolytes put another tunic over him and strapped a belt around it.

'Ave!' They both saluted him. Alfred looked up at Swithun, puzzled.

'You're a Roman now, Alfred,' Swithun explained with a smile. 'A consul. Successor to Julius Caesar, no less.'

Despite his smile, there was a look of respect in his eyes and he fell in behind as they walked back down the church. The soldiers too looked at him in a different way. Something had happened on that papal throne which had both raised up and isolated him. *This must be what a king feels like*, he thought.

But such thoughts were soon put away. Swithun came to his room that evening. 'We have done all we came for,' he said. 'Now it is time to go back home.'

5. Borderlands

The campaigns against the Welsh had gone well enough, Aethelwulf thought. Inconclusive, but then campaigns against the Welsh were normally inconclusive. They always had their mountains to which they could retreat. They had done so the previous year at the approach of the Wessex fyrds but had returned over King Offa's dyke this year, encouraged by further signs of Mercian disunity. King Burgred was still having difficulties in persuading his ealdormen to accept his authority. It was ever thus in Mercia, or had been since Offa's death. To be angered by Mercia's disunity was as pointless as being angered by the sea being wet – it was, and one had to act accordingly.

Had he been right to accept an alliance with Burgred so readily? Did he have a choice? Burgred was the one who had emerged from the chaos following the pagan capture of London and Beorthwulf's deposition, He had as good a right as anyone to be king. Were Aethelwulf to give his support to anyone else, it would only make matters worse. Observing the Mercian ealdormen close to, he couldn't see an alternative. They were a grasping, narrow-minded lot, concerned solely with their own advantage, whatever noble motives they might awkwardly profess when he met them. At least Burgred gave the impression that he had higher aims. And his ability to keep his thoughts and emotions under close check was, although frustrating for a prospective father-in-law trying to gauge his worth, a strength in this treacherous environment.

And to do Burgred justice, he did seem pleased to see him, both last year and now. He was clear and open in his gratitude and willingness to accept protection from a senior king. Of course, he was partly doing so to show his ealdormen that he had such protection, but even so, such an obvious alignment of interests, with Wessex recognised as the senior partner, was welcome to Aethelwulf. He was in a good mood at the welcoming feast which Burgred held in Shrewsbury for him, listening to speeches and poems in his honour. The next day, he agreed to lead a punitive expedition against the Welsh, who had disappeared back over the dyke again at his approach.

They marched through empty moorlands for days, meeting no-one. It was desolate country – wide expanses of peaty bog, which often made their progress painfully slow. In this open country, they would be clearly visible for miles to hidden watchers in the hills. Aethelwulf had the impression of being watched the whole time by an invisible enemy. Every village they came across was deserted, which suggested the inhabitants had seen them coming. He thought uneasily of the pagans at Aclea and wondered if they were marching into a trap.

Burgred, however, was reassuring. 'It is the Welsh way,' he said. 'If it comes to an open fight, they disappear. They're too disunited amongst themselves to launch a concerted attack on a large force. The king of Powys is old, with his thoughts on God. His sons are busy eyeing one another to see who will succeed him. That may be the reason behind their recent attacks on us – one of them trying to win support over the others. But they could all be disappointed. Rhodri, king of

Gwynedd, is the old king's nephew and known to be ambitious.'

'What do we do then?' asked Aethelwulf, a little exasperated at this tale of more disunity. The Mercians and the Welsh seemed to be well-suited to each other.

'We find a traitor,' Burgred replied coolly. 'There are usually plenty of those in Wales when the kings and princes are at war with one another.'

And in Mercia too, no doubt, Aethelwulf thought, but did not say, wondering afresh at the fate of Beorthwulf. Burgred certainly seemed to know his way around this sort of warfare. But that was no bad thing. Maybe they'd had it easy in Wessex since his father, King Egbert, had united the kingdom. It had not always been so. If you cannot tame men's ambitions, then you have to know how to use them if you're going to survive.

Burgred's optimism proved well-founded. A man came into their camp one nightfall with news of the old king's movements. 'He's heading towards the border with Gwynedd,' Burgred reported to Aethelwulf. 'Either for the protection of the mountains or because he doesn't trust his sons. Or both. If we march all night, we can intercept him at the river.'

'We're going to march all night through the bog?' It was hard enough to make progress in the day.

'This man knows a dry path through.'

'And you trust him?'

'He knows he'll be the first to die if he leads us astray.'

'And what's he getting from us?'

'Ten head of cattle. Do you not think it's worth it?'

'For a king, it's a good price.'

'I thought so, too.'

And, sure enough, they were led true and straight to the old king and his small guard, whom they overcame without a fight in the early morning by the river. One of the king's guards drew his sword but the king, seeing the force which confronted them, touched his hand to dissuade him.

For Aethelwulf, his meeting with the old king of Powys transformed what had been a tiresome, if necessary, expedition into something much more worthwhile. Burgred had spoken right when he said that the old king's thoughts were on God. You could see it in his shining eyes and the calmness with which he accepted his captivity. Aethelwulf felt himself drawn to this man with a look of peace which nothing seemed to disturb. During the day, as they rode eastwards, he tried to talk to him. The king spoke little English and he no Welsh, but they both spoke some Latin, although with hesitance on both sides. This hesitance, this shared effort of communicating in a language foreign to them both, did bring them closer together. When talking at least, the fact of Welshness and Englishness had to be put aside to struggle with something different. Aethelwulf found it frustrating when he couldn't find the words to say what he wanted to. But the old king, whose name was Cyngen, seemed more amused than frustrated at any inability to communicate.

'I am sorry,' Aethelwulf said slowly, 'that we have had to take you captive.'

Cyngen shrugged slightly. 'It is war,' he said. 'It happens.'

'I hope the war ends soon."

'So do I. I always do.'

That evening at dinner, Aethelwulf found further common ground with the captive king. He had been asking about Cyngen's sons, questions which Cyngen answered with bland vagueness. But they had perhaps prompted a deeper response within him, because he suddenly drank deeply from the cup of wine before him.

'I am old,' he said sombrely. 'Old men can outstay their welcome, particularly kings. But it doesn't matter. I am ready to go.'

'You are not old,' said Aethelwulf, wondering uneasily if he was much older than himself. 'You will rule for many years yet.'

'I hope not,' Cyngen responded bleakly. But then, catching the look on Aethelwulf's face, he smiled and his tone lightened. 'I've wanted to go to Rome for many years. I've always thought that those kings of yours had the right idea – the ones who left off fighting while they still had time and went as common pilgrims to seek the Lord before they died. For years, it has not been possible for us Cymri – our differences with Rome prevented that. But we have no differences any more. A Cymric king could go. And I plan to be the first!' His eyes shone brightly in the firelight and he looked ten years younger.

'I want to go as well!' Aethelwulf exclaimed. 'I've been planning it for years.'

'You? You're still young.'

'I don't feel it. I've been fighting since I was a child. I know that we are not just put into this world for,' he looked around, trying to find the right word, 'for all of this. And who knows when death may come for any of us? What did Bede say? This life is like a small bird flying into a warm, lighted hall from a winter storm and remaining but a moment before flying back out again.'

'He took that simile from a Cymric poet,' Cyngen responded with a smile.

'What does that matter if it's true?'

'It doesn't matter, I suppose. Except to poets.'

'I expect your Cymric poet took it from someone else.'

Cyngen laughed. 'I expect you're right. There's nothing new under the sun. Except Our Lord, who is always new. I hope we do both make it to Rome, my lord king. It would be good to kneel side by side at the tomb of one greater than either of us.'

'I hope so, too. You've made me more determined than ever to go. And if there's anything I can do to aid your journey, then you have only to say the word.'

'A safe passage over your lands would be welcome. As you can see,' he added wryly, 'my safety in Cymru is no longer assured.'

'You shall have safe passage through Mercia and Wessex. I will make sure of that. And I will write to the king of France and the emperor and ask them to ensure the same for you over their lands. That is, if you plan travelling overland.'

'I do now,' replied Cyngen. 'Thank you, my lord king. I am even more pleased that we met.'

The following day, envoys arrived from King Rhodri of Gwynedd, seeking to negotiate the release of King Cyngen. A few days later, envoys also arrived from Cyngen's sons. Aethelwulf did wonder if the sons would have sent envoys had King Rhodri not done so. The sons might have endured their father in the hands of the English. In the hands of a powerful Welsh neighbour, who also had a claim to the throne of Powys, was a different matter entirely. Aethelwulf had decided to leave the negotiations to Burgred and take little part in them himself. It would help Burgred's authority to have him seen as the person dictating terms of settlement to the Welsh. But he did arrange for his son, Aethelberht, to act as an assistant to Burgred.

Berti had acquitted himself well enough in his first campaign. True, there had been no fighting but he had survived the rigours of the march and the night ride without ill effect. So long as his health held up, Aethelwulf had no doubt that he could be a leader. He had the intelligence and the courage – it was only physical strength that he lacked. And that might not matter so much if he was able to command the loyalty of those with the strength to defend him. Aethelwulf had not noticed any sign of dissension amongst the men he had assigned to Berti's command. Well, one could only do so much. It was all good experience. As were the negotiations – Aethelwulf had no doubt of Berti's abilities there and listened with interest to his accounts of those in private at the end of each day in his tent.

'There's no love lost between the Welsh,' Berti told him. 'The sons' envoys spend the whole time arguing with those from Gwynedd. I can see why the old king might want out. The problem is what he leaves behind.'

'What's Burgred doing?'

'Leaving them to argue – it drives up the price.'

Aethelwulf frowned. 'Security is more important than money.'

'There's compensation for the sack of Shrewsbury to think of.'

'That was the sons' doing?'

'I think there's little doubt of it. The Gwynedd envoys keep acknowledging that it was an act demanding compensation, and they wouldn't do that if it was

Rhodri's doing. But, even so, they're offering more for the king than his sons.'

'Is Burgred tempted?'

'Difficult to say. He's very hard to read.'

'He can't hand the king over to Gwynedd. That's effectively agreeing to Rhodri taking over Powys. Better arguing princes on your borders than an over-mighty king.'

'What's to be done then?'

'We need to take it away from the envoys. We need Rhodri and the sons here to hammer out a general peace treaty. That's more important than the exact level of compensation for Shrewsbury.'

'Will they come?'

'They'll have to. They have no choice. We hold the person they're all hoping to succeed.'

And come they did. The sons hostile and suspicious, Rhodri good-natured and magnanimous. And, Aethelwulf could see at once, far more dangerous. With the sense to realise that now was the time for politeness and expressions of goodwill. Rhodri had time on his side. The English would not be here forever.

Aethelwulf had persuaded Burgred that it was necessary to put up with the bad grace and hostility of the sons and accept less money from them than he could have got from the charming and smooth-spoken Rhodri.

'I will make good the difference for you in my daughter's dowry,' he told him.

This assurance of his forthcoming marriage drew a rare smile from Burgred. 'Thank you, my lord king.'

'But we need to do more. We need to sort out the succession while we have the chance. I want that old man to be able to go to Rome, not die surrounded by his squabbling family.'

'The old man is probably the main reason why Rhodri hasn't invaded already.'

'So, we make Rhodri agree to the succession while we have him here in an amenable mood.'

'You think he'll agree to that?'

'If we present it as necessary to enable Cyngen to go to Rome, I think so. He'll look like an enemy to religion if he doesn't. Whether he'll keep to any agreement when we're gone is a different matter. But I think it's the best we can do. At least it will make things more difficult for him. If Cyngen stays and the sons continue fighting amongst each other then he'll just pick them off one by one and take over when Cyngen dies.'

He was aware of only half-believing his reasoning as he advanced it. He suspected that Rhodri would take over Powys at some stage whatever they did. He had that look. But Aethelwulf wanted Cyngen to be able to go to Rome before that happened. Rhodri might want that also. He did seem to have some respect for his uncle. Unless he was just a very good actor. Oh, all these worldly calculations – how tired he was of them all! How much less important they were than his conversation with Cyngen before the fire. And yet, how much of his time he had to devote to them.

They secured an agreement that Cyngen's eldest son would be appointed regent while his father was in Rome. Any objections that the younger sons might have had to this appointment were stifled by the genial presence of Rhodri. Maybe even they were beginning to realise that if they didn't hang together, they'd hang separately.

Rhodri expressed delight at the agreement enabling his uncle to depart on his long-planned pilgrimage. He insisted on putting his name to the agreement as a witness and supporter of it. Which means, Aethelwulf thought wryly to himself, that when the agreement falls apart, as it almost certainly will, he'll have a better justification for invading as its upholder. There were definite seeds of greatness in that young man. Well, maybe it will at least buy a little time. And Cyngen can go to Rome. The release from bondage of that old man was important. Almost as important as his own. He was determined he would not be delayed much longer. He would oversee Elsa's marriage to Burgred. And then, at last, it would be time for him.

*

Blade stood on the low cliff at Reculver, looking out across the deadly stretch of water, to which pagans flocked like ravens to a corpse. In the two years since he had been here in the east – not yet a king, his father still denied him that – a month had not passed by without some incursion of pagan ships. He had come to loathe this flat, marshy land, so defenceless against the sea, and the rivers which snaked so treacherously into its heart. How easy it was for the pagans in their agile craft to penetrate these sheltered waters, carry out their deadly raids and be gone before any effective resistance could be mounted. Even when Blade and his men managed to capture and destroy some of the pagan ships, there were always more to take their place. Close to Francia, on a direct route back to the pagan homelands, it was too tempting a target.

A few years ago, this coastland had been well cared for, feeding and housing communities of farmers, fishermen and religious. Now, it was almost deserted – the fields returning to scrub, the abandoned houses and monasteries beginning to fall down, with only the occasional fishing boat making its tentative way over the dangerous sea.

Like those around him, Blade felt a combination of deep anger and a growing but never openly acknowledged helplessness at the endless pagan raids, which were slowly bleeding the kingdom of its life. How much easier it had been at Aclea, where all had been decided in one fight. With Ealdorman Elchere, he had tried to counter the raids by building more ships and manning the old sea forts. But the coastline to be guarded was so great and the men who could be spared for the task so few that it was never enough to keep the pagans out.

So now, standing on the cliff beside the abandoned abbey, looking across the treacherous channel to a pagan fleet on the island's shore, he had mixed feelings. At least this would be a fight. The pagans were becoming bolder, more reluctant to leave the land which gave them such rich rewards. They had overrun the island, massacred or enslaved its remaining inhabitants, with a view to settling permanently on such a convenient, defensible refuge. Their confidence was such that ships containing their women and children had already landed. From where he stood, Blade could see the smoke from campfires a few miles behind the ships lined up to face them. An incentive to his men, he thought grimly. Enough of them had lost their own wives and children to the pagans. Who knows? They might even find some of them in the pagan camp.

But he was getting ahead of himself, assuming a victory before the battle had even begun. If the past two years had taught him anything, it was to keep a cold heart when facing such a cold-hearted enemy. Very well, but he would not think of defeat. He would be dead long before then. He went over in his mind for the thousandth time why they would defeat the pagans. They outnumbered them at least three to one. Not only the fyrd of Kent, but that of Surrey too, under Ealdorman Huda, had been raised to expel this intrusion. His initial worry had been that the pagans would sail away when they saw the force which confronted them, as they had done so many times before. But they hadn't.

Why? The question nagged. Was it just over-confidence and a desire for land? Or did they have some secret knowledge, or more men than spies had reported? Perhaps reinforcements were waiting out at sea over the horizon until the battle had begun. His brother Athelstan had been killed by just such a stratagem in this very place.

He shook his head angrily to dispel such womanish worries. This was different. The channel of water separating them from the island was only a couple of miles wide. Their boats were smaller than the pagan ships but the number of them crossing would give no room for clever pagan manoeuvres. If more ships came, they would have to join the fighting on the island.

He didn't want to think about it any more. He felt an urgent desire to be in his boat and speeding across to the island where all the answers lay.

Elchere and Huda were climbing the hill up towards him. It must be time.

'Is all ready?' he asked a panting Elchere when he had drawn up beside him.

'It is my lord prince,' Elchere confirmed. 'The tide will turn in an hour, and the wind is favourable for us.'

'Then let's been on our way,' Blade replied, almost running down the hill towards his boat.

His crew were waiting for him, leaping to their tasks. The sail was hauled up to catch the fitful breeze as the men at the oars pulled as one. The boat shuddered into movement, lurching forward under its heavy load of armed men. If Blade had looked around, he would have seen other boats hurrying to follow his lead. But his attention was focused forward. He joined the group of warriors in the bow. So much depended on how quickly they could cross the channel. If enough of them could make the island's shore without being stopped by the pagans then surely their numbers would prevail? But if they were held up in the channel, the turning tide and the pagans' – curse them! - better seamanship might change all that. He stared intently at the ships now making their way in a line to meet them.

'Oh, to go faster!' he muttered to himself. His oarsmen were straining every sinew, but the sail flapped loosely. The light breeze was slackening further.

The pagan ships were coming on with only the smallest of gaps between them. If they tried to sail between, they'd be attacked from both sides. They would not make the island without a fight.

Blade looked around him for the first time. Their boats were on either side, only a short distance behind. If his boat veered off course, it would obstruct them and cause confusion before battle had even been joined.

He looked straight ahead at a large ship with a black figurehead of some snarling pagan god.

'We board that one!' he shouted.

The boarding irons were brought out, ready to be thrown. The men around him drew their weapons, summoning their powers. Blade, spear in hand, stared at the ship they were bearing down upon. He could see the men on it drawing their own weapons, getting ready to repel them. Any moment now. . .

A fierce roar as the irons were thrown. Blade hurled his spear at a pagan who had rushed forward to try and dislodge an iron hook. No time to see if he'd hit the man. A shout warned him of a pagan spear thrown at him. He ducked behind his shield and felt the sharp jar of something glancing off it. For a few moments, the sky was raining spears. But the irons were holding the craft together.

Now was the critical time, and now the pride of Beornhard the Strong, whose land was on the island, to be the first onto the pagan's ship. A mountain of a man, with the battle fury upon him, he jumped across with a mighty cry, crashing into three men who tried to stop him, swatting away their spears like so many pinpricks, carving a way through with his sword, Vengeance.

Other men followed Beornhard, leaping behind him with their own cries to fill the gap he had made and push further into the pagan ship. But the pagans had rallied. They launched themselves at Beornhard with sword and spear, pushing him backwards. Suddenly, there was no longer a gap to jump into, just a confused crush of straining men.

'Wait!' Blade shouted at a man about to jump. There was nowhere for him to land, just a forest of spears, swords and bodies. Too late. The man leaped without a thought, crashing into the back of one of his fellows and knocking him to the ground. Stumbling backwards himself, with no sure footing, he was caught between the craft, helpless. A quick-witted pagan lunged forward and speared him through the throat.

Blade cursed. 'No-one else is to jump until I say so!' he shouted. 'We fight them from here.' To prove his point, he picked up a spear from the pile on deck and threw it at one of the pagans. This time, he saw the strike, the man crumpling to his knees. The men behind him gave a roar and followed by throwing a further volley of spears. Blade looked down at the spear pile. Almost gone. They'd have to go now. But the volley had eased the pressure on Beornhard, who was pushing forward again. There was space behind him.

'All right!' Blade shouted, picking up one of the last remaining spears. 'Jump now!'

He stayed where he was, watching the warriors jump into the ship and join in the push forward. The pagans were giving ground now. They could no longer stem the surge of bodies coming over. In some deep dark place of his own, which was also somehow the battle's heart, he watched the death struggles on the pagan ship. Beornhard was like some mighty wind, cutting down all before him now. Some of the pagans were even jumping over the side to escape. Blade stayed where he was. This battle was almost won; there would be others.

'Do we go now, my lord?' The oarsmen around him now.

'No. I need you to row when the fighters are back. We must get to the shore quickly. But you two, he said to two of the youngest and slightest, 'go and collect as many spears and weapons as you can and bring them back here. Don't go where there's fighting. Just where it's over. We've thrown a lot of spears. We need to get back what we can. Don't take armour – there's not time. Just weapons.'

So much could get lost or forgotten in the battle's rage. Being able to stay calm in the heat and remember small things – that it what won victories and kept you alive.

In ten minutes, it was over. The fighters were back, bloody and victorious, the pagan ship beginning to sink. The way to the island was clear now, the other boats around them still locked in their individual struggles. Should they stay and try to help? No, the whole idea had been to reach the island. When the pagans saw that a boat had done that, they would surely lose heart.

'Straight for the shore,' he confirmed to the helmsman.

Nearing the island, he felt a twinge of doubt. There weren't many people on the shore and some were already beginning to run. Should he have stayed on the water until it was clear that the battle was won?

The boat was already beginning to scrape onto the stony beach. Beornhard and some others leaped out and started running towards the fleeing pagans.

'Wait!' Blade shouted. Not heard; or if heard, ignored. With a sickening lurch of the stomach, he realised the mistake he had made. There were just old men and children left here. And a camp full of women less than two miles away. Beornhard and the others would not stop running until they had reached that. Intent on vengeance, they were lost to any fight now.

'Just when I was thinking myself so clever,' he muttered. He'd thought of the camp as an incentive; he'd forgotten it could be a distraction as well. He looked back at the boats still locked in struggle mid-channel, and then around at the men still with him, the rowers exhausted from their pulling, a few of the

younger warriors looking doubtfully at him. Well, they couldn't stay here gathering seashells.

'We go back,' he barked at the helmsman, trying not to catch anyone's eye.

Back in mid-channel, he saw a pagan boat drawn up beside Ealdorman Elchere's boat and in the process of boarding it.

'Head there!' he pointed to the helmsman.

This time, Blade went over with his warriors, anxious to make up for the time he had wasted. The pagans were swarming all over the deck of Elchere's boat. He caught sight of the old ealdorman himself with two companions, desperately trying to fend off attacks from at least five pagans. He cursed. If Elchere was killed, then even if they won this battle, he would be to blame.

'Forward!' he shouted to his warriors, leaping into the fighting mass on Elchere's boat and cutting his way towards the hard-pressed ealdorman. Attacking from the rear, he scythed down two pagans with his sword, Bloothirst. But then more turned to face him and thoughts of reaching Elchere were forced from his mind by the need to defend himself. The deadly present flowed in, wiping out both past and future. A tall pagan thrust a spear at him, while another launched himself at him with a cry and upraised sword. Dodging the spear, he managed to parry the sword with his shield, but the force of the blow knocked him backward. Had it not been for one of his men rushing forwards and attacking the spearman before he could thrust again, that might have been the end for him. The advantage of surprise was over. There were still plenty of pagans on this boat well able to defend themselves. A solid phalanx now faced him.

'Lock shields!' Blade cried to those around him. 'We fight as a wall.'

It was back to Aclea. Except this time the pagans knew of the enemy behind and had men to keep them away. The numbers were about even. As always in a shield wall, time had disappeared and the world shrank to the man you were facing, and the ones on either side of him. Those who could kill you, or those you could kill. How long was spent in thrusting shields forward and trying to make a gap in the opposite wall, or taking the thrust of the other and parrying the seeking spear or sword? Blade had no more knowledge than those around him. Knowledge was no longer important. Willpower was all. Who had the most desire to stay alive?

And then, in the scramble of thrust and counter-thrust, Blade sensed a flicker of distraction in the man before him. Pushing forward, he caught the man with shield askew. It was enough. The man stumbled and Blade brought Bloodthirst down across his exposed neck. The men on either side had pushed with him and suddenly the momentum was theirs. The pagans were falling back. Still with his attention locked, Blade was vaguely aware of movement at the far end of the boat. Some more of their men were boarding. Too many for the pagans now. The resistance in front of them melted away and Blade reached Elchere at last.

The ealdorman lay dead in a pile of corpses, a bloody wound in his chest. Blade stared in dismay at the man who had, in the past two years, been better than a father to him. Certainly, better than his father. Always encouraging, competent, generous and supportive. Had that rash push to the island. . . ? No, he would not think it. And no one else would say it, either, whatever they might think. 'Kings and princes do make mistakes,' he remembered Elchere telling him once. 'But they can't afford to let anyone say so.' Elchere would not have blamed him. And who could say for sure whether an earlier attack would have saved him? He would not accuse himself.

The battle on board Elchere's boat was almost over. The last pagans were outnumbered and surrounded now. Blade looked across to the other boats and ships. A sight of chaos – some burning, others smashed and beginning to sink. The tide was sweeping into the channel now and the air was full of the cries of men in the water, struggling in its grip. The fighting was just about over. The pagan fleet was destroyed but they'd exacted a heavy price. The loss of boats and ships on either side looked similar. It was only their greater number which had prevailed. And who were the men crying out in the water? Friend or foe? They would try to rescue those of their own. He was reluctant now to leave the water and head for the island once more.

The next hour or so was spent rescuing those of their own men that they could. Some had already drowned. Others half-dead were hauled on board to lie gasping unheeded while others were sought. And when they found pagans, they pushed them away with sword or spear. Some preferred to be speared than left to drown. A desperate look in their eyes, trying to climb onboard with the last of their strength. Blade scowled – they showed no mercy, they would receive none.

At last they could hold no more and had to head for the island to avoid sinking themselves. Fearful cries of those left behind rang in his ears.

'We'll be back!' he shouted. Even so, they had to fight off others trying to climb aboard. Some of them crying out in English.

By the time they reached the island, unloaded their cargo of men and returned, the sea was quieter. Some corpses were floating on the surface. With a stab of the heart, Blade recognised Ealdorman Huda of Surrey. His boat had been sunk. Both ealdormen dead. A costly battle, indeed.

'Pull him in,' he commanded grimly. He wouldn't take a live man's place. There weren't that many left. They pulled out a few more who still showed signs of life. Some of them died on board. Other boats were now in the channel searching for survivors. They could finish the job. He needed to get back to the island and organise those on the shore.

'Let's go back.'

At least the men on the shore were too exhausted to have followed Beornhard's example and charged off to the pagan camp. They were sitting around on the stony beach, staring dully at the water. Already a few more dead bodies among them.

Collecting a band of those still able to march and leaving the others to manage as best they could, Blade headed off to the pagan camp, wondering what he would find there.

It did not take long to find out. Even before they reached the camp, he could tell that Beornhard and his companions had left their mark. The thin smoke of cooking fires he'd seen before was replaced by an ugly black cloud, caused by bigger fires. As they approached, the smell of smouldering wood and straw filled their nostrils. And then, the expected sight – the makeshift pagan huts collapsing into ashes, the ground between them strewn with the bodies of women and children. Blade looked down at the corpses – some of the women's fingers had been cut off, and there were bruises around arms and necks. Jewellery collection. It's a lesson they taught us. Beornhard's sword was not called Vengeance without reason.

Where was Beornhard? He hadn't returned to the beach so he must still be here. Unless he had disappeared with his hoard, and no doubt a woman or two. This had been his land – he might still have a boat hidden away on it somewhere.

A sound of sobbing was coming from one of the huts to escape the flames. Two men went into the hut and brought out a woman with a baby in her arms. The baby was dead, its throat cut, but the woman still hugged it to her breast, her face a mask of despair.

'God damn you all! Murderers!' she cried in a Kentish voice.

One of the men drew his sword.

'No!' Blade shouted. The man sheathed his sword. 'Bring her here.'

The man brought the woman to him, still holding her dead baby. Young. A beauty, were it not for the agony in her eyes and etched upon her face. She avoided his gaze.

'What's your name?'

'Go to hell, murderer!'

One of the men shook her. 'Show respect to the king, bitch!'

The king. Blade felt a moment of pleasure. If the men had started calling him king, then it wouldn't be long before he was.

'He killed my boy,' the woman muttered, a little calmer.

'I didn't kill him,' Blade replied. 'Nor did I order this,' he gestured around at the bodies and burning huts. 'But I'm not surprised at it. Do you know how many English villages have been left like this by pagans?'

At this, the woman looked up and stared straight at him. Light blue eyes. 'Yes, I do.'

'Because you're English yourself, aren't you? That's why the man who killed your child didn't kill you. Didn't touch you.'

'I told him to kill me,' the woman replied, the pain in her eyes blazing forth. 'Twice this has happened to me. My family and friends killed by pagans. I'm taken captive, raped and abused for years. Finally, I win through to a new life and find it is still possible to love. And then my own people come and destroy my life once more.' She gave a bitter laugh. 'There's nowhere left for me to go now. So have one of your brave men unsheathe his sword and finish the job.'

'You are still young,' Blade said softly.

'No, I'm old. I've seen too much of men and their ways to want to go on living. You think you're different from the pagans? You're just the same.'

'Your boy is dead. Don't you want to bury him?'

The woman looked puzzled. 'What do you mean?'

'We are all burying bodies, lady. We'll bury your son as well. And these women, and their children.'

'And you think that will make it right?'

'No, it will never be right. It never is. You've lost a son in this fighting. I've lost someone who was better than a father to me. All these men here have lost someone equally dear. But we don't think there is nothing left for us to do but die.'

The woman's face crumpled and she looked as though she was about to cry. 'What is to become of me, then?'

'I'll put you under my protection. You can join my household. Until you decide what you want to do. Tochar, you'll take care of her?'

'Yes, my lord.'

Blade moved on. He didn't want to spend too long a time with the woman. People were quick to draw conclusions. Already a few knowing smiles around him.

'An attractive woman,' said Derwin, one of his companions.

'Yes,' Blade agreed. Such speculation wouldn't do any harm. It would protect the woman, at least. Maybe he was interested in her? Those blazing eyes had aroused certain emotions in him. Not straightforward, though. Connected somehow with his own loss. A need to acknowledge grief, for gentleness in the most unlikely circumstances. The truth would most likely be more damaging to an almost-king than a simple assumption of physical attraction.

There was shouting ahead. A tall man. Beornhard and the others who had gone with him. Still here.

'God be praised, my lord.' Beornhard bowed to the ground on approaching. If he was nervous, he didn't show it. 'We thought we were to come on here. We didn't realise you were heading back onto the water.'

'No,' said Blade. It might be true. He didn't want to dwell on it. He had already decided he was not going to punish Beornhard for desertion. And as for destroying the pagan camp, well that had to be done. There was a blood price to pay. His men would expect nothing less for what they had suffered at the pagans' hands. Better for vengeance to be exacted in a raging fury than in cold blood. But there was one matter outstanding.

'Where is the treasure?'

'My lord?' Beronhard did his best to look uncomprehending.

'You know what I mean. Pagan camps always have treasure from what they've seized. And I can see you've taken rings from fingers. But there's nothing here. So, where is it? You know that treasure taken in war is for the king to dispose of, not some common soldier.'

'My lord, we took it to a safe place. We've only just found out that you were here. We can bring it to you immediately.'

'Any women? And slaves?'

'A few,' Beornhard admitted reluctantly.

'Bring them as well. A lot of people have been fighting today. Some for a lot longer than you. I'm sure you would wish for them to be rewarded for their valour.'

'Yes, my lord.' Beornhard made to go.

'And Beornhard . . .'

'Yes?'

'If you keep anything back, you die.'

'But my lord, I fought as well. Am I to get nothing?'

'You will be rewarded as the king sees fit.'

'The king is not here,' Beornhard muttered, a rebellious look in his eyes.

'Seize him,' Blade said to the men around him.

It took four men to hold him but they did so at last.

Blade drew Bloodthirst and held it to Beornhard's throat.

'I am the king's representative,' he said calmly. 'Ealdormen Elchere and Huda are dead. As far as you and your men are concerned, I am the king in this matter. My father would expect me to deal with a mutiny without recourse to him. And I will do so, if necessary. Do you understand?'

Beornhard had stopped struggling. 'Yes,' he said sullenly.

'Yes, what?' Blade said, keeping Bloodthirst to his throat.

'Yes, my lord prince.'

'Go with him,' Blade said to the men around him. 'And make sure you get everything.'

In that, he felt confident of being obeyed.

*

'Not long now,' Osburh smiled brightly at her daughter. The past few weeks, few months even, had seemed to consist largely of smiling brightly. She'd suppressed thoughts of her illness to supervise Elsa's wedding to Burgred of Mercia. The illness was still there – she could feel its grasp reaching further within her every day. But she was determined not to let it prevent her from supporting her daughter as she made the first, irrevocable steps away from her childhood and home. Still so young – two years younger than she'd been when marrying Aethelwulf, and two years is a lifetime at that age. Her child's face solemn, a look of foreboding deep within her eyes. Too intelligent not to realise that what lay ahead was very different from what she knew, and too uncertain of herself not to doubt her ability to cope with the change.

Even at the best of times, Elsa had never been jolly. But she couldn't afford to be a frowning, reluctant bride. Her future life's ease depended on her husband's regard. And if she couldn't win that at their wedding, then when would she?

And so, Osburh set to work with tales of the delights of married life. Of how love often began in the midst of fear and doubt, how it can creep up on one unawares, taking root in the heart and growing with the years.

'Did you feel frightened?' Elsa asked.

Osburh thought back. It was pleasant to do so. Her overwhelming memory was not of fear, but of a triumph which was overwhelming. To be marrying the king! But there had been times when she was frightened. At night, when the guests had gone, and she'd been left alone with him in their broad bed, his thick fingers on her shivering skin. She'd been frightened then.

'Sometimes,' she could reply truthfully. She was determined to be truthful with Elsa, not to leave a source of reproach. It had been different for her, and Elsa knew that. But there were women at court who had been more reluctant than her, yet learned to love their husbands. Osburh arranged for them to tell Elsa their stories, to reassure her that there were many different ways for love to find her.

'You are bound to feel differently than your mother,' Osburh heard one of her friends say to Elsa. 'Your mother was not the king's daughter.'

It seemed to be having an effect. Elsa smiled more often, even making a joke on occasion. And her companions helped – the friends she would be taking with her to Mercia. They fluttered around her with compliments and gossip. Osburh listened to their chatter and laughter with approval. Elsa would survive. When she relaxed and accepted that she was worthy of love, she was not unattractive. Her grave, grey eyes – Aethelwulf's eyes – inspired tenderness. And she was so intelligent. She would find a way into the inscrutable Mercian's heart.

A week ago, they had ridden up to the royal manor at Chippenham, near the border between the two kingdoms. Every day brought more guests; every evening, the great hall was more crowded. No one could remember a more important wedding. Osburh's own, with a disapproving father-in-law, had been small-scale in comparison. But for most of the people crowding into Chippenham, Elsa's wedding was more about an alliance between old enemies, Wessex and Mercia, than it was about the bride and groom. The ealdormen, bishops and thanes from each kingdom who filled the tables on either side of the great hall in the evenings, eyeing each other with varying degrees of suspicion, had little thought for the future of the young girl who had brought them here.

Osburh had decided that there would be no high table until after the ceremony. With King Burgred not arriving until the morning of the wedding, there was too great a risk of the Mercians taking offence at being presided over by the king of Wessex alone. After the ceremony, they would have a high table and Elsa would sit at it with them, beside her husband. She would have people considering her then. Osburh's heart fluttered slightly at the thought. Hopefully, a mood of celebration would flood over both sides and bring them together. In the meantime, she did what she could as hostess, moving around the Mercian tables, greeting and complimenting their great men and thanking them for coming. A few of the churchmen followed her example – a number of them had met one another at church councils. It was easier for them to forget their differences in shared concerns and higher loyalties. But the ealdormen and thanes stayed where they were. The memories of battles past could not be put aside so easily.

Only at night could she let her bright smile slip away. Since her illness had taken hold, she had been sleeping apart from Aethelwulf. He had not objected to this. He was very considerate – asking her how she was feeling at least once a day, sometimes more. A good man. But she had not forgiven him for sending Alfred away and never would. Not only the cruel act itself, but the knowledge it had brought her that, behind all his smiles and little kindnesses, he didn't care what she thought. Not if it ran counter to what his precious religion told him, or what he thought it told him.

But she knew it wasn't good for her to revisit her anger. Whether it had caused her illness or not, it would certainly fuel it if allowed to. Somehow she must learn to live with the loneliness and betrayal.

The last few months, concentrating on Elsa's wedding, had helped, providing a reason for going on. What would happen when it was over and Elsa gone as well? She didn't want to think about that. Yes, there was Redi and, if Mother Frige still listened to her prayers, Alfred would be coming back soon. But Redi spent all his time these days with Ceolwulf, the Mercian's son. Anxious to escape the constraints of childhood, he had little time or need for her. And who knew what Alfred would be like after months in the almost exclusive company of monks? Would she even recognise him as her little boy? And, if she did, how long would it be before Aethelwulf sent him away from her again?

With such cold thoughts, Osburh lay awake long into the night, sleeping fitfully before waking early, in readiness for another day of smiling brightly.

The wedding day dawned grey and overcast. Osburh went early to Elsa's room. Some of her companions were already there. Lioba, the matron, twice married, with a twinkling, appraising gaze. Osburh had been relying on Lioba to acquaint her daughter with any facts she might not know about sex and men's desire. Her own attempts had been met by Elsa with furious blushes and hurried assurances that she knew all about that. It was a price she paid for never having been very close to her daughter – there were certain secrets and confidences she wouldn't be trusted with. She could only hope that others would be. Lioba certainly had the experience, if possibly not the intelligence, to help her. Listening to her salty comments alone would teach Elsa a fair amount. And the rumours which attached to some of the other companions suggested that she would not have to rely upon Lioba alone.

Anyway, certain things must be experienced – there was only so much that talking could do to prepare a girl. All really depended on the kind of man her husband was, and only Elsa would find that out. But he seemed to be a patient man. He might even wait to sleep with her – she was still so young.

The time has come for me to step back and not get in her way, Osburh thought. Her new life is beginning. I might have wished it later had things been different. But as it is, it is better now.

And so, she did not stay long with Elsa that morning. Long enough to smile on her a few more times and tell her how beautiful she was looking. The companions all chimed in with enthusiastic agreement and Elsa looked happy. Ready for her day.

Osburh left her daughter to the laughing care of her companions and walked out of the manor. It was still early. The men would not be stirring for an hour or more. The grey sky was unbroken but did not smell of rain. Not unpleasant or inauspicious, she thought. Calm. Neutral. There were worse days on which to get married.

She walked the short distance up the hill to the church. A bustle of activity inside as final preparations were being made. She stood near the entrance and idly watched the activity, feeling distant from it somehow. A group of men were engaged in raising banners above the rood screen. White dragons for both Wessex and Mercia. The Mercian banner looks a bit more spiky than ours, she thought. At least they'll mask most of that fearsome scene of the Last Judgment on the ceiling. Why do Christians delight in painting their churches so? Who wants to get married under a picture of everlasting torment?

Women were arranging lilies around the church. Symbols of purity, supposedly. Osburh didn't much like lilies. Didn't see them as pure. Blatantly sexual the ways their petals opened. And that strange, sickly smell they had.

She had better go. She wasn't doing anything here, apart from indulging a certain hostility. One of the priests recognised her and detained her for a while with nervous questions as to whether she approved of everything. She reassured him and escaped back to the manor.

Aethelwulf was up. He greeted her fondly with a kiss. 'How are you feeling?'

'I'm well, thank you.'

'And Elsa?'

'She's happy. Smiling.'

'That's good.'

A sound of horses and men arriving in the courtyard outside. They looked out.

'The bridegroom.'

'I'll go and welcome him,' Osburh said.

'I'll follow you once I'm dressed.'

'Let him get settled first. It will have to be a formal meeting with you. There are so many Mercians about.'

'All right,' he smiled. 'Let me know when I'm allowed to see him.'

Pleased with himself for being so amenable. Amenable in the little niceties which women deal with so well, she thought. Immoveable on anything he saw as important.

The next few hours passed swiftly in a sea of details – greeting the grave King Burgred, arranging for the housing of him and his attendants, checking with the royal staff and cooks on the feeding of the waking guests, trying to resolve a dispute among the musicians, accompanying Aethelwulf for the formal reception of Burgred and then returning to the church to check on the seating arrangements. When she left the church, she saw some of the guests starting to leave the manor and walk up the hill. Merciful Frige, the ceremony must be about to start and she didn't even have on her wedding clothes! She hurried back down the hill, trying to ignore the greetings of those coming up and rushed inside the manor to her room, hurriedly changing into her best gown. Dressed in a few moments, she made her way back to Elsa's room. Gone. No time for any last words. The next time they spoke, she'd be married.

Outside again and just in time. She could see Burgred and his men arriving at the church, but the horses were only now being brought round for the bride's party. Aethelwulf was already mounted. Servants were fussing around Elsa and her companions, helping them up onto their horses. Osburh scrambled up onto her horse. As she did so, she felt a sharp, stabbing pain in her stomach that almost made her cry out. The illness, ignored all morning in the rush of events, reasserting its hold. She gritted her teeth. At that moment, Elsa, safely up on her horse, looked over and smiled at her. She tried to smile back, but heaven knows what it looked like. Most likely a grimace. Her skin was prickling with sweat.

They rode the short distance up to the church. Osburh stumbled down off her horse, pleased that she did not form part of Elsa's procession. She hurried into the crowded church, looking at no one, and made it to her seat at the front, almost collapsing into it, her head spinning. She closed her eyes and breathed in deeply – a few moments, that's all she had before Elsa would make her entrance and she'd have to stand up. A few moments to regain control. *'Please, Mother Frige,'* she prayed. *'Help me get through this. I can't faint here.'*

Mother Frige must have heard, because by the time the pipes sounded to announce the bride's entrance, her head had stopped spinning and the stabbing pain in her stomach eased a little. She was able to stand up, turn and smile as the bridal procession entered the church. Glancing across at King Burgred, she was pleased to see that he looked nervous. Memories of her own wedding came flooding back when the time came for Elsa and Burgred to stand before the priest. Two young lives. What would fate bring them? She was suddenly crying. She ducked her head down, dabbed her eyes dry, and looked up in time to see Burgred place a ring on

Elsa's finger and the priest pronounce them man and wife. She sighed, and the pain leaped back. In her chest now. She suddenly realised with complete clarity that she did not have long to live, that her disease was fatal. *'Just let me see Elsa on her way,'* she prayed. *"It's only another day."*

Somehow she made it through the celebrations and the feast that evening. Elsa and Burgred joined them at the high table. He was attentive to her. But he was bound to be here – he was a careful man. Osburh caught a shy smile from Elsa to her husband which calmed her heart for a few precious moments. The long poems of Wessex and Mercia tested her strength, but she managed to remain sitting throughout them, her mind spinning away into dark corners, with only the occasional phrase registering.

> *"I bind together nations,*
> *bring new life to the strongest,*
> *dispense the wine of gladness,*
> *and give the future to my lord.*
> *But what is my name?"*

That was about the easiest riddle she had ever heard. Diarmait being a courtier. She smiled over at him and saw Elsa blushing from the corner of her eye. And then Burgred bend to kiss his bride, accompanied by a cheer from the hall. Well done, Diarmait. And a lot shorter than those seemingly endless poems about battles. I wouldn't vouch for its truth, though. Just one of those sweet things which men say to women on occasions like this. Even a royal bride can't give the future, unless it's her own the riddle refers to. That she certainly has to give.

*

Osburh's prayer was answered. She survived long enough to see Elsa depart the following day for Mercia with her husband and companions. She rose to see them off, her smile in place. But when they had gone, and the last Mercian departed, her smile slipped away and she was aware of falling into a deep well of pain. The outside world was flickering strangely, becoming less real. The world inside her seemed to be taking over from it. As if in a dream, she stumbled into her room and collapsed onto the bed. By the time Yetta found her there, curled up around her pain, murmuring incoherently, saliva gathering around her loosened lips, she was barely conscious.

Yetta's cries brought others to the room and between them they eased off Osburh's outer clothing and put her into the bed. By the time the news reached Aelthelwulf, the royal doctor was examining a patient who would not argue with him any more. He met Aethelwulf at the door of the room with a grave face.

'The illness is far advanced,' he said. 'If she had accepted treatment . . .' He paused. It wasn't the time to continue that argument. Besides, he wasn't sure it was right. He had seen this disease before, and never managed to cure it. 'It probably wouldn't have made any difference,' he admitted. 'I think she's kept going on willpower alone these past few weeks.'

'Is there nothing you can do? Would bleeding help?'

It never had with this disease. And recalling Osburh's vehement objection to bleeding for Alfred, the doctor was reluctant to endorse it now she could no longer object. She was going to die, and soon. Better for the king to get used to that idea now than to raise his hopes with pointless activity. And were she to die after being bled, who would be blamed?

'I have given her a draught of poppies and black alder to ease her pain,' he replied. 'Do not hold out great hope, sire. A priest is more appropriate than a doctor now.'

Aethelwulf blinked. A priest? What would Osburh have to say to a priest? His wife's paganism, never openly acknowledged between them but certain to him nonetheless, suddenly loomed large and terrifying. Where would she go? What was the future for her soul? If Swithun was here, he would find a way to help her – she trusted Swithun. But he was still away with Alfred. They should be back soon, but if what the doctor said was right, then soon would be too late.

He went into the room. Osburh was lying in bed with her eyes shut. Yetta was sitting on a stool beside her head. Spinning wool into thread with a spindle. Aethelwulf motioned for her to leave and she gathered up her wool with one hand while continuing to spin with the other.

He sat down on the stool vacated by Yetta and looked down at his wife. She was not breathing as calmly as he'd thought. A lot of resistance there – something harsh and unknown, the disease within. Quietened perhaps for a while by the doctor's medicine, but not departing. He took one of Osburh's hands into his own. How thin it had become, the bones prominent beneath the pale skin. Her face too was peaked – cheeks sunken, lines of stress around her eyes and mouth. He sighed. He had known she was ill, but not as ill as this. Only a few months ago, when he'd last held her in his arms, when she'd last let him embrace her, the soft roundness of her flesh had thrilled him as so many times before. All gone now – eaten away by some inner demon. How had he not noticed the extent of such a change? She'd kept him at bay. Insisted on sleeping alone, barely let him touch her. He'd thought it was because she was still angry with him over Alfred. He'd seen the anger more than the wasting flesh – or maybe equated the two? She'd been so active these past few weeks. He'd even thought she was getting better. And with Alfred on his way back, maybe they could have returned to how they were before?

Osburh groaned and shifted a little in her bed.

'Osburh, it's me. Your Wulf.'

Was that a slight flickering of her eyelids? No change around her mouth – her familiar expression gone. How far away was she?

'Osburh, I'm frightened,' he continued. 'Will you see a priest? For me.'

Was that a tightening of her lips? Impossible to tell. But the harshness of her breathing was louder now. Someone coughed in the doorway to attract his attention. The priest who only yesterday had presided over Elsa's marriage. The doctor must have sent him up. Aethelwulf beckoned him into the room.

'Sire, I'm so sorry.' Quite a young man. Nervous. The wedding had been a strain for him. And now this.

'Do you have the sacrament?' Aethelwulf asked bleakly.

'I do, sire.'

'What about confession. She can't speak.'

'When did she last go to confession?'

'I don't know.' Probably not for a long time, he thought. And then only because it was expected of her.

'I can administer the sacrament without an individual confession in these circumstances.'

'Which means she'll die in her sins.'

'Do you have any concerns, sire.?'

'Father, my wife was baptised a Christian, married a Christian, and brought up our children as Christians. But I know that in her heart she clung to the old religion.'

'That is not unusual, sire.'

'And praying to the goddess Frige instead of our Lord Jesus Christ, what about that?' Aethelwulf cried, his voice rising in pain. 'How can that be forgiven by a God who demands we worship Him alone?'

The priest looked troubled. 'Only God can see into the heart, sire.'

'Then why do we have confession at all?'

'It is safer. A guarantee of forgiveness.'

'Well, can't you see that I want that for my wife? She is a good woman. I love her. But I'm frightened for her. And I blame myself. We argued and . . . I couldn't do anything. I thought she'd come round in time. But now there is no more time. Just eternity stretching ahead.'

The priest considered. 'Are you able to communicate with her? I have known it with husband and wife, even when one cannot speak.'

'I don't know. What difference would that make?'

'If you can communicate with her then she can make her confession through you.'

Aethelwulf turned urgently back to his wife, taking one of her skeletal hands gently in both of his. 'Osburh, can you hear me? If you can then please squeeze my hand.'

Her expression did not change but was that the slightest movement of her fingers?

'My sweetest love, you're going to die and leave me here alone. I want us to be together again. But you need to say you're sorry for your sins, and for praying to Frige instead of Jesus. Will you do that?'

No movement. He stared at her anxiously, her breathing becoming more impersonal. 'Please?'

A sudden twitch of her whole hand in his. He turned to the priest, who was watching intently. 'She says yes!'

The priest nodded. 'It is enough.' He raised his right hand over her and pronounced the prayer of absolution before administering the final sacrament.

Aethelwulf was strengthened by the thought that he was fully united with Osburh in Christ at last. He sent for Berti and Redi to come and say goodbye to their mother. Berti was pale, Redi stone-faced, determined not to cry. If Osburh recognised them, she gave no sign of doing so. The doctor came back and confirmed he did not think the end would be long.

Aethelwulf invited those of Osburh's friends and attendants who were there to join the family and crowd into the room around her bed. The priest said prayers for the repose of Osburh's soul and Aethelwulf then permitted the friends and attendants to say their weeping goodbyes.

Finally, they were all gone. Aethelwulf resumed his seat at the head of the bed and gently placed one of his hands back over one of his wife's. Lost in thoughts and memories, aware less of the shrunken figure beside him than the spirited girl and woman he had loved. An hour or two passed and then his attention was snatched back to the present by a choking sound and a sense of struggle on the bed.

'Osburh!' He bent over and took her in his arms.

She was trying to rise. Her eyes opened suddenly and she looked straight at him. A terrible stare, unseeing but intense. She opened her mouth and tried to speak some word. What was it? His name? That of Frige? Jesus? Lost in a choke. A sudden spasm passed through her and rattled in her throat. And then she was gone, all tension fled, limp and lifeless in his arms.

6. A Time for Giving

It was a cold homecoming for Alfred. During the long journey back from Rome, he had been sustained by the thought of seeing his mother again. He had so much to tell her. So much to try and understand. She would explain it all to him, and be once more that warm, gentle source of love and knowledge, not the intense and rather frightening person who had said goodbye to him. She had been ill then; she would be better now, and as she was before.

Instead of which, she was dead. No more. He would never see her again. His mind struggled to grasp the loss. Swithun broke the news to him. And then his father, stiff and formal, confirmed the brutal fact. Talking of God again. Why should God want to take his mother away? And forever.

'You will see her again, Alfred,' Swithun reassured him.

'When?'

'When we all rise again at the Last Judgment.'

It seemed a long time to wait. What was he to do in the meantime? It suddenly felt as though there was nothing for him to do. From being the centre of attention, a prince anointed by the Holy Father himself, he was now back to being a little boy, ignored by most. His father was locked in consultation with his counsellors for most of the time, Berti was away in the eastern kingdom with Blade, and Elsa was married and in Mercia. Redi's hostility to him was as strong as ever. He continued to jeer at him as a little priest and refused to let him join the hunting expeditions he went on with Ceolwulf, the Mercian.

'You should be in church on your knees, Little Elf. That's the place for priests.'

Deprived of attention, lonely and lost, he found some company among the servants and slaves. He sat with his old nurse, Yetta, listening to her tales of his mother. But they only made him miss her more. Diarmait tried to teach him harp playing, but his heart wasn't really in it. It took such an effort to make even the slightest of pleasant sounds. And listening to Diarmait play would sometimes make the sorrow within him much sharper. On the whole, studying with Colman was better. Trying to pick out meaning from strange Latin words and negotiate a path through all the rules governing word endings, tenses and cases was more impersonal. He could lose himself in trying to solve the problems presented. A correct solution gave a quiet satisfaction. Reading English was more emotional. Once in a while, he would take out the book of poems his mother had given him and leaf through its pages, allowing a bitter sweetness to rise within him.

He found some relief from his loneliness at the stables and kennels, watching the grooms and dog-handlers tending to their animals. Horses were too valuable for him to be able to do more than watch them. It would be at least a couple of years before he might be allowed a horse of his own. Despite all the riding he had done on his journey, he was still thought of as too young to join in a grown-up hunt. But the dogs were less jealously guarded. And the chief handler, Acca, had children of his own and was able to recognise a lonely boy rather than an interfering prince. He was happy to take time introducing Alfred to all the dogs, telling him their names and characteristics.

Alfred noticed that Acca always passed over one dog – a black, shambling animal, which pushed forward eagerly for the attention it didn't get.

'What's that one called?'

'That?' Acca grunted. 'He's called Sideways. He can't run in a straight line. He always veers off to the right and bangs into other dogs. I'm going to have to get rid of him. You can't take him hunting – he confuses all the others.'

'Can I have him?'

'You?' Acca considered. 'I don't see why not. No one else will want him. But I can get you a better dog than him.'

Alfred looked at the black dog, left behind the other dogs crowding around Acca. He did look lop-sided. But he had a hopeful, friendly expression. 'I want Sideways.'

Over the following months, he lavished a lot of attention on Sideways, trying to get him to run in a straight line, devising all sorts of exercises, even at one stage digging a trench for him to run along. But the exercises and trench-running were to no avail. He still veered off to the right.

Aethelwulf meanwhile was making arrangements to go to Rome. This time he would not be denied. Osburh's death only gave him an added incentive to be gone. Painful memories of past happiness beyond recall, feelings of emptiness and guilt all combined to make the present even more intolerable to him. To stay was only to be waiting for the grave, surrounded by endless frustrations. But to be gone, while he was still young enough for the journey, held out both the prospect of new experiences and the fulfilment of old desires. To say nothing of his promise and dream. Everything pointed the same way.

Swithun, fresh from Rome himself and full of the sights he had seen, made no attempt this time to dissuade the king. Other counsellors were less supportive. Ealhstan in particular was hostile to the idea.

'A king should not desert his country,' the old warrior said gruffly. 'What signal will that give to the pagans? They are growing stronger. We have invasions to deal with every year. If the king doesn't fight them, why should his people?'

'I am not deserting my country!' Aethelwulf snapped. 'I will return, and stronger than before.'

'You intend to recruit foreign mercenaries?'

'Spiritually stronger. With the blessings of God and the Holy Father.'

Ealhstan looked unimpressed by the thought of spiritual strength making any difference in a fight against pagans. Not for the first time, Aethelwulf wondered at how the Church could countenance the most irreligious man he had ever known being its Bishop of Sherborne. Not that he was a bad man. No one fought more bravely or loyally than Ealhstan. But his indifference to any other consideration but physical force made him narrow.

'My lord bishop,' Aethelwulf continued, 'a king must look outside his country on occasion. We have been isolated from our neighbours for a long time. They fight the pagans, too. I shall discuss these matters with the king of Francia. The emperor, too, possibly.'

'Other people can do that for you.' Ealhstan was not to be persuaded. Aethelwulf gave up any attempt to do so.

'I'm afraid my mind is made up. As you know, I have been planning this a long time. I mean to go. In the New Year, after Easter.'

Ealhstan scowled. 'Then why ask me here if you've already decided?'

'I must make arrangements for interim governance in my absence. No one is better able to hold the kingdom for me than you. Your bravery and skill at arms is legendary. I propose appointing my son Aethelberht to be regent of Wessex while I am away. But he will need to rely on you as his general.'

'Your son Aethelberht is young and untested in battle. His brother Aethelbald is older and a valiant warrior, who has proved himself on many occasions. He fought under me at Aclea and I have personal knowledge of his bravery. If you leave, then he is the one who should be regent, not Aethelberht. My loyalty is to the eldest. You should not pass him over.'

'I don't intend to pass him over. But he is already established as ruler in the eastern kingdom. I propose that he should be king there, and remain king there, even when I have returned from Rome. In the same way as I ruled in the east while my father was still alive.'

'If he is made king then he will have to rule the old kingdom. The men of Wessex will not accept the eastern kingdom being ruled by someone more senior than their own ruler.'

Aethelwulf considered. There was something in what Ealhstan said. If Blade was made king in the east then he might seek to take the west away from Berti, particularly as he would most likely be supported by Ealhstan and some others. They would use Berti's inexperience as an excuse. If he was hoping to rely upon Ealhstan's strong right arm in his absence then he couldn't afford to overrule him in this as well.

'I hear what you say, my lord bishop. There is wisdom in it. I do not intend making either of my sons kings yet. I am not abdicating. But if you believe that my eldest son should be regent of Wessex while I am away rather than his brother then I will take your advice. But the eastern kingdom is currently facing more pagan attacks than the west. As you say, Aethelberht has less experience in combat. He will not be able to rely upon your support in the east.'

'He will rely on the ealdormen, as Aethelbald has done.'

'The ealdorman of Kent is new.'

'He's been fighting pagans since he was a child. That's no guarantee that he will continue to be able to prevail against them now. As I say, the pagans are getting stronger every year. But if you are to lose one kingdom in return for your spiritual well-being, much better for it to be the east than the west.'

'He's angry,' Aethelwulf reported gloomily to Swithun. 'I thought I could rely on Ealhstan. I'm not so sure now. And yet, I must go!'

Swithun considered. 'Ealhstan is one lord,' he said eventually. 'A very important one, it's true, but only one. There are plenty who don't think like him. In the Church especially, but also amongst the fighting men.'

'What are you saying?'

'What is your concern about Ealhstan? That he won't fight the pagans for you?'

'He'll always fight the pagans. It's in his blood. He's been doing it all his life.'

'That he'll usurp the kingdom while you're away?'

'Not in his own name, no. He has too much respect for my father's house for that. But we've never been close, despite all the battles we've fought together. And he likes Blade, who is . . .' Aehtelwulf searched for the right word, 'impatient. Blade could seek to usurp the kingdom while I'm away, with Ealhstan's support.'

'So, you need to ensure that Ealhstan's support won't be sufficient. He's a great fighter, but he has enemies among the lords. He's ridden roughshod over many. And even Ealhstan can't make a king on his own.'

'So, what's your advice, my friend?'

'Were you going to be making any gifts before you left? To the Church, perhaps, for the success of your pilgrimage?'

'Yes, of course. You know that.'

'Be generous,' Swithun advised. 'Very generous. More generous than any king has been before you. And not just to the Church. To your lords, as well.'

'Particularly to those who don't like Ealhstan?'

'I would not limit your generosity to them. You want to leave as many as possible with fond thoughts of you. And I would try and find a way to ensure that your larger gifts will take some time to come into effect. Have some extra system for approving charters to transfer land, for example. People can forget the generosity of a year ago. But if they're still looking forward to the effects of the generosity by the time you're coming back from Rome, then they're less likely to have forgotten it. It would give them a good reason, if they needed one, for not wanting to support a change of king.'

Aethelwulf rarely laughed, but he gave a harsh bark of laughter at this advice. 'Lord preserve me from holy men! The journey will be expensive enough, as it is, with the amount of presents I'm taking with me.'

'True. But you're a great king, and a great king must be generous. And you've been wanting to make this journey all your life, haven't you? It's a once in a lifetime event. So you can't afford to stint it. Particularly if you want to have a land to come back to.'

'Your advice is as excellent as ever, my friend,' Aethelwulf acknowledged with a rueful smile.

'I made you laugh. The Lord loves a cheerful giver.'

'And I shall be one. It is a great opportunity to show to the world that there is more to this life than worldly wealth. And I shall have to divest myself of greater riches.'

'Such as?'

'You, my lord bishop and friend. I had hoped to take you with me so we could share the journey together. You would be able to explain so much to me. But I need you here to help safeguard the kingdom. There is no-one I trust as much as you.'

*

The church at Wilton was crowded with men who had travelled from every corner of King Aethelwulf's kingdom. All of his sons were there. Blade and Berti had ridden over from the Kentish coast a week ago, leaving the new ealdorman, Elchere's brother, Ethelmod, to resist the seemingly endless raids from the pagans, now encamped on the Isle of Sheppey. Redi, stern and solemn, kept close to Blade. Alfred gravitated towards Berti as a sympathetic presence.

As well as the king's sons, most of his ealdormen and bishops were present in the church, along with thanes from the depths of rugged Cornwall, the moors and costs of Devon, the meadows and marshes beyond Selwood, the rich lands fed by the great river on the Mercian border, the southern forests and seashores. Men from the hills, from sweet, secret valleys, marsh-girt islands, wooded strongholds, shingle beaches and clifftop lookouts. All had heard news that the king would be making a great announcement at Wilton on the Sunday after Easter, and that it would be wise for them to be there.

There were men too from beyond the kingdom's bounds – representatives of Burgred from Mercia, of ambitious Rhodri from Gwynedd, of the uncrowned Edmund from East Anglia. And from Francia, the genial Abbot Lupus, who had been staying at court, and whose presence gave rise to even more rumours than were flying around already. Was the king about to give up his crown for a pilgrim's staff? It had been done before by kings of Wessex. If so, who would succeed him? His eldest son, surely? Everyone's eyes were drawn to Blade, who was grave and self-contained. The past two years of command in the east had changed him. He looked like a king in waiting. He kept his own counsel, seeming to pay little attention to those who flocked around him, trying to catch his eye. And yet, one sensed, it would not be wise to assume he didn't see everything – his gaze when it did come to rest on someone was piercing, and there was an intensity in his stillness.

In fact, Blade was in an agony of impatience. So near, and yet who knows? Ealhstan had assured him that he would be appointed regent of Wessex in his father's absence. And yet his father had said nothing to him in the week he had been at Wilton. His conversation restricted to bland enquiries about the east. Was he even now dreaming up some trick to deprive him of his birthright? If he wasn't appointed regent, it would be the gravest of insults. And yet, how many of the men now trying to catch his eye could be relied upon if someone else was given the prize? Would they not immediately gravitate to whoever his father appointed? But who? Berti was the only other possibility, and Berti couldn't rule on his own. But he could with Ealhstan. The thought struck him unpleasantly. Ealhstan might prefer Berti as regent; it would mean more power for Ealhstan. But what about his assurances of support? Lulling him into a false sense of security? Blade shook his head angrily, temporarily alarming some of those around him. Such thoughts can lead to madness. There was nothing for him to do but wait. It would not be long now. Possess your soul in patience, he told himself. It was a phrase his mother had said to him once when he was a boy, complaining about something. It had stayed with him for some reason. The thought of Osburh took him away from immediate concerns. He would have liked to have seen her before she died. So much left unsaid.

The sound of the monks' singing announcing the beginning of mass was not unwelcome. Blade had spent most of his childhood impatient of the religious rituals which his father so valued. But now, as a ruler and a man, he could see that religion had its uses. If he was about to make a major announcement to a large number of people and was uncertain as to how it would be received, he'd too make them have mass first, he thought. He felt a sudden sympathy for his father.

Those agonised calculations of loyalty he'd been wrestling with a few moments ago – his father must have had to face those all his life.

Aethelwulf entered the church without ceremony before the religious procession and took a seat some distance away from Blade, who was unable to see his face. No matter – it would show nothing beyond devotion to the Lord. Religion had that advantage, too – one could lose oneself in its ritual. Blade, still in the reflective mood which thoughts of his mother had prompted, let the rhythms of the service wash over him, allowing his mind to rest in remembered tenderness. Memories of Osburh gave way to thoughts of Gytha, the Kentish woman who'd entered his household after Beornhard's raid of the Viking settlement on the Isle of Thanet. Entered his bed, too. A beauty he could not resist. He had not forced her, left her alone to grieve her son. But the weeks passed and they grew accustomed to one another's presence. She had made herself useful, appreciating the surroundings of a royal household and the space he gave her. She had not wanted to leave. And then one evening, it happened. Her light blue eyes watchful, but no longer hostile. His own desire and need for a woman's touch. Her sadness perhaps, as well. The careful resolutions he'd made all gone, swept away in a hungry embrace. She was not surprised, not resistant. Held on to him in the night and kept him warm, his limbs glowing with gratified desire. She smiled at him, murmured his name, but he sensed her sadness still there. He ought to find her a husband, give her a chance of a new life, but to renounce her sweet skin, the softness of her breasts, her sudden intake of breath, would not be easy.

Swithun was talking of sacrifice, Blade realised with amusement. But churchmen always talk of sacrifice. And always the same one – Jesus sacrificing his life for us all. An example to be applied to everything we do. The sacrifice of a kingdom, perhaps? *My kingdom is not of this world.* Well, mine is. Or might be.

He put such thoughts aside. He needed to prepare himself, not indulge in idle daydreams. He forced his mind back to the service – the eucharist, the moment of transformation, a bell ringing to announce the presence of God come down amongst them. He went up meekly with the rest to eat His flesh and drink His blood. Knelt like his father on his return. Wishing all his sins away.

The mass was over. Swithun was announcing in a loud voice that they should go forth in peace and love to serve the Lord. But only the monks left. Everyone else remained, awaiting the king. Swithun himself stepped aside to make room for him, but Aethelwulf remained where he was, seemingly lost in thought or prayer. A certain restlessness began to grow amongst the congregation. Blade felt it himself – the calmness which the mass had engendered began to leach away from him. What was his father thinking of?

Swithun looked tentatively at Aethelwulf. 'Sire,' he prompted.

Ealhstan frowned. 'My lord king, you must bestir yourself,' he said sharply. 'Your people are waiting.'

At last, Aethelwulf stepped forward to below the rood screen separating the nave and choir and turned to face the assembled men. He began speaking immediately, loud enough to be heard but without any particular emphasis. Almost remote, as if he was still wrapped in a reverie. He spoke of the need for God's favour and protection. Of times past when England had been a chosen vessel of God, bearing His light and learning throughout the world. Of its great saints and scholars – Bede and Alcuin in the north, Chad and Cedd in the middle lands, Aldhelm and Boniface from this kingdom.

'A few names only. But there were thousands of good and holy men in their days. And God looked kindly on our country. There were no pagan invaders to kill our men, carry away our women and children, lay waste our land. The great St Boniface and others went out from here, with no thought for themselves, to bring the light of Christ to those very lands from which those pagans who now afflict us come. But when that great and holy generation was called home by the Lord to take their reward, where were the others to take their place?

'The answer is that no one took their place, my people. We had become lost in our own concerns, our own comforts. We forgot the Lord. And the tide of poison and hatred, which had started to recede before the example of our holy men, has now come flooding back and threatens to overwhelm us. The Lord is a jealous God. When Israel and Judah forgot him, He handed them over to pagan conquerors. He can do the same to us.'

There was silence in the church now, all restlessness gone. The king's sombre voice held all. It was like the voice of doom. Above him, the rood screen showed Christ at the Last Judgment with the saved on His right floating up to heaven and the damned on His left being cast into hell.

Aethelwulf modified his tone a little. 'And yet Judah was not totally destroyed. The Lord saved a remnant of its people because of His love for David. And we have not gone so far as Israel and Judah in our sins. We do not serve foreign gods or sacrifice our children in the fire. But every year, the distance between ourselves and God grows greater. Why should he save us? Why should he concern himself with the fate of strangers?'

He paused to let his words sink in. And then he told them of his dream, of the priest and the children reading books with lines of blood. 'All my life, I have wanted to go to Rome as a pilgrim. Indeed, I promised to do so the first time I had this dream. But the concerns of this kingdom have always prevented my going. Now, I know I must go. It is my duty as well as my desire to rededicate our land to the Lord and to beseech His protection for us. And I ask you, my people, to turn back to God. We all need to seek His forgiveness before it is too late.'

So it was true, Blade thought. Despite all the rumours and assurances of people close to the king, he had never really allowed himself to believe that his father would be going. He had talked of it for so long without doing so that Blade had come round to the view that he never would. It was a pretence, a gesture of piousness. But now, having announced it to the kingdom, he must go. He couldn't back down now. Blade looked over at Ealhstan. A face of stone.

Aethelwulf was continuing to speak. Blade concentrated again. The important part would be coming soon.

'As part of my preparation for pilgrimage, and the rededication of this country to the Lord, I hereby give one tenth of all my possessions, all the royal revenues and lands, to the Lord.'

What was that? *A tenth?* Of everything? Blade was aghast. No king had ever done that before. The royal revenues were thin enough as it was without a tenth being given to churches to buy more candlesticks and lands which wouldn't yield warriors.

'An inventory of the royal lands and revenues has been drawn up. I have appointed the holy bishop of Winchester,' Aethelwulf bowed to Swithun, 'to be the administrator of my wishes in this matter during my absence. He will arrange for the distribution of one tenth of my wealth for the relief of the poor, for the saying of prayers and masses for our safety and God's favour, and for the sustenance of the kingdom.'

The sustenance of the kingdom? What was that? Money for the relief of the poor and the saying of prayers and masses would go to the Church. But where will money for the sustenance of the kingdom go? Blade looked curiously at Swithun. Was there more than piety behind this? Will this holy man be rewarding warriors as well as churchmen during the king's absence? His father normally found a way of combining pious pronouncements with self-interest. He'd certainly made the bishop of Winchester considerably more powerful than he would otherwise have been. Blade foresaw potential clashes ahead. Maybe he'd have to follow his father's example and start studying the Bible more closely.

But he was getting ahead of himself. There was still the most important issue – the regency. Whatever his father might do to try and tie the regent's hands, he still had to appoint one. And surely even he couldn't presume to pass over his sons and appoint a bishop to fight his battles?

The announcement of the king's tithing had caused something of a stir in the church. Blade looked around. Many faces looked impressed, moved even, by Aethelwulf's words and intentions. An old man cried out, 'May God bless your mission for us, my lord king! And remember us in your prayers.'

'I will do that, Osgar,' Aethelwulf replied gravely. 'You can be sure of that.'

Maybe a few faces unimpressed, or assessing possible advantage. Not many, though. A general sense of fervour and affection in the church. Aethelwulf had calculated and spoken well. There was no question but that his announcement had met with general approval. He would be setting out with the goodwill of the vast majority of his people. But he would be setting out; that was the most important thing.

'I hope that my absence from my beloved kingdom and you all will not be long. But we are all in God's hands and it is right that I make provision for rulers to be appointed in my absence. My eldest son, Aethelbald, will take my place as ruler here in Wessex. I know he has the benefit of your love and confidence. He will of course be guided in his rule by our great men, but I appoint two of my closest advisors, standing before you now, as his particular counsellors. Ealhstan, our great and mighty bishop of Sherborne, will be the commander-in-chief of our armies. And the noble Swithun, bishop of Winchester, will oversee all matters relating to the Church in Wessex, and the distribution of my property which I have announced today.

'In the eastern kingdom, I appoint my son, Aethelberht, to take his brother's place as ruler. I have watched Aethelberht grow in wisdom and stature these last few years. These last few months, he has been sharing his brother's rule in the east. He is well-loved there and I have every confidence in his ability to protect and nurture that kingdom in my absence. He will, of course, be guided by the great men of our eastern kingdom, in particular, our noble primate Ceolnoth, and the ealdormen Humbert and Ethelmod. As always, we pledge the support of this mighty kingdom to our brethren in the east. Although I have seen fit to renew the division of rule which existed until recently for the period of my absence, we are proud to be one land, one people. It is as one people that I take you all in my heart and in my prayers to Rome and to God.'

*

Alfred was told at the last minute that he was to be accompanying his father to Rome. Swithun, observing the boy's misery at the loss of his mother, had persuaded Aethelwulf that it would be a kind act to take his youngest son with him. Aethelwulf, exuberant at the prospect of finally fulfilling his heart's desire, was not against having one of his sons along to share his happiness. Or maybe two.

'What about Redi as well?' he suggested. 'He could be spared.'

'They would argue the whole time,' Swithun replied. 'I wouldn't take both if you want a quiet life. Redi is happy here; Alfred isn't.'

'Very well, it shall be as you say. Alfred's done the journey before. He can be my guide,' Aethelwulf added with a chuckle.

Alfred wasn't sure what he felt about going travelling again. There was more jeering from Redi to endure about definitely being made a priest this time. It didn't seem to matter what he did; it wouldn't bring his mother back. And he was sad to be leaving Sideways behind. Whilst they were taking some hunting dogs with them as a present for the Frankish king, Sideways was not one of them. 'Gifts are meant to be welcome,' Acca explained.

'I could take him with me.'

'He'd confuse the other dogs.'

The old excuse. But despite the sorrow of saying goodbye to Sideways, when the day of departure came round, he was glad to be going. Not excited – just relieved not to be left to cope with Redi and the feeling which a motherless home gave him. It was a much grander departure than the one he'd made with Swithun. An army of men was accompanying the king on his pilgrimage and lines of wagons bearing gifts and provisions streamed out behind them. Alfred rode in one of the wagons with Colman for much of the journey to the south coast. With his father present, he was no longer the centre of attention as he'd been on the first journey. Just a camp follower.

Aethelwulf had decided to depart from Hamwic. It was a longer sea crossing, but less of a landward journey to Verberie, the great palace where King Charles himself was to greet them. It felt right to Aethelwulf to be leaving his kingdom from the heart of Wessex, rather than its eastern extremity. Down the same double tide river which had brought his ancestors, Cerdic and Cynric, to this land so many generations ago.

Stepping into the ship which would take him to Francia, he felt the years dropping away from him. He was young again, or at least no longer old. Leaving behind the endless worries and calculations involved in holding on to a kingdom. Other people would have to struggle with them. For the first time since his youth, he was free – able to look ahead in simple anticipation of pleasures to come. There would come a time when he would have to think again of his kingdom and its responsibilities, but not now, on the outward journey. He had resolved to let go of all he could, at least for a few months, to make space for the new to revive his soul.

And so, he did not look back as his ship cast off from the land. It was a clammy, misty morning. Not ideal sailing weather – poor visibility and little wind. The flotilla of ships huddled closely together, making its way slowly down past the coast of the great island which lay below Hamwic. Despite his resolution not to think of the past, Aethelwulf could not prevent his thoughts resting briefly on his dead wife. The island was her ancestral land, its inhabitants her people. Although they had hardly ever visited it during the course of their marriage, it had seemed to become more important to her as the years passed. It was the source of her paganism, the cause of a deep historical resentment which gradually became more apparent to both of them. The difference between us, he thought – forgotten for a long time in the happiness of youth and love, but never wholly departed and becoming ever clearer as they grew older together.

It looked like an Isle of the Dead, its crouched shape looming in the mist. He crossed himself as he turned away, pleased to be leaving this behind as well. Away from the island and out on the open sea, the mist thinned but the grey, hazy light remained. They were inching their way forwards, the sound of the crews straining at the oar benches cutting through the heavy air.

'My master, King Charles, is very much looking forward to meeting you, sire.'

The abbot Lupus. Aethelwulf had grown rather fond of this Frankish cleric in the few weeks he'd been at court, sent as an emissary to welcome a brother king. Highly intelligent, but also transparently acquisitive. Many of the higher churchmen affected to be uninterested in gifts or favours, wrapping themselves in a sort of spiritual superiority which irritated Aethelwulf. Lupus had none of that. An avid collector of books for his library and treasures for his monastery, he made no secret of his pleasure at the gifts which came his way as his king's representative. Aethelwulf had begun to suspect that he'd volunteered for the mission in order to add to his collections. But he didn't begrudge him that. This was a time of giving. And while, as Swithun said, the Lord loves a cheerful giver, the giver tends to like a grateful recipient.

'I have never met your king,' Aethelwulf replied. 'I knew his father, and his grandfather, but only as a boy knows great men. I was born at Aachen, in the reign of Charlemagne. He welcomed my father as a guest after the Mercians drove him into exile. We owe much to the House of Charlemagne, as does all of Christendom. But I left the emperor's court when I was younger than my son, Alfred, is now. And I have not left England since. A kingdom can swallow its ruler up, my lord abbot.'

'Your father and you have made the kingdom of Wessex a name to be reckoned with throughout Christendom, sire.'

Aethelwulf gave a slight shrug. It was an easy compliment. He'd make this genial cleric work harder for his presents.

'Tell me about King Charles,' he said. 'He must be over twenty years younger than me. In the prime of life. But it can't have been easy for him.'

He could see caution creeping into Lupus's friendly face. 'I don't know what you mean, sire.'

'To rule so great a kingdom from such an early age; and as the youngest son, as well.'

'It is the Frankish way, sire. The inheritance is to be shared between all the sons.'

'He had to fight for his share, though, didn't he? When barely more than a boy. Against his own brothers.' Aethelwulf's holiday mood was making him a little mischievous.

'It was an unprecedented situation,' Lupus said awkwardly. 'So great an empire to be divided. Everyone was finding their way. Kings are often tested at the beginning of their reigns. And, as you say, King Charles was very young. But he proved himself worthy. And has ruled us well ever since. At peace with his brothers.'

'Indeed,' Aethelwulf agreed. 'It is an impressive achievement. To have survived with so little support, and so many enemies.'

'The king has the support of the whole country,' Lupus replied stiffly. 'He has no enemies.'

'Kings always have enemies, my lord abbot. What of the Aquitanians, the Bretons, the pagans?'

'There are always some on the edge of a great kingdom who will try to resist its rule. But the heart of the country is united, and solidly for the king.'

'I rejoice to hear of it. Now tell me something of the king himself. I have heard tell of his wisdom, and of his friendship for scholars.'

'He is one of the most intelligent men I have ever met,' Lupus replied simply. 'He knows more of theology than many who have spent their lives in its study. He speaks at least eight languages, including

Greek, thanks to John of Erin. And he has, through his own efforts and example, re-established the love of learning in our land. The Palace School is once more creating great scholars, the king's own children amongst them. He has built great churches and noble palaces, and sponsored writers and craftsmen. And all this in the time he has left over from governing the country. He is a worthy successor to his noble father and grandfather, sire.'

'The king's children attend the Palace School?'

'They do, and are expected to compete with the brightest in the land.'

'I have heard of the Princess Judith. My men met her at Rheims.'

'She is his eldest child. She takes after her father in her intelligence and beauty.'

'The king is a handsome man?' Aethelwulf was beginning to tire of the panegyric.

Lupus looked a little hesitant again. 'You may have heard, sire. . . It is no secret. . . The king suffered an illness as a child. His hair fell out and has never grown back.'

'I have heard some such thing,' Aethelwulf admitted. The baldness of the Frankish king was notorious throughout Europe. His enemies cited it as a curse from God, his supporters a sign of God's especial favour. Jokes about hairless swine and babies' bottoms had at one time been commonplace. But after the king had ordered that five monks, convicted of circulating the jokes, have their eyes put out and their hands, tongues, ears and genitals cut off, they became less so. Each of the mutilated monks was placed, still alive, at the gateways of five of the great towns of the kingdom, where they bled to death. The king insisted that the bodies remained where they were until their flesh had rotted away. Only then would he permit burial. After that, jokes about the king's baldness tended to be restricted to lands outside his rule.

*

'My youngest son, Alfred.' Aethelwulf was introducing him to the Frankish King Charles. Alfred was aware of a pair of piercing blue eyes staring at him. He tried not to stare back, which was difficult. Colman had warned him that King Charles was bald. That was all right; there were bald men at his father's court, to say nothing of tonsured monks. But normally they had hair somewhere – the side of their heads, moustaches or beards, the backs of their hands. The Frankish king was, as far as Alfred could see, completely hairless. His pink skin shone brightly in the afternoon light. He must be quite a lot younger than his father – there was a brisk, youthful air about him – but his total lack of hair made him seem ageless, from a different world than the one he knew.

It added to the sense of strangeness he already felt on returning to Francia. The long, grey Channel crossing had been followed by a river journey, snaking their way through fields and woods, all the way to the palace at Verberie. The palace itself, situated on high ground and surrounded on three sides by forest, was immense. They had to pass through three gateways to reach its heart. Only after passing a small village of servants and craftsmen, and then a training ground flanked with soldiers' barracks and stables, did they reach the great inner square with stone buildings running down either side of it. At the end, the king's residence, church and fortress with mighty towers was so much grander than anything he had seen before. Even the vast buildings of Rome, being from a different time and falling into decay, hadn't made such an impression on him. This was new – it had been built by the grandfather of the smooth-faced man now scrutinising him. It had an energy which Rome did not. But what the source of that energy was, Alfred didn't know.

'You've become quite a traveller for one so young, Alfred.' King Charles had finished his scrutiny and was smiling down at him. He had a pleasant smile, a slightly sharp voice. 'And how did you find the Holy Father?'

'I liked him. He was kind.' *He didn't strike me dead*, he thought.

'Would you want to be like the Holy Father when you grow up?'

He didn't understand the question. He couldn't imagine being like that old man in the enormous church. He remembered what Swithun had told him about not asking questions of strangers when you don't know the answer. He thought it probably applied to not answering questions from strangers when you don't know why they're being asked also.

'I don't know,' he said, keeping his gaze on the floor to avoid the king's eyes. 'I don't know what I will be.' He sneaked a glance at his father. He'd always assumed that his father would decide what he was to be when he grew up. He didn't imagine he would have any choice in the matter. So, why was this strange foreign king suggesting that he might?

'Alfred is still very young,' Aethelwulf said. 'But he has a great love of the Lord.'

'We should all hope to cultivate that,' King Charles said with a faint smile. 'Youngest sons, in particular.'

Alfred didn't understand that either. He remembered Princess Judith telling him that her father was a youngest son. Was he referring to himself? King Charles made him feel uneasy. So different from anyone he knew. He was not unhappy when the king's pale blue gaze returned to the adults, dismissing him from his attention. Shortly afterwards, he and Colman were led away by servants to the royal nursery.

Even the nursery was grand in this palace. A long, high-ceilinged room, almost as big as some of their great halls back home. Two large fires were burning at either end, but it was still cold. Princess Judith was not there, but the king's other children were. Four boys of a similar age to Alfred crowded around him curiously. A younger girl, doing some drawing at a table with a teacher, glanced at him briefly before returning to her drawing. An even younger girl was practising walking backwards and forwards along a rush mat, watched by an admiring nurse. King Charles was not short of children. Maybe that was behind his comment about youngest sons?

Alfred relaxed a little. It was rare for him to be amongst anyone younger than himself. King Charles's eldest son, Louis, might be a year or two older than him, but he had a stammer, which made him seem younger. The other boys listened politely as Louis negotiated his way around a formal speech of welcome. Alfred was listened to with equal politeness when he made a stumbling reply in Frankish. Maybe such formality was unnatural, but at least he didn't feel threatened by these well-behaved children.

Louis was in the process of showing him a book, which Alfred recognised as a psalter, when there was a noise at the far end of the room. Princess Judith had entered and been immediately recognised by the youngest girl, who gave a cry of welcome and promptly fell over. The cry of welcome was succeeded by a squawk of complaint. Judith bent down to fuss over the little girl and reassure her that she wasn't hurt. Alfred stared across the room. Judith had grown since he'd last seen her – she looked like a woman. Luxuriantly dressed – a deep blue robe and gold torque. Dark hair shining in the firelight as she played with the little girl, coaxing her back to good humour.

'M-m-m--y sis-sis-sis-sister Ju-Ju-Judith,' Louis explained.

'We've met before, at Rheims,' Alfred said, forcing his attention back to the psalter. Beautiful illustrations.

The little sister was back on her feet again, proudly resuming her progress back and forth along the rush mat. Judith watched her for a few moments before leaving her once more to the care of the nurse and joining her brothers and Alfred.

'P-P-P-P . . .' Louis took his duties as host seriously.

'Thank you, Louis,' Judith said gently. 'I've met Prince Alfred before.'

'In R-R-R . . .'

'Yes, in Rheims. He's told you, I see.' She turned to smile a welcome at Alfred. Deep blue eyes. 'You've grown,' she said pleasantly.

Her polite brothers looked at him with respect, as if this was particularly clever of him. Alfred wondered if he should tell her that she'd grown in reply and decided against it. Princess Judith had a knack of making him feel confused. He remembered her being bright and challenging before. She wasn't like that now. With her brothers and sisters, she was patient and understanding. Clearly the eldest – they all looked to her for approval. One of the younger boys, Carloman, who up until then hadn't spoken, was encouraged to talk of his first time out with the hawks. The others chipped in with their own tales of hawks, becoming more enthusiastic, more like young boys. Even interrupting one another. Alfred watched Judith manage the conversation so that no one felt left out. He recognised the skill, could remember his mother doing the same. His mother – a sudden pain.

'Do you have hawks, Alfred?' Judith asked, including him in the conversation.

'Yes.'

'And dogs, too? The English are famous for their dogs.'

She persuaded him to talk about Sideways, which wasn't hard for him to do. And then the boys responded with tales of their own dogs and it was as if they had known one another all their lives. They were still discussing dogs when Colman, who had been sitting quietly reading all this time, stirred himself and said that they ought to be getting ready for dinner.

'I will come and show you to your room,' said Judith. 'Your baggage will have been delivered there by now.'

She led the way out of the nursery, along a passageway and up a flight of stairs, ensuring that Alfred was beside her and Colman a little way behind.

'Are you pleased to be travelling with your father, Alfred,' she muttered abruptly. Alfred was aware of a certain tension in her voice. The calm mother-like figure of the nursery had been replaced by someone more urgent.

Alfred didn't know what to say in reply. 'Yes,' seemed safest.

'I'm told he's a religious man,' Judith continued. 'Is he also a good man?'

Alfred looked at her, uncomprehending.

'Ah, you don't understand.' She was still speaking quietly but the tone of exasperation in her voice was unmistakeable. 'You're too young. Well, I'll try to explain. My father is a religious man – he attends mass every day, he builds great churches and talks theology with the bishops and John of Erin. But,' she hesitated, staring at him intently for a moment, 'he's very strict with us, the boys especially. They are all terrified of him. That's why poor Louis has his stammer. Are you terrified of your father, Alfred?'

Alfred considered. His father could be distant – less so on this journey where he was seeing more of him than ever before. But no, he was not terrified of him. He didn't think he would do him harm.

'No,' he said. 'I'm not. He's a good man.'

Judith's blue eyes glowed their thanks. 'That's something, then,' she said softly. 'This is your room. I may see you at one of the dinners, but if I do, we won't be speaking. Our conversations have to be carried out on the sly, Alfred. We haven't had this one either, have we?'

He sensed a note of entreaty in her voice. This time, she wasn't telling him what to do, she was asking him for a favour. It made him feel important. 'No,' he replied.

A trace of her old bright smile and then she was gone.

'What was she talking to you about?' Colman asked when they were alone in the room. 'I couldn't hear – she has a very soft voice.'

'She was asking about our family,' Alfred replied. Which was sort of true.

*

Aethelwulf stared in astonishment at the man sitting opposite him. He had heard tell that this Irishman propounded strange and unsettling doctrines, but nothing as outrageous as this. He half-expected him to burst into flames. He looked over at King Charles to see if he was equally outraged, but the Frankish king had a smile on his face and was looking at John of Erin as a trainer of hounds might look upon his favourite dog.

Aethelwulf struggled to control his temper. This must be some kind of test. These Franks were peculiar people – too clever for their own good. Add in a showy Irishman and you had a rich mixture.

'I don't understand,' he said to John of Erin. 'How can you say that God does not exist?'

'Not me, my lord king,' John of Erin replied. 'St Denis.'

'Our founding saint,' King Charles added. 'St Paul's Athenian convert.'

'No saint would ever say that God does not exist.'

'I understand your reaction, brother king. I had the same reaction myself when John first expounded this doctrine to me. I had a mind to send him to be tried for heresy.' King Charles smiled pleasantly over at his court philosopher. 'But he has since convinced me that it is not heresy, but rather mysticism of the highest order. I honestly believe that it has helped me to come closer to the Lord.'

'How can saying someone does not exist bring you closer to that person?'

'It does sound shocking at first,' John of Erin admitted. 'And paradoxical. But the Bible is full of paradoxes.'

'Nowhere in the Bible does it say that God does not exist.'

'Ecclesiastes comes close,' observed King Charles.

Aethelwulf was beginning to feel out of his depth. He wished Swithun was here; he missed his wisdom. He looked over at Abbot Lupus and tried to gauge his reaction. No use – his face was wooden. That amiable man had no desire to argue with his king. John of Erin might have a certain licence to challenge King Charles, but Aethelwulf suspected that other members of the French court would be reluctant to do so. There was a certain menace about the man, despite his friendly manner. That story of the tortured monks stuck in the mind.

The vast hall was almost empty. A few figures were moving near the entrance, but it seemed that most of the Frankish warriors slept elsewhere in the palace complex. Only at the high table was there still light. The musicians had been sent on their way a long time ago. King Charles was fond of after-dinner discussions amongst a few chosen companions.

'It is not a doctrine for the many,' King Charles continued. 'I won't be authorising John here to be preaching it in the pulpit any time soon. It would be easily misunderstood, as matters of the spirit often are. But for the proficient, for those advanced on the spiritual path, it has great value. Would you like John to explain it to you, as he explained it to me?'

Aethelwulf had little choice but to say that he would. In fact, he would have much preferred to have gone to bed and leave these Franks to argue over their troublesome doctrines, but that was hardly the act of an honoured guest.

'The problem is really in the concept of existence,' John of Erin began. 'What do we mean when we say something exists?'

'We mean that it is,' Aethelwulf replied slowly. He tried to concentrate his tired mind. He had a feeling that this Irish wordsmith would soon set it spinning.

'Very well, and how do we know that something is?'

'We just do,' said Aethelwulf, a little helplessly.

'Our senses tell us, or our mind, or our faith,' said Abbot Lupus, coming to the rescue.

'Very good,' said John of Erin. 'But none of those would be sufficient proof for Euclid. Our senses can be mistaken, and our minds.'

'But not our faith,' said Abbot Lupus.

'Our faith can be mistaken as well,' John of Erin rejoined. 'Otherwise, there would be no such thing as heresy. Is Gottschalk not mistaken?'

'Let's leave Gottschalk out of it,' said King Charles with a smile. 'Things are complicated enough as it is. I think you've been toying with our guest long enough, John. What proof would be sufficient for Euclid?'

'Would you accept that something exists if it doesn't not exist?' John of Erin asked Aethelwulf.

'Yes, of course.'

'In doing so, you accept that there is such a thing as non-existence.'

'I suppose so.'

'It makes sense, doesn't it? This table, for example. It's solid enough, isn't it? It exists. But there was a time when it didn't exist. A craftsman had to make it. And before that, a tree had to grow in the forest. So, there was a time when this table did not exist.'

'Yes, of course, but I don't see what that has to do with God. Material things come into being, but God doesn't. He's eternal.'

'But you accept that there is such a thing as non-existence?'

'Yes, but it's not important.'

'St Denis would disagree with you. He would say that non-existence is extremely important. Without it, we cannot tell whether anything exists. We define everything in this world by having something to contrast it with. When we say that something is light, we have the idea of darkness, which it is not. When we say that something is fast, we have the idea of slowness, which it is not. When we say that something is, we have the idea of not is, which it is not.'

Aethelwulf had expected his head to be spinning, and it was. 'But what has any of this to do with God?'

'How would you define God?'

'Not not God?'

John of Erin nodded. 'That would seem to make sense, wouldn't it, given what we've agreed? But if you define God in that way, then you are limiting God. You are saying that there is such a thing as not God. If God is universal and omnipresent, then how can there be such a thing as not God?'

Aethelwulf had the feeling of being tricked by some sleight of hand which he couldn't identify. He wasn't sure that he cared that much. He wanted to go to bed. Probably the quickest way to achieve that would be to let this Irishman finish his word-splitting proof. 'So, how would you define God?' he asked.

'I wouldn't,' John of Erin replied. 'God is beyond definition. That is the whole point of what St Denis says. And if we say He exists, we are limiting Him by implying that there is a state which He is not.'

'The state of non-existence?'

'Yes, but that is a real state. And it often depends on the beholder whether something exists or does not exist. Someone sitting where we are sitting a hundred years ago wouldn't have this table between them. It wouldn't exist.'

'It seems to me to be arguing about nothing.'

John of Erin gave a rare smile. 'It is arguing about nothing, that is precisely the point. But nothing is extremely important.'

'Why?'

'When we say God *is* something – be it God is good, God is just, God is wise, we are limiting Him. We are applying our own limited concepts to someone who is unlimited.'

'So, now as well as saying God doesn't exist, you're saying He isn't good, either.'

'It's not my doctrine; it's that of St Denis. God includes goodness, of course, but He is not limited by it. He is, if you like, beyond goodness, just as He is beyond existence. Whenever we attribute any quality, even existence, to an unlimited Being, we are in effect using metaphors. We are applying ideas we think we understand to a Being we certainly do not understand. The only thing we can say for certain about God is what He is not.'

'And what is He not?'

'Anything we seek to define Him by, because that inevitably involves a limitation of His Being.'

'It sounds like a recipe for anarchy.'

'Well, as my lord king says, it's not a doctrine to be proclaimed from the pulpit. Positive assertions about God do have value, even if they are only metaphors. Metaphors can have great value. It is always easier to latch on to something we think we understand than to something we don't. But for the seeker after truth, St Denis's doctrine has great value.'

'I don't see why.'

'It teaches humility.'

Somehow, humility wasn't a virtue that sprang immediately to Aethelwulf's mind in connection with this challenging philosopher.

'Why humility?'

'We become wary about telling God what He is. Which is often, unsurprisingly, what we would like Him to be. Instead, we admit that we do not know Him, but ask for His love nonetheless. We pray in darkness, not light; in blindness, not sight; in ignorance, not knowledge. We seek to empty ourselves of everything, including our concepts of God. Only then is there space for God to fill us, only then can the new wine be poured.'

Aethelwulf was silent. It had been worth staying up for. All the verbal games and confusing questions had been leading somewhere. He looked over at the great fire, which was now just a few embers. There was a comfort in this darkness, something which might help him to live whatever time was left for him on this earth. His sight would be fading, his weakness growing. To learn to accept that was no small thing.

'And that is St Denis's doctrine?' he asked, after a while.

'One of them, my lord king.'

'It does have value,' he admitted.

'It does, doesn't it?' said King Charles, pleased. 'I've authorised John to translate it from Greek into Latin. It deserves to be wider known. Amongst those who are able to understand it. Such as you, my brother king.'

*

'And so, my lords prince and bishop, it is clearly the case that whilst this land may have been grazed by cattle belonging to Ealdorman Eanwulf, and even occupied by his men, it has never been formally allocated to him. If it had been, he would have a charter recording the allocation, and no such charter has been shown to you. In the absence of any such allocation, the land belongs to the king. The king, before he left on pilgrimage, made a tithe of all his property to the Church and appointed the bishop of Winchester to administer the tithe. The bishop of Winchester has ruled that, as part of the tithe, this land should be given to the abbey at Glastonbury.'

'*If* the land belongs to the king,' growled Ealhstan, studying a piece of parchment with Swithun's ruling, which had been submitted by the monk before him.

'Indeed,' the monk replied smoothly. 'The gift is made conditional upon the land being the king's to give, which is the reason for this hearing. But, in the circumstances, it is for the ealdorman to show that the land is his. This he had failed to do. Therefore, it must be the king's to give.'

'What do you say to that?' Blade asked the thane representing the ealdorman.

'Sire, you have heard the testimony of aged men to the effect that this land was owned by the ealdorman of Somerset in the time of their fathers. Tradition has it that it has belonged to the ealdorman of Somerset since it was won from the Britons in the days of King Ine. It has never been royal land and the Church has been unable to produce any witness to show that it has. The Church relies solely on the lack of a charter. Not every piece of land has a charter. The king must make the charter.'

'And until he does, the land is his,' the monk responded.

'Sire, we are talking about land that has belonged to the ealdormen of Somerset for over a hundred years. It was not your father's intention to dispossess his most loyal supporters.'

Blade and Ealhstan were sitting at high table in the great hall at Somerton, hearing a dispute between the abbot of Glastonbury and the ealdorman of Somerset over ownership of a hundred hides of good grazing land near Taunton. It was a warm early autumn day and Blade would have much preferred to have been out hunting in Selwood. Acting as arbiter between quarrelling subjects was not his favourite royal duty. It was impossible to please everyone – someone always went away hurt and offended by the king's justice. And yet cases had to be decided, otherwise the arguments went on forever, consuming the energies of all around. For Blade, it was a rather ignoble balancing act – calculating the gain of one person's pleasure against the loss of another's disappointment. You saw the worst of people at such times – their pettiness and greed.

Arguments over land were the most difficult, much more difficult than criminal cases. With criminal cases, there was often a general agreement as to what needed to be done, and he was only required to endorse a decisions which had effectively already been reached.

But the arguments over land which reached him needed a royal decision, and it was invariably a decision which risked angering one valuable supporter or another.

'Very well,' he said, wanting to bring the matter to a close. 'We have heard your arguments. You will now leave us and I will confer with my lord bishop. When we have reached our decision, you will be sent for.'

The monk and thane bowed and left the hall. Blade turned to Ealhstan. He had come to rely upon him heavily in matters such as this. The old bishop was more than a fighter; he had been deciding cases amongst subordinates since long before Blade was born.

'I've lost count of the number of cases which we've had to judge because of my father's grant to the Church,' he complained. 'I wonder if he was aware of the amount of trouble he was going to leave behind with his grand gesture. And then to put a churchman in charge of the allocation. He must have known that a churchman would favour the Church whenever he could.' Like many others, Blade tended to forget that Ealhstan was, officially at least, a churchman.

'He's concerned for the future of his soul,' Ealhstan observed.

'Then he should have abdicated. That's what kings concerned with their souls have done before. Instead of which, he's been over-generous in giving away the kingdom's resources, encouraging the Church to be as grasping as only the Church knows how. And after he's processed through Europe and spent as much of our money as possible, he intends to come back here and take up power again. With the result that any decision I make is always going to be subject to appeal to the king when he gets back. He's made it impossible for me to govern at all.'

Ealhstan looked at Blade appraisingly. 'Your father's position on his return from Rome, if he returns from Rome, will be most unusual. Unprecedented, even. As you say, kings of Wessex who have left for Rome before have abdicated. None of them came back to rule again. If he is going to do so, he will need all the support he can get.'

'What are you saying?' Blade asked slowly.

'What do you want to do about the ealdorman of Somerset's land?'

'Tell that sly monk to go hang himself.'

Ealhstan gave a wintry smile. 'You should always be polite to the Church. Particularly when ruling against it.'

'Do you think I can? He's right about the charter, isn't he? I can't say charters don't matter, otherwise everyone will be claiming land they haven't been given.'

'Then grant the ealdorman a charter. Say that having heard the case, you are satisfied that it was not your father's intention to deprive the ealdorman of land which has been in the possession of his family for generations, but to clear up any doubts, you are granting the ealdorman a charter in respect of the land. The ealdorman, I'm sure, will be willing to pledge you further support in return. And be very grateful to you personally.'

'The abbey will be furious.'

'Whose support would you rather have?'

Blade laughed. 'That's easy! The ealdorman controls over five hundred men, not to mention the Somerset fyrd.'

'And who knows when you will need those men and the fyrd? More than you need the prayers of a few well-disposed monks.'

'But what about my father? He won't want to antagonise the abbey. Particularly when he's on pilgrimage.'

'He left you in control of the kingdom. He can't complain about decisions made in his absence. And he won't want to antagonise the ealdorman of Somerset by trying to take back a charter you've already granted him. As I say, he will need all the support he can get on his return.'

Blade was silent, considering a new world of power which the old bishop's words had opened up for him. 'You know,' he said eventually, weighing his words carefully, 'my father's grant to the Church has left a lot of people unhappy, not just Ealdorman Eanwulf.'

'Such gestures often do, sire. But you are in a position to ensure that your father's generosity does not unknowingly cause injustice. A king's first duty is to ensure justice for his subjects.'

7. Pilgrims' Goal

Alfred's second journey to Rome made less of an impression on him than the first. They followed much the same route and memories of the previous journey would intrude and cause him confusion. He kept expecting Swithun to be there and had to fight off feelings of disappointment when remembering that Swithun wasn't with him now. Instead, there was his father, but he couldn't ask his father the things he used to ask Swithun. His father, living the life he had dreamed of for so long, was caught up in feelings of his own. Aethelwulf's brightness and enthusiasm for everything they encountered on their journey was puzzling to Alfred. It was so different to how he was back home. Quite often his father would call him over in order to show him something which he found remarkable. It was hard for Alfred to match his enthusiasm, particularly if it was something he had seen before with Swithun. But if he didn't try and pretend that he was as excited as his father wanted him to be, then there'd be a look of disappointment in his father's eyes and he'd often be quite brusque with him for some time afterwards. As a result, memories and impressions got mixed up and overlaid with an anxiety which made him wish for the journey's end. At least he would see the Holy Father again. The old man's twinkling eyes and the anointing ceremony at St Peter's were his most precious memories of all, and ones that his father would be unable to touch.

Crossing the Alps was less eventful this time. It was later in the year and the snows much retreated, leaving more of the mountains' grey spines exposed. No snowfalls now, and not even a hint of bandits – the size of their force enough to ensure that. Even so, there was no need for him to feign excitement when his father called him over at the top of the pass to look down through cloud at the fields of Italy stretching out below them. This was a view that would always catch the heart.

They followed the same route down off the mountains and towards Rome, stopping again at the hostel in Pavia, where they were greeted by the same jovial guestmaster as before. Alfred noticed that he made no reference to the tomb of Queen Eadburh this time, and when they went into the church, the wall which contained her memorial plaque was covered by a tapestry of Mary Magdalen washing Jesus's feet with her hair. Should he mention the plaque to his father? He saw the guest master shooting a worried glance at him when he saw where he was looking. No. Why disturb the dead?

At Pavia, they received the unwelcome news that the pope had died of a fever a couple of months before. Alfred felt a chill in his heart when he heard. The one person he'd been looking forward to meeting in Rome was gone. He thought of his mother. Why did people always die before he could reach them?

Aethelwulf was also disturbed by news of the pope's death. Who would meet him now? Travellers fresh from Rome brought news that a new pope, Benedict, had already been elected. Those of Aethelwulf's guard who knew the emperor were concerned when they heard of the election of Benedict.

'It's too soon,' said Markward, a churchman from the imperial lands, who had been acting as one of the party's guides. 'They can't have consulted the emperor. He will feel slighted.'

Some fifty years before, on Christmas Day, the emperor's grandfather, the great Charlemagne, had been anointed the first Holy Roman Emperor by a pope whom he'd rescued from deposition. And since that date, in return for protecting the Holy See from its enemies, Charlemagne and his successors had expected to have a deciding say in the choice of a new pope. But the Holy Roman Emperor was hardly ever in Rome. And he wasn't a Roman, but a Frank from the northern lands, descendant of the old empire's barbarian enemies. So the temptation was always there for the clergy and people of Rome to elect their bishop (who just also happened by virtue of his office to be pope) from amongst themselves, and then to send a delegation over the Alps to wherever the emperor might be to seek his ratification of a decision which had already been made. By the Holy Spirit.

'Wasn't the last pope elected without the emperor's approval?' Aethelwulf queried. 'The emperor accepted him.'

'That was different.'

'Why?'

'The Saracens were storming the city. It was a crisis. The emperor accepted that the city had to have its leader in place as quickly as possible and couldn't wait for his agreement. There is no such crisis now. If the emperor allows this election to go through also, he'll be seen as accepting that he has no real role in choosing a new pope, whatever the situation. He won't want to do that.'

'You'd better go on ahead and see what it's like in the city. We'll follow more slowly and wait at Viterbo. Come to us there with your report.'

They left Pavia, seen off by the entire congregation of monks. Aethelwulf had been generous to the hostel which had sheltered so many English pilgrims over the years. The guest master's smile was broader than ever, and Queen Eadburh's plaque remained behind its tapestry.

At Viterbo, Markward met them again. 'The city's tense,' he reported to Aethelwulf. 'But it always is between popes. Too many people have a stake in the outcome. The emperor has his supporters, or those who think they'll gain more from a different pope.'

'Did you meet Benedict?'

'Yes.'

'What's he like?'

'Nervous, but resolute, I think. He does have a lot of support in the city, and most of the higher clergy. But he doesn't stray much from the Vatican. It's more easily defended than the Lateran Palace, thanks to the new walls.'

'We'll be protected by those as well.'

'Yes. I think you'll like what the old pope has done with the money you sent him previously. Your quarter is looking much better than when I last saw it. There's been a lot of new building there.'

Aethelwulf considered. 'I ought to go there and be with my people. Has a delegation been sent to the emperor?'

'Yes. It was sent immediately after the election. It should be back in a week or two.'

'Is there any news of the emperor's reaction?'

Markward shook his head. 'Not yet. Everyone's waiting.'

Aethelwulf made his decision. 'We'll have to wait as well. But we'll be better waiting in Rome than here. If the emperor sends an army, this is on its route.'

'I don't think it will come to that,' said Markward. 'He's more likely to seek to impose his will by supporting opposition within Rome. But the trouble is more likely to be in the old city than the Vatican. Benedict looks to be fairly secure there. You'll be under his protection.'

Aethelwulf frowned. 'I don't want to be under any pope's protection. Particularly if there's a chance of his being deposed. But I can't stay here. I'm on pilgrimage to Rome, not Viterbo.'

'I think it will be all right,' said Markward. 'You're here as a pilgrim. So there's no need for you to take sides.'

'How can I not take sides? I'll be living next door to Benedict.'

'Yes, but he won't want to quarrel with you. And it's reasonable for you to delay making any formal contact with him until his appointment has been ratified. After all, you set out to see the old pope, not him. Just keep your guard about you. Don't disband anyone. A body of soldiers could yet prove useful.'

Aethelwulf sighed. 'And I thought I was escaping such considerations by going on pilgrimage.'

Markward gave a sympathetic smile. 'I don't think that's possible, sire. Not in this world. And certainly not in Rome.'

For Alfred, his second entrance into Rome was much grander than the first. Then they had ridden in almost unnoticed, just another band of pilgrims, albeit one with an armed guard. But a king entering the city, particularly at a time when all was uncertain – that was a different matter entirely. Crowds surged around them as they passed through the Porta Flaminia, jostling their horses and staring up at them.

'*Il imperatore!*' someone shouted, which cry rippled through the people, causing them to press ever more insistently against them. Alfred could feel his horse twitching beneath him at the mass of bodies and unaccustomed hubbub all around. How had he ever thought of Rome as an empty city? It seemed as though the whole world was suddenly here.

'*No, non è il imperatore!*' Markward shouted down. '*Siamo solamente dei pellegrini.*'

The crowd was not convinced; they looked more like soldiers than pilgrims. Why should the emperor not smuggle himself and his troops into the city in the guise of pilgrims? And these newcomers were definitely from beyond the mountains. The mutterings and arguments increased. But all of Aethelwulf's force was now through the gate and making its way through the crowd and deeper into the city. Alfred bent over his horse's neck and whispered soothing words into the animal's ear. He tried not to look around him but knew that the hill to their left was covered with people looking down at them. All watching and waiting. A sudden movement might set them off.

Aethelwulf, however, was oblivious to the tension and noise around him. This was a moment he had been waiting for all his life. During their approach to the city walls, through the mighty ruins, he had said nothing, in the grip of deep emotion. This is what human beings had once been capable of; and if once, then why not again? And now through the walls and into the city itself, it was as if his mind was hurtling back through time. The present – the restless, surging crowd, his nervous companions – had slipped from his view. Instead, the past was unhooking itself from these ancient stones and coming to meet him. He would not have been surprised to be confronted by a mighty Caesar, or to feel the stare of a sharp-eyed apostle upon him.

He stopped beside a large, crumbling castle, where he sensed the past strongly.

'What is this?' he asked.

'Er, the Mausoleum of Augustus,' said Markward, looking around.

'How wonderful!' Aethelwulf exclaimed. 'Is that where he is buried?'

'Yes.'

'Can we go in and have a look?'

'Sire, we really ought to keep moving,' Markward urged. The crowd had eased a little, but he would not feel secure until they were over the river and within the confines of the Vatican and Saxon Quarter. 'We need to arrive first. Your people are waiting for you.'

'Oh, very well,' said Aethelwulf, disapointed. It seemed rude to be passing Augustus by without stopping to greet him. But then he was a pagan. Perhaps it was best not to make one's first visit in the city to a pagan temple.

A little further and they became lost in a maze of streets near the Capitol, trying to find a bridge over the river. After two failed attempts, Markward was becoming more anxious than ever. Much more of this and they would all be dispersed. He had a nasty feeling that they had already lost a number of the guard. Once they stopped and started drinking wine with the locals, who knew if they'd ever come back?

Aethelwulf remained oblivious to his guide's concerns and in no hurry to cross the river. After their second attempt to find the bridge had failed, they stumbled into a square, at the far end of which stood a building, the like of which he had never seen. Fronted by a colonnaded porch, it was round and roofed by an enormous dome. Some Roman's name was proudly displayed on the front of the building, but Aethelwulf's enquiries revealed that although it had once been a temple, it was now a church, dedicated to Mary and all martyrs. That decided him; he was not going to pass this by as well. Ignoring Markward's protests, he dismounted from his horse and walked into the hybrid temple church.

Inside, it was dark. There was a hole at the top of the dome through which some light came, but otherwise the only light came from hundreds of small candles in niches all the way round the church's circular interior. Each niche dedicated to a different martyr. Aethelwulf suddenly felt uncomfortable. He did not find the darkness welcoming. There was too much death in here. And the circularity was disconcerting also; it led nowhere and was so different to what he knew. He said a quick prayer and hurried out, willing to be shepherded along by Markward now.

Markward had ordered guides ahead to find the bridge. They had met up with a papal guard sent to welcome them. Together, they processed to the bridge and then over it into the safety of the walled Vatican enclave, which was to be their home.

A group of Saxon residents had assembled to greet them and gave a cheer at their arrival. The area had indeed changed much in two years. An air of desolation had hung over it then, but now new buildings stood where once had been blackened ruins. The streets were clean and a sense of calm pervaded in contrast to the noisy, jostling city they had passed through.

Aethelwulf gave a brief speech of thanks to the residents for their welcome and said how pleased he was to be among them. Most of his audience was old. People tended to go on pilgrimage after they had raised their families, expecting to die at their place of pilgrimage and hoping that proximity to so many saints would ease their passage through purgatory.

Aethelwulf finished his speech and there was some more applause. They were now being invited to prayers at the Saxon church of St Mary's, founded by King Ine over a hundred years before. The church had a proud position beside the river. Once inside, Aethelwulf's soul, still a little troubled by its experience of the temple church, began to relax and expand. The light interior, the straight lines leading up to the altar – these he knew, this was home. The church had been shut two years ago due to fire damage. But now, like the streets outside, it had been restored and offered the reassurance of the familiar to those who had travelled far.

The prayers lasted an hour or so and from there they proceeded to the house where they were to stay, a new building constructed especially for the king. Markward and some of the guard met them there. Others of the guard were lodged elsewhere nearby.

'Well, we have arrived, my friend,' Aethelwulf said to Markward with a smile. 'Our thanks to you for seeing us safely here.'

'I rejoice to see you safely at your destination, sire,' Markward replied.

'And you will stay to act as our intermediary with the Holy Father?'

'Yes, sire. I will call on him at the earliest opportunity to explain your position, and how you are unable to call on him and present your offerings until his election has been ratified. I'm sure he will understand.'

'I don't know how I'm going to manage to avoid him in this small space.'

'The Holy Father usually keeps to St Peter's or the Castel Sant' Angelo at present.'

'So, I should avoid those two places?'

'I would advise so, yes.'

'Coming on pilgrimage to Rome and not visiting St Peter's!'

'Sire, there are many other sacred sites in Rome. And we must hope that it will only be for a short time. The delegation should be back from the emperor any day now.'

But the return of the delegation did not bring a resolution of the situation. Indeed, it made matters much worse. Not only had the emperor refused to accept Benedict's election but, furious at what he saw as an act of rebellion, he had appointed his own pope, Anastasius. Anastasius returned with the delegation and promptly installed himself in the Lateran Palace. From there, he called on the citizens and clergy of Rome to arrest the usurper, Benedict, and do homage to himself as their divinely appointed leader. Rome now had two popes, one at either end of the city.

*

The royal party settled into its accommodation in the Saxon quarter of the city. To begin with, they didn't stray far from the walled security of the Vatican area. There was a long journey to recover from and a new set of subjects for the king to get to know. It was a rare privilege for the Saxon pilgrims to have their king amongst them and many of them seemed determined to make the most of it. From morning until night, there were callers at Aethelwulf's residence, either seeking favours from him or more often just wanting to make themselves known to him. As they dined most evenings with the king and accompanied him to daily mass at St Mary's, Aethelwulf would have had to have been extremely forgetful not to recognise them all after a very short time, but that was a risk many seemed unwilling to take.

'Why do you put up with these people calling on you the whole time?' Alfred asked his father after a particularly tedious visitor had taken up the best part of an hour, talking about the family he'd left behind in Wessex. A tall, gloomy-looking man, who nevertheless interspersed his account with interjections of 'Alleluia!' and 'Praise the Lord!' for reasons Alfred was unable to understand.

'A king must be available to his people, Alfred,' Aethelwulf replied.

Alfred decided that as he was unlikely to ever become a king, he didn't need to be as available as his father and escaped as often as he could from the constant callers. In the morning, after the expedition to mass, he would have lessons with Colman. After the midday meal, the late summer heat drove adults to their beds, but he never felt tired. The heat didn't trouble him – it was such a welcome change from cold, damp England.

When the adults were settling down for their siestas, he would leave the house and go exploring the quiet streets around it. His father had agreed to him going out on his own so long as he kept to the Saxon quarter. He was safe enough there. The city across the river was forbidden territory, guarded by bridge-keepers and gate men.

Alfred was happy enough to keep to the area around their house. It held more than enough to interest him. Little streets snaking their way through tightly-packed wooden houses, suddenly emerging into open ground, littered with the stone remains of an earlier world. Mostly, he had the place to himself – a few people occasionally hurried by on errands and cats would stalk past him on missions of their own. But neither humans nor cats seemed concerned by his presence. It was too hot for most to be curious – the city baked in silence, broken occasionally by a burst of shouting from one of the houses. Alfred, keeping to shaded areas where possible, would wander from street to street, marvelling at the dazzling light and sudden shadows, the dusty stones and unknown, pungent smells.

His father had told him to keep away from St Peter's. He would have done so anyway – his memories of the place were a mixture of dread and awe. Mixed with sadness for the kind old pope who had died. But the walls built by that pope were an endless source of fascination – a massive creation in stone which harked back to earlier, grander times. When the worst of the heat was beginning to ease, he would invariably be drawn to one of the series of steps leading up to the battlements. The sentries knew him and paid him no heed. Once at the top, there was usually a cooling breeze. And he could look down on the river boats and across to the shimmering city, which he'd been told held so many dangers.

But whatever dangers the city held, they were not sufficient to dissuade Aethelwulf from wanting to start visiting its sites. It was what he had travelled across Europe to do. Who knew how long it would take for the papal situation to resolve itself? Possibly years. He wasn't going to stay stuck in his house, playing unwilling host to a lot of elderly pilgrims for that length of time. He had an armed guard. And Romans were used to pilgrims in their city. As Markward had said, there was no reason for him to get drawn into the struggle between the city and emperor.

And so, a couple of weeks after arriving, Aethelwulf began to cross the river and visit the holy places, accompanied by his guard and a large number of fellow pilgrims. Alfred ensured that he and Colman were always invited along on these expeditions, although he soon began to find them rather depressing. They always seemed to be visiting cemeteries or places of martyrdom. He wondered why Rome was seen to be such a holy city, given the number of Christians it had killed. There were days when they just seemed to be processing from one death to another. They visited the tombs of the kings of Wessex, Caedwalla and Ine, who had died in Rome. He remembered them from poems which Diarmait sang about them on special occasions, but it was hard for him to relate those poems with the dusty cemetery which held their bones.

The places of martyrdom were often fairly indistinguishable from their surroundings, but Alfred began to dread when they arrived at one as their guide would launch into a detailed account of the tortures and death suffered by each particular martyr. Alfred listened with a mixture of horror and disgust to stories of people being flayed alive, roasted on gridirons, boiled, burnt, mutilated, torn apart by wild animals, crucified and generally hacked to pieces. What felt worse was that he seemed to be the only member of the party to have these feelings. Everyone else listened to the guide with an attitude of devout attention. The man who said 'Alleluia!' and 'Praise the Lord!' at regular intervals said them even more often, and he was not the only one to do so. Alfred even noticed his father muttering piously to himself after one particularly grisly account.

Visiting the churches was something of a relief. Once his eyes had grown accustomed to the gloom, he started to pick out sumptuous decorations and mosaics glittering in the light of candles or lamps. Their guide told them stories of the churches also, but they tended to be gentler stories than those of the martyrs' deaths, full of wonders and miracles – visions of the Virgin Mother, magical snowfalls in the middle of summer, treasures brought back from the Holy Land, such as the True Cross on which Our Lord was crucified, the crib in which He was born, the Ark of the Covenant which God first made with man. Stories of healing and reconciliation.

One day, they were visiting a monastery at the top of a hill facing the old city's centre. This, Alfred had been told, was a particularly important place as it was the home of St Gregory. From here, he had decided to send missionaries to England, and had directed the successful mission by letter and instruction.

'Without this man, England might still be pagan,' Colman said.

Alfred looked around in some bewilderment. The fact that the stories he had heard came from a place which you could visit, as they were doing, took some getting used to.

They were walking in the monastery's terraced garden, looking over at the ruined palaces and pine trees on the hill opposite when Aethelwulf suddenly gave a cry of recognition at the sight of an old man being helped to slowly walk up the hill towards them.

'King Cyngen!'

The old man stopped and waited for them to join him. Alfred could see that he was leaning heavily on the arm of a boy beside him. He looked thin and gaunt, but his face was smiling.

'My lord king,' he said as Aethelwulf came up to him. 'How good to see you again! And in happier circumstances than when we last me. We both made it!'

'Indeed we did. And I'm flattered that you should be coming to pay your respects to the apostle of the English.'

Cyngen laughed. 'Yes, well. It's probably the time to put such distinctions aside. For me, at least. I am no longer a king, just a simple pilgrim. I will not be returning to Powys. The journey here almost killed me; the journey back certainly would. Indeed,' he continued with a wry glance ahead, 'I'm not even sure about the journey up the rest of his hill. It's very steep, isn't it? And, now you come to mention it, would the apostle of the English want to be visited by an old Welshman?'

'I'm sure he'd be honoured. And he was a great pope as well as being apostle of the English.'

'Yes, I must admit that was more of a consideration for me. And the abbot up there has been very kind to me. I wanted to say thank you to him before I go.'

'I thought you said you were staying?'

Cyngen gave a slightly apologetic smile. 'A slip of the tongue. I'm not getting any younger, my lord king.'

Aethelwulf looked at him intently. 'Are you well, my lord king?'

'In my heart and in my soul, better than I have ever been.'

'And in your body?'

'I have been ill,' Cyngen admitted. 'The doctors tell me I have recovered.'

'And have you?'

'The fever has passed. That's why I'm out, making the most of it. But since you ask, I will tell you. There is no reason not to. Death is close to me, my lord king. I do not expect to last through another winter. I will die this year. It is no sadness for me. I am where I want to be.'

Aethelwulf's face softened. 'Let me lend you my arm, my lord king. We will get you to the top of this hill.'

Cyngen was living in a cramped pilgrim's hostel near the Colosseum. Aethelwulf, when he saw the noisy, dirty place, immediately invited the Welsh king and his small retinue to come and lodge with him over the river. But Cyngen refused the offer.

'You'll have to forgive me, my lord king. It is not pride and I mean no offence, but my people would not forgive me if I ended my days as a guest of the Saxons. And this place suits me well. I am but a pilgrim, amongst his kind.'

But he did not object to frequent visits from Aethelwulf, and to their two groups joining together to visit the holy sites. The atmosphere in the city was becoming more hostile. Pope Benedict had responded to the proclamations of the emperor's pope, Anastasius, by declaring him excommunicated. Street battles between supporters of the rival popes were breaking out almost every day. The traditional protection afforded to pilgrims could no longer be depended upon. Any individual or small group was at risk if they happened to be in the wrong place at the wrong time. The Welsh group around Cyngen was small and elderly, with the exception of a boy called Owen, who was only a few years older than Alfred. Without the protection of the Saxon guard, they would have been in danger every time they left the hostel. In the circumstances, Cyngen saw nothing wrong in accepting a degree of Saxon protection. There were pilgrims of all nationalities here and differences which might seem insuperable at home became less important when compared with the goal they shared. Besides, he liked Aethelwulf's company.

But the old king was becoming daily more frail and on some days kept to his bed. This is what happened on a day in September when Aethelwulf had decided on an expedition to the early Christian catacombs on the Appian Way, south of the city.

'He's going to stay where he is,' Aethelwulf reported to his party outside Cyngen's hostel, having gone in to see him. 'Huw and Owen will look after him. Efan, Elisyth and Bryn are coming with us.'

Alfred enjoyed their ride through the city streets. They always started out on an expedition in the early morning to avoid travelling in the heat of the day. At this time, the city was mostly quiet with people still indoors. The past was always present in Rome, but usually as something sad and lost – gigantic ruins which spoke of a mastery long gone. But in the glitter of morning dew, the remnants of the past still held the promise of something new. Looking across at the ruined forum and the wooded hills of the Palatine above, it was possible to imagine that they were only quiet because it was still so early. The shops and temples in the forum would be opening soon, great men and women in the palaces above would be emerging from their dreams of conquest, and in an hour or two, the whole place would be humming with the bustle of a thousand years ago, not standing in reproachful desolation.

They kept to the right below the hill on which St Gregory's monastery stood. To the left, lay the Lateran Palace and the great church of St John Lateran. Places becoming daily more dangerous for those travelling east from the Vatican. But safe enough at this hour. They were soon out of the built-up area and picking their way through ruins and open land towards the old city walls.

At the old walls, they passed through a gate and out onto the Appian Way. The most famous of all the ancient Roman roads was now a bumpy, dusty chaos of broken stones and weeds. Horse and man had to concentrate on where they were putting their feet.

They stopped at a church where, according to their guide, St Peter had been stopped from fleeing Rome by a vision of Christ walking in the opposite direction. From there, it was only a short distance to the first of the catacombs. Off their horses, they followed the guide in a torch-lit procession through underground tunnels to the burial places of martyrs and popes. Many of them buried in secret with a few cryptic signs, only to be understood by the few who believed in the underground faith. The occasional beautiful fresco came as a surprise. Mostly it was dark and gloomy, with the more susceptible members of the group sensing ancient terrors still hanging in the air.

After leaving the last of the catacombs, it was time for the midday meal and a rest while the sun blazed down from its zenith.

'We ought not to leave it too late before returning, sire,' Markward advised Aethelwulf after a couple of hours. 'We should try to get through the city while there are still not too many on the streets. Late afternoon is often when the trouble starts.'

Aethelwulf scowled. Running scared between city mobs was not how he had envisaged his visit to the Holy City. 'Very well,' he replied. 'Let's get going.'

Even at the city gate, they could sense a difference from the morning. A group of people stared up at them as they rode past. The Saxon guard adjusted their weapons, sensing they might be needed. As they rode through the ruins towards the centre, they could hear a growing noise up ahead, as well as an ominous plume of black smoke.

Markward looked worried. 'We'd better send a guard on ahead to see where the disturbance is. We may need to go round it.'

'If there's trouble, then we're better facing it together,' said Aethelwulf. 'We don't want to split up. Besides, we have to get the Welsh back to their hostel.'

'They can come with us until it's blown over.'

'What about Cyngen?'

Markward looked uncomfortable. 'No one's going to attack an old sick man in his bed,' he muttered, looking far from convinced. Who could predict what a mob would do once its blood was roused?

'Owen!' shouted one of the Welsh. The Welsh boy was running down the hill towards them.

'Something has happened'" Aethelwulf exclaimed. 'What is it, boy?'

Owen had pulled up, panting, beside them.

'There's a battle going on!' he gasped, recovering his breath. 'It started by the Colosseum but it's spread all around the hostel. Some of the nearby buildings are on fire.'

'Is the hostel burning?' Aethelwulf demanded.

'Not yet, but . . .'

'Where's King Cyngen?'

'He's still in his bed. We can't get him out. It was hard enough for me to get through the fighting. I don't know how we can get a sick man out. I said I'd try to find you. He . . . he's not well, sire,' the boy's eyes showed his distress. 'I think he may be dying. And this may well finish him off. But if we can't get him out, he may burn to death.'

'That will not happen,' Aethelwulf declared. 'We'll get him out. You can show us the way.'

'Yes, sire.'

They made their way hurriedly towards the centre. Turning the corner below the hill of St Gregory's monastery, they suddenly saw a mass of shouting men facing up to one another. Some were throwing stones, others had makeshift spears or knives in their hands.

'Can we get round another way?' Aethelwulf asked Owen. 'Maybe by the Lateran?'

'There'll be more men coming from there,' said Markward. 'Anastasius's supporters advance from the Lateran and Benedict's from the Vatican.'

The hostel was on the north side of the Colosseum. They could see the smoke from there billowing ahead of them.

Aethelwulf looked around him rather helplessly. 'What do we do, then?'

Alfred felt a sudden pain in his heart seeing his father at a loss. His father always knew what to do, always made the decisions. But now he seemed to be asking someone else to do so. An old man seeking direction from others.

'We'll cut our way through, sire,' said Osric, captain of the guard. 'It's no different from what we've done a hundred times before. This rabble will soon part when they see real soldiers coming at them.'

'Yes, of course,' said Aethelwulf. 'You're right, Osric.' He encouraged his horse a few paces forward.

'Sire,' Osric said tentatively, 'there's no reason for you to risk your life in this. It will be easier for us if we have only one king to look out for. Owen can show us the way.'

'That's good advice,' said Marward approvingly. 'There is your son to consider also, sire. And these people,' he indicated the other pilgrims. 'They need to be got to safety. I can lead you round by the river to the Vatican while your guard rescue King Cyngen and bring him to you there.'

Aethelwulf sat motionless on his horse for a few moments. 'Very well,' he said, a little sadly. 'It shall be as you say.' He looked over at Owen. 'Do you know how to ride, my boy?'

'Yes, sire.'

'Then take my horse,' said Aethelwulf, dismounting. 'He's a steady animal. He won't take fright.'

'But what will you ride, sire?' asked Markward.

'I will walk. Like King Cyngem, I am but a pilgrim. And the distance is not far.'

They watched Owen, Osric and the guard ride down into the shouting mass of men and saw it part before them. Then they turned and followed Markward as he led them down to the river and along small streets back to the Vatican bridge.

Osric and the guard brought Cyngen on a makeshift litter to Aethelwulf's house in the Saxon quarter. The ailing Welsh king was too weak to ride a horse. Osric and his men had cut their way through to the hostel where he was lying helpless, carried him out and placed him across a horse until they had ridden back out through the fighting crowd, whereupon they rigged up a slightly more comfortable means of transporting him the rest of the way.

Cyngen was only barely aware of his surroundings, certainly no longer in any condition to object to Saxon hospitality. Aethelwulf arranged for him to be installed in his bed and examined by his doctor.

'He has a fever,' said the doctor, reporting back. 'It's most likely been made worse by his being moved. He shouldn't be moved any more.'

'Is there anything you can do for him?'

The doctor looked doubtful. 'I have given him borage and camomile for the fever. The problem is that he is very weak. Normally, I would bleed for a fever, but he is too weak for that.'

'Do you expect him to live?'

The doctor suppressed a scowl. It was a question he hated, and one that people always asked. What did his expectations have to do with anything? Time would tell soon enough.

'He's an old man,' he replied. 'And he's very weak, as I say. He may pull through, but . . .' how to put it? The king was religious. 'The Lord may have decided that it is his time.'

Aethelwulf nodded. 'He said himself he was going to die soon.'

'I'll look in on him again tomorrow,' said the doctor.

Aethelwulf found accommodation nearby for the rest of the Welsh party, who took turns to sit with and tend their king. Aethelwulf spent time himself sitting at Cyngen's bedside. He didn't know why he felt such tenderness towards him. He hardly knew the man. And yet he had sensed a kind of fellowship with him on their first meeting. Another royal pilgrim. It was as if he was looking at himself in a few years' time. There were lessons to be learned at his bedside, even if Cyngen never spoke again.

Outside the sick room, attempts were being made to resolve the conflict between the rival popes and their supporters. Markward reported back to Aethelwulf on the progress of these. 'Neither's going to back down, but they can't afford to let the fighting go on. It's very damaging for the reputation of the Church to have the Holy See a battleground.'

'It's taken them this long to realise that?' Aethelwulf's views on the sanctity and wisdom of Rome had taken a blow over the past few weeks.

'I think that each was hoping to scare the other away, but that's clearly not going to happen. So, they're going to have to have another election between the two candidates.'

'Who will vote?'

'The same as before.'

'Then Benedict's bound to win, isn't he? Rome won't accept a pope foisted on them by the emperor, unless the emperor is at its gates with an army.'

Markward gave a thin smile. 'You have a firm grasp of the workings of the Holy See, my lord king.'

'So, the emperor's given up?'

'I think his legates have decided that they can't just continue on their present course. The emperor's action in appointing his own pope without consulting anyone else has always put in a difficult position. Benedict is becoming ever more popular. If he wins another election, then it will make it easier for those who've been opposing him to change course and declare their support. The Holy Spirit will have spoken.'

'He spoke before.'

'Well, yes, but without consulting the emperor. If He says the same thing despite the emperor's response, then it's more convincing.'

'And the emperor?'

'Is a long way away. And, it's understood, not in the best of health.'

'Well, the sooner it's sorted out, the better,' said Aethelwulf. 'I came here to pay my respects to the Holy Father. I wasn't expecting to have to make a choice.'

The holding of another election increased the tension in an already febrile city. Aethelwulf decided to stay in his house until it was over. He had no desire to be caught up in another street battle. Markward brought him reports, but he wasn't that interested in them. He supposed he wanted Benedict to win, but the whole business sickened him. The thought of pledging his country's allegiance and presenting a significant amount of its wealth to someone who owed his position to a Roman mob was galling in the extreme. It was hard to see the working of the Holy Spirit in this blatant power struggle.

But people still came to Rome with faith in their hearts. Still wanted to die here, believing it to be more sacred ground than that from which they came. Cyngen, for example. Whoever was elected pope would make no difference to him. It was becoming increasingly clear that he was never going to rise from his bed again. And yet one morning, as Aethelwulf was sitting beside him, the old man opened his eyes and looked at him with recognition. The fever appeared to have left him.

'You have been very kind to me, my lord king,' he smiled. 'Are my men nearby?'

'They are. Would you like to see them?'

'I need to see Huw. I have some instructions for him. I have no control over what happens to my kingdom. But there are some private matters which he will be able to deal with for me.'

'I'll send for him.'

'Before you do,' Cyngen propped himself up in the bed a little to look more closely at Aethelwulf. 'I must ask for your kindness once more.'

'Anything I can do for you, I will.'

'I am going to die, I know that. This may be the last time I can speak to you. I want to be buried at St Priscilla's cemetery. There are other Cymru there. Huw has all the details.'

'It shall be done.'

Cyngen nodded. 'I know I can rely on you. Huw will return to Powys to deal with my private affairs and convey news of my death. He will be trusted. Efan, Elisyth and Bryn are old, like me. They will want to stay on in Rome.'

'I will ensure they are cared for.'

'That will not be necessary. With me gone, they can be simple pilgrims. The city is used to such. I can leave them enough to guard them from starvation, and that is all they need. It is Owen I seek your help for.'

Aethelwulf waited while Cyngen gathered his strength to continue.

'His family was killed in a raid. He has no one. It is not easy in Cymru for someone without family. If he goes back there, he is likely to face servitude whoever comes to power. And he's a bright lad – he deserves better than that. I'd hope to find him a position of his own, but,' he gave a slight shrug, 'there's no more I can do for him now.'

'I will find him a place in my court,' Aethelwulf replied. 'A place of honour. He will remind me of you.'

Cyngen smiled again. 'Thank you, my brother in Christ. Now, if you don't mind, I need to speak to Huw while I'm still able.'

Shortly after speaking to Huw, Cyngen slipped back gently into unconsciousness. He lingered for three days, watched over by his attendants, before dying at the same time as the streets outside erupted in noisy celebration. The results were in and Pope Benedict re-elected with an overwhelming majority.

*

As the months passed, Alfred began to feel bored in Rome. At first, it had been exciting – the heat, the massive stone buildings and ruins, the quick, dark people with their explosive language, so unlike the Latin he studied with Colman. And the danger of the streets with the sudden massing of men, the unaccountable angers, the riots and rumours of riots – frightening at times, but not boring. But with the re-election of Pope Benedict, the violence in the city ebbed away as swiftly as it had arisen. The stifling summer gave way to a serene autumn. News from the north was reassuring for the city – the emperor had died. His successor would have his hands full in securing his own position. He'd not have the opportunity to seek to impose his will elsewhere for a number of years. Benedict and Rome were safe. The knowledge of having won this particular battle infused the city with good humour. The emperor's death, presaged by two shooting stars, was seen by many as a sign that God was with His Holy City and its chosen pope.

And so, the streets were safe now for pilgrims. Which, for the Saxon party, meant more trips to churches. Aethelwulf was determined to make the most of the opportunity to pray at every church in Rome. Alfred had not known it possible for one city to contain so many churches. At times, it felt that all he had done in his life was visit churches, and that it was all he was ever going to do. The sense of frustration he felt at entering yet another dim interior, with yet another dark-eyed priest assuring them that their salvation would be assured by the protection of the particular saint to whom the church was dedicated (often someone he'd never heard of until then), the 'Alleluia's and 'Praise the Lord's of the tedious pilgrim who always seemed to be in the party . . . troubled him. He wondered if it meant he was a bad person. To begin with, he'd enjoyed the churches. Now, they irritated him. Nothing had ever compared to that morning in St Peter's when he'd been anointed by the old pope. He began to fear that nothing ever would.

He was disappointed, too, in the new pope. Benedict was a small, sharp-featured man with none of the warmth which Alfred told himself he remembered from the old pope. He didn't smile, or if he did, he didn't smile at him. Even the amount of gifts which Aethelwulf presented him with – the gold, the silver, the jewels, the precious fabrics – provoked only the briefest of acknowledgements, as if they were merely payments due. Alfred wondered how this small, cold man could have provoked the passions he'd seen in the streets outside.

He began to feel homesick. He wondered how Sideways was getting on without him. He even wondered about Redi. Would he be grown up and a warrior by the time he got back home? Would he ever get back home? His father showed no sign of wanting to leave.

The days before Christmas were a distraction. The weather broke and the rain, with its reminder of home, was somehow reassuring. It also discouraged yet more expeditions to far-flung churches. They stayed close to the Vatican and went to the Advent services in St Peter's. Alfred felt the excitement of those around him as the days grew darker and the great day of the birth of light drew closer.

Christmas Eve was wet and windy. The great night service, presided over by the pope, began at sunset in the basilica church of St Mary Major on the Esquiline Hill in the old city. They rode through lashing rain past streets of ruins to take their place in the great marble church, which housed five plain sycamore planks – the holy crib from Bethlehem. Throughout that long night of prayers, readings and chants proclaiming the wonder and mystery of it all, Alfred was happy to share some of his father's devotion. He felt the presence of another world, in which time and troubles had no meaning. Maybe he wasn't such a bad person after all if he could feel that. Even the pope looked grander and more noble in his red and gold vestments at the centre of the ceremony.

After an outburst of joy and celebration at midnight, when his father embraced Alfred with tears in his eyes, the pope said his first mass. And then they proceeded with torches through glistening streets to a smaller church on the Palatine Hill, where they prayed and waited for the dawn, when the pope said the second mass. Then, in the grey light of Christmas morning, they made their way back to St Peter's for the third and final mass.

When all the celebrations of Christmas had subsided, Aethelwulf fell ill. Alfred had not known his father ill before and an icy fear gripped his heart. Something told him that his father might not mind dying now. That's what kings of Wessex did, wasn't it? They went to Rome to die. But what would happen to him if his father died? Would he ever get back home? Or would he be made a priest and have to stay in this foreign land, as Redi had taunted?

The following weeks were anxious ones in the Saxon quarter as the king lay ill in his bed and the rain churned the streets outside to mud. Doctors gathered in the house and conferred. Alfred stared at them nervously as birds of ill omen. Even the pope came to visit the sick man. He gave Alfred a searching glance on leaving, which made Alfred even more uneasy. Had they been discussing him? He needed no encouragement from Colman to join the pilgrims in the Saxon church of St Mary's in the daily prayers for his father's recovery. But then he was praying for himself as well.

Whether it was due to his people's prayers, the ministrations of the doctors, his own resilience, or a combination of all three, Aethelwulf began to recover. Alfred had not been allowed to see him for weeks while the illness was at its height, but one morning he was told he could do so.

His father was lying in bed, propped up on some pillows. He looked tired and his face was more lined than Alfred remembered. It was something of a shock to see him lying in bed.

'Are you going to get better?' It sounded stupid coming out like that. But he wanted to know.

His father smiled wearily. 'I think so, Alfred. I believe the Lord has a few more things for me to do before he calls me home.'

'Can we go home? We've been here a long time.'

Was that a look of pain in his father's eyes? Or irritation? 'In time, Alfred. In time.'

He had to be content with that. He knew that his father would need to recover his strength before embarking on the long journey home. The following weeks saw his father leave his bed, but he gave no indication of planning their return. Perhaps it was the lingering effects of the illness, but he was lethargic and passive, uninterested in anything beyond the daily round of services which occupied the Saxon pilgrims of St May's. Alfred fretted with impatience. When his father had said that the Lord had more for him to do, surely he meant more than counting down the days until Ash Wednesday?

He confessed his impatience to Owen. The Welsh boy was a few years older than him, but he was still by far the nearest to his own age amongst all the pilgrims. He might have some other hope for his life than to die in Rome.

But Owen was used to waiting, and having his future dependent upon the wishes of others.

'Nothing will happen until after Easter, Alfred. Winter is not the time for kings to make long journeys. Not unless they have to.'

'He doesn't even think of leaving after Easter. He's not said anything about doing so.'

'He will want to hear what Markward has to say first.'

'Markward? Is he coming back?'

The cleric had left them months ago on hearing the news of the emperor's death. Alfred hadn't expected to see him again.

'If he doesn't, your father won't move. We have to travel over imperial lands. Markward is a guarantee of the emperor's protection. There's a new emperor now. Any old guarantees are worthless. And there's King Charles to consider as well.'

'King Charles is our friend. We stayed with him coming out here.'

'He may be your friend, but he's also the new emperor's uncle. Your father will want to know what the relationship is between them before travelling over both their lands. A new reign can be a dangerous time, Alfred.'

The months passed. Lent came with the spring. Alfred found it difficult to pay much attention to the sombre church services, but he identified with the emphasis on waiting and looking ahead. Easter would bring resurrection, he was told. Perhaps, it would also bring Markward? The waiting was hard. Less hard than dying on a cross, though.

Markward arrived back in Rome on Palm Sunday. Alfred couldn't help thinking more of this than of Christ's entry into Jerusalem as he waved his palm in celebration. Nothing would happen until after Easter. But at least it might happen then.

Holy Week seemed to take over the whole city of Rome, the entire population entering into the drama of God's last days on earth. Alfred, reassured by Markward's return and seeing a connection somehow, joined those around him in letting the events of hundreds of years ago in a different place, with their oft-repeated emotions of rejoicing, despair, guilt, agony, loss and mysterious triumph, flood through him.

After Easter, Aethelwulf remained closeted in meetings with Markward and others for a number of days. Alfred waited nervously before being rewarded at the end of the meetings by his father telling him, somewhat gloomily, that their time in Rome was ended. They would be leaving the following week, stopping once more with King Charles at Verberie, before continuing back home to Wessex.

8. Hospitality

King Charles was used to people predicting his imminent demise. He had not been expected to survive a sickly childhood. But he had, much to the annoyance of his elder half-brothers, who were already men, ruling their own lands, when he was born.

His only supporter throughout his vulnerable childhood had been his father, Emperor Louis, son of the great Charlemagne, who had grown tired of the ingratitude and rebellions of his other sons and determined that his youngest would not be deprived of a share in his inheritance. Charles was the only son who had not rebelled against his father, perhaps because he was too young to be in a position to do so.

The emperor's attempts to secure a patrimony for Charles had provoked further rebellions from his outraged elder brothers, Lothair and Ludwig. Emperor Louis had managed to eventually suppress the rebellions and have Charles declared king of Western Francia. But the emperor's death shortly afterwards had left Charles vulnerable once more. He had only just become a man and the loyalty of his nobles was untested. Had his brothers combined against him, they could easily have deposed him.

But the greatness of the empire forged by Charlemagne was only matched by his descendants' mistrust of one another. If the new Charles was deposed, then who would rule the lands he had been given? The new emperor, Lothair, had no doubt that he was the man. His brother, Ludwig, king of Eastern Francia, disagreed. Charles, who was not a man to bear unhelpful grudges, saw his opportunity. Quicker-witted than either of his brothers, he persuaded Ludwig that Lothair had designs on Eastern as well as Western Francia. It did not take a great deal to convince Ludwig of his elder brother's likely treachery. He entered into an alliance with Charles and together they defeated Lothair, forcing him to sign a treaty guaranteeing their rule over Eastern and Western Francia respectively. Lothair had remained as emperor but his rule was restricted to the Middle Kingdom and Italy.

Since Lothair's defeat, twelve years ago, King Charles's rule in the west had been fairly secure, at least as far as attacks from his own family were concerned. But his kingdom was under regular attack from northern pagans, who sailed down its great rivers in their terrible longships, dealing out death and destruction everywhere they landed. Early in his reign, they had even penetrated as far down the Seine as Paris, plundering the city and only retreating after payment of a heavy ransom. Over the years, King Charles had deployed any number of means to contain the pagans – he had fought them, he had bribed them, he had formed alliances with them, he had spied on them, encouraged treachery and dissension amongst them, and even tried to blockade the rivers down which they sailed. He had had some success, but it was never total. The pagans always came back, in what seemed an inexhaustible flood, descending from their icy strongholds. The struggle against them was draining the land of its wealth and the people of their spirit. Charles was well aware that there were many in his kingdom who were beginning to ask themselves whether the crippling taxes required to defend against or pay off the attackers were worth it when they didn't protect against the ongoing violence and disruption. Deals were being made with the pagans by small groups and even nobles for protection. And those deals could in time, if co-ordinated by an intelligent pagan leader (of which he knew there were several), lead to insurrection.

And now Emperor Lothair had died. There was little to be feared for the moment from his son, the new emperor. Like all new rulers, he would be intent on securing his authority over the lands he had inherited. Ludwig, however, was another matter. The East Frankish king was now the oldest member of the family. Charles knew that Ludwig had grown to resent the adroit alliance against Lothair into which he had been manoeuvred. Like all of Charlemagne's descendants, he had ambitions to be sole ruler of the mighty empire. To do so, he would have to deal with his slippery younger brother once and for all. And now, with the new emperor otherwise engaged, was the propitious time to do so.

Charles could guess the way his brother's mind would be working. From spies, he knew that merchants from East Francia had been seen visiting various nobles in his own kingdom. He could not be sure that they were agents from his brother but he had his suspicions. Certain nobles could never be trusted. Robert of Anjou had ambitions of his own, which Charles had always checked. He might have calculated he would do better under the rule of a distant Ludwig. And Pepin of Aquitaine, whom Charles had imprisoned, had recently escaped and was back in his own lands. He would certainly be willing to come to an understanding with Ludwig.

All these thoughts were in King Charles's mind as he sat in his study at Verberie, listening to a report from Count Baldwin on the latest pagan attacks down the

Seine. A useful man, this Baldwin. Charles prided himself in being a good judge of people – he would not have survived as long as he had were he not. Baldwin was young but had already proved himself a fierce fighter. He came from forestland in the north-east of the kingdom. Not wealthy, which had its advantages in a soldier. It meant he was more likely to be loyal. He still had his way to make in the world, and the best way he could do that would be to win battles for his king.

Baldwin was intelligent as well as brave, capable of executing the more subtle tactics which Charles often preferred to counter the pagans. Particularly at a time like the present when, due to the scheming of nobles such as Robert and Pepin, he had less men to call upon than he would have liked. His summons for troops had only been patchily answered. The nobles whose lands were far distant from the Seine always found reasons why they could not respond. He didn't have that many troops and he needed to keep some back in case Ludwig took the opportunity of his engagement to invade. But he badly needed a victory against the pagans to quell the rising discontent.

So, what to do? Try to divide the pagans so there were less of them to attack? He had done it before – the pagans were a shifting alliance of war bands, who nearly always split up in their attacks to cover the widest area and capture the most booty. The problem was knowing where they were going to attack before they did so. But there was a solution to that if one could only find the right pagan, willing to earn his gold in a less strenuous manner than attacking villages and churches. The pagans' fondness for gold often outweighed their loyalty to one another, particularly those from another war band.

For the past weeks, King Charles had posted men up and down the Seine to shadow the pagans, learn what they could about them, and try and establish contact with a leader willing to sell information about attacks. And now it seemed that this policy may have borne results. Count Baldwin had ridden in with news of a successful contact with one of the pagan leaders.

'You're sure of this information?' Charles asked. He was not about to believe something just because he wanted to.

'I am, sire,' Baldwin replied.

'You've met the man?'

'I have.'

'How?'

'I went to their camp disguised as a peasant with a couple of my men and some sheep. The pagans are used to such visits.'

Charles nodded. He might disapprove, but he could understand. If he was a peasant with a pagan war band in the vicinity, he might decide to take them presents as well. 'And who is he?'

'His name's Bjorn. He's the leader of one of the war bands. I found out from one of his men that he'd had a fierce argument with Sydroc, who leads the other band, over some allocation of booty a couple of weeks ago. They patched it up but I was told that there's still bad blood between them.'

'And you think that's the reason?'

'Well, he's not doing it for nothing.'

'How much did you give him?'

'All I had. I was in no position to haggle. And I promised him as much again if we had a victory.'

'How are you going to fulfil that promise?'

'I was hoping that you would do that, sire. He's a valuable acquisition. And the prospect of future gain might lessen the chance of his having an attack of conscience and telling Sydroc to cancel the attack. You don't need to pay him any more if you don't want to. But it might make the prospect of future deals with pagans less likely.'

Charles frowned. He didn't like being told what to do. This young man was a little too full of himself. But he had done well. It took a certain coolness to enter a pagan camp and negotiate a betrayal with its leader. And the north-east was a long way from Anjou or Aquitaine.

'So, where are they heading?'

'Up the Eure to Chartres.'

'When?'

'Bjorn said he could delay it for a week or so.'

'That should give us time, then.'

'Yes, sire.'

'Stay here until I call for you again.'

There was no harm in reminding the young man who was in charge.

'Welcome back, Alfred.'

Princess Judith, smiling at him. There was something different about her, but he couldn't decide what. Was she a little taller? Still small for her age, with the bright assumption of superiority he remembered. Her face a little finer? Her hair was certainly different. She looked older, he decided – the gap between them didn't appear to be lessening. He suspected that, however far he travelled, she would always be treating him as one of her baby brothers.

She didn't ask him about Rome. Already, the time he had spent there seemed distant. The journey back to Verberie had not been easy. It had rained constantly, except in the mountains, when it had snowed. His father had fallen ill again and they had had to stop in a monastery until he was well enough to continue. Alfred had felt his own illness rising in his gut during the procession of muddy days, but he gritted his teeth to beat it down. If he fell ill, he wasn't sure his father would think him important enough to stop for.

There were other hazards to the journey as well as the weather. As Owen had said, a new reign is a dangerous time. Bands of armed men were at large in the imperial lands, their allegiance uncertain. On some days, the returning pilgrims were forced to stop because of warnings of men up ahead. Markward and others would ride on to negotiate a safe passage. Alfred understood that payment of a certain amount of gold was often necessary to enable them to continue their bedraggled journey. The helpless look in his father's eyes, which he had seen first in Rome, appeared more often now. If only they could get back home and put this sense of being at the mercy of others behind them.

It was a relief when they reached Verberie. Alfred would have preferred to have kept on going. His longing for home was becoming more acute, even though he didn't know what would be waiting for him there. Sideways, hopefully. For the thousandth time, he regretted having been made to leave his lopsided friend behind. He was tired of being surrounded by strangers.

But his father, having reached the security of Verberie, showed no signs of wanting to move on. King Charles held a great feast in his honour, plying him with questions about Rome and Alfred sensed his father's spirits reviving in the warmth of his reception.

A few days after their arrival, Alfred was heartened by the appearance of a familiar face. Swithun! Surely, that must mean they'd be going home soon? Why else would Swithun be coming to see them?

Swithun came to find him the following day.

'You're looking well, Alfred. Did you enjoy seeing Rome again?'

'I want to go home, Father. Why can't we go home?'

'There are some things which need to be sorted out first. You've been away a long time.'

'I know! That's why I want to go home.'

Swithun ran an affectionate hand through Alfred's hair. 'Soon, Alfred, soon. Is Princess Judith looking after you?'

'She's bossier than Elsa.'

'Prerogative of the elder sister.'

'And she thinks she knows everything.'

'She is a very accomplished young woman. But even accomplished young women need friends. Are you her friend, Alfred?'

Alfred looked at his old guardian in puzzlement. Why was he asking that? 'I suppose so,' he said eventually.

'Good.' Swithun didn't seem to be expecting anything more.

'I don't think she needs me as a friend,' Alfred continued, still puzzled. 'She has plenty of friends.'

'Maybe so, but she'll need you, Alfred. She'll need your goodwill. You'll give her that, won't you? I know you will.'

'I don't understand.'

'No, I don't suppose you do,' Swithun gave a tight smile. 'But you will. And then you'll remember this conversation.'

He clearly wasn't going to explain further. Alfred dismissed such adult mysteries. What did it matter what he thought of Princess Judith? He wouldn't be in her strange country much longer. 'Are you going back home, Father?'

'Yes, tomorrow.'

'Can I go with you?'

'No. You need to stay here a little longer, Alfred. Try and enjoy yourself – not many boys have seen as much as you have.'

'I want my dog.'

'Ah, I'm sorry. I should have brought him with me. He's being well looked after. Don't worry, it won't be long.'

The evening after Swithun's departure, Alfred was told that there would be a great feast at which he would sit beside his father at the high table. He was to have a bath and a fine new tunic was put out for him. It reminded him of the preparations made before his presentation to the old pope.

After his bath, he put up with servants fussing around him. The warm water had left him feeling hazy. It was nice to be treated as important again. It hadn't happened much recently. Once his various attendants were satisfied that he looked presentable, he was escorted down some stairs towards the great hall. But before he could get there, another servant approached and said that Princess Judith wanted to see him in her chamber.

Princess Judith? That wasn't usual. For all her domineering ways, she'd never summoned him to her before. He remembered the curious conversation with Swithun and for the first time felt uneasy. Had Swithun been trying to tell him something? Was this evening about Princess Judith? And him? Why else was he going to be sitting at the high table? He dismissed the thought. It wasn't possible. She was so much older than him. And she'd told him when they first met that she wouldn't be marrying him. But such things did happen when kings wanted to seal alliances. Normally, the male was older, but not always.

She was sitting at a table, looking more regal than he had ever seen her, a golden coronet in her dark hair, golden earrings, a necklace of pearls, a sumptuous white gown. A maid was still arranging tresses of her hair. 'It's all right, Jeanne, you can leave us.'

The maid left. Alfred remained standing.

'You wanted to see me?'

'Yes.' She looked up at him, her eyes troubled. He suddenly realised that she was nervous. 'I wanted to tell you before my father makes his grand announcement this evening.'

He gazed at the glowing pearls around her neck, not wanting to meet her eyes any more. So it was true. Why had no one told him before?

'I am going to marry . . . I am going to be wed to . . . your father.'

His father! He stared at her in astonishment. 'I don't believe it!'

'It's true.'

'But he's so old!'

Her eyes glittered but she said nothing.

'And . . .' he struggled to find words to express what he was thinking. It wasn't just that his father was old in years. In the last few months, he'd seen him ageing rapidly in spirit also. That helpless, resigned look in his eyes. He'd wanted to stay in Rome. His heart was no longer in the present, let alone the future. So, how could he think of marrying this bright, challenging girl? It didn't make sense.

He saw Princess Judith still looking at him, a fixed expression on her face, the glitter in her eyes becoming tears. *She'll need you, Alfred. She'll need your goodwill. You'll give her that, won't you? I know you will.* 'And you're so young,' he concluded lamely.

She smiled through her tears. 'I know that, you know that, but I'm old enough as far as my father's concerned. He's been planning to marry me off for years. And when your mother died, your father became his first choice. His coming out here and their getting on so well sealed the matter. My father is in need of allies, particularly against Uncle Ludwig. I knew then that if your father returned from Rome, I would be marrying him. I've had a lot of time to get used to the idea. But I wasn't sure if you knew. I didn't want your first knowledge of it to be when my father announces it to the world this evening. Did you not suspect anything?'

'Nothing,' said Alfred bitterly. 'You kept your secret well.'

'It's not my secret,' she replied sadly. 'Nothing of it is mine.'

He left Princess Judith's chamber in a sombre mood. What on earth was his father thinking of? And why hadn't he told him of his intention? Did he think it didn't concern him? His feeling towards his father had undergone a lot of changes in the past year, but this was the first time he had made him angry. When they met outside the great hall, he stared resentfully at him.

'So, you know,' Aethelwulf said simply.

'I found out. Not from you!'

'It's a matter of state, Alfred. An alliance between countries involving much negotiation. You have to learn that as a king's son.'

'And Princess Judith?'

'She has always known it.'

Which was true, he thought, sitting beside his father at the high table, listening to King Charles announce the engagement. She had always known that she was a pawn, to be deployed by her father to his best advantage. Just as Elsa had been married to a Mercian king over twice her age. But his father must be four times older than Princess Judith! Easily old enough to be her grandfather. Was he the only person to see the discrepancy as they stood to receive the acclamations of the Frankish court? His father's large, stooped frame and weary eyes; Princess Judith tiny and bright beside him, glittering with gold and jewels, a fixed smile on her face. Playing her part.

*

King Charles was in a good mood. The pagans had been been seen heading up the Eure towards Chartres, as predicted. Bjorn had delayed them long enough for preparations to be made for their reception there. That man had done well – he would definitely reward him. If things went as planned, Bjorn would certainly not be welcome amongst his own kind again. If some of the pagans could be made to swear fealty, then it would be worth a little land to set them fighting against one another. Charles was well aware from his own experience that blood loyalties can count for little against self-interest.

But he should not get ahead of himself. There was the present action to accomplish first. He had sent Count Baldwin ahead with a strong contingent of mounted men to the woods before Chartres. From there, they should be invisible to the pagans coming up the river. Baldwin had orders to delay his emergence from the woods until the pagan ships were in sight and to intercept them at a ford before the town where the water was shallow enough for horses to cross. When confronted by well-armed men on horses, pagan war bands intent on plunder normally retreated back downriver, relying on the speed of their accursed ships to soon outdistance any attackers. And away from the ford by Chartres, the Eure was too deep for horses to cross.

King Charles was relying upon the pagans retreating back down the river. Baldwin had strict orders to prevent them landing and continuing on overland. It was doubtful that they would do so. To do so would be to leave their ships in enemy hands and a pagan prized his ship almost as highly as he did his life, certainly more highly than other people's lives. With a ship, he could strike almost anywhere and melt away at will. Without a ship, he was just another man to be hunted down.

Even so, if the pagans realised that they had been betrayed they might, if their leader was intelligent, avoid doing the obvious. If men had been positioned in front of them in the woods before Chartres, what was to stop men being positioned behind them downriver as well? And although there was not time to blockade the river entirely, obstacles could be placed in it to be impede the pagans' progress and piers erected from which archers could shoot into the ships. King Charles had had some success against pagan war bands with such tactics before. Would this Sydroc be aware of that? And if he did, would he have the coolness to avoid retreating back into a trap when confronted by Baldwin's attack? Might he not break through and proceed on to Chartres? Or even – he had heard of it being done – cut out across country with his men carrying their boats to land them on another river? Well, Baldwin was there to prevent that. And Baldwin had sworn to accomplish his task, or die in the attempt. Which was only sensible – if the pagans did break through after all these preparations then Baldwin might just as well be dead. Charles hadn't needed to spell that out. Baldwin was no fool. And he was a good fighter. This was his chance to show it.

Charles was confident enough of success to invite his guest and prospective son-in-law along to witness the engagement. There would be no harm in having him return to Wessex with memories of a successful Frankish attack on the pagans. It would show him that he was not the only one who could trap and destroy them. The completeness of Aethelwulf's success at Aclea had resounded throughout Europe and Charles hankered after something equally impressive. And not just as a warning to his brother, Ludwig.

He decided also that it was time for his eldest son, Louis, to witness combat, and this was a suitable occasion as he could be kept at a safe distance. The news that Louis was to go had led to Alfred beseeching his father that he be allowed to go too. Aethelwulf was reluctant but Charles was impressed by the vehemence of Alfred's pleading.

'Let him come,' he said to Aethelwulf. 'He'll be safe enough with Louis. We should accustom our boys to what fighting is about. Who knows when they'll have to take over from us? Something tells me that boy of yours is not destined for the Church. And, even if he is, churchmen need to know about fighting, too.'

They rode out from Verberie, passing through a quiet and nervous Paris – Alfred noticed burnt buildings here as well – to the banks of the Eure. The pagan ships had passed through towards Chartres. The place where the royal party stopped was now full of activity. Men were piling rocks into the river, carpenters were sawing and hammering away building piers. Armed men were assembling. Alfred felt a thrill of excitement charged with fear. His first battle. Would it happen? Would he get to see those terrible pagans who had killed his brother, whose threat hung over all their lives?

He could tell that he was not alone in experiencing such feelings. The excitement and fear he felt within him was visible on the faces of those around him, particularly the younger men, whose first engagement this might be. Many of the older men seemed withdrawn, lost in their own thoughts, preparing themselves for what might come. But the eyes of the young glittered with the same emotions Alfred felt within himself. The very air seemed to taste of anticipation.

King Charles was calm and methodical, inspecting the work and issuing orders. To begin with, Alfred, Louis and Owen followed around in the group surrounding him and Aethelwulf, until Charles noticed them and ordered them taken away to some high ground overlooking the river, a bowshot away from any danger. Alfred was secretly not unhappy to be ordered to follow Colman and other non-combatants away from the river and he sensed that Louis felt the same. Owen, however, bristled with irritation at being forced to accompany them.

It was a fine, sunny day. The heat was building. It would have been enjoyable to be basking in the sunshine were it not for the steadily increasing tension which now infected everyone. As the hours passed, King Charles grew more irritable. He came up to the high ground where Alfred and the others were on a number of occasions to try and view some signs of activity further up the river. But a wooded bend a mile of so upstream hid any sign of what might be happening. The Eure glinted lazily in the warm sunshine, a picture of peace. Scouts from Baldwin's force should be arriving by now with news of the pagans retreating back downriver. None had arrived.

King Charles scowled. He'd never trusted Baldwin. The man was all show.

Midday came and went. King Charles was debating with himself whether he should send more scouts out to try and discover what was happening. It would be a sign that he was worried, that things were not going to plan, but his men would know that already. An army waiting to go into battle is sensitive to the slightest shift in expectation. They would all know that the pagans should have been turned back by now.

It had grown quiet. The work was done and everyone now was waiting. A dangerous time. A time when questions as to the commander's wisdom tend to be forming. King Charles paced up and down. It was no good. He had to know the worst, and now.

Suddenly, the ominous silence was broken by shouts coming from the direction of the river. Yes, a scout had arrived. God be praised! He tore down the hill, outdistancing his attendants.

The scout had dismounted from his horse and was surrounded by a pressing mass of people. They parted to let the king through.

'Well?' Charles demanded of the scout, who was still panting from his breakneck ride.

'They're coming!' the scout gasped. 'They tried to break through us. It was a fierce fight. Count Baldwin . . .'

Charles turned away. He could hear about Count Baldwin later. For the moment, there was a job to finish.

'Everyone to their stations by the river!' he commanded. 'They'll be here any minute.' A galloping horse would outdistance longships but the distance to cover was not far.

Sure enough, the first ship was soon spotted rounding the bend in the river. For Alfred, watching from his vantage point, it was a fearsome sight. Crowded with warriors, most of them pulling at an oar, it sped across the river at a pace he would not have believed possible. The warriors who weren't rowing ranged along each side of the ship, swords and spears in hand.

Everything then happened very quickly. Even from a distance, Alfred felt, for the first time, the disorientation of a battle where time and space seem to melt away. He saw the first ship crash into a rock in the river and then try to manoeuvre its way through as archers on the piers unleashed volleys of arrows at the men aboard. He saw his first man die – one of the pagans pierced by an arrow in the throat, blood erupting through his gaping mouth. He felt the pent-up fury of the men in the boat, like animals caught in a trap. He understood the decision of their captain to give up the attempt to get through the blocked river and to steer instead straight for one of the piers and the archers loosing their deadly arrows. With a roar, the pagans leapt onto the pier and started to scythe down those archers who had not been quick enough to get away. But King Charles was ready for them. The archers gave way to spearmen who threw themselves at the pagans, pushing them backwards by force of numbers, toppling many into the river from which they had come.

Other pagan ships were arriving but there was nowhere for them to go. The river ahead of them was a seething mass of bodies, arrows and rocks. One tried to crash its way through all the obstacles but only succeeded in running aground, its men spilling ashore to be butchered by the spearmen. One ship did manage to reverse its course and head back upriver, its men abandoning the ship before reaching the ford. They struck out across country, but away from their ship, in a strange land and isolated, they would be easily hunted down.

Alfred sensed Louis flinch at the slaughter of the helpless pagans. He himself did not flinch. He felt as though he was in a long tunnel, passing untouched through the dead and dying, uncertain of their reality.

And then it was over. The bodies strewn along the river bank were real enough. But Alfred and Louis were not allowed back down to the river. They had witnessed a battle, which is what they had come to see. Now they were being shepherded into carriages for the triumphant return to Verberie.

King Charles had achieved his victory. It was a fine one, but he knew that it would be no more than a temporary check to the flood of pagans invading his land. Next time he might not be so fortunate. But he had sent a signal, both to the pagans and his brother, that anyone who took him on would have a fight on their hands. And he had impressed the king from Wessex, showing him the wisdom of their forming an alliance. He was in a good mood for the whole of the journey back.

Summer had given way to autumn. The weeks following the victory over the pagans on the Eure were taken up with preparations for the marriage between Aethelwulf and Judith. King Charles was determined that this royal wedding would surpass any that had gone before. Like his victory, it was to be a sign of his power. And, for Charles, it was a more satisfying sign than any battle. He had taught himself to be a soldier in order to survive; he had not needed teaching in how to spend money well. A lover of the beautiful, he had transformed his grandfather's forbidding palace at Verberie, installing mosaics and statues, hanging rich tapestries on the walls, furnishing it with costly pieces from the royal workshops.

And now he had an event to stage worthy of such a setting. The great men of the Frankish kingdom were converging on Verberie. Outside in the terraced gardens, carpenters were busy constructing a grand pavilion with a huge stage in front. This wedding was too big for the palace church. There were too many people who wished to see the union of the house of Charlemagne with that of Wessex. And so, on the stage overlooking the gardens, a stone altar was lifted into position and thrones installed for the royal couple to occupy once they were joined in matrimony.

'Will Judith be a queen?' Alfred asked Colman, watching the preparations in some awe.

'Certainly, she'll be a queen,' Colman replied. 'Why do you ask?'

'My mother wasn't a queen.'

'Your mother wasn't the King of Francia's daughter.'

It will make her even more bossy, Alfred thought. But he had little opportunity to find out. He hardly saw Judith. When he did, she was remote, surrounded by her companions, dressed in ever-increasing finery. As though she was leaving what she had been, in order to take up a new role on the stage being prepared for her.

Archbishop Hincmar arrived from Rheims. As the greatest clergyman in the country, he was to conduct the marriage ceremony. He recognised Alfred with a grave bow and said, 'We meet again, my lord prince,' but didn't waste any further time on him. Alfred represented no one but himself now and there were more important people to occupy the archbishop's attention. He spent most of his time closeted with King Charles.

The day of the wedding dawned cloudy. It was late in the year for an outside ceremony. Even King Charles was unable to arrange the weather. Just before Michaelmas, on the cusp of change, when the sun shone, it was serene and golden. But everyone knew that the season of storms was approaching and a cloudy morning brought nervousness and frequent glances up at the sky. If a storm broke on this day of all days then what sort of omen would that be? Even the bishops and clergy clustering around Hincmar were not insensitive to the threat from older gods.

The gardens had been filling up since early morning. It seemed as though half the country was gathering to see their king's daughter married. Seats in front of the stage were put out for members of the family and the most important guests. Everyone else just spread out over the wide terraces and courtyards. Down by the river, fires were lit and breakfasts consumed. For some, the feasting had already begun.

Alfred had been woken early, bathed and given a new suit of clothes for the occasion. The fact that he was the only member of the groom's family present had temporarily increased his importance. He was even allowed Owen as a companion to sit with, which made him feel a little more grown up. But Colman was still with him also, as though a reminder of his junior status. Would he be expected to call Princess Judith mother? The thought made him shiver.

They hung around the great hall for an hour or more, waiting for something to happen. People came in and out with pre-occupied looks on their faces. King Charles appeared once, deep in consultation with Hincmar. Of Aethelwulf, there was no sign.

Eventually, a servant took charge and ushered them out to the seating in front of the stage. The wind had picked up, scudding clouds across the sky. The seating was fairly sheltered but even so Alfred felt the coolness of the day. But it didn't feel as if it was about to rain. The seating filled up around and behind them. Alfred forgot about the weather with the presence and conversations of those around him. He saw Louis and King Charles's other children being shown to seating across an aisle. It would not be long now.

Next to him, Owen was whittling a piece of wood into the shape of a cockerel. Alfred envied the Welsh boy's skill at whittling. He could create any animal from wood. When Alfred tried, he always ended up cutting himself. But more than the skill, he envied Owen's ability to lose himself in the task. He did not get nervous or impatient waiting for things to happen if he had a piece of wood to work on. Colman disapproved, saying that it showed a lack of respect, but Owen did not regard himself as subject to Colman, and no one else seemed to mind, if they noticed. He was an unobtrusive whittler.

Behind them was the sound of people being disturbed by latecomers making their way to seats in the middle of a row. Alfred glanced round and saw the large, red-haired figure of John of Erin, the king's philosopher, with a companion, heading for the seats directly behind them. John was beaming genially in all directions, seemingly delighted by the disapproving looks cast at him. Eventually, he gained his seat and settled into it with a satisfied sigh. Once seated, his companion pulled his cloak around him with a shiver.

'Late in the year for a wedding,' he muttered. 'And to have it outdoors as well. We'll be lucky if we don't all catch a chill.'

'It is late,' John of Erin agreed in what he presumably thought were suitably quiet tones, although Alfred heard him easily enough and expected others did as well. 'But it's appropriate. Autumnal weather for an autumnal wedding.'

Alfred wondered what he meant. Was he referring to his father? But the thought was lost in the beginning of the mass. The unearthly singing of the monks processing down the central aisle between the seating to the pavilion sent a thrill through him, as always. Behind the monks was a whole troop of clergy –

acolytes, deacons and priests. And bringing up the rear was Archbishop Hincmar, in robes of gold and white, bearing a crosier taller than him. Still no sign of Aethelwulf or Judith.

The mass began with scriptural readings interspersed with psalms. And then Hincmar rose from his chair on the stage and made a speech about the sanctity of marriage, his strong voice reaching to the far ends of the gardens, now crowded with people. When he stopped speaking, the sound of horns and trumpets issued from the direction of the palace and everyone turned their heads in expectation. Yes, there they were at last. Two columns coming slowly towards them. The first led by Aethelwulf, stern and mighty in his battle armour, Osric and the rest of the military guard lined up behind him, as though advancing on some ritual combat. The second was led by Judith, tiny in a white gown, with her father beside her and her companions behind. Although King Charles was also wearing armour, it was light and burnished with a soft sheen, not dissimilar to the silk tunic he wore underneath it. The soldiers who followed behind Princess Judith's companions were interspersed with brightly dressed courtiers and relations. While the Saxon column might have been on its way to battle, the Frankish one looked as though it was off to a court entertainment.

'A meeting of worlds,' Alfred heard John of Erin say behind him. He had no difficulty in understanding and agreeing with that. He felt a moment of shame at the rough figures his countrymen cut compared to the elegant Franks. He saw looks of amused contempt pass among some of the well-dressed dignitaries around him.

But that moment passed as his father drew closer and he could see his face. Firm, authoritative and serious, with none of the weakness or hesitancy which Alfred had witnessed in the past few months. He looked like a king, and a king who had won many battles. one beyond the judgment of people who had not. He saw the smiles disappear from the faces of those around him and an air of growing seriousness take hold. Any spy reporting back to King Ludwig of Eastern Francia would be obliged to admit that his brother's new ally looked as though he could fight. And that, for King Charles at least, was the principal object of the exercise.

The two columns had reached the base of the stage. Aethelwulf, Osric, Judith and King Charles mounted some steps onto the stage and took their place in front of the altar, facing Hincmar, who stood before it. The rest of the columns stayed standing where they were so that John of Erin's two worlds remained lined up behind their respective leaders.

Hincmar's strong voice was calling down blessings on the bride and groom, his arms raised aloft, as though by that act alone he could join two countries. Alfred listened in wonder as his father repeated the wedding vows read to him. When it came to Judith's turn, he could barely hear her. Those a few rows back would have heard nothing. But Hincmar seemed satisfied and pronounced them man and wife. Alfred was a little disappointed. He would have expected more ceremony to accompany so significant an event. Even the monks' singing of a *Te Deum* after the pronouncement of marriage didn't sound that different to the psalms they had sung previously. And the mass which followed, although it contained a number of references to Aethelwulf and Judith, followed the same course as every other mass, with Christ's sacrifice at the centre, as always. Alfred would have expected King Charles to have made more of the occasion with such a large audience and after such preparations.

But King Charles was not finished. The wedding itself was but a prelude, which he was content to let the Church manage according to its long-established custom. Before God, the wedding should be acknowledged as being between a man and a woman. Before the huge crowd filling the palace gardens, it needed to be more than that. The two columns of followers still standing before the stage bore witness to that. No one left when the mass was over. The trumpets and horns sounded once more, accompanied this time by drums and pipes, to announce a grander stage of the proceedings. Hincmar remained standing where he was but Aethelwulf and Judith turned to face the crowd.

Hincmar was praying again, but this time his prayers concerned Judith alone. He called upon God to purify and strengthen her for the mighty task to which she had been called. The thrones were being moved into position in front of the altar. An acolyte approached Hincmar with a flask of oil on a gold tray. Hincmar took the flask, opened it, made a sign of blessing and then poured the contents over Judith's head, saying in a loud voice, 'May the Lord crown you Queen of Wessex, joint ruler with your husband, the mighty King Aethelwulf.'

The trumpets, horns, drums and pipes burst out again and this time Alfred did feel a shiver of awe pass through him at the motionless figure of Judith with the anointing oil glistening down her dark hair. He was not the only one. An inarticulate murmur passed through the crowd. Attendants from the back of the stage brought forth a gold crown and jewel-encrusted robe. Hincmar placed the crown upon Judith's head as a physical manifestation of her new status. The attendants draped the gown around her. Aethelwulf took her hand and she turned her face to look at him, her first movement since being anointed his Queen. He led her gently towards the thrones, where they sat, side by side. The two columns of followers now moved together to become one and proceed up onto the stage to pay homage to the joint rulers. Ushers appeared to direct the rest of the crowd onto the stage to pay their respects to the royal couple seated in their thrones. When it was Alfred's turn to pass before the girl who was now his mother, her gaze was fixed and inward, as though still contemplating the change which had come upon her. Her smile was distant from her eyes. His father was similarly remote.

On leaving the stage and returning to the palace with Colman and Owen, Alfred was aware that something had happened, but he wasn't quite sure what. Owen had finished his cockerel but he wasn't happy with it. 'Too much going on,' he said when showing it to Alfred. 'I couldn't concentrate on it properly.'

Having achieved his objective, Aethelwulf was anxious to return to Wessex with his bride before the onset of winter made crossing the Channel hazardous. The wedding celebrations were cut short after two days and the Wessex pilgrims, augmented by Queen Judith and her companions, set out on the final leg of their journey back home. If Aethelwulf was happy and triumphant after his prestigious wedding, he showed no sign of it. He spent much of the time glancing up at the sky, his thoughts turning back to what might be happening in his kingdom after his long absence. As for Judith, the few times Alfred saw her, she looked anxious, very different from the confident person he'd known before. He'd feared that being crowned queen would make her even more overbearing, but it seemed to have had the opposite effect. The few questions she asked him about life in Wessex were timidly put, as though she was afraid of what his answers might be.

Aethelwulf had decided to cross the Channel at its narrowest point given the time of year. Kent had the added advantage of being ruled over by Berti. He was confident that his second son would welcome him home; he was less sure what his eldest son's reaction would be.

After three days of waiting at the coast for an October gale to blow itself out, a day dawned calm and fair which the ships' captains pronounced fine for the crossing. They boarded the ships. A wind did pick up when they were out on the water, but it was from the south and landed them on the Kent coast in good time without alarm.

9. Homecoming

A grey November day. Those leaves which remained on the trees were at their most spectacular, shining against the dull sky in cascades of copper, gold and vermilion. Even Aetheluwlf, his mind pre-occupied, registered their beauty. But with no real pleasure. 'They will be gone soon,' he thought. 'The first sharp wind will blow them down.'

He was riding in the centre of a heavily armed group of men with his wife, Judith, and his son, Berti, beside him. They were entering the forest that straddled the border between Sussex and the old kingdom of Wessex. Outlaw country. It was no place for Judith. He had told her to stay behind at the fortified manor where they had spent the night, but she had refused. It had not taken Aethelwulf long to realise that his young wife had no intention of accepting a subsidiary role. She had been crowned a queen of Wessex, and a queen of Wessex she intended to be. She had met his warnings of danger with an angry retort.

'You think a woman does not have your courage?'

'It's not your place.'

'It's my place as much as it is yours.'

He couldn't afford to cross her. There were Frankish soldiers in his guard, who would most likely withdraw their services at any slight to their queen. And she did after all embody one of his strongest bargaining counters – his newly forged tie with the House of Charlemagne. So, maybe it was for the best that she came along. He tried to convince himself, but it only added to his creeping conviction that he was no longer master of his own domain.

Berti at least he could rely on. His second surviving son had welcomed him home with unfeigned pleasure, willingly resigning his authority back to his father. But Blade was a different matter, as Aethelwulf had feared he might be. Swithun had travelled to Canterbury to tell him so.

'He will not resign,' Swithun had told him. 'He says it is for you to resign to him. And he has support.'

'Who?'

'Ealhstan.'

Aethelwulf dismissed Ealhstan with a wave of the hand. 'Ealhstan is a great fighter but he has few warriors at his personal command. I've always made sure of that.'

'Eanwulf also.'

'Eanwulf?' Aethelwulf looked concerned. Unlike Ealhstan, the ealdorman of Somerset had many warriors at his personal command. His retinue was second only to the king's. 'Eanwulf has always been loyal to me.'

'Not any more.'

'What has happened to change him?'

'There was a dispute with the abbey at Glastonbury over some land. Your son ruled in Eanwulf's favour. And he's helped him in other ways, too. Not unintelligently. Eanwulf is beholden to him. It is in his interests that your son remains king in Wessex.'

'That was the sort of thing you were supposed to prevent!'

Swithun spread his hands. 'I did what I could, sire. But Winchester has little authority beyond Selwood. I made some grants of land there in your name, but had no means of making sure that they took effect. Ealhstan's influence in the west is very strong. Add in the ealdorman of Somerset and you have a formidable combination. Enough to make any western thane nervous.'

'What about Wiltshire and Hampshire? You had influence there, I trust.'

'I had influence, yes.'

'Enough to prevent them joining a rebellion against me?'

Swithun was silent for a while. 'If you were ruling in Hampshire then it would be loyal,' he said eventually. 'But your son is established there. He has made inroads. It's hard to say how great. That would only be apparent if it came to a test. I would say that most people in Hampshire are hoping that it won't.'

'And Wiltshire?'

'The same, but more so. It's closer to Somerset.'

'So, you're saying that there's no one in the western kingdom on whose loyalty I can rely? After nigh on twenty years of ruling them.'

How do you tell a king that you'd told him so? Swithun contented himself with a murmured, 'You always knew there would be difficulties on your return, did you not, sire?'

'I will meet him,' Aethelwulf decided. 'On some neutral ground. That can be arranged, can't it?'

'Yes, sire.'

'These rebellions often fall away when a king confronts them in person. I will show my son I am not afraid of him.'

He had spoken confidently then. He was less confident now, making his way to the neutral ground selected, a hunting lodge in the Forest of Bere. Blade had agreed to the meeting readily enough. Too readily. As though he had nothing to fear from his father's presence. Was he hoping to profit from it? Aethelwulf couldn't believe that even Blade would seek to capture him in order to get his way. But such things did happen. He thought of Cyngen, abandoned by his sons; and the House of Charlemagne was notorious for its family disloyalty. But not in Wessex, where the bond between father and son was held sacred. How could Blade hope to command the loyalty of others if he betrayed his own father? Even so, Aethelwulf decided to ensure that he was accompanied by Berti to the meeting, along with a heavily armed guard.

Swithun met them in a clearing just before the lodge. He took in the size of the guard with an approving nod.

'It's going to be crowded,' he said.

'How many men does my son have with him?' Aehtelwulf asked.

'About the same. More within easy call.'

The lodge was just over the border in Wessex. That shouldn't matter, Aethelwulf thought. I am the king. And I need to show I have returned.

'Are they all there?'

'Prince Aethelbald and Bishop Ealhstan are.'

'And Eanwulf?'

'The ealdorman is not there, no. But he has sent a contingent of his men.'

That suggested Eanwulf was not entirely sure how things would transpire. Unless Blade had not wanted him to witness the meeting with his father. Either way, it was some comfort that he had stayed away.

They followed Swithun to the hunting lodge. A large body of men was already encamped outside it. They stood and watched the new arrivals in silence, a certain tension in the air.

'There is a bur just over the ridge,' Swithun said. 'The prince has directed that you be accommodated there. With your men. And the princess,' he said, with a bow to Judith.

'The queen,' she said.

'I beg your pardon, my lady,' Swithun replied awkwardly. 'The queen.'

'Where are we to meet?' Aethelwulf asked.

'At the lodge,' Swithun replied. 'The prince has directed me to escort you there once you have recovered from your journey.'

Aethelwulf frowned. This was not how he had envisaged the meeting. His son was arrogating to himself the role of host. But as he was already installed in the lodge, there wasn't much Aethelwulf could do about it. Withdrawing from the meeting in protest at such presumption was an option, but it might be something of an over-reaction. And it would leave Blade still in control of Wessex. After all, what did it matter who went to whom? Even so, it was not a good beginning. Impressions were important with so many witnesses. And the way in which Swithun seemed happy to follow Blade's instructions was troubling also. Whose side was his confessor on? He glared suspiciously at Swithun, who did not appear to notice.

'Will you let me show you to the bur, sire?' Swithun asked.

They couldn't stay where they were. It would not take much to set the two troops against each other. There was already some muttering going on between them. He nodded shortly and they followed Swithun over the ridge to the bur, where they dismounted. He led Judith into the building, followed by Berti and Swithun, while the guard positioned itself outside.

'So, what is my son's position?' Aethelwulf asked, once seated at a table with a cup of wine in his hand. 'Does he acknowledge my authority now?'

'He is prepared to acknowledge you as king,' Swithun replied. 'And ruler of the eastern kingdom.'

'And the west?'

'The west he will not give up. He requires you to acknowledge him as ruler of the western kingdom. He does not insist upon the title of king.'

'How very noble of him!' Aethelwulf exclaimed harshly.

'And he expects you to name him publicly as his successor.'

'As a reward for his treachery. And what of my wife?'

'He made no mention of her, sire.'

'My wife was crowned Queen of Wessex, not of the eastern kingdom.'

Swithun did not reply, but remained staring at the floor. The king he knew; the queen he did not.

'Well?' Aethelwulf asked eventually.

'I do not know about your wife,' Swithun replied slowly. That was true; he didn't know. He could guess, but it would not be wise to do so. 'Perhaps you might wish to raise that with him yourself?'

'I will do so,' Aethelwulf replied with decision. 'And now. I've had enough of this foolishness. Come, my dear. Let us go and confront this rebel son of mine. You, too, Berti. A loyal son I will always reward.'

If Berti was pleased by the compliment, he gave no sign of it. He had been grave and silent all morning, and he remained so. But he followed his father and Judith out of the bur. Aethelwulf signalled for his men to follow him back down the ridge to the lodge.

Whether they quarrelled with his son's men or not, he wanted them near to him.

Inside the lodge, it was dark and smoky. A fire was smouldering in the centre of the long room in which Blade received them. He himself was sitting at a table at the far end of the room with Ealhstan beside him. Candles burned on the table but did little to dispel the gloom. Aethelwulf could not remember having been in the lodge before; it struck him as a mean place. He walked briskly past the fire and up to the table where his son was sitting. Blade waited until he was at the table before standing to greet him.

'Welcome, father,' he said, before sitting down again.

'Are we to remain standing while you sit?' Aethelwulf demanded, his face growing red.

'Not unless you wish to,' Blade replied. 'Frick, Golding, bring up some chairs for my father and his companions. 'Hello, Berti,' he said, greeting his brother. 'It's good to see you again.' His gaze rested briefly on Judith.

'This is my wife, Queen Judith, daughter of King Charles of Francia,' said Aethelwulf.

'I'm very pleased to meet you, my lady,' Blade said without expression.

'Judith was crowned Queen of Wessex at a ceremony before her father and the whole Frankish court,' said Aethelwulf, sitting down opposite his son. He had decided to tackle the matter head on.

'There are no queens in Wessex.' Ealhstan rather than Blade replied. The old warrior looked stern and formidable. 'There have been no queens in Wessex for over fifty years. Your first wife was not a queen, my lord king, and neither was your father's wife. It is for the people of Wessex to decide whether they have a queen, not some foreign court.'

'You insult my wife, old man!' Aethelwulf exclaimed, half rising from his seat in anger.

'No insult to the lady is intended,' said Blade smoothly. 'But what my lord bishop says is true. We do not recognise queens in this country. I am sorry if you were led to believe otherwise, my lady,' he said, addressing Judith. 'As my father's wife, I respect and honour you. But I do not recognise you as a queen; and neither does my people.'

'*Your* people!' Aethelwulf said scornfully.

'Yes, my people,' said Blade, ignoring the scorn. 'The people I have ruled for the past two years and whom I intend to go on ruling. The people I know better than you do, father, if you thought they would accept a queen imposed upon them by a foreign power.'

'How dare you say that Judith has been imposed upon this country!'

'I am sorry you have to witness this disagreement, my lady,' Blade said to Judith. 'But as my father chose to bring you with him to this meeting, it is best you hear the truth at it.'

'I asked to come along,' Judith replied in a small voice, her face white. 'This matter concerns me.'

'Yes,' Blade acknowledged. 'Yes, it does. Well, as I say, I am sorry if you or your father were misled. That was not my doing.'

'Judith was not misled,' Aethelwulf replied with quiet fury. 'It is impertinent of you to suggest it. She was crowned a queen and anointed with sacred chrism. She is a queen before God.'

'I can well believe it,' Blade replied, looking with a certain admiration at the pale young girl before him.

'But a queen before God is not the same as a queen of Wessex. That requires the people's consent, which they will not give.'

'Will you be so good as to tell me why not?' Judith enquired tightly.

'The last queen we had was imposed on us by a foreign power. And she proved cruel and oppressive. She was expelled from the country. Since her time, the people have sworn to have no more queens.'

'In my country, the people accept what their king tells them to,' Judith observed.

'It is not the same here,' Blade replied. 'A king rules by consent. He does not ignore the wishes of his people.'

'It seems a poor sort of kingship.'

'Perhaps,' said Blade, unruffled. 'But it is the custom of the country, and custom is important here, my lady. You may find us very slow. I'm told your father's court is full of brilliant people. But if you wish to live amongst us, you will need to adapt to our ways.'

'Your impertinence knows no bounds,' said Aethelwulf angrily. His son's assumption of calm authority both goaded and worried him. It suggested a confidence unlikely to give way easily. 'Not content with defying your own father, you seek to defy this lady's father, who is the greatest monarch in Europe.'

Ealhstan snorted, which caused Aethelwulf to round on him. 'What do you mean by that, old man?'

'Everyone knows the West Frankish king is fighting for his life,' Ealhstan replied solidly. 'His own brother plans to depose him. You don't frighten us with him.'

Judith's pale face flushed scarlet. Blade turned on Ealhstan. 'You go too far, my lord bishop. That is an insult. My lady, please accept our apologies. We are a blunt people; we say what we think.'

'It's not a virtue to dissemble,' Judith responded, her eyes bright, but not tearful. Blade found himself admiring her more and more. Much too fine for my father, he thought.

Aethelwulf had stood up at Ealhstan's words. 'Come, Judith,' he said. 'I will not have you listen to any more of this impertinence.'

Judith looked up at him, and then across at Blade. Her slowness to rise to follow her husband detracted from the dignity of his exit and left Blade with a most pleasant feeling.

'They'll be back,' Ealhstan said when the king's party had left the room.

'I do hope so,' Blade murmured.

Back at the bur, Aethelwulf gave vent to his anger, railing against his son's disloyalty and calling down all manner of curses upon him.

'And his rudeness to you, my dear,' Aethelwulf said to Judith. 'That was unforgivable.'

'He wasn't rude to me,' Judith replied. 'He went out of his way not to be. The old bishop spoke slightingly of my father but your son apologised for that.'

'Sheer impertinence!'

'Was it true what he said? About the people not accepting a queen?'

'The people will accept you, my dear. You can be sure of that.'

'I don't see how I can be queen of Wessex. Not if your son remains its ruler.'

'He will give way to me.'

'He didn't seem about to.'

'He will be made to.'

'How?'

Aethelwulf was silent. That indeed was the question. He had hoped to overawe his son; that was clearly not going to work. If anything, Blade had seemed to be enjoying their confrontation. So, was he prepared to fight him? And plunge the country into civil war for an authority he had been anxious to divest himself of less than two years before? Did hurt feelings and a sense of betrayal justify that? And who would follow him if he put them to the test? He was getting old. Might they not prefer a younger leader? Even those in the eastern kingdom?

He looked over at Berti, his loyal son. 'What do you think, Berti? You've said nothing all morning.'

'I think you need to agree terms,' Berti replied.

'And reward him for his rebellion?'

'It's only rebellion if you choose to see it as such. He is your eldest son. He would inherit the rule in Wessex anyway, unless you tried to disinherit him. And many would say you have no grounds for doing so. He's been ruling in your place while you've been away, and ruling well. Why should that be a source of discontent? An orderly transfer of power confers honour on the person who secures it.'

All of which was true. Were it just a matter of his own pride, he could learn to let that go. He would have to renounce more than pride soon enough. But the young girl sitting before him, whose life was just beginning, did make a difference. Had he not led her to believe she would be Queen of Wessex if she married him? The charge of misleading her which Blade had so coolly levelled had been the one to wound him the most. He was an honourable man. And Judith had been crowned queen. How could he ignore that? Would she ever respect him again if he did?

'But Judith . . .' Aethelwulf began tentatively.

'Judith can be your queen,' Berti replied. 'She will rule the eastern kingdom, alongside you. It was never envisaged that she would rule alone.'

'My son will not recognise her as queen. You heard him.'

'I don't think my title matters,' Judith said. 'If the people of this country do not accept queens, then what is the point of calling me one?'

Aethelwulf looked at her a little hesitantly. 'I did not seek to mislead you, my dear.'

'It was my father who insisted on my coronation,' Judith replied. 'Perhaps it would have been better if he had not. I can see how it might be resented here. And that rough old bishop might be rude, but he's right. My father will not invade this country on my behalf. He'll never exert himself for me.'

They were making it easy for him. Berti would not want to fight Blade. Why should he? Berti was the second son; and he had never been ambitious. But Judith? Was this not as great a humiliation to her as it was to him? He looked with some puzzlement at the composed figure of his young bride. No, he did not understand her. She had been insistent on her right as queen to accompany him here; now, she seemed unconcerned at letting her claim on the title go.

Had he known her better, Aethelwulf might have realised that Judith felt the humiliation of Blade's defiance as keenly as he did. But she had learnt from her father how to hide her emotions. And it had only taken one meeting to convince her that Aethelwulf would never prevail against his son. The difference in their manner told her that – the son calm and self-assured, the father blustering and angry. Even had Aethelwulf promised to fight for her honour, she would not have believed him, or wanted him to. So why continue the humiliation? Aethelwulf might have thought that Judith was making things easy for him, but that was not her way. She was instead mentally resolving to have as little as possible to do with him, and that included not sharing his worthless protestations.

When Swithun called in and added his voice to that of Berti, recommending recognition of Blade's rule in the west, Aethelwulf felt he had no alternative but to do so. Judith remained silent. He even asked her once if she agreed with them but she would not be drawn on expressing any further opinion. 'You must do as you see fit,' was all she would say.

And so he did, with conditions designed to disguise his capitulation. Judith would rule as a queen in the east, Blade would rule in the west on his father's behalf. He would remain a prince but was nominated Aethelwulf's successor in the west ("not in the east!") and Aethelwulf was recognised as the senior ruler, retaining his title as King of Wessex. Berti and Swithun were tasked with continuing the negotiations as Aethelwulf no longer wished to speak in person with his rebellious son.

Blade agreed to his father's conditions readily enough. He had what he wanted – continued rule in the west and formal recognition of his right to succeed there. As for the rest, well if Judith could persuade the east to accept her as a queen, then good luck to her. Berti had renounced his rule in the east to their father. Blade had never intended to claim that while their father lived.

When he died, Blade was confident that Berti would accept him as overlord, whatever their father might try to do in the meantime. Berti was no fighter; and he wouldn't want the kingdoms split. The west was the senior kingdom. It had conquered the east. If his father wanted to fool himself that he could remain the senior monarch only ruling in the east, then let him do so. He was unlikely to live for long.

Terms agreed, Aethelwulf was anxious to get away from the scene of his capitulation as quickly as possible. Blade suggested a feast to celebrate their agreement, primarily (as far as he was concerned) to enable him to see some more of Judith. His father's young royal bride had aroused a definite interest in him. But that pleasure at least Aethelwulf was able to deny him. He insisted on keeping to his bur that night and returning to Sussex the next morning with only the briefest of farewells.

'It's been a great pleasure for me to meet you, my lady,' Blade said gently to Judith in the moment he was allowed to say goodbye to her. 'I hope you will learn to love our country.'

He was rewarded with a slight flush on her small face. A sign of anger, as it had been when Ealhstan had dismissed any threat from her father? Possibly. He would accept anger from her for the moment.

'You are most kind, my lord prince,' she replied stiffly, in a tone which suggested the opposite, before turning deliberately to Aethelwulf, who was in a hurry to get away.

Blade stood in the doorway of the lodge with Ealhstan, watching them ride away with Berti towards their guard.

'She will be trouble,' Ealhstan said sombrely when they were out of earshot. 'What possessed the old fool to marry her?'

Blade smiled to himself but did not reply. He could think of a reason or two. All in all, it had been a most satisfactory meeting.

It was a gloomy ride back into Sussex. Aethelwulf was silent and brooding, trying to come to terms with the events of the previous day, asking himself if there was anything he could have done differently, if maybe there still was. Judith was similarly silent. Berti tried to keep up a conversation with her, feeling it was duty to try and show she had not been forgotten. But it was hard work, and often easier to let the silence hang in the air. He found his own thoughts drifting away to Canterbury and the comfortable concubine waiting for him there.

They reached the manor of Steyning that evening. A large, pleasant manor situated between the Downs and the sea, its lands were among the most extensive in Sussex. Aethelwulf had already decided it would be his main residence when he was in the east; now it looked as though it would be his main residence permanently. The south coast was less prone to pagan attack than the east, being further away from their homelands. As such, it was a suitable place for a retired king. Not that Aethelwulf saw himself as retired, but his eldest sons did. It suited Berti, as well as Blade, to have their father resident in Steyning. Although Berti had resigned his rule in the east on his father's return, he had done so fully expecting to be asked to continue as effective ruler in Kent. The Kentish coastline bore the brunt of pagan attacks and he had correctly assumed that his father would not want to take up again the task of repelling them. It was a task Berti had become used to over the past two years. Although not a fighter himself, he was a skilful reader of men and had formed a good relationship with Ethelmod, the ealdorman of Kent. Between them, they deployed thanes and fighting men along the coast to beat off the pagans when they landed. A never-ending task, but one he had become used to. And it was worth being busy to maintain his freedom and not be dependent on other members of his family. The recent meeting with Blade only strengthened him in that feeling.

And so, when that evening at Steyning, his father confirmed that he wanted him to return to Canterbury and continue the work he had been doing, he did his best to hide his satisfaction. Only the sight of Judith, pale and silent at the dinner table, gave him pause for thought. What on earth was she going to do? He had little doubt that his father, once he had come to terms with his rebuff and hurt pride, would adjust to his reduced role and perhaps even secretly be relieved by it. The manor at Steyning was a considerably more comfortable retirement location than the monk's cell afforded most kings whose lives outlasted their rule. But what was Judith to do here? Her life was just beginning. Away from any influence, with nothing to occupy herself with but checking estate accounts and trying to please (or cope with) an elderly husband, she might well feel she had been buried alive.

He dismissed the thought. There was nothing he could do about it. She had been aware of his father's age when she married him. And no one can guarantee the continuance of power, particularly in these difficult times. Part of Berti's wisdom consisted in knowing when not to interfere. If he concerned himself with her situation, it would not do her any good and it could easily cause harm. So, he spoke to her as carefully as she spoke to him and largely dismissed her from his mind when riding east the next morning, his thoughts returning with relief to Canterbury.

*

Another return for Alfred, this one less hard than the last. No one he knew had died while he'd been away. Sideways welcomed him back with his familiar lopsided friendliness. It was good to be back in England. To begin with, he was happy enough living with his father and Judith at Steyning. He went out walking with Sideways, exploring the countryside around this new home. They climbed up onto the Downs and could see for miles out to sea. On the whole, he decided he preferred being on land looking out to sea than the other way round. He was even taken out on his first hunt, although Sideways remained banned from hunting as a confusing influence on the other dogs. But Alfred enjoyed himself He was complimented on being a good horse rider, which he should be, he thought, given the amount of miles he had ridden on his travels. The tang of excitement when the hounds caught a scent remained with him. It was an experience he would like to repeat.

His father had gone back to being remote. He saw little of him outside of meal times, and sometimes not even then. He spent a lot of time in his study, but what he was doing there, Alfred didn't know or care. He saw more of Judith, who seemed much older and sadder than she had been in Francia. Perhaps that was what marriage did to a woman – his mother had been like that at the end. He still found it difficult to think of Judith as his father's wife. That made her his new mother. Impossible! He would never think of her as that. Swithun's curious comment came back to him at times, almost like a reproach, *She'll need your goodwill. You'll give her that, won't you? I know you will.* What could he possibly give to her? He did notice that she read a lot. She could read Latin fluently, which seemed like magic to him. He was still labouring through sentences with Colman. She looked up from her book one time to see him staring at her in wonder.

'What's so surprising, Alfred?'

'You looked like you were in a different world.'

'I was. I'm always in a different world when I'm reading. Aren't you?'

'I don't read very well. I do have some books but I mostly look at the pictures in them.'

'Show me your books.'

He went and collected the book of poems his mother had given him and the psalter from his father and showed them to her. She was delighted by the book of poems, holding it carefully in her hands and leafing through the pages.

'It's so beautiful!' she exclaimed.

'My mother gave me that when I was ill,' he said proudly.

'Do you miss your mother?'

'Yes, very much.'

She nodded and seemed to understand. 'That's as it should be. Well, I'm sure she'd be very proud of you – all the things you've done, the places you've seen.'

He hadn't thought of that. The thought of his mother being proud of him suddenly brought her closer to him, and the sense of her loss. He turned away from Judith to hide a tear in his eye.

She gave him time to collect himself before asking him gently if he could read her a poem.

He knew the poem about the battle with the dragon by heart so he could pretend he was reading it. He took the book and recited the poem to her as he had so often recited it to himself.

'You read very well,' she said with a smile when he had finished. 'You hardly need to look at the pages.'

Was she teasing him? He decided he didn't mind if she was. It was nice to see her smile.

'That's a psalter,' he said, indicating the book from his father.

'Yes, I know.' She seemed less keen to hear him read from the psalter, which was just as well as he'd have trouble negotiating even the simplest Latin.

'What are you reading? There are no pictures in it at all, are there?'

'No, pictures aren't always necessary, Alfred. You form the pictures in your head.'

She made it sound even more like magic than ever.

'Is it a sad book?'

'Why do you ask that?' she said, surprised.

'You looked sad when you were reading it.'

'You're very observant,' she said with a fleeting return of her smile. 'I shall have to be careful. Yes, I suppose it is a sad book. Certainly it was written in sad circumstances, the saddest possible.'

'What were they?'

'The man who wrote it had been condemned to death unfairly. The book is his attempt to come to terms with his fate. And he succeeds. So, although it is sad, it is also a comfort for those who have to suffer much less than he did.'

'Can you read me some of it?'

'In English?'

'Can you do that?' he asked, surprised. 'It's in Latin, isn't it?'

'You don't understand Latin, though, do you? If you give me some time, I might be able to translate a little of it for you.'

He watched in awe as she took a pen and a scrap of parchment from beside her, stared at her book for a while, dipped the pen in some ink and scratched a few words on the parchment, correcting a few, writing some more. This was different from anything Colman had taught him. He kept silent, hardly daring to breathe, for the fifteen minutes or so that she was engrossed in her task.

'All right,' she said eventually, looking up. 'This is one of the poems the prisoner writes when the Lady Philosophy first appears to him:

> *Then the night ended*
> *and I saw the light once more.*
> *As when a north-west wind*
> *which has hidden the sun in cloud and rain*
> *is checked by a wind from Thrace*
> *which attacks the darkness and frees the sun*
> *to dazzle our startled eyes.'*

The poem over, Judith remained where she was, frowning at the piece of parchment as though not sure whether her translation was correct. Alfred felt the image of the vanquished storm keenly but one question nagged at him.

'Where's Thrace?' he asked.

'What?' Judith was still pondering her translation. *Was 'startled' right?*

'Where's Thrace? Where the good wind came from.'

'Oh, Greece, I think.'

'Is that where the prisoner came from?'

'No. Maybe he'd been there. The ancients often referred to places in Greece, especially in poetry. It's a way of linking their work with that of earlier writers. Poetry came from Greece.'

'You know so much.'

'My father insisted on all his children being highly educated. Quite why, I'm not sure.'

'I wish I knew what you did.'

'Education isn't always a blessing, Alfred.'

'You can read all sorts of books, can't you?'

'Yes,' she acknowledged.

'And they help you, don't they?'

'I suppose they do,' she said, looking at him with renewed interest. 'Go on.'

'I think it is good to know,' he said. 'The bad as well as the good. Otherwise, how can you really value the good? Isn't that what the poem is saying with the different winds?'

She stared at him intently. 'Out of the mouths of babes,' she murmured. 'God bless you, Alfred. You know more than you might think.'

'I know very little. And I want to know so much! Will you teach me? You know more than Colman. He only knows what he's been told.'

'I have a feeling you'll soon be teaching me. But, yes, why not? We can teach one another.'

But in fact there was little opportunity for Alfred to have lessons from Judith. Aethelwulf did not see it part of his new wife's duties to teach his son; he had a tutor for that. The age difference between Judith and Alfred was not great enough for her to take the place of his mother. An elder sister such as Elsa perhaps, but he was getting to the age where he should be breaking away from feminine influences. The country had more need for its princes to be warriors than Latin speakers. If Aethelwulf had ever thought of Alfred becoming a priest, his pilgrimage had put an end to that. Anyone could be a priest – there were good priests and bad priests, as with every other occupation. And the boy seemed healthy enough – his travels had toughened him up. He enjoyed hunting and being outdoors. There was no reason why he should not train to be a warrior like his brothers. Even Berti seemed to be managing well enough as a warrior, and Berti had been frailer than Alfred. A leader of men needed intelligence as much as a priest, even more so. But he needed strength also, to retain the respect of his men. Aethelwulf was still smarting from the meeting with Blade. The best response to a disloyal son would be to ensure that his other sons were capable of rule. He had been forced to acknowledge Blade as his successor in the west, but Blade had no heirs. Who knew what the future might bring?

And so, Alfred found that although his lessons with Colman continued, they became less frequent. Instead, he was encouraged to go out riding more with Owen and taken on more hunts. And three times a week, a soldier from the king's guard would give them training in combat using blunted swords. Alfred enjoyed the change as evidence he was being treated more seriously as a man and less likely to be expected to become a priest. He would be better able to fend off Redi's taunts, as well as any blows, when they next met.

Redi came to stay at Steyning for Christmas, along with Ceolwulf the Mercian, his constant companion.

But Alfred had a companion of his own now, Owen, who was about Redi's age and bigger than him. Whether it was because of Owen, the passage of time, or just because he felt more confident in himself, Redi was less hostile to his younger brother than when they had last been together. He even seemed quite pleased to see him and listened to Owen's tales of their adventures in Rome and Francia with every show of interest. And when he heard of their training with the king's guard, he even chuckled.

'So, you're not going to become a priest, Little Elf,' he said. 'You'll be a muddy-arsed fighter with the rest of us.'

'I never wanted to become a priest,' Alfred replied.

They went out hunting together over Christmas and Alfred was pleased to show he could keep up with the others. Redi treated him more as an equal than an encumbrance. Alfred was aware of his brother having changed over the past two years since he'd last seen him. He was much taller. A spurt of growth had given him the height of a man, if not yet the heft. He was rougher in some ways. Mixing with soldiers may have contributed to that – he had spent most of his time out east with Ethelmod, who had taken him on expeditions to repel the pagans. Having seen action seemed to have calmed him down and given him less need to prove himself. Maybe it's similar to what I feel, Alfred thought – he likes being treated as a man, as I do. Redi had his own world now. Alfred felt little desire to tag along after him in it but he was happy that they could meet up with less of the tension there had been when they were always together.

At times, he saw signs of the old Redi – flashes of exasperation or scorn – but on the whole these passed by quickly, and someone less attuned to a brother's moods might not have noticed them. They were enough for Alfred to think it might be best for them not to spend too long a time together. On one occasion, he saw a side of Redi he had not noticed before. It was when he was being introduced to Judith. In the past, Redi had greeted strangers with a breezy self-assurance, but before Judith, he appeared tongue-tied and even blushed fiercely. It was almost as if he was frightened of her. I'm not like that with her, Alfred thought, and she's a lot older than me than she is Redi. Maybe it was just that he was more used to her – they'd known one another quite a while now. But this evidence of his brother's timidity with someone he knew well struck him oddly. It was more evidence that their worlds had grown apart.

After the Christmas period, Redi returned east with Ceolwulf. Alfred was sad to see him go. It looked like Redi was the person who was having adventures now. But Aethelwulf had decided that Alfred, too, would learn more away from the quiet surroundings of Steyning. He had no intention of sending him to the court of the rebellious Blade. Instead, he resolved that Alfred and Owen should go to Mercia to be with Elsa and Burgred. Experience of a different court is always valuable, and a further link with Mercia might prove useful. Aethelwulf was still turning over in his mind whether to take any punitive action against Blade to reassert his authority in the western kingdom. If he chose to do so, Prince Burgred would have a part to play. Alfred was too young to be an active intermediary. But the boy was observant. His impressions of how things were in Mercia would be worth having. And it would show Elsa that she had not been forgotten by her family.

Alfred was pleased to be leaving Steyning. It had been enjoyable enough for a few months but he was beginning to feel bored. It was quiet and there wasn't a great deal to do. There were few people his own age, and after Christmas the hunting became less frequent. His father had lost interest in hunting and a court takes its lead from its head. It would be interesting to be with Elsa and see how much she'd changed. And to see Mercia as well – he'd heard so much about it.

Owen was less keen on the trip. 'Mercians don't like the Welsh,' he confessed to Alfred.

'But you're one of us now.'

'They'll know I'm Welsh the first time I open my mouth. Maybe before.'

'I'll protect you,' said Alfred, before thinking it sounded ridiculous. Owen was so much bigger than him. 'I mean, you protect me. We're a team, aren't we?'

Owen gave a somewhat bleak smile, 'Yes, we're a team,' he said.

10. Mercia

Travelling again, through the muddy roads of early spring. Alfred and Owen had been assigned a guard commanded by Osric to escort them as far as the great river which formed the border with Mercia. As they headed north-west on the Roman road, Alfred felt a thrill of anticipation piercing the high Downs that sheltered Steyning. New territory once more, and this time he was allowed to take his dog with him. Sideways kept up an erratic progress beside his horse, occasionally getting lost or left behind and having to be retrieved by irritated members of the guard. Alfred's dog was not popular with anyone but Alfred, but his cheerfulness seemed proof against any amount of cursing.

After crossing more hills, they reached the river and the border, where another guard was waiting for them. It was commanded by Cynehelm, the father of Ceolwulf, Redi's companion. Alfred knew that there was some sort of alliance between Cynehelm and his father – the fact that Ceolwulf was growing up in Wessex was evidence enough of that – and so he was not worried when Osric and the Wessex guard departed, leaving them in the care of the Mercians. Rather, he was excited. Now he was truly away from his father's influence.

Cynehelm was very respectful. Alfred had the pleasant feeling of being the centre of attention, which he had not felt since his first trip to Rome with Swithun. He was a representative of Wessex again, but this time better able to observe those around him. He noticed the deep lines on Cynehelm's face when he turned to talk to him. Although younger than Aethelwulf, he had a similar air of weariness. A frequent refrain in his conversation was the phrase 'these troubled times'. Alfred, happy to be on the move to somewhere new, couldn't see what was so troubled about them, but nodded solemnly because it made him feel important.

Cynehelm had a manor not far from the river. They made their way there to spend the night. At the manor, there were more new people to meet – an ealdorman called Mucel and his wife Eadburh, who was Cynehelm's sister. The name Eadburh was familiar somehow. Alfred tried to remember where he had heard it before. Of course, the wicked queen of Mercia who was buried at Pavia. He wondered if this new Eadburh was a relation. She looked harmless enough – large and fair, with a sympathetic air. She had her daughter with her, Ealhswith, a girl a year or two younger than him. The same fair colouring as her mother. Alfred felt a stab of pain seeing mother and daughter together, Eadburh's head bent listening to some confidence. It didn't happen so often now, but such sights could bring back the loss of his own mother with sudden sharpness.

Ealhswith was not allowed to stay up for the evening meal, but Alfred and Owen were treated as the guests of honour. Mucel was a jovial man, with none of his brother-in-law's careworn manner. He talked a lot about himself. Alfred realised that this wasn't due to vanity, but rather a desire to put them at ease. Owen in particular was wary of Mercians. It was as if Mucel was telling them all about himself to reassure them that they had nothing to fear from him. With Cynehelm's tendency for brooding silences, the meal might have been a strained affair had it not been for Mucel's flood of reminiscences.

They learnt that Mucel, his wife and daughter were returning from visiting his wife's homeland in the west.

'My own land is in the north-east,' Mucel told them. 'Close by the border with Northumbria. But my wife, and Cynehelm, come from the opposite end of the country, the land of the Hwicce. Do you know this land?'

'No,' said Alfred. Owen said nothing.

'It borders your own land of Wessex,' Mucel continued. 'And Wales,' he added with a nod to Owen. 'It is a land of a great river, like this one. But it has more hills, in the south at least. My wife would say that it is the most beautiful land in the country, but then she is prejudiced,' he said with a fond smile at her. 'It is less stark than my own land, it is true. Good sheep country on the hills.'

'Who are the Hwicce?' Alfred asked.

'The Hwicce are a tribe. Mercia is a land of many tribes, Alfred. Our great kings united the tribes under their rule but family connections with them remain.'

'What tribe do the kings belong to?'

'The kings have come from different tribes. The Hwicce have contributed kings to Mercia in the past. My wife and Cynehelm are of their royal line. But our recent kings have come from further north. The heartland of our current king is around Nottingham.'

'In Wessex, our kings come from the same family,' Alfred said.

'It hasn't always been so.'

'Yes, it has. We have a poem which names the kings going back to the very beginning.'

'And were all these kings of the same family?'

'Yes, I think so. It sounds as if they were.'

'Then the poet has done his job well,' said Mucel with a slight smile. 'Wessex has certainly been fortunate to have your family ruling it, Alfred. Your grandfather was a truly great king, as your father has been. And now your father is arranging a peaceful transfer of power to his sons while he is still alive. Not every country is so fortunate to have so wise a ruler.'

Alfred considered. His father didn't seem so happy about their move to Steyning. And he always spoke harshly of Blade. Maybe things weren't as straightforward as he had thought?

'Why do you change your kings?' he asked.

'That is a difficult question,' Mucel replied. 'What would you say, Cynehelm?'

'A king rules with the consent of his people,' Cynehelm said promptly. 'If he loses that, he may be replaced.'

'Doesn't that make things worse?"'Alfred asked.

'Why do you say that?' asked Mucel.

'Wouldn't it cause division?'

'It can do,' Mucel agreed. 'But sometimes there is no alternative. A king may be killed, leaving no one to succeed him. Or he may not be able to defend his people from aggressors. Such things are often not known until they're put to the test.'

'So, King Burgred may not always be king?' Alfred said slowly.

'No one can say for certain what the future holds but we have every confidence that he will be our king for as long as he lives,' Mucel replied. 'He has proved himself as a brave warrior in battle and a wise ruler in peace. We hope to share Wessex's good fortune in having a strong royal family ruling us from now on, don't we, Cynehelm?'

'Oh, certainly. A strong king is the greatest of blessings a land can have. Particularly in these troubled times.'

They travelled on the next morning, Mucel and his family travelling with them on the road to Tamworth, the Mercian capital. Alfred gained the impression that Mucel's travels in the south-west had not just been prompted by a desire to see his wife's relations. He talked knowledgeably of the Welsh tribes whose lands bordered those of the Hwicce, more knowledgeably than might be expected from an ealdorman whose land was at the opposite end of the country. And he spoke warmly of Burgred. Alfred wondered if he had been on some kind of royal mission. His father always wanted to know what was happening on the borders of his land, away from his immediate supervision. And the more Mucel talked, the more Alfred sensed a purpose behind his genial conversation. He did not tend to ask direct questions but rather encouraged confidences in return for his own. He even managed to elicit information from the wary Owen with his talk of the kingdoms of Gwent, Glywysing and Brycheiniog.

'It is not land I know,' Owen said suddenly. 'I come from further north.'

'Brycheiniog shares a border with Powys,' Mucel observed.

'Powys no longer exists,' Owen replied. 'Since my master's death, Rhodri of Gwynedd rules there now.'

'Powys exists,' Mucel replied. 'Powys will always exist, whoever might rule there. Rulers come and go, the land remains.'

'Perhaps,' said Owen, seeking refuge in silence once more.

Mucel continued the subject when they stopped for the midday meal. 'You may meet some of Rhodri's men in Tamworth,' he told Owen. 'King Burgred has formed an alliance with him against the pagans.'

'I had heard as much,' Owen admitted.

'Our king is a great one for alliances,' Cynehelm said. Alfred had the impression that he was less a supporter of Burgred than Mucel was. There was a certain dryness in his voice whenever he spoke of him. So many impressions to store up in this new world.

'King Rhodri always speaks highly of your master,' Mucel continued in his gently probing way.

'Despite taking his land.'

'The land of his sons,' Mucel corrected, 'who were fighting bitterly amongst themselves. Rhodri has brought peace to Powys. From what I've heard of your master, he would have appreciated that. His sons rebelled against him when he was alive. There is nothing to be gained from supporting them. Their own people have deserted them. Those who show no loyalty always end up commanding none.'

Owen shrugged. 'I have no connection with Powys any more. Not since my master died.'

'A man always has a connection with the land of his birth.'

Three days later, they rode through the gates of Tamworth in the late afternoon. Alfred looked around with interest at the Mercian capital. From here, King Offa had exercised dominion over most of England. The town itself was protected by a wide ditch and tall ramparts topped with a spiked palisade. A large castle stood guard on a hill overlooking its tightly packed streets. The stone was darker here than at home. Over the course of their journey, Alfred had noticed the stone darken through various shades of brown until now it was a mixture of grey and gloomy red. Most of the houses were made of wood, but even they seemed to share the sombre colouring of the stone. More than he had done since leaving Wessex, he felt as though he was in a foreign country. The voices in the streets spoke in unfamiliar tones, sharper and more nasal than what he was used to. Some of the languages swirling around him, he did not understand at all. But Owen brightened at the sound of some soft voices heard in passing. 'Cymric,' he smiled to himself. 'There are Welshmen here.'

They rode up to the castle, only to be told by a steward that the court was at Lichfield to celebrate a saint's feast day. They were expected back in a day or two but most of the household had accompanied the royal couple. 'There is an inn in the town where the king's visitors often stay,' the steward added.

'The Boar,' said Mucel. 'I know the place. Very well, we will go and stay there until the king and queen return.'

At *The Boar*, they were made welcome, the landlord delighted to have such distinguished guests. He provided them with his best rooms and set aside an area for them to dine in private, away from his other customers. But Mucel, always interested in new surroundings and people, took Alfred and Owen with him into the public room to have a drink before their meal.

The public room was crowded and smoky, the carcass of a pig being roasted on a spit over an open fire at the far end. People were eating at long tables in the centre of the room, while to one side was a bar at which drinks were being served. Mucel led the boys towards the bar but before they could reach it, they were stopped by a fight breaking out at one of the tables. A young man, only a little bigger than Owen, suddenly smashed his fist into the face of another sitting beside him. The other responded by getting to his feet with a roar, a knife in his hand.

'Stop that!' an older man shouted, but the other man was now on his feet as well and grappling for control of the knife.

Mucel strode towards the fighting men and caught the wrist of the one holding the knife, twisting it sharply and causing him to drop it with a cry. The older man who had cried out was holding on to the other and pulling him away.

'What's this about?' Mucel demanded, his arms gripping his man to prevent him reaching for the knife again.

'He called me a dirty Welsh spy!' panted the one being pulled away by the older man.

'He is a dirty Welsh spy. They all are!' cried the other, twisting and turning to escape Mucel's grasp. An onlooker bent and picked up the knife, taking it out of reach. Mucel twisted the whole of his captive's arm behind him, causing him to give a howl of pain. He then shoved him back down into the chair he had risen from.

'It's Huw,' said Owen in a tone of wonder.

'What?' Alfred had edged towards the bar.

'Huw,' said Owen, pointing at the older man, who was now pulling his companion away towards a further end of the table. 'You remember. From Rome. He was one of our group.'

Alfred looked again. He would have had difficulty recognising the flustered, worried face from the calm, competent person he had seen in Rome. But Owen had lived with him for months and so must know.

'What's this about?' Mucel repeated. The two assailants were quiet now, regarding one another sullenly from across the table.

'It's as Rhys said,' the man recognised by Owen as Huw said wearily. 'The man called him a dirty Welsh spy. Rhys is young, he has a hot temper. He reacts badly to insults, that one in particular.'

'Why did you call him a spy?' Mucel asked the man before him.

'Because he is. They all are. Speaking their pagan tongue. Planning their next raid.'

'We were speaking Welsh,' Huw admitted. 'Rhys is more comfortable speaking Welsh; he is from Dyfed, a long way from the border. But we are not spies. We are simple farmers and traders. I have a licence from King Burgred to trade in sheep and wool. That is why we are here. I can tell you the names of my customers. They will vouch for us.'

'You trade in sheep and wool from Dyfed?' Cynehelm had entered the room, drawn by the noise.

'No, from Powys,' said Huw, turning to face this new questioner. 'Rhys is my nephew. His father has died. He lives with me now; I am teaching him a livelihood.'

'You could do with teaching him how to behave.'

'I know. I am sorry. He is young and hot-headed.' Huw looked hesitantly at the man sitting across the table staring at him. 'If I can pay some form of compensation. . .'

By way of response, the man spat deliberately on the floor.

The mood of the room was hostile. Alfred remembered Owen saying that the Mercians didn't like the Welsh. A number of faces in the room were staring intently at the Welshmen.

'Are you staying here?' Mucel asked them.

'No, in town with friends,' Huw replied.

'Then you'd best go there now. And don't come back.'

'Yes, we'll do that. Thank you, my lord. Come on Rhys,' Huw pulled his young charge towards the door.

Mucel turned back towards the bar with a sigh. Such confrontations were not uncommon. King Burgred's alliance with Rhodri of Gwynedd was unpopular with many of his subjects and Welsh traders who ventured this far into Mercia in its wake often met with a hostile reception. When he was last in Tamworth, three men had been killed in a brawl at an inn like this one. Not the best impression of Mercia for this young prince from Wessex. Well, even princes have to learn how the world is.

Owen was tugging at his hand.

'What is it, boy?'

'My lord, I know the older man. Let me accompany them back to their lodgings. The streets may not be safe for them.'

Mucel looked over at the centre of the room. The man with the knife he had restrained was no longer there. A number of other men had disappeared also. He felt a burst of exasperation. Why were people so stupid? But this young Welshman was in his charge. He couldn't allow him to put himself in danger.

'No,' he said, but it was too late. Owen had already left for the door. 'Stop!' he shouted but Owen paid no attention and dived swiftly out of the door.

'Let him go and be with those of his kind,' Cynehelm said.

Mucel frowned. But he wasn't about to go rushing after Owen. He would send a couple of his men but who knew where those Welshmen were heading? Tamworth had plenty of hiding places. And what a lawless place it had become. No, he corrected himself, Tamworth had been a lawless place since the death of King Offa. King Burgred's accession hadn't changed that. 'Take the prince to our dining table,' he said to Cynehelm curtly. 'I will join you shortly.'

Alfred followed Cynehelm to the dining area which had been set aside for them. Eadburh and Ealhswith were seated at the table waiting. Ealhswith's eyes were wide with excitement.

'What's happened?' Eadburh asked Cynehelm.

'There's been a brawl between some Welshmen and the locals. Our young Welshman has gone haring off after his countrymen.'

'Where's Mucel?'

'I think he's gone to send some men after them. He said he wouldn't be long.'

Sure enough, Mucel joined them after a few minutes, accompanied by an apologetic landlord. 'I'm so sorry, my lord. Most regrettable. Such disturbances are very rare here.'

Mucel grunted. He had no desire to listen to the landlord's lies. He was quite put out of his normal good humour. He had a nasty feeling that things weren't over yet. Why did that Welsh boy have to run off the way he did? His mood discouraged conversation and they ate in silence. Only Ealhswith looked as though she was enjoying herself. Maybe she didn't normally have exciting things happen around her.

Halfway through the meal, the landlord entered again. 'I'm sorry to disturb you, my lord, but one of your men says he needs to speak with you immediately.'

Mucel got up and left the room, leaving a host of questions behind.

Outside the door, Blythe was waiting for him.

'What is it?'

'We've found them. It's bad. Two men dead. The ones involved in the fight.'

'God! And the boy who was with us?'

'He's there. It looks as though he killed the Mercian. We're holding him and the old man. The others fled before we got there.'

Worse and worse. At least the prince hadn't gone with his friend. 'Take me there,' said Mucel grimly.

Blythe led him through dark streets down to the river and an open space in front of a large watermill. There were men holding torches in the open space and by their light, Mucel distinguished two bodies lying on the ground. He cursed softly to himself.

The Welshman and the boy were standing beside the watermill with a couple of his men beside them, but they showed no sign of trying to escape. When he drew closer, he could see that they both appeared bewildered. He had seen men look like that before at the scene of a murder.

'What caused this?' he asked.

'We were attacked,' Huw said. 'There was a whole group of them. Rhys tried to fight them off, to protect me. And was stabbed . . .' He paused, his eyes wide with shock. 'Killed.'

'There are two bodies,' Mucel said.

'I killed the other,' Owen said. 'I heard the shouting and caught up with them just as they were being attacked. I saw that Mercian kill Rhys. And I killed him.'

'It was self-defence!' Huw burst out. 'They would have killed us all.'

'Was it self-defence?' Mucel asked Owen.

'I was protecting Huw,' Owen said. 'They would have killed him. And yes, me too. I'm a Welshman. Huw is my friend. He has always looked after me.'

Mucel was aware that beyond the ring of torchlight, people were gathering to see what would happen.

'This is a matter for the king,' he said. 'His peace has been broken. He will decide the consequences. In the meantime,' he said, looking at Owen and Huw, 'you will be taken to the castle and kept there to await his decision.'

'But Rhys, what will happen to Rhys?' asked Huw.

'He will be given a Christian burial, along with the other.'

'You'll bury him with fellow Cymru, won't you?' asked Owen.

Mucel scowled. He was not going to take orders from a self-confessed killer. 'That also is a matter for the king,' he replied. 'Take them up to the castle,' he said to Blythe. 'I will follow you when I have seen to the bodies.'

Blythe and some of his men formed a guard and escorted Huw and Owen away. They made no protest. They would be safe in the castle. Their lives would be cheap anywhere else in Tamworth tonight.

Mucel stared out into the darkness. 'Is there a priest among you people?'

An elderly man shuffled into the ring of torchlight. 'I am a priest,' he said simply.

'Father, can you arrange for the burial of these bodies?'

'Yes.'

'You had best bury the Welshman tonight. Is there somewhere appropriate?'

'There is a graveyard which has other Welsh in it.'

'Good. Bury him there. Keep it as quiet as possible. The other,' Mucel looked down at the young face, still showing the bruise where he had been hit at the inn. 'Do you know him?'

'Indeed, I do,' the priest sighed. 'Poor Cenred. His parents will be heart-broken.'

The crowd of onlookers was moving forward into the light. Mucel had a desire to be gone before Cenred's parents arrived.

'Get some of these men to take Cenred to his church,' Mucel said to the priest. 'You can sort out a funeral with his parents as you wish. But the Welshman needs to be buried tonight. And quickly. I'm not having his body violated.'

The priest nodded. 'I understand, my lord. I will attend to it myself.'

'Is there someone with a cart?'

'I have a cart,' a large, honest-looking man came up to them.

'You'll take this body on it and go with the priest to bury it?'

'I will.'

'Good.' Mucel handed the man some coins. 'This is for your trouble.'

The man looked pleased and hurried off to collect his cart.

'Take as few with you as possible,' Mucel said to the priest. 'Just that man and one or two others you can trust to dig the grave. Anyone else, direct to help with Cenred.'

'It will be done as you say, my lord. You can rest assured of that.'

'Thank you, Father.' Should he give the priest some money as well? No, that would look bad. 'I'll call on you, Father, in the next day or two. Which is your church?'

'Saint Chad's.'

'Thank you once again.'

Mucel left the scene with the rest of his men and headed up the hill to the castle. The same steward greeted him as had done a few hours previously. He assured him that the Welshmen were locked up safe. 'Do you want to see them, my lord?'

'No.' It had been a long day; Mucel had no desire to prolong it further. 'I will return in the morning. You expect the king back tomorrow?'

'Tomorrow or the next day, yes.'

Mucel made his way back to *The Boar*. As he reached the inn, he heard cries of lamentation and anger coming down from the river. He hoped the priest had got away with the Welshman in time but felt no desire to investigate further.

Alfred was shocked to hear that Owen was being held in the castle, having killed a man. He had been sent to bed as soon as Mucel returned, grim and uncommunicative, that evening. But it was not possible to keep the news from him the following day. The town was full of it. And Owen's absence had to be accounted for.

'I must go and see him!' he exclaimed when Mucel told him what had happened.

'You can't. Not until the king comes back and decides what should be done with him.'

'Why not?'

'It's not safe. Feelings are running high against him in the town. The boy he killed was the son of a prominent man.'

'But why would Owen do such a thing?'

'They were attacked. At least, that is what he says, and I suspect it's true. The young Welshman was killed also.'

'Then he's not to blame.'

'That's for the king to decide.'

Alfred was left full of questions, which none of the adults were willing or able to answer. Cynehelm just shrugged. 'These things happen, Alfred. A Welshman will always side with his kind.'

'But he's my friend.'

'Blood is thicker than water.'

He received a more sympathetic audience for his bewilderment from the young girl, Ealhswith. 'It happens at home as well,' she said. 'Particularly with traders. We often have trouble when pagan traders visit.'

'The Welsh aren't pagan; they're Christian like us.'

'Yes, but they're different. They come from somewhere else. And many of these people will have fought them in the past. It's not so easy to forget that. Especially if family members have died.'

Alfred looked at her with interest. Her face was young and innocent, but her words suggested a certain wisdom. Maybe she was repeating something her mother had said.

'I like Owen,' he said, feeling as he said it that it was a childish response. But she smiled at him in sympathy. A nice smile; it stayed with him.

King Burgred returned from Lichfield two days later to find his capital still on edge and two Welsh prisoners in his castle.

'Did anyone see what happened?' he asked Mucel in a private conference with him that afternoon.

'The Welshmen say they were attacked by a group. When my men arrived there was no one else there but they would have had time to flee after Cenred was killed. No one has come forward; they're probably frightened to.'

'So, there's no-one to contradict what the Welshmen say?'

'No, and it makes sense. Would one man have attacked two? And the Welsh boy was killed as well.'

'A life for a life.'

'The people in town don't see it that way.'

'No, they wouldn't,' Burgred agreed. 'A Welsh orphan against the son of a well-liked local family.' He sighed. 'This Huw, what do we know about him?'

'He was a close companion of the old King Cyngen. He was with him on pilgrimage when the old king died. As was the other, the one who's admitted to killing Cenred. That's where he met your wife's brother.'

'Yes,' said Burgred slowly. That connection was a problem also. 'They're friends?'

'They are. Alfred was most upset when I told him yesterday. He wanted to come up here and see him immediately.'

King Burgred was silent for a while. Mucel said nothing. He knew his king well enough not to intrude on his considerations. He could guess at some of them but there would be others that he knew nothing of. Burgred was a careful man; even with trusted subordinates, he kept a lot to himself. 'Going back to Huw,' he said eventually, 'how has he managed since returning from Rome? With a new ruler in Powys."

Yes, Rhodri, thought Mucel. The reaction of that powerful neighbour would certainly play a part in Burgred's considerations. The alliance with King Rhodri might be unpopular with many Mercians but it had proved its worth to Burgred. Only a few months ago, Rhodri had defeated an invasion force of pagans coming from the west before they could reach Mercia.

'I think he's managed well enough,' Mucel said in response to Burgred's question. 'King Rhodri has not touched his land. He's been careful not to offend those men of Powys prepared to accept his rule.'

'And Huw does that?'

'As far as anyone knows. He's not given any sign of rebelling. That tends to be a young man's occupation,' Mucel added wryly. 'And, as far as I can see, no one in Powys supports King Cyngen's sons. They spent their whole time fighting one another. Rhodri has brought peace.'

'Yes, peace is certainly worth a lot,' Burgred agreed.

'I don't think Huw has the influence with Rhodri that he did with Cyngen,' Mucel continued. 'Maybe that's why he's taken to trading with us. I checked his licence; it's valid. His customers vouch for him also.'

'Let's banish him,' Burgred decided. 'Tell him to return to Powys and stay there. Withdraw the licence; there's reason enough for that.'

'The boy as well?'

'He can't stay on here now, can he? Alfred will be with us for some time.'

'Yes, I see that,' Mucel agreed. 'Can I let Alfred see him before he goes? He'll be unhappy if he's not allowed to.'

'I suppose so, Burgred replied, a little impatiently. 'But do so today. I want them gone by nightfall. The sooner they're gone, the sooner things will settle down.'

Alfred stared mournfully at Owen, who was sitting on a bed in the room where he was being kept in the castle. It was a secure, thick-walled room but not a dungeon. Light filtered through from outside. Huw had tactfully withdrawn to the far end of the room to give the friends some privacy for their goodbyes.

'You're leaving me,' Alfred said reproachfully.

'I have to,' Owen replied. 'The Mercians would have my blood if I remained here. Ealdorman Mucel was right – it's not so easy to leave behind the place of your birth. I am Welsh, I'll always be Welsh. Even with all the kindness you and your father have shown me, I've never felt at home in England. The English will never accept me as one of them.'

'I do.'

'You are different, Alfred,' Owen said with a fond smile. 'I am sorry to leave you but I have no choice now. The life of a man is between us. Hopefully, we will meet again one day.'

'What will you do in Wales?'

'Huw has kindly offered me Rhys's place as his assistant. Your father agreed to take me into his court because I had no one in Wales who would support me as kin. I do now.'

'I'll miss you.'

Owen bit his lip and stared at the floor. Alfred was still young; there was much he did not understand.

As if sensing that now was the time to intervene, Huw came over from his side of the room to join them. 'It's very kind of you to come and see us, my lord prince,' he said.

Alfred stared back at him with his clear gaze. 'Why would I not come and see you?' he replied. 'Owen is my friend. I don't think he's done anything wrong. He was defending you. I'm sorry about your nephew.'

'Thank you,' Huw replied. He hesitated. Something about the boy's artless candour moved him to consider a solution to a problem. Could he ask it of him? Was it fair to ask a boy? But he wouldn't get into trouble, would he? And he could always say no. "Would you. . . would you be willing to do something for us, my lord?'

Alfred's gaze narrowed. Artless he may be, but he was no fool. 'What are you asking for?'

'Rhys has been buried in secret. I can understand the reason for that. But. . . I would like to know where. I may be able to come back here one day. And if I am I would like to visit his grave. And there are other members of his family still alive who would wish to do the same.'

Alfred's gaze cleared. He nodded. 'I can do that,' he said. 'It is right for you to want to know. But how can I get the information to you?'

'The family we were staying with down by the river have Welsh kin. If you pass the information to them, it will reach me.'

'All right, I'll do that,' Alfred replied. He was pleased by the request. It was a small adventure to enliven what he saw as dull days ahead without Owen. And it was a token of ongoing friendship.

Owen seemed to think that also. He got up from the bed and gave Alfred a hug. 'God bless you, Alfred,' he said. 'I'll miss you, too. You're going to be a great man.'

That was rather like Redi saying he was going to be a priest; he wasn't sure he wanted to be a great man if it meant being lonely. But looking at Owen he realised that his friend was happier than he had ever been in Wessex. He had a new life ahead of him, one where he would not be in exile. So, he would have to let him go and learn to be happy for him also.

'God bless you, too,' he replied. 'I wish you both a safe journey.' He shook hands with Huw and left the room. Short goodbyes were the best. Not that he didn't think of Owen many times over the following months. When he had discovered from one of the grave-diggers where Rhys was buried, he would often include it on his walks with Sideways and stand by the freshly dug earth for a few moments, wondering about the world beyond the border, while his dog looked up at him with lopsided goodwill.

*

With the king and queen back from Lichfield, Alfred and his travelling companions moved into the palace adjoining the castle to be with them. It had been four years since Alfred had last seen Elsa. He had difficulty recognising her to begin with. Her first words to him were that he had grown. She had, too; she was a woman now. A queen no less; Wessex didn't have one of those. And yet as the days passed, he began to see traits in his sister which he remembered from when they were younger. He had expected her to be bossy, which she was, although in a calmer way than before. Her status meant that she was used to being obeyed, and she no longer had to contend with older brothers. But she still had a certain irritability and impatience, which she did her best to keep hidden, but which surfaced from time to time in unguarded moments. Life had improved for Elsa, but it still held many areas of frustration. She would tell Alfred about these when they were alone sometimes, with an honesty which he remembered as another of her qualities.

About Burgred, she said little. He paid her every attention but he was so self-contained a man, it was always difficult for an outsider to gauge what he was feeling. If Elsa knew, she didn't say. 'He is a good man,' she said in a rare confidence. 'He deserves a son.'

That, Alfred soon learned, was Elsa's principal frustration. After three years of marriage with no pregnancy, she was beginning to fear that she was barren. It had had the effect of making her more religious. She prayed to God for the blessing of fertility and made frequent visits to the cathedral at Lichfield. But her religious concerns did not blind her to the world around her, through which her husband had to plot their course. Alfred soon received confirmation from her of the divisions in Mercia at which Mucel had hinted. Cynehelm behaved towards her with extreme courtesy, but when he had left to return home, she confessed her distrust of him to Alfred.

'He's a plotter,' she said. 'He'd like to see us gone.'

Alfred was shocked. Wasn't Cynehelm his father's friend? Why had he been chosen to escort him to Tamworth if he was an enemy?

'Oh, he's safe enough at the moment,' Elsa said in response to Alfred's questions. 'We ensure that he's kept on a tight leash. And he's been useful to father as a spy – that's where his talent lies. But his family has no love for my husband's – they're only waiting for an opportunity to rebel against him. As is half of Mercia. It's not an easy land to govern, Alfred. Too many of its lords believe they have a claim on the crown. Burgred has to spend most of his time keeping them in check.' A rare smile crossed her face. 'But he's good at that.'

About Mucel, she was more complimentary. His lands adjoined those of her husband's and he had supported Burgred in his ascent to the kingship. As Mercian lords went, he was one of the more reliable. His wife could have been a problem, coming from Cynehelm's troublesome family, but Elsa didn't think she was. 'She's a good woman,' she said, which in this context meant someone content to follow her husband's lead.

Mucel and his family departed Tamworth a week or so after Cynehelm. Much of that time Mucel had spent in conference with Burgred. Alfred could see from the fond good wishes of the departure that he was high in the king's favour. 'He protects our back in the east,' Elsa said simply. Alfred was pleased to have his good impressions of the man confirmed and joined in the general wish that they have a safe journey back east.

With his travelling companions gone, Alfred adjusted to his new life, which wasn't so different from the old one. He went for walks with Sideways and observed the Mercians going about their daily lives. At least there was more going on in the streets of Tamworth than the quiet confines of Steyning. The watermill was a particular source of fascination and the millers became used to the sight of the young boy with the dog staring in wonder at the large wheels turning the shafts and interlocking cogs to the enormous millstones grinding the grain. There was always activity around the watermill; along with the market, it was one of the major sites of social interaction in the town with a steady stream of customers. Alfred learnt much about the people of Tamworth from watching the negotiations and arguments over the buying and selling of flour.

Elsa ensured that her brother did not have too much time to spend on his own. The military training which he had started in Wessex continued with a group of young Mercians. Alfred was small for his age but his travels had toughened him up and he was a quick learner. He soon learnt that there was more to physical combat than just strength. Waiting was important – not letting fear lead you to over-commit. So many people sought to banish the fear of confrontation by an immediate all-out attack. He learnt how to keep that out while staying calm himself, waiting for an opening. Often an opponent's strength could be used against him if a move was made at the right time. After one such occasion, when he had managed to get his blunted sword past a large Mercian's guard, he even received a rare commendation from the gruff thane who oversaw the training. 'You don't look like much, but you'll do.'

And he enjoyed expeditions out of Tamworth. Sometimes these were undertaken as part of the training, when they would camp out and be expected to fend for themselves. On other occasions, Burgred took him along as part of his court travelling around the kingdom and even beyond it. They rode into the Welsh borderlands and met with King Rhodri, about whom he'd heard so much from the Mercians. He was a jovial man with a glinting smile – a lot less frightening than Alfred had expected him to be. He had hoped he might see Owen at King Rhodri's court but there was no sign of him and it didn't seem right to ask after him, given the circumstances in which he'd left Mercia.

In Mercia itself, they met with local leaders and Alfred compared his impressions of them with Elsa's accounts of their loyalty. With the ones she distrusted, he tried to discern signs of unreliability or hostility in their welcoming faces. It wasn't easy to do so. He wondered how Burgred managed.

Burgred himself didn't say a lot to him, but then Burgred didn't say much to anyone. He did treat him as a family member and ensured that he was well looked after. Alfred learnt to trust his taciturn brother-in-law.

At Chester, close to the borders of both Wales and Northumbria, Alfred admired greater town walls than any he had seen since Rome. They were Roman, he learnt, but unlike many of the old Roman constructions, looked as though they were still fit for their original purpose. Perhaps the town's proximity to two borders gave its inhabitants an incentive to keep its walls in good repair.

As part of her campaign to secure God's blessing of a son, Elsa wanted to see a hermit who lived in a remote cell by the river near Chester. Burgred and Alfred both accompanied her to the cell. Alfred had expected the hermit to be ancient with a white flowing beard, like the pictures of holy men in his psalter. He was surprised to find he was a young man of about Berti's age, dressed in fine clothes and with a number of books on a shelf in his comfortable cell. He came from a noble family and had been a monk at the monastery in Northumbria where St Bede had written his famous books over a hundred years ago. Plegmund, as the hermit was called, was a scholar himself and might have followed in the great Bede's footsteps had the monastery been as secure as it was in the saint's time. But the coast of Northumbria was increasingly prey to pagan raids, with undefended monasteries being a favourite target. After one such raid, Plegmund had escaped with a sackful of books from the burning library and made his way back to the greater safety of his Mercian homeland. Rather than join another monastery after his experiences in the north, he had felt the call of the solitary life and had established himself as a hermit on an island in the middle of a marsh. Should pagans reach this far inland, they would have some difficulty reaching his cell and he would have plenty of notice of their approach.

But the remoteness of Plegmund's cell did not deter visitors. Indeed, it may have encouraged some. Wandering Irish monks, with which Mercia was well-stocked, often called in on Plegmund in the course of their travels. As a consequence, he was unusually well-informed about goings on in Ireland and often had news of whatever foreign parts his visitors were returning from. Most of their visit was taken up with a wide-ranging discussion between Burgred and Plegmund covering recent events in Ireland and Francia. Alfred listened with ears wide open. He learnt that Ireland suffered badly from pagan raids also, one even reaching the monastery of Clonmacnoise, which both Plegmund and Burgred referred to with reverence as the home of saints and scholars.

'They managed to save their library,' Plegmund said. 'Unlike Jarrow,' he added mournfully, casting an eye on the books on his shelf. He saw Alfred looking at them in wonder also. 'Do you like books, my lord prince?'

'Yes,' Alfred replied.

Plegmund went to the shelf and took down a volume bound in calf skin. 'This is a history of our land by the great St Bede. Every ruler should have a copy by their side. Do you read Latin, my lord prince?'

'A little,' Alfred said defensively.

Plegmund handed him the precious volume and returned to his discussion with Burgred. They were talking about Francia now and Alfred heard names he recognised – King Charles, Hincmar and John of Erin. But he was only half paying attention now with this magical book in front of him. He turned the thick pages slowly, wishing he could decipher the regular columns of black lettering. Why was Latin such a difficult language to learn? Colman had not accompanied him on this trip to Mercia. He had almost stopped having lessons with him anyway, their place having been taken by the military training. There was no real expectation on him to continue studying. And yet, the thought of so much information and learning lying just beyond his grasp was a constant reproach. He remembered the look on Judith's face as she was reading. In a different world. He would ask Elsa to find him another teacher.

Burgred and Plegmund were still talking about Francia. Apparently, there were rumours that King Charles might be facing an invasion by his brother, the East Frankish king. Plegmund didn't seem to think that any invasion was imminent. 'It won't be until next year at the earliest,' he opined.

Burgred seemed to think he had obtained sufficient information from this well-informed hermit. Or maybe his wife's impatience had communicated itself to him. Elsa had been growing increasingly restive at the prolonged discussion of foreign affairs. She had wanted to visit this cell for a blessing from a supposedly holy man. But the holy man seemed far more interested in discussing worldly events with her husband. She wondered where his reputation for holiness had come from. Had he, perhaps, successfully predicted the outcome of a battle in the past?

But Plegmund's manner changed on being informed by Burgred of his wife's wish for a blessing from him. He became quieter and more considered. He led Elsa through a series of prayers and called on God to grant her the blessing of fertility which she and her husband craved. Even so, Elsa found the visit dissatisfying.

'He talked a great deal for a hermit,' she said to her husband after they had left the cell.

Burgred looked uncomfortable. 'Hermits often do talk a lot when they have visitors. Most of their days are spent in silence.'

'So, they need to talk a lot when they have visitors?'

'No. But people come to them for advice. And I was interested in what he had to say, even if you weren't.'

'It didn't seem to have much to do with God.'

'God is interested in this world also, my dear.'

Back in Tamworth, Elsa found a religious more to her liking in a young priest from Lichfield called Werferth, who reminded Alfred of Colman. He had the same quiet, deferential manner, which adapted itself easily to life at a court. That he was not someone who would spend his time discussing the affairs of various kingdoms with her husband was a mark in his favour, as far as Elsa was concerned. She appointed him her confessor and also tutor to Alfred, who had confided in his sister his wish to continue studying. As he got to know him better, Alfred revised his opinion that Werferth was another Colman. Underneath his quiet manner, Werferth had a searching intelligence which made his lessons considerably more interesting than those of Colman, who often resorted to learning by rote. With Werferth, there was always a reason for the tasks he set, always a connection to a wider world. From the breadth of his references, Alfred realised that he must be a considerable scholar in his own right and he determined to make the most of having him as a tutor. On the occasions under Werferth's guidance when he was able to coax meaning out of a forbidding Latin sentence, he felt a sense of achievement and revelation which made the grind necessary to get there more than worthwhile.

Werferth also translated stories to Alfred, particularly from the history of St Bede, which Plegmund had shown him in his cell. From these he learnt of a different England than the one he knew, where battles were fought far away in the north and where, although Christians might die in the fight, their religion marched triumphantly on. After a reading from Bede, he would imagine himself a Christian warrior vanquishing pagans in his military training. Werferth encouraged him to write down the stories that inspired him – more hard labour, scratching shaky letters, very different from the smooth, neat script of the book. He would never make a scribe. But it was some form of communion with a greater world. He remembered his conversation with Colman on the road to Rheims about how books could keep your memory alive for a long, long time.

The months passed and spring gave way to summer. Mucel returned to Tamworth. There was some trouble with Welsh tribes to the south, who were not party to the alliance with Rhodri. Despite the fact that his land was at the other end of the country to the border with south Wales, or maybe because of it, Mucel was Burgred's favourite representative for dealing with disputes that arose down there. The two men remained in close conference for a couple of days and the king held a banquet for his ealdorman on the eve of his departure.

'Can I go with you?' Alfred asked Mucel at the banquet.

'What's that?' Mucel smiled genially down at him.

'Can I go with you? You're going to the land of the Hwicce that you told me about, aren't you? I've not been there.'

'You like to travel, Alfred, don't you?'

'Yes.'

'Well, I don't know. Have you asked the king? Or your sister?'

'They'll say yes if you do.'

Mucel looked at him appraisingly. 'If they agree, I don't see why not. It's good for a prince to see the country.'

Burgred and Elsa made no objection so Alfred left with Mucel the following morning, pleased to be on the move again to somewhere new. As they travelled south, he noticed hills off to the right, breaking up the flatness of the landscape. They reached the great river of which Mucel had spoken and followed its course towards the sea, the stone becoming lighter – a pale, golden colour – and other hills appearing off to the left.

'That is the land of my wife's family,' Mucel said, indicating the hills on the left. 'Good for breeding sheep. And stubborn people,' he added with a smile.

They continued down the river valley to the town of Gloucester, which Mucel had chosen as his base for negotiations with the Welsh. 'This is the furthest south you can cross the river safely,' he told Alfred. 'It's a treacherous river, where the tide comes in very quickly. It kills many each year. So a place where you can cross it safely is important to whoever holds it. That's why the Romans built a fort here.'

From Gloucester, they travelled over the river to meet with the Welsh tribal leaders. The land over the river was the principal cause of the current trouble. It had been borderland for hundreds of years with both Welsh and English laying claim to it. When Mercia was strong, the Welsh were pushed back behind the dyke King Offa had built to keep them out. But when Mercia was weak, they crossed the dyke and sought to reclaim the land which had been theirs before the Saxons came.

'It may not look it, but it's valuable land,' Mucel explained, as they rode over scrubby ground dotted with clumps of trees. 'Mostly for what lies underneath.'

'What's that?' Alfred asked.

'Iron. And coal. Half the swords in the kingdom are forged here. The Welsh have always wanted a share of the resources. And as the river isolates this part of Mercia from the rest of the country, it's not easy to defend.'

Over the next few weeks, they met with various Welsh leaders, usually in forest clearings or other remote locations. The meetings were invariably friendly. Mucel was well-known to the Welsh from previous visits. He remembered them, asked after their families, and listened more than he spoke. Alfred could see that he was a skilled negotiator, his natural good nature helping to smooth over grievances and disagreements. With the Mercians, he had a more difficult job. They had been subject to raids, were angry and wanted revenge. Alfred watched Mucel lead them gradually to an awareness of their vulnerability, and the need to come to some sort of accommodation with the Welsh. Moving between the various groups, agreeing compensation, trading rights and privileges was a tiring and time-consuming business, but after a couple of months, the Mercians had agreed to accept compensation for the raids and the Welsh had agreed to withdraw in return for a guaranteed supply of iron from the mines. Alfred realised that much of the money needed to secure the agreement was being provided by Burgred. He asked Mucel why when they were riding back to Gloucester after the final agreement had been reached.

'Because securing a peace is often cheaper than continuing a war,' Mucel replied. 'Not always; but here, we have calculated that it is.'

'Won't paying the Welsh to stop their attacks only encourage them to launch some more?'

'It might,' Mucel acknowledged. 'These agreements don't last forever.'

'What happens then?'

'Then we have to decide again whether buying a peace is cheaper than waging a war.'

Despite his observations of Mucel's negotiating skills, it didn't seem a very sustainable way of proceeding to Alfred. He remembered Cynehelm's wry comment that

Burgred was a great one for alliances. 'Is it just a question of what's cheaper?' he asked.

'No, it's a question of a hundred and one things,' Mucel replied, a little sharply. 'As you'll have seen if you were keeping your eyes open.'

They rode on in silence for a while until reaching the outskirts of Gloucester, where Mucel recovered his good humour. 'Come on,' he said to Alfred. 'It's time for you to see what all this has been about.'

He led the way down to a stone building near the river. As they drew closer, they were hit by a wave of heat reaching out to them. The air filled with clangs and shouts. In front of the building, were a number of rough cylindrical furnaces a few feet in height, which were giving off blue flames and smoke. A few men were standing by the furnaces, watching the flames and occasionally shovelling coal onto the fire. Other men to one side were smashing at rocks with hammers. As they drew closer, their horses became skittish at the noise and heat so they dismounted, going forward on foot.

As they reached the building, there was a shout from one of the fires. They watched as a thick golden liquid began to seep out from a hole at the base of one of the furnaces.

'Is that iron?' Alfred asked, fascinated by the glowing liquid, which seemed possessed by a life of its own, moving in heat.

'Not yet,' Mucel replied, as a man reached into the hole with a large pair of tongs and extracted a glowing bloom from the fire's heart. Everyone drew back as he lifted his dangerous load onto an anvil. Then two more men came forward and started hitting the bloom with hammers, drawing off sparks of what could have been anger.

'Come on,' said Mucel. 'That will take some time. There's something else I want you to see.'

He walked into the stone building with Alfred following. Inside were more fires, although smaller than the ones outside. This was where the wrought iron was forged into weapons and tools. At one anvil, a blond giant of a man was hammering metal into the shape of a sword. He stopped when he saw Mucel approaching and grinned down at him.

'So, you're back again, are you?' he said. 'And who is this you've brought with you?'

Although his English was good, he spoke with a strange accent which Alfred did not recognise. Close up, his hair was as much grey as it was blond, and his face was lined, but he still looked a powerful man. On hearing Alfred's name and lineage, he smiled again. It was a challenging smile, of one used to life's ironies.

'A prince of Wessex,' he said. 'I fought your father once.'

The man's name was Olaf and he was a pagan from the north. Alfred stared at him with barely-concealed wonder. It was his first sight close to of one of the terrible northern pagans who dominated so many people's fears. It seemed appropriate that it should be in a place of fire and smoke.

Olaf was a veteran of a hundred battles in Francia, England, Wales, Ireland and the Pictish lands. He had fought under Ragnar Lothbrook, at the siege of Paris over ten years before.

'Have you heard of Ragnar Lothbrook?' he asked Alfred.

'No.'

'Ach, what do they teach the young these days?' Olaf exclaimed in disgust.

'You're not as famous as you think you are,' Mucel observed.

'Me? I'm nothing. But that man was a leader, the greatest there has been.'

'Where is he now?' Alfred asked.

'In Valhalla, like so many others. But he left three sons. You will hear of them, I assure you.'

Alfred felt a chill pass through him, despite the heat. What was this enemy doing amongst them here?

Olaf enlightened him. He was happy to tell his story. After the death of Ragnar Lothbrook in a raid, he had drifted north with various war bands, never settling. In Ireland, he had offended one of Ragnar's sons, Ivarr, at a banquet and had to leave in a hurry with Ivarr's men on his heels. He crossed over to Wales on a boat full of monks off to populate a new monastery. His previous experiences of monks had been brief and bloody and they were all terrified of him to begin with. But the Christian religion lays on its adherents the strange obligation to love their enemies and a couple of the braver monks had engaged with this alarming stowaway. When they learnt that he was on the run from his fellow pagans, they decided he was ripe for conversion and Olaf spent the rest of the voyage learning about Christianity. He had always been curious about other people, and had never understood how Christianity, which seemed such a defeatist belief, had managed to become so widespread in all the lands he'd been attacking over the years. The monks were happy to enlighten him and invited him to join them at their monastery. As he had nowhere else to go, he accepted and spent six months in the unlikely surroundings of a religious community. It was a pleasant enough place to rest up and learn about a country from the inside. He was a strong man, who had been a farmer before he had taken to raiding, so he was able to earn his keep working in the monastery's fields.

But after a while the novelty of the religious services wore off and the rigidity of the monks' routines grew tiresome. It was a barren life they led; the joy he saw in some monks' eyes was as much a puzzle to him after six months as it had been at the beginning. And he missed the presence of women. Any religion which cut itself off from the pleasures and comforts of women had to have something wrong with it. He had a brief relationship with a woman he met in the fields, but the need for secrecy was distasteful to him. And when the woman started expressing feelings of guilt, using the very same Christian arguments he'd heard from the monks, he decided it was time to move on.

Ivarr had left Ireland and so he could have returned there. But his time at the monastery had worked a change in him; or maybe it was a change that would have happened anyway. He was no longer young. There was nothing waiting for him back north, but he felt a growing need to settle somewhere, to stop wandering. A monastery wasn't the place for him, but he decided to keep his eyes open for somewhere that might be. And so it made more sense for him to head east, towards the more settled Saxon lands. He fell in with a group of traders, who travelled between the Welsh gold mines and Mercia. They needed guards for their valuable cargo. A powerful, unattached pagan, used to fighting, and with some knowledge of the land and languages, was a welcome recruit. He worked for them for the next year, travelling throughout Wales and

Mercia, and learning more about the metal-working trade. Gloucester was a frequent stop and something about the place appealed to him. He had been born on the banks of a similar, unpredictable river. And it was a centre for metal-working, which interested him more than farming. The fire and smoke was congenial. He found a girl, whose father made swords and was not averse to taking on a willing apprentice.

'And so here I am!' Olaf concluded with a laugh. 'Making swords for Mercians to use against one another.'

'I hear that Ivarr is back in Ireland,' Mucel observed.

'Yes,' said Olaf. 'They can't have been saying their prayers.'

'Is he really that terrible?'

'So the stories say. But you shouldn't always believe the stories.'

'You knew him, though.'

'He was young when I knew him. Just arrived in Ireland. Making his way, with little but his father's name. Or so I thought. That was my mistake,' he added wryly.

'Why do you say that?'

Olaf stared at Mucel. 'What a one you are for questions! I suppose that's your job. Information-gatherer for the king of Mercia.'

Mucel reddened. 'Should we not want to know about our enemies?'

'Ivarr's not your enemy. Not yet. He has enough to keep him busy in Ireland.'

'He's not our friend.'

'No,' Olaf agreed. 'But then Ivarr is no man's friend. He's a cold man. He doesn't look like much, you know. He's tiny compared to his father. And he has weak, bandy legs, caused by some childhood disease. Some of his men call him The Boneless One. Behind his back, of course. You don't insult Ivarr to his face. As I know only too well. I was lucky to get away. A year later, I wouldn't have. But then a year later, I would have known him better.'

'How does he get men to obey him if he's physically weak?' Mucel asked.

'He's not weak,' Olaf replied. 'He's as tough as iron and his arms are as strong as anyone's. On a horse, the weakness of his legs don't matter. He can lead a charge. If anything, his disability has made him stronger. He has had to be strong to survive. He cares for no man. So, they all fear him. But more than that, they obey him because he is a brilliant commander. He has never lost a battle. His coldness helps him there. Having conquered his own weakness, he knows how to exploit the weaknesses of others.'

Olaf turned back to his anvil with the air of one who had said all that he intends to say. He picked up his hammer and resumed smashing it down on the rough sword before him.

11. The Bride

Princess Judith headed towards the great hall at the sound of harp music. Listening to Diarmait practising was one of the pleasures of her quiet life. He would give impromptu recitals for her and the cascade of notes took her away to a brighter place. The old man was an exile like her but he was in contact with his homeland whenever he played his instrument or sang one of the old songs. But much as she liked hearing Diarmait play, Judith liked talking to him as well. He was something of a gossip and a valuable source of information about the family in which she found herself. He had been a harpist at the Wessex court from a time when even her husband was young; from before he was king, when his father, King Egbert, the great restorer of Wessex power, ruled the land.

'A gloomy, stern man,' Diarmait said in response to Judith asking about King Egbert. 'But he liked a tune and was good to me. Everyone respected him. They said he was hard, but fair. You find that in people who've had to make their own way.'

'I'm told he didn't approve of my predecessor.'

'Osburh?' Diarmait gave a reminiscent smile. 'He would have preferred her to be a princess, it's true. Like you, my lady,' he looked fondly at her. His eyes noticed something. 'You're wearing Osburh's brooch.'

'Oh,' Judith was embarrassed. 'Yes. The king asked me to. He said he liked to see it being worn.'

As a peace offering, Blade had sent Osburh's jewellery back to his father. It didn't make Aethelwulf speak any more fondly of him, but he did not reject the jewellery. He showed it to Judith, passing items tenderly through his hands as if they brought back something of their previous owner to him. He had wanted Judith to wear some. She was reluctant to wear a dead woman's jewels – it made her feel like an interloper. But the hurt look on his face when she refused made her feel guilty and so she'd agreed to wear the brooch as the most neutral piece – it wouldn't be touching her skin. And it was a pretty object of delicately worked gold set with dark red garnets. It wasn't much that he asked of her; he could have asked more. So far, he had not insisted on his rights as her husband. He had treated her with a gentle courtesy, for which she was grateful. Perhaps he was waiting for her to grow older and the difference in their ages to become less stark – the thought made her nervous. Or maybe he was still pining for his dead wife? That thought might have made her relieved, but it didn't. It made her feel like an object, a commodity to be traded. What had she come all this way for? What was this marriage? If it had made her a queen, as her father intended, then it might mean something. But it hadn't even done that.

And so she spent her time reading and listening to Diarmait with a sense of her life having become detached from its course. She was still so young. She listened to her companions chattering about their new-found or past loves with a sense of irritation. As a married woman, she was meant to have passed beyond that stage of youthful infatuation. She hadn't even been through it. From time to time, she caught herself thinking of her husband's estranged oldest son. That look on his face when he said goodbye to her after that disastrous conference in the forest. . . she had known what that meant. That was the look of someone who saw her as something more than a commodity. But what was the point of dwelling on such things? She had been given to the father, not the son.

As the weather improved, she started to go out riding with some of her companions, usually accompanied by Osric and one or two members of the king's guard. She was aware of some romances between her companions and members of the guard. Depending on her mood, she would either make it easy or difficult for them to ride together. There was no romance between herself and Osric, but she liked the old soldier's company. Old? He must be at least ten years younger than her husband but he had the shrewd, slightly weary air of someone who had seen a great deal. Like Diarmait, he could be persuaded to talk of his past. She learnt of battles past and many of the personalities of Wessex, whom Aethelwulf occasionally mentioned. Although he had moved east to Steyning with the king, Osric came from the old kingdom in the west, the land now ruled over by the rebellious son. He talked of its fields and towns with the nostalgia of an exile.

'It's pretty here,' Judith said. She was an exile herself, but one of the consolations she found was in the landscape – the bright, shingle coast and the green swell of the steep Downs inland.

Osric looked around with an unimpressed look on his face. 'It's poor land,' he declared. 'Much richer to the west.'

There seemed little prospect of her being able to travel west to verify the statement. But on days when the sun was shining, when riding over the top of the rippling Downs gave her the sensation of sailing on the nearby sea, that seemed no hardship.

She was enjoying just that sensation one morning when Osric suddenly reined to a stop. At the same time, two men from the guard following rode up to him. They were pointing out to sea at a longship coming from the east.

'Pagans,' Osric replied in response to her query. 'We need to get back, my lady.'

'Is there any danger?' she asked, not sure if the slight tingling in her body was fear.

'Not from one ship. But there could be others following behind.'

They rode back to Steyning, where Osric reported the boat's presence to Aethelwulf. It had continued travelling west. Lookouts reported no signs of other ships following.

'Most likely just spying out the land,' Aethelwulf said when she asked him about it that evening. "No cause for concern.'

'Is that what Osric says?'

He frowned. 'Osric always worries.'

His tone discouraged further questions but she decided to ask Osric about it the next day. Ever since they had settled in Steyning, Aethelwulf's thoughts had been occupied more with the past and the future than the present. He had told her he was writing his will. 'It is a time to reward those who have been loyal and punish those who have not,' he said. The thought that he was spending most of his time providing for what would happen after he had died made her feel uncomfortable. It emphasised the gap between them – her life had barely begun, whereas he was contemplating the ending of his. Demands of the present were an irritation for him, a distraction from his major concerns.

'The ship didn't land,' Osric told her the next day. 'It went as far as the island then turned back east.'

'They've not come this way before, have they?'

'Not for a long time.'

'Do you think they'll come again? Maybe with more ships?'

Osric looked at her. 'It's possible,' he admitted.

'And if they landed, would we be able to fight them off?'

She was intelligent, no doubt about that. Her questions honed in on exactly his concerns, which the king had dismissed. But the king did not want to know.

'Well?' she asked with a slight frown at his delay in replying. She was his mistress as much as the king was his master. And from what he had seen of Frankish royalty, they expected to be obeyed and have their questions answered fully.

'The king believes so,' he said eventually.

'What do you think? They're your men.'

'You're asking me to contradict the king?'

'I'm asking you to tell me the truth. As you see it. What did you tell the king?'

'I said we needed more men.'

'Why?'

'The harbour is thinly defended. If the pagans landed there, they could cause a lot of damage.'

'And if that ship was on a spying expedition, which the king seems to think, it would have seen that.'

'It might have.'

'So, we need more men, don't we? Why did the king not agree? His son, Prince Aethelberht, has a duty to defend him.'

'Prince Aethelberht is facing constant pagan attacks in the east. He has no men to spare. And he's a long way away.'

'Prince Aethelbald, then. He's nearby. And he's not under constant attack, is he? We've a joint interest, don't we, if the pagans start attacking the south coast?'

'The king would rather die than ask Prince Aethelbald for help.'

'And the rest of us are to die as well? Just because of. . .' She paused. Perhaps the rest was best left unsaid.

Osric was watching her closely. 'What would you have me do, my lady?' he asked softly.

She felt a moment of pleasure pass through her. She may not be a queen but if the king wasn't going to act then Osric, at least, seemed prepared to accept his orders from her.

'You still have contacts in Hampshire, don't you?' she asked.

He nodded. 'My family is there.'

'And you know the ealdorman. Wulfstan, isn't it?'

'Yes. We were close once. Before I accompanied the king on his pilgrimage.'

'So, if you or your family make the ealdorman aware of our need for men to guard the harbour, could that not be arranged by him as a local matter? Without need for the involvement of Prince Aethelbald?'

Osric smiled. Yes, she was certainly intelligent. 'It could be presented as such,' he said. 'But if the king were to discover we had Hampshire men here, he might not like it.'

'You're a Hampshire man, aren't you?'

'Yes, but I've been in his personal service a long time.'

'We have a duty to ensure the king is adequately defended,' Judith decided. 'I think it unlikely that he is going to enquire where any new members of his guard have come from, particularly if they are deployed on the coast rather than at court. His mind is occupied with other matters. But if he does, you can say that it was my decision and that you were obeying my specific orders. If he has any issues, he can raise them with me. Is that sufficient for you?'

'Yes, my lady. Thank you. I will arrange to contact Ealdorman Wulfstan without delay.'

The next few days were nervous ones for Judith. It was the first time she had asserted herself independently of the king. He might be angry if he found out. Had she put herself in Osric's power? No more than he had put himself in hers. And it was the right thing to do, she had no doubt of that. The king might not be concerned about the present, but he had a duty to protect those in his care. And if he didn't, then it was right that she did. The appearance of two more pagan ships a couple of days later confirmed her in this view. She sent Osric and members of the guard down to the harbour to scare them away from landing. He obeyed her readily enough. The ships continued sailing west as before and didn't land. Even so, it made her anxious for a reply from Wulfstan.

When it came, it was accompanied by a request for a meeting. She didn't like that. It was one thing to put in a request to the ealdorman of Hampshire without the king's knowing; another to meet with him in private. But Osric was reassuring. 'It is the way we do things,' he said. 'He's not had dealings with you before.'

'You told him that the request didn't come from the king?'

'I had to. Otherwise, he would have replied to the king.'

'And what did he say when you told him?'

'He said he could understand the need. They've been concerned by the pagan ships themselves.'

Judith considered. After all, what difference did it make? The ealdorman of Hampshire was an old man. And it would be useful for her to meet him also and assure herself of his loyalty and dependability. Even so, she hesitated.

'How can I meet him?' she objected. 'I can't travel into a neighbouring kingdom, one the king regards as hostile.'

'There's no need for that,' Osric replied. 'He can come here.'

'Here?'

'Well, the border. We can go out riding and meet him by accident.'

'Accident?'

'An arranged accident,' Osric acknowledged. 'The border between our two lands is fairly flexible. People go to and fro the whole time. Hunting parties often cross over; there's no reason why riding parties shouldn't also. And if your party happens to run into that of the ealdorman of Hampshire, then it's only right that you should greet one another. The king couldn't object to that – Wulfstan is one of his oldest subjects.'

Judith stared at Osric. She had always thought him a bluff, straightforward soldier. Maybe most people have a talent for conspiracy when it's in their interest. It was best that he had that talent for the current task. But she knew from her father's court that once people started to conspire, they often found it hard to stop.

'Is it safe?' she asked softly, her eyes fixed on his face.

'Safe?' Osric shifted a little uncomfortably under her scrutiny. 'Why, yes. Of course, my lady. As I've said. . .'

'Because if it isn't,' she said, moving closer to him, 'I will survive. The king and Prince Aethelbald will see to that. But you won't. You will be tortured most horribly. I will see to that.'

Osric's face was sweating. He dropped to his knees. 'My lady, I swear to you I will protect you. May I be tortured to death if I fail in that task.'

Judith nodded. 'Good,' she said calmly. 'That's what I wanted to know. It's best we understand one another. Very well, you may arrange the meeting.'

Three days later, she rode out early with Osric and a small guard westwards towards Hampshire. They reached the beginning of the forest which divided the two kingdoms. The forest which had been the scene of her husband's unsuccessful negotiation with his son. But she was confident of being a better negotiator than her husband. And she was asking for less.

They kept to the outskirts of the forest, riding north through heathland and glades, keeping well within the boundary of the eastern kingdom. Judith was aware from the tension of Osric as he rode beside her that they had reached the planned meeting ground. The trees provided some shield from casual observers.

The sound of riders approaching from the left caused her to turn her head. Yes, they were led by an old white-haired man. That would be Wulfstan. But who was that young man riding beside him? He looked familiar. She turned to Osric with quiet fury. 'You have betrayed me!'

'My lady, I have not!' His eyes were terrified. 'I was not told the prince was coming.'

Wulfstan was greeting her with an apologetic smile on his face. 'My lady, it is a great pleasure for me to meet you. When I told my lord the prince of your request, he insisted on coming with me in person to assure you that we would do everything in our power to assist you.'

Blade was very different from when she had last seen him. Then, he had been calm and in control, amused even. Now, he looked awkward and nervous, aware that he was not welcome. She did not disabuse him of the fact.

'I did not know that the prince would be accompanying you,' she replied stiffly to Wulfstan. 'Had I known, I would not have come.'

'My lady,' Blade said hoarsely. 'I will explain my presence which is so unwelcome to you.'

'There is nothing you can say to explain it,' she retorted.

The other riders had dropped back, leaving them alone. She looked around for Osric; he had disappeared.

'It appears I'm your prisoner,' she observed coldly.

'No,' he replied. 'I'm yours.'

She did feel a moment of fear at those words. His hostility she could endure, might even welcome. His love? She didn't know about that.

She rode on. He kept pace beside her.

'You must know that your coming here will cause me trouble,' she said. 'My husband is bound to be told of it. A meeting with the ealdorman of Hampshire could be accepted as an accident; a meeting with you, never.'

'I had to see you again,' he said. 'I have not stopped thinking about you since we last met.'

'You're mad!' she said, looking at him with glittering eyes. 'I am married to your father.'

'That is an unnatural marriage. He is almost in his grave. What could he possibly give you?'

She felt tears gathering and blinked them away angrily. 'It's cruel of you to say that. His eldest son.'

'The fact that I am his eldest son gives me the right to say it. You should have been married to me and not him. He is the one who has prevented that. His selfishness and his mistrust of me.'

'Is he not right to mistrust you?'

'Why? Because I want to rule, as is my right, and am not prepared to let him pass me over? I have proved myself worthy. I have fought for him; I have governed for him. But he's never liked me. I don't know why. Maybe I've not told him enough times that he's doing God's will. He knows that I'll make a better king than Berti. But he's doing his best to deny me that. As he's tried to deny me everything else.'

There was genuine hurt in his voice. He looked young and surprisingly vulnerable when she glanced at him. She did not doubt what he was saying – it rang true to her. He had opened himself up to her in a few brief moments more than Aethelwulf had ever done. And he was right, wasn't he? She should have been married to him. Then she wouldn't be living this half-life – a pawn in old men's games. She would have her own existence. Who knows? Even children. Her heart was beating uncomfortably. But what could she do?

Blade was watching her closely, a growing look of triumph on his face. 'You agree with me,' he said. 'I can see that you do.'

It was too much. She suddenly burst out crying. She wasn't quite sure why. Maybe it was just the emptiness of her life brought home to her by this vigorous young man at her side. And the impossibility of change. Even if she had wanted to marry him, it was too late. God and all His saints stood in the way of that.

Blade was further encouraged by her tears and reached out an arm to her.

'Oh, go away!' she snapped. 'Haven't you done enough damage already? What can I do?'

He was calm now, no longer nervous. Back to how he had been at his meeting with Aethelwulf in the forest.

'You've already done it,' he replied. 'And I bless you for it.'

Had she given herself away? Certainly, the self-control which had governed her life since her marriage had deserted her.

'What can I do?' she repeated woefully. 'You've even scared my guard away.'

'They're still here,' he said. 'As is Osric. He will be scared of you. But he had no knowledge of my coming today, I swear to that on my love for you.'

'Your love,' she repeated. 'Your love is inconvenient, my lord prince.'

'I know,' he gave a happy smile, which suggested a warmer, simpler world to her. 'I will do my best to minimise its inconvenience to you, my lady.'

'And how do you suggest I explain this meeting to my husband?'

'You will find a way, my lady. I have every faith in you.'

Riding back with Osric and the same guard who had accompanied her out, Judith was silent for a long time. She could see that Osric was anxious. Well, let him sweat for a while. Eventually, she spoke to him.

'You abandoned me.'

'My lady, I did not,' Osric protested hurriedly. 'But you were angry with me. I was afraid. I swear I did not know the prince would be there.'

'Even so, I did not ask you to drop back and leave me alone with him.'

'No, my lady.'

'So, why did you?'

'It was clear that the prince wanted to speak to you alone, my lady. Wulfstan saw that also.'

'And you take orders from the prince and Wulfstan, do you?'

'No, my lady. But if I had stayed with you then others would have done also. And whatever it was he wanted to say to you, I felt it best that no one else was there to hear it.'

There was sense in that, she had to admit.

'And did anyone hear it?' she asked.

'No, my lady. Wulfstan and I ensured that everyone kept their distance.'

'Even so, there are plenty of witnesses to our having met and had words.'

'Yes.'

'So,' she hesitated, but there wasn't anything really to decide. She still needed Osric's help. 'How is that to be explained to my husband?'

'I would suggest telling him what happened, my lady.'

'Really?'

'We had hoped to keep the meeting secret from him. But I don't think that's sensible now. Too many people will talk of the prince's presence. A reason needs to be given for the meeting and the real reason doesn't involve the prince. He came along uninvited. You didn't welcome him – there are witnesses to your saying you would not have come if you had known he would be there. You can tell the king that you were concerned about the need for more men to defend the coast, and that I suggested a meeting with Wulfstan. I hope you will still protect me from any anger of the king, my lady.'

She considered. Yes, it was good advice. Sometimes the truth was the best policy. Up to a point.

'Did Wulfstan say anything about the men?' she asked. She had forgotten about the reason for the meeting.

'Oh, he promised those immediately. That was never in doubt when the prince came with him. Of course, the king may not accept them once he knows about them.'

'No.' That seemed a lesser problem now.

Aethelwulf was angry, angrier than Judith had ever seen him. 'This is treachery!' he exclaimed when she told him of the meeting on their return. His eyes bulged with fury.

'If it was treachery, I wouldn't be telling you about it,' she replied. She steeled herself to remain calm, but was uncomfortably aware that calmness might not be enough. He was hurt in a matter of family pride, a place where reason often cannot reach.

'Conspiring with my son, that wretched traitor!'

'I didn't know he would be there. I wouldn't have gone had I known. I told him that. Ask anyone who was there.'

'What use would that be? Conspirators always lie to save their skins.'

'The conspiracy, if you insist on calling it that, was to ask Wulfstan for men to help protect your kingdom. Wulfstan, not your son.'

'You must have known that Wulfstan would refer any request coming from you to my son.'

'I did not, no.' Should she have known? Did Osric know?

'How could you be so stupid? You know that they will seize any opportunity to humiliate me."

'Surely not?" She faltered. What could she say? *Don't mention Prince Aethelbald.* 'I thought Wulfstan would want to help. Haven't you said before how loyal he was?'

'That was before my son stole Wessex from me. Men's loyalty is to those who can harm them.'

She bit her lip. Should she continue to argue with him? He seemed to be calming down a little.

'I thought Wulfstan would want to help,' she repeated. 'His land is threatened by the pagans also.'

'I told you the pagans weren't a concern. Their ships appear from time to time. And then they disappear. I've been fighting pagans all my life. I know when precautions need to be taken against them.'

She was silent.

'You don't believe me?' he continued. Calmer, but the anger was still there. They were on safer ground, though.

'I. . . I was worried,' she said quietly. 'I've heard of what those ships can do.'

'And you don't trust me to defend you?' He was closer to her now. A big man. She was more aware of his physical presence than ever before. His broad shoulders were stooped but still powerful, his skin rough with age and pinpricked with little points of red. His eyes, which often seemed weary, looked younger – sharper and more commanding; perhaps that was the effect of his anger. She felt more frightened of him than she had ever been before, even on the day of their wedding. The effect of his closeness told her more clearly than any words that she was in his power. But, in case there was any doubt, he added the words.

'I have been very considerate to you,' he said softly, his breath on her face. 'Too considerate. You take it for weakness. You would betray me to my son.'

'I swear to you I would not!' she cried.

He bent down and kissed her fiercely on the mouth, stopping any more protestations.

'No, you will not,' he said pulling away, and looking at her panting and fearful face. 'You will not have the opportunity. You will not go riding again. Your place is at my side.'

He came to her room that night. She knew enough about men to have expected him to do so. An assertion of ownership. Well, it wasn't so bad. The darkness of night has its mercies. He was rough to begin with, but she soon realised that he was nervous, too. That made it more bearable – the sense that what was being done was greater than both of them. The weight of his body upon her made her gasp and she cried out in pain as he thrust within her. He whispered endearments in her ear, his hot, possessive breath spreading out over her small body. She clenched her teeth against the pain as his excitement grew and his seed burst deep within her. She was conscious of liquid everywhere, within and without – blood, semen and sweat. The smell was cloying, intimate, overwhelming..

Aethelwulf lay as though dead on top of her, his arms flung wide. She wriggled out from beneath him and lay unburdened on her back, staring into darkness. One of his arms reached out for her, a hand cupped around her breast. She shivered but did not try to remove it. She allowed his caresses, aware of having left her childhood behind.

The following months were difficult for Judith. Any news about Prince Aethelbald aroused fresh suspicions in the king. It may have been that no one had heard what the prince said to her on that fateful afternoon when they had met, but that they had been alone together, and that the prince had very much wanted to speak to her was common knowledge. She knew that for Aethelwulf, increasingly aware of the comparisons being covertly made between him and his son, and with the sensitivity to ridicule of an old man who takes a young bride, it was more than enough to prove her guilt. He didn't ask her what had passed between his son and her. She wished he had – she had not encouraged Blade. Better the truth than whatever the king's suspicions were telling him.

Clearly, Aethelwulf had decided that fathering another son would be the best response to whatever people were saying about him. It would show that he was still vigorous, a man to be respected, and provide another royal contender to set against Blade. As Judith knew, a son whose mother was a Frankish princess would have a strong claim to rule. And so her husband made several more visits to her room to assert his rights and she learnt more lessons in the art of loveless intimacy. Did she hate him? No, part of her felt sorry for him. He was a victim, as well as she. She was aware that the act of love was becoming an increasing strain for him. But he had chosen his victimhood; she hadn't chosen hers. She had not had many illusions about marriage, but she hadn't thought it would be as bad as this. There were times when she felt little more than an object, to be used and then discarded. She didn't know which she feared more – becoming pregnant, or not becoming pregnant. If no son arrived to fulfil Aethelwulf's wish, then she knew he would blame her. But if one did, how would she feel towards him?

Added to which, the pagans had returned. Their ships were now a regular sight offshore and after they had landed and raided a settlement only twenty miles away, even Aethelwulf had decided that more men were needed as a defence force. He had, needless to say, rejected the offer of men from Wulfstan and, in addition, he had dismissed Osric following the meeting with Blade. The new commander of the guard, Keane, was young and inexperienced. But Aethelwulf had called for support from his other son, Aethelberht. Berti had arrived from Canterbury with a contingent of men to patrol the coast. If he resented having to divert men from the east coast to the south, he didn't show it. Judith liked Berti. Although he seemed quite frail, certainly in comparison with Blade, there was something reassuring about his calm response to threats and dangers. She felt comfortable with him and appreciated the look of respectful sympathy in his eyes when he talked to her. And Aethelwulf relaxed a little with Berti there. He was not jealous of Berti, who had plenty of experience in listening to and validating his father's opinions. Judith was not the only one sorry to see Berti go, but the effect of his visit and the reinforcements he had brought lingered for some time, leaving Aethelwulf less irritable and suspicious.

*

The year was drawing to an end. The first full year of her married life, Judith realised. Maybe the year when her marriage had truly begun, when it had stopped being something in which she was only incidentally involved. It was definitely hers now; or, more accurately, she belonged to it. What did she feel? Nothing much. A grey dullness which matched the weather outside. What a cold, miserable land this was for much of the time. At least it made Aethelwulf's prohibition on her riding easier to bear. She read, and wandered around the estate, finding some consolation in the bustle of the farm and its animals. But even these could prompt unwelcome thoughts. She stopped looking in on the pigs in their sties. Their trusting eyes and genial snuffles had cheered her to begin with. But with the Christmas feast approaching, their days were numbered, their betrayal nigh.

Aethelwulf had gone back to spending a lot of time in his study with books and charters. He still seemed to be working on his Will, often consulting with scribes and priests. Perhaps he felt more in control of events doing that? He came to her room less often, for which she was grateful, although it made her feel more redundant than ever.

She was reading in her bur one morning with two of her companions, Marie and Elise, who were doing needlework by the fire. Judith had so far avoided taking up needlework. When she did that, she thought, her life would definitely be over.

The bur had a window overlooking the courtyard before the hall and the king's study. She would break off from her reading occasionally to look out into the courtyard and watch the comings and goings. She heard the sound of a horse clattering into the courtyard and looked up to see Keane, the new commander of the guard, hurriedly dismounting and making straight for the study. That was unusual – Aethelwulf didn't like being disturbed by his guard when he was at work.

Unusual enough to make her nervous. She stood up. Marie and Elise looked at her.

'I'm just going to check on something,' she told them. 'I'll be back soon.'

Outside, Aethelwulf was already in the courtyard and calling for horses and his steward.

'What is it?' she asked.

'Pagans,' Keane replied. 'They've landed at Shoreham.'

'Shoreham?' It was only about five miles away, at the mouth of the river which flowed past Steyning. 'What are you going to do?'

'We're going to beat them off,' said Aethelwulf, whose steward had come up and was helping him into a coat of mail. He looked more vigorous than Judith had ever seen him.

'But what about us?'

'Keane is going to ride along the coast and raise some more men and then he'll come back here and look after you. We're blocking the river with carts and will be between you and the pagans.'

'What if there are more of them?'

'If there are more of them, they'll be spotted. Keane will have everyone on alert. Don't worry, you'll be perfectly safe.' He spoke with a certain impatience and yet, at the same time, she had the impression that he was rather pleased she was needed his reassurance. He certainly showed no fear himself as a groom brought up a horse for him, which he swiftly mounted. Other members of the guard were gathering around him, awaiting his lead.

'Don't worry,' he repeated, beaming down at her. 'We'll be back in no time. The pagans won't know what has hit them.'

She watched him ride away with the guard.

'I'll be back soon, my lady,' Keane said, on his horse again.

'Yes,' she said, not sure how much of a reassurance that was. He was only a little older than her. 'And what do we do in the meantime?'

'I would gather everyone in and around the hall. I've already sent word that all the hands should come in from the farm. They will protect you in my absence. Not that you'll need protecting,' he added hurriedly.

'All right,' she said. 'I'll go and collect everyone.' It would give her something to do. 'Come back soon.'

'I'll be with you again before you know it, my lady,' Keane replied. 'And I'll bring more men with me.'

He clapped his heels into his horse's side and rode away at speed. It was an opportunity for him to show his worth. Let's hope he has some, Judith thought as she went back to the bur to collect Marie and Elise.

After she had passed messages on to a number of people, the hall began to fill up with the household servants. Outside, the farm hands were gathering, many of them bearing the most warlike of their tools – axes, hammers, knives, a few spears. The mood was sombre. This land had mostly been spared pagan raids but everyone had heard the stories and there were few who did not know someone with experience of them. Tales of their cruelty and indifference to death hung in the air.

Part of her would have liked to have remained out in the open with the men. Inside the hall, among mostly women and children, the atmosphere was more palpably one of fear and helplessness. Some were weeping quietly, others murmuring prayers. At least for some of the smaller children, too young to know the reason for their all being allowed into the hall, it was a great adventure and they ran around the worried adults whooping with excitement.

Diarmait at least was calm. 'I'm an old man,' he said in answer to Judith's query. 'I've seen lots of these raids come to nothing. And I believe in the king. He's beaten the pagans many times.'

How little of her husband's life she really knew.

'Would you like me to play some music?' Diarmait continued. 'It might help.'

'That's a good idea,' she replied. The harp was on its stand near the king's table. 'But avoid battles.'

'Yes, my lady,' Diarmait smiled. 'With this audience, I shall sing of love.'

The music did help. Diarmait sang Irish ballads, which took them away to a gentler place. Intrigued by the novelty of being played to, even the tensest faces began to relax a little. Judith allowed her own thoughts to be enchanted by the old man's music. Life could yet hold a great deal in store.

There was a stirring amongst the men outside. Perhaps Keane had returned? He must have been away for over an hour. She went to investigate.

'What is it?'

A man lay sprawled on the ground, panting for breath.

'He says pagans are coming from the west,' reported Marden, one of the farm supervisors.

'From the west?' Shoreham was due south.

Marden nodded. 'It's a different band, my lady. They must have landed further down the coast and struck inland.'

'Where's Keane?' Judith asked, trying to keep her voice steady.

'He's riding to intercept them. He sent this man back to warn us.'

Judith's head was spinning. She must keep control. 'How many men does Keane have?' she asked.

'A handful.'

'And the pagans?'

'Fifty or so.'

'He won't hold them, will he?'

'No, my lady. He's going to try and catch them by surprise to kill a few and then fall back here.'

'He should have come back here when he first saw the pagans,' Judith said. She had been right to distrust him. Too young; trying to prove himself.

Marden looked uncomfortable.

'We must call the king back.'

'Yes, my lady.'

'Has anyone gone?'

'We've only just heard the news.'

'Well, someone go for God's sake! Who's the quickest?'

'I'll go, my lady,' a thin young man came forward.

'Get him a horse.'

'I'll be quicker running,' he replied. 'I know a short cut to Shoreham.'

'All right, run. Like the wind!'

The young man tore off. Judith turned back to Marden.

'Do we have any horses?' she demanded, aware that all the good ones were likely to have been taken by the guard.

'There's Strider,' Marden replied. 'She's about the best one left, but she's old and not fast. Dale might well be quicker running.'

'Get someone on her anyway.' The farm hands looked around among themselves. Horses were a noble's prerogative. But one of the ploughmen, who was at least used to being with horses, volunteered. Watching him being manoeuvred onto his elderly mount instilled no sort of confidence in Judith. The pagans would be upon them before that horse got halfway to Shoreham.

'The rest of you get ready,' she said. 'They could be coming any time.' She ought to go back inside the hall but was reluctant to do so. At least here, she could hear and see the worst. The men seemed solid. No obvious signs of fear. Resentment, yes, but people could fight from resentment. What about herself? She didn't know. She realised Diarmait was still playing his harp. No, she wouldn't go back into the hall. Let them continue listening to music.

Would she die? It hadn't been much of a life. Very different from what she had imagined. But maybe it would be better to die than be taken by the pagans. She had heard what they did to women.

'Give me a knife,' she said to Marden.

He hesitated.

'Give me a knife, I said.'

He handed her his own knife. She ran her finger along the blade. Sharp enough. With this, she had a choice.

The entrance gate to the courtyard had been shut and barred. The men with spears formed a line behind it. The pagans might cut the gate down, but it would delay them if they tried to get through that way. But would they? The central buildings were only surrounded by a timber stockade. Easy enough to cut through or set alight. In the courtyard, she felt like a rat in a trap, meekly awaiting its fate.

Judith saw some men climbing onto the roof of the great hall. That would be better. At least she could see what was coming from there.

'How did they get up there?' she asked Marden.

'There's a ladder, but it's steep and you then have to pull yourself up over the roof overhang.'

'Show me.'

'It's dangerous.'

'You think staying here is safe? Show me.'

He took her to the ladder and followed her up it, his body blocking the sight of the drop. The overhang onto the roof looked impossible. Judith could barely reach past it. But Marden called down one of the men on the roof who reached down and grasped her wrists and with him pulling and Marden pushing they got her onto the roof, where she lay panting on the thatch.

'You're as light as a feather, my lady,' said the man who had pulled her up, a grin on his broad face, which made her feel better. They showed no fear, these farmers. She clambered up and followed him to his vantage point on the other side of the roof.

Judith looked across to the west and the trees on Chanctonbury Ring. Hard to distinguish, but yes, that could be men coming down from the hill. No sign of Keane.

'How long before they're here?' she asked Marden, who had come up after her.

'An hour or so at that pace. Maybe less if they speed up.'

They walked round to look south towards Shoreham. No one was coming back along the road. Aethelwulf had spoke confidently of being back in no time. He had been gone a number of hours already. If the pagans had divided their forces deliberately to attack in the rear, might not those on the shore keep up the fight to make things easier for their companions? The land dipped before the sea. She couldn't see what was going on down there. Dale must have reached them by now. It was only a few miles. Less if he knew a shortcut.

The minutes passed with her thoughts darting backwards and forwards, seeking encouragement, trying to avoid discouragement. She remained on the roof, watching the pagan band draw ever closer.

After half an hour or so, one of the men on the roof broke the silence by crying out.

'What is it?' she asked sharply.

He didn't reply.

'What is it?' she repeated.

'Don't look, my lady" Marden said.

She had thought it a god. She had heard that pagans often marched into battle behind an image of one of their gods. But now she saw that it was a head. A human head. Keane's head, cut off and fixed to the end of a spear. She did not cry out, but bile rose in her throat and her blood ran cold. She fingered the blade of her knife once more. Unless the king returned soon, they were doomed.

The pagans were before the gate. She watched them confer in front of it. Rough, wild-looking men. A leader started gesturing to either side. Yes, they were going to storm the stockade. A lot easier than trying to knock down a barred gate. Marden started to edge back round to the side of the roof where the ladder was.

'I need to tell the men,' he said to Judith. 'We can spread out behind the stockade. Don't worry, my lady. They won't find it easy. They don't know the layout and they'll only get a few through at a time. We can pick them off.'

She nodded, not knowing whether to believe him or not. 'I'll stay up here,' she said. 'I can signal to you where they're trying to break through.'

He nodded. 'Yes. Nevin, you stay up here with our princess. The rest of you, follow me down.'

She watched them hurry back down the ladder. The men in the courtyard were already beginning to fan out to the stockade as the pagans started to hack away at it. It wouldn't take them long to cut a way through. And if Marden and the others did succeed in keeping them out, then there was another way. She watched an old man in a hollow some distance away, crouching before a pile of wood. Summoning Loki, the god of fire. Even as she watched, a thin plume of smoke began to rise up from the hollow.

The first pagans had cut their way through the stockade and a fierce fight was taking place. She cast her eyes around. Other pagans were attacking different parts of the stockade but no one else had yet managed to find a way through. Marden was right – they would not find it easy. He hadn't said anything about fire, though. Already torches were being brought from the hollow towards the stockade. She looked south again. Still no sign of any people coming back. Surely, Dale must have reached them by now?

No sign from the south, but from the west, more people were coming. Some men on horses, followed by other men running. She felt sick. That was it, then. Even if the king came back now, he would be too late. At least she still had Marden's knife.

But the pagans seemed confused by the approaching men. A number of them stopped, lighted torches in hand, to stare towards them. An unreasoning hope began to stir in her breast. Could they be? But how was it possible? The king was in the south. He would not have looped round to the west to get back here. And Keane had been killed. Even if he'd managed to raise a few men, there weren't that many in the scattered dwellings to the west. And these men were being led by someone. There was a definite purpose to their advance.

'It's Osric!' Nevin said with a laugh from beside her. 'With men from the Hampshire fyrd. They must have tracked the pagans here.'

Osric! After his dismissal by Aethelwulf, he had returned to his homelands in Hampshire. She had not expected to see him again. And yet, here he was, come to rescue them with the men whose help Aethelwulf had spurned. Her heart burned with a fierce exultation. Her husband might not value her, but there were others who did.

Sure enough, the pagans had stopped their assault on the stockade and were turning to face the advancing men, who were almost upon them.

*

King Aethelwulf was in a black mood. The pagans at Shoreham had put up a much fiercer fight than expected. For hours, battles had raged along the shoreline, their outcome in doubt. The effort needed to dislodge the pagans and the tension involved had exhausted him. He felt too old for such battles. These were all young men trying to make a name for themselves. Why should he be having to resist a new generation? That there might be an answer to such a question; that it stemmed from his refusal to accept help from a rebellious son was not something he was prepared to acknowledge. And yet, deep down, there may have been an unspoken awareness of this, which only added to his weariness and bad temper.

And then, in the midst of an almighty effort to force the pagans back into their ships, a panting young man had arrived to tell him that another band of pagans was advancing on Steyning. What could he do? They had no men to spare. Trying to disengage now would be disastrous. All he could do was urge his men to redoubled effort and hope that Keane and the farmhands would be able to keep the pagans out of Steyning long enough for them to get back.

But it was another two hours before they forced the pagans back onto the water and there was no certainty that they would not seek to land again as soon as they'd left the shore. But he couldn't delay any further. Feeling sick with worry and giddy from exhaustion, he galloped back along the road to Steyning with his lead nobles.

And when he got there, what did he find? That the pagans had been put to flight and his estate and wife rescued by Osric, the man he had dismissed for being in league with his accursed son. Judith had been loud in singing the praises of Osric, who had stood there with a satisfied smile on his face, as though expecting to be rewarded for his treachery. Well, he couldn't punish him in the circumstances, but he certainly wasn't going to reward him. He dismissed him with curt ill humour and told him to return with his men to Hampshire as they weren't welcome in his land. That had led to another argument with Judith, who accused him of rudeness and ingratitude. Unkingly behaviour, no less! What did she know of the behaviour of kings? Her father was notorious for his disloyalty to those who fought for him. He had thought she was becoming accustomed to her position of dependence but this whole unfortunate event had reawakened a wild defiance in her. She thought that the pagans' attack had proved her right and him wrong. Why should he have to spend energy he couldn't spare in defending himself against her? Her role was to support him not attack him. Osburh would never have criticised him in such a way before other people. His suspicions about her being in collusion with his son flared up again.

He wished he could just dismiss everyone and go to bed. He had never felt more tired than he did now. There was a deep weariness in his bones. But he could not ignore the men who had fought under his command. There needed to be a feast to celebrate the pagans' defeat and reward those who had secured it. He wished he could bar Judith from the feast, but that wasn't possible either. She had, in name at least, led the successful defence of the estate. If she wasn't given the credit for that then who would be? Osric? Impossible. Marden? Equally impossible. The king's honour could not be seen to be in the hands of his farm workers. If Keane had survived, he could have been given the credit, but he had been killed before the attack began.

Feeling pressurised by Judith, he had given a brief speech of thanks to the farm hands for their defence of the estate and directed that they have their own celebratory feast in the courtyard. She would have had them in the great hall itself, which showed how little she understood the ways of kings.

And so, as he sat at the head of the long table in the great hall, with his wife at the other end, he could hear the sound of laughter and singing coming from the courtyard. Those outside were enjoying themselves considerably more than those inside. The king's black mood infected those around him. He had tried drinking to lighten his mood and make him less tired, but it had

had the opposite effect. He felt dull and heavy, just waiting for the evening to end. He stumbled through another speech of thanks and offered a toast to those who had fought so bravely and to remember those who had died. 'May Christ take them to His holy bosom,' he concluded and sat down, feeling he had done his duty.

But those furthest away from the king, at the end of the table presided over by his wife, were less affected by his sombre mood. Some of the younger nobles were there and drink did not weary them in the way that it did the king. For many, it had been their first major fight and worthy of celebration. As well as the wine, their closeness to Princess Judith, small and glittering in her finest robe, was an additional stimulant. Her own role in fighting off the pagans should surely not be overlooked at an occasion like this? After the king's toast, it was open to others to propose their own toasts. Those closest to the king realised that he would not welcome any other toasts and kept to their seats. But those around his wife felt no such constraint. Encouraged by those around him, a young man called Rudd got to his feet and with a gallant bow to Judith, offered his own toast, 'To our brave and resourceful queen!' he cried. 'May she continue to defend our home and hearth as she has done today.'

There was a stiffening at the king's end of the table. Some of the servants had started to refer to Judith as the queen but, since his meeting with Blade on his return, Aethelwulf had not done so. She was his wife, Princess Judith. But after today it seemed that others, in addition to a few servants, wished to acknowledge her as queen, despite the evil precedent set by Wessex's last queen. Eyes around the table warily watched the king to see what his reaction would be to this unfortunate toast. It was not always the custom for the king to participate in toasts made by others but if he did not join in a toast to his own wife, what would that mean? And would he punish those who did.? Aethelwulf stared down the table at Judith but did not move. Silence hung in the air and no one else made to rise.

Judith's face reddened. It was not possible to tell whether it was through shame or anger at the king's lack of a response.

'Rudd is very kind to propose a toast to me,' she said, her chill tone audible throughout the silent hall. 'But the king is right not to rise. He knows that he owes the preservation of his estate to the valour of the men he has feasting outside this hall. And, most of all, to his former captain Osric, who came to our rescue with men from the Hampshire fyrd, and was rewarded for his loyalty by the king telling him to go away and never come back.'

Aethelwulf's face flushed a dark mottled red. 'You are impudent, woman,' he said, his voice thick with anger. 'You know that I dismissed Osric for treachery. I could have had him killed.'

'Osric never betrayed you,' Judith responded crisply. She didn't care what he did now; she would have her say before witnesses. 'All he did was accompany me to a meeting with the ealdorman of Hampshire to ask for military support against the pagans. The need for such support has just been demonstrated, but you refused it through pride, and dismissed Osric for the same reason. You would rather your wife was killed and your people enslaved than admit the need for help. Fortunately for us, Osric doesn't bear grudges. Unlike you.'

Aethelwulf's face darkened even further so that it was almost black. 'You met with my son!' he cried out.

'The son who has betrayed me. You are in league with him against me.'

'That is a lie. I didn't know your son would be there. I told him so and told him I would not have gone had I known he would be. Any number of witnesses will tell you that. But you choose not to listen.'

This time, Aethelwulf did get to his feet. He staggered up, fury in his face. He looked as though he might rush down to where Judith was sitting and throttle her with his bare hands. Rudd, still standing, fingered the handle of his sword. What would he do? The rest of the table looked on, appalled.

But, once standing, Aethelwulf made no further movement. His hands pressed down on the table, as though requiring its support. He glared down at Judith with a terrible look. 'You. . .you. . .you,' he choked with anger.

Or was it anger? Something was wrong. The awareness showed in his eyes, which lost their focus, turning inwards. His face began to twitch and his lips were flecked with saliva. Sounds of concern issued from around the table and a number of men around the king rose from their chairs to assist him. But before they could do anything, Aethelwulf gave a stifled gasp and pitched forwards, face down onto the table.

'Get a doctor!' someone cried.

'And a priest,' Judith muttered, her face white.

12. The Followers of Guernir

'Welcome back, Alfred. You've grown. Mercia has done you good.'

Swithun looked frailer than Alfred remembered. If he had grown, Swithun appeared to have shrunk. The lines on his face were deeper and he had a definite stoop. But his eyes still had a lively sparkle and he smiled with pleasure at seeing his young charge again.

'How did you find our neighbouring kingdom?' Swithun continued.

'Very interesting,' Alfred replied. He didn't know what else to say. Two years had passed since he had left Wessex with Owen – he had left as a child. And returned a man? No, not yet. Something in between. Still subject to the directives of others, but more aware of the fact; and more aware of them.

'And how is your sister, the queen?'

'Happy. She has a son.'

'So I heard,' Swithun's smile broadened. 'That is always a blessing.'

It certainly had been for Elsa. She had begun to despair of ever becoming pregnant. Alfred had noticed that although Burgred behaved towards her as courteously as ever, they were together less often. 'He'll put me aside,' Elsa confided to Alfred one dark night. 'A king needs an heir.'

But then her prayers and entreaties had at last been answered. Alfred remembered the morning that she had come into his room, her face flushed and beaming to tell him. Happier than he had ever seen her before. She had something of her own at last.

Months of anxiety had followed, which affected him also. He had grown close to Elsa. She treated him as an equal and told him things which no one else did. Having lost his mother, it was good to find a sister, with whom he could share hopes and fears. But if she lost her child, how would she react? Would she even survive?

But she did not lose the child. She gave birth to a healthy baby boy at the appointed time, and her life changed. Burgred delighted in his son, and the wife who had provided him. Alfred was pleased and relieved for Elsa but found it difficult to share her delight in the squalling baby. Inevitably, his relationship with his sister changed. She now had someone else to care for, someone who took precedence over him. Her world revolved around the baby. Their confidences, which he had grown to enjoy, dried up. She had no need for them any more. He escaped from the castle in Tamworth as much as possible. When he was there, he was often bored and lonely.

So, Blade's summons for him to return to Wessex was welcome. Mercia had been interesting and it had been good to get away from home at the time. But it was good to return now also. So much had happened since he had been away. So many rumours of wild happenings had whetted his curiosity. Hopefully, Swithun would be able to explain things to him. He always had in the past.

Swithun's smile faded, aware of the need to move on to more difficult subjects. 'You've come from Steyning, I understand?'

'Yes, I thought I should go there first.'

Swithun nodded. It was hard for the boy. To have lost both his mother and father while away from them. And so young still.

'That was the right thing to do, Alfred,' he said. 'I'm only sorry that you could not be at the funeral. But. . .' he hesitated, 'it was not an easy time for anyone. It was best that you stayed where you were.'

'I've heard rumours he was poisoned.'

'That is a wicked lie!' Swithun snapped, suddenly angrier than Alfred had ever seen him. 'Started by the malicious and spread by the foolish. Your father was not poisoned, Alfred. He died of exhaustion, having bravely fought off a pagan attack, as so many times before.'

'Why should people say he was poisoned?' Alfred persisted. Swithun was his best hope of finding out the truth.

'He collapsed at a celebratory feast. The credulous always suspect poison in such circumstances. But he lived for days after his collapse with doctors attending him constantly. They found no sign of poison. They are all agreed that his heart just gave way, having borne so much and for so long.'

'And why accuse Princess Judith of poisoning him?'

Swithun looked uncomfortable. The boy had grown into a relentless questioner. But if he had heard such tales then best deal with them now. He would be meeting Princess Judith soon enough.

'Your father collapsed in the middle of a public argument with the princess, Alfred,' he replied. 'After a disagreement which unfortunately continued during the feast. So, it was witnessed by many people. When your father collapsed, it was an opportunity for those who wish the princess ill to spread lies about her. But I don't know of anyone who was at the feast who believes the lie about poison. It has been spread by people who weren't even there.'

Alfred's mind teemed with further questions, but he sensed that there would be a limit to how many more Swithun would be prepared to answer. But there was something else he needed to know, a question Swithun would be expecting, but which he might find more difficult to answer. How to ask it? Stay away from rumours.

'Do they wish her ill because she has married Blade?'

Swithun did not reply for some time. Eventually, he said quietly, 'It's possible.'

'Do you think that was the right thing to do?' It was a cruel question. He knew that Swithun had refused to officiate at the wedding. Ealhstan had done so in his place.

Swithun looked at him with more than a shade of reproach in his eyes. 'I can't answer that.'

'The Bible says a man should not marry his father's widow.'

'It does.'

'So, why did they marry? And so soon after my father's death?'

'The princess was expecting to return to Francia after your father's death, Alfred. She was making arrangements to do so. But your brother. . .' he paused, 'declared his love for her.'

'At the funeral?'

'So it seems.'

'That's not right,' Alfred said stolidly.

How rigid the young can be, Swithun thought. Until they fall in love themselves. 'He knew he had to act quickly,' he said gently. 'Otherwise he would have lost her. As I say, she was planning to return to Francia as soon as she could after the funeral. Once there, he would never have seen her again.'

'But surely you don't approve of what they did?'

'It's not for me to approve or disapprove. The Bible also says you should not set yourself up as a judge of other people. Judgement is for God.'

'I don't understand.'

The boy looked bewildered. How to explain to him that people you look up to don't always do what the Bible tells them to? It was a lesson he needed to learn, and soon.

'Your brother might have expected to marry the princess in any event,' he said. 'He is a lot closer to her in age than your father was. Your father marrying her himself would have been a shock to him. He may even have seen it as a provocation. You know well enough that there was animosity between them.'

'So, it's not surprising that people should suspect my father was poisoned?'

'It may be a reason why some give credence to the lie. But, as I have told you, it is a lie.'

'But why should she marry him?' Alfred continued, more to himself than Swithun this time. His mind went back to the times he had been with Judith in Steyning, in particular when she had translated and explained to him the poem about the prisoner being comforted by the Lady Philosophy. 'She didn't have to, did she? She's an intelligent person. She must have known that people would say it was wrong.'

Swithun sighed. 'We are straying into territory where a cleric is not the best person to answer your questions, Alfred. Perhaps you should ask the lady herself? She may think she owes you an explanation. Just remember what I said about avoiding judgement. There are all sorts of reasons why people do what they do.'

In the royal manor a few miles south of Winchester, not far from where Alfred was having his discussion with Swithun, Judith was nervously awaiting his arrival. When Blade had decided to recall him from Tamworth, she experienced a fresh outburst of the feelings of guilt which had afflicted her at the time of Aethelwulf's funeral and her subsequent wedding to Blade. She knew all about the mutterings occasioned by so rapid a remarriage. It was not seemly; she should have been in mourning for at least a year. But she could not remain in Wessex for a year unattached. Her father was expecting her to return once he learned of King Aethelwulf's death. She would not have put it past him to send soldiers to abduct her if she did not return of her own accord. And for what? To remarry her as quickly as possible to some elderly count to shore up his support. Her father would not wait a year: he could not afford to. The rumours were thick that his brother, King Ludwig, was preparing to invade his kingdom. Wessex was a haven of peace compared to what she could expect if she returned to her father. And the thought of another loveless marriage to someone old enough to be her grandfather repelled her. Surely, she could do more with her life than accept being a pawn in her father's increasingly frantic manoeuvrings?

Not on her own she couldn't. A girl in a foreign land with no supporters, but already some enemies, who blamed her for causing Aethelwulf's death. Whether by poison or simply by disagreeing with him hardly seemed to matter. She needed a protector if she was to remain. And the one person who could offer her adequate protection was eager to do so. Arriving at Steyning for his father's funeral, Blade had lost no time in declaring once more his love for her. When he had done so before, she had refused to even consider the possibility, married to another man. Which had made Aethelwulf's suspicions and accusations even more hurtful. But now he was dead, she looked on his son with new eyes. He was handsome, young, brave – a considerable improvement on anyone her father might have in mind for her. Her life might have some meaning married to him. And he was in love with her. The very fact that he was willing to brave the Church's disapproval by marrying his father's widow showed that.

Once she allowed herself to look, she found herself a prey to new feelings. Of sudden mirth and bursts of happiness. And a certain carefree recklessness. People thought that she was in collusion with Blade? Very well. She would give them reason for such thoughts. The Church would disapprove? Let it disapprove. The Church had sanctioned her unnatural marriage to Aethelwulf, so clearly it must be wrong. It had condemned her to old age before she'd even had her youth. She would have it now.

She expressed reluctance and hesitation to Blade, but he knew with a lover's insight that he had won her. He stopped her objections with kisses and responded to her fears and reservations with a young man's confidence. Love made everything easy. She was infected by his confidence and began to share it. By the time he left Steyning two weeks after the funeral, he had her consent.

But before he left, she insisted that he tell his brothers and obtain their approval before they returned east.

Disapproval from the Church and from some of Aethelwulf's followers, she was prepared to weather – with Blade's support. When she was married to him, she would be protected from it. But families are different. Their resentments are fiercer and more long-lasting. And Aethelwulf was their father as well as Blade's.

Berti expressed nothing but pleasure at having Judith as his sister-in-law. She knew him as naturally courteous and quite capable of saying one thing and thinking another. But she believed him. She remembered the sympathy in his eyes when he had been with her and Aethelwulf. He was a man of the world; he knew the nature of her marriage to Aethelwulf. He would not hold it against her, entering another so soon after his death.

Redi she hardly knew. He had only stayed with them briefly at Steyning. She recognised that he was at that awkward age on the cusp of manhood when a boy becomes aware of sexual feelings and often reacts with embarrassment when confronted with a young woman. The whole idea of marriage still seemed rather peculiar to him but he showed no hostility to the thought of Blade and Judith marrying. She sensed that he was still very much under the influence of his brothers, particularly Berti, and would follow their lead. Apart from his brief visit to Steyning, Redi had not seen his father for a long time and did not seem particularly distressed by his death.

That left Elsa and Alfred in Mercia. Of Elsa, she knew nothing beyond what Aethelwulf had told her, which was little enough. But she was queen of another kingdom and her interests would be concentrated there. Alfred was a different matter. He was the one she knew best, and also the one who had been closest to his father. Had he not shared the long journey to and from Rome with him?

She was secretly relieved that the family had decided it was not worth Alfred returning from his stay in Mercia for the funeral. Her wedding to Blade, six months after the funeral, had been a quiet occasion. The Church's disapproval had seen to that, although Bishop Ealhstan had been willing enough to preside over it. But everyone knew he was much more a warrior than a churchman. It had seemed a little odd seeing his scarred hands raised in blessing over Blade and her. As if they were going into a battle. Well, maybe they were. But the smallness and privacy of the ceremony was reason enough not to call Alfred back for it either.

But after a year, Blade had decided that it was time for Alfred to come back. He could not remain in Mercia forever. He was a prince of Wessex and should be learning his duties here. Leave him in Mercia much longer at that age and he might start seeing himself as a Mercian. And although, as expected, Berti had agreed to Blade's overlordship as the elder brother and ruler of the senior kingdom, the fact remained that there were two princes in the east and only one in the west. Added to which, Blade was aware there was still some discontent over his marriage to Judith. With Alfred at his court and under his influence, there would be less scope for any malcontents to seek to build him up as an alternative ruler. Blade had not seen Alfred for a number of years – he remembered him as a docile, sickly child. The sort that might be easily influenced. If so, then he, Blade, should be the person doing the influencing. Redi's deferral to Berti at the funeral had not escaped his notice. Alfred's support could be useful.

At least, until he and Judith had a son, and time had accustomed the Church and others to their marriage.

He explained all this to Judith and was surprised when she expressed some concerns at having Alfred back with them.

'I thought you liked him.'

'I do like him. I. . . I just don't know what he'll think of me. The last time he saw me, I was married to his father. Your father.'

Blade took her in his arms. He knew it was something difficult he had made her do. 'You don't regret marrying me, do you?'

'No, of course not.' She smiled up at him. 'It's just hard to explain to others sometimes.'

'I don't see why. Just some stupid rule of the Church's. Your being married to my father was a lot more unnatural than your being married to me.'

It was true. The happiness she had felt growing within her was evidence enough of that. In Blade's arms, she felt safe and cared for. She loved his natural candour, so different from that of her father or Aethelwulf. With him, things were easy. But away from him, she still had moments of feeling guilty and fearful of retribution. Perhaps she was just unused to being happy? The feelings had been receding over the past months, but the prospect of Alfred's return brought them back.

'Berti and Redi were happy for us to be married, weren't they?' Blade continued.

'I know, but Alfred is different.'

'How?' Blade frowned. He realised that she knew his brother better than he did. 'Is it the Church?' Alfred had been a lot in the company of churchmen. He'd spent over a year with Swithun on the first pilgrimage to Rome. And then going again with his father. There had been a time when they'd thought he was destined for the priesthood. Maybe he still was?

'No, I don't think so,' Judith replied. 'But he's a deep thinker. And he worries over things that he doesn't think are right. Berti and Redi. . . I got the impression that they weren't concerned because they didn't think it affected them. Alfred's not like that.'

'It doesn't affect Alfred any more than it affects Berti and Redi,' Blade responded.

'No,' Judith admitted. It was hard to explain. Particularly to someone who wanted people to be as straightforward as he was.

'You will persuade him. If you don't think it's wrong, then he won't.'

He had more confidence in her powers of persuasion than she did. But she didn't think it wrong, whatever the Church might say. Not for one moment had she regretted her decision to stay in Wessex and marry Blade. The long-expected invasion of her father's kingdom by her uncle Ludwig had taken place and her father had been forced to flee to the south. Francia was in a state of civil war. She had concerns for her brothers and sisters, but not for her father. He would survive; he always did. But the thought of being shackled to him, or to one of his elderly supporters, at such a time made her shudder. At least her father's troubles meant that he was in no position to object to her marriage.

So, that only left Alfred. Who was just a boy. So, why should she fear his disapproval? Because he knew her before she was married to anyone?

A servant came in to announce Alfred's arrival. She had decided to see him alone to begin with. In the presence of his brother, Alfred was unlikely to express an opinion. With her, he might.

'Show him in, Maeve.'

He had grown since she had last seen him, but was still slight and small for his age. Not very robust. He took after Berti more than Blade, prone to illnesses and with a weary look already in his eyes. But intelligence also; he had seen a great deal for one so young.

She embraced him warmly. 'I'm so pleased to see you again, Alfred.'

He looked at her with his intelligent green eyes. Like a cat, she thought. Something unreadable in them.

'You look happy,' he said.

'I'm happier than I was,' she said. She knew that with Alfred she would have to be totally honest. He would see through anything else.

'Happier than with my father.'

'I didn't want to marry your father, Alfred. You know that. He was a great deal older than me. My life with him was not easy.'

'Were you happy when he died?'

'No,' she said, shocked. 'How can you say that? Oh. You've heard stories.'

'Swithun tells me that they're lies.'

'Of course they're lies!' she said with an explosion of anger. 'How could you even think they might be true? Do you not know me at all?'

His eyes did flinch a little at that. She knew her anger could scare men. It came and went like a lick of fire.

'You were unhappy with my father,' Alfred said. Not by way of an explanation, but as a fact from which he intended to progress. There was something stolid about him, she thought. A typical Englishman. One who would not be hurried in his reasoning.

'I was not always unhappy with your father,' she said. 'I've told you I didn't want to marry him, which you knew. But women often have to marry men they don't want to, particularly royal women. We have to learn to adjust our expectations of life.'

'Everyone has to do that,' he said, a flicker of interest showing in his eyes. She remembered he liked his philosophy.

'Well, there you are, then,' she said. 'We are no different. And your father was a good man, Alfred. I knew that. Some women are married to cruel, uncaring and violent men. Your father was none of those things.'

'But you were arguing with him when he died.'

'When he collapsed, yes.' She recognised this as another of his stepping stone facts. 'Shall I tell you why?'

'Yes.'

She did so, leaving little out. She told him of the pagan ship, the expedition with Osric to Wulfstan, Blade's appearance, Aethelwulf's reaction, Osric's dismissal, the pagan attack on Steyning, Osric's reappearance and her subsequent argument with Aethelwulf, at which he collapsed. Alfred listened intently, saying nothing.

'I see,' he said when she had finished.

'Do you?' she asked urgently. 'Do you understand why I was arguing with him?'

'I think so, yes.' He frowned. 'He was wrong to dismiss Osric. It was because he thought he was working for my brother, wasn't it?'

'Yes.'

'Was he?'

'Not when he arranged for me to meet with Wulfstan, no. Osric was as surprised as me when your brother turned up to that meeting. He was afraid.'

'And yet my father was right to be suspicious, wasn't he?' Alfred continued.

Judith blushed. 'No he wasn't,' she replied sharply. 'I had nothing to do with your brother before your father's death.'

'But now you're married to him.'

'I know what some people say but I don't feel the need to apologise for our marriage. I was going home, but your brother persuaded me to stay. He said he loved me. I won't deny that the idea of being married to someone who said they loved me was attractive. My father would not require that of any future suitor he might choose. Had he arranged with your father for me to marry your brother in the first place, instead of your father, my marriage to your brother would have been seen as perfectly natural.'

Alfred pursed his lips. He recognised faulty reasoning when he heard it. 'But that didn't happen,' he responded. 'And, as you said, we have to adjust our expectations to life as it is.'

'We do, but there are occasions – rare enough, indeed – when the possibility of an alternative life presents itself. If one accepts such a possibility, it usually involves upsetting or offending those who expect us to continue with the life we've been given. I accepted such a possibility and, sure enough, it has upset and offended some. But I don't regret my decision, or feel the need to apologise for trying to be happy. Happier than I was.'

She didn't learn whether he accepted her right to be happy or not because Blade chose that moment to enter the room. Had he been unwilling to leave them alone too long? He greeted his younger brother heartily. More heartily than he had ever done before. Judith watched as Alfred dutifully replied to his brother's questions about Mercia and his journey back. It was hard to know what he was thinking. But she had said what she intended. It was the only explanation she could give him.

*

Alfred settled into life in the royal manor near Winchester. It wasn't so different to life in Tamworth. Blade was often away, travelling to different parts of Wessex. Alfred had barely known him as a child; his brother was already a young man at the time of his birth and often away from their father's court. He had been nervous of meeting him again, given his father's hostility. Would he prove to be as evil and treacherous as his father said he was? Elsa had told him not to worry and he soon felt she was right. Blade had been very welcoming and imposed less restrictions on him than his father, or even Burgred, had done. It did feel a little odd at first, being treated as a valued family member by someone who had hardly noticed him before, but maybe that was the difference which being a king made to someone. Was he being disloyal to his father in accepting a position at Blade's court? It was an awkward thought. He had not felt the crushing sense of loss at his father's death as he had at that of his mother. He still thought of his mother from time to time, whereas his father already felt remote. A figure from the past, whose dislike of Blade seemed increasingly irrelevant.

Adjusting to his new life was made easier by a new friend. Aethelnoth, the son of Ealdorman Eanwulf of Somerset, was spending time at the king's court. As he was about the same age as Alfred and of a cheerful disposition, the two quickly became close friends. They attended military training and joined in the king's hunts together.

On one such hunt, Alfred's horse had taken fright and bolted away from the rest. Aethelnoth urged his horse after him. By the time Alfred's horse had calmed down, they were both a long way from the rest of the hunt and in country neither of them recognised. Attempts to return the way they had come only resulted in their becoming even more unsure of where they were. A steep hill rose before them.

'Let's go up there,' Aethelnoth suggested. 'We'll be able to see where we are from the top.'

As they crested the top of the hill, they saw a settlement of a few tents grouped around a couple of huts, surrounded by a simple fence. Such settlements were not unusual, often housing traders or drovers for a day or two as they passed through the country or rested from their travels. What was unusual was the queue of people waiting outside one of the huts. Locals, suspicious of strangers, normally avoided such places, but in the queue outside the hut, Alfred recognised a couple of workers from the king's estate. Curiosity made him edge his horse forwards.

'Shouldn't we avoid it?' suggested Aethelnoth.

But Alfred had recognised someone else walking across the compound.

'Colman!' he exclaimed in surprise.

Colman stopped, recognised his former pupil and came out of the compound to greet them.

'My lord prince,' he said. 'It does my heart good to see you again.'

'But what are you doing here?' Alfred asked in puzzlement. 'What is this place?'

'This is the temporary residence of Guernir and his followers. Gifted us by Ealdorman Wulfstan.'

'Who is Guernir?'

'Guernir is a holy man and a healer, my lord prince. He lived as a hermit on the east coast until forced out by pagan attacks. He has been making his way westwards to find a new place to settle. In the course of his journeying, he has attracted followers, mostly other religious men whose houses have been destroyed by the pagans. We have become a community.'

'But your house wasn't destroyed, Colman. Steyning still exists; I visited it on my way back here.'

'Steyning still exists,' Colman acknowledged. 'But with you gone and your father dead, there was nothing for me to do there any more.'

'But they would have kept you on, surely? You could have moved with Princess Judith when she married my brother.'

'I chose not to do so,' Colman said softly.

Alfred didn't ask why. The Church had opposed the marriage and Colman was a churchman. A number of people had left the king's service following the marriage, either in obedience to the Church or because of loyalty to Aethelwulf. And when people leave the king's service, they have to go somewhere.

'You could have gone to another estate,' Alfred continued. 'There are plenty of nobles' children who need teaching. Or Berti could have found a place for you.' A number of Aethelwulf's men had joined Berti in the east. Steyning was, after all, part of the eastern kingdom.

'He did offer to take me,' Colman replied. 'But I felt I had done enough teaching of the young. And then I met Guernir and realised that the Lord was calling me to a different life.'

'What sort of life?' Alfred asked, looking over to the queue outside the hut. 'What are those people over there waiting for?'

'Healing,' Colman replied. 'Healing of the body or healing of the spirit – it is all the same. Guernir has the gift of healing. That is what we are engaged in. This country needs a great deal of healing.'

'Do you heal people?' Alfred asked. Colman had certainly changed from the conventional tutor he remembered.

'I preach repentance of sins. We all do that. It is the first step to healing.'

Aethelnoth shifted nervously on his horse. 'We ought to be getting back, Alfred,' he said. 'I think I can see the route we should follow from here.'

'Come and meet Guernir first,' Colman said. 'It would be good for you to meet him. Then maybe you might understand.'

'Isn't he busy?' Alfred asked, looking over at the queue, which was still long.

'He will make time to see you,' Colman replied. 'Those people will be willing to wait.'

'All right, then' said Alfred and followed Colman through the fence gate and into the compound, where he and Aethelnoth dismounted. A young man in a religious habit came up to take charge of their horses.

'This is Neot,' Colman said, introducing him. 'I believe you are related.'

Alfred looked at the young man with surprise. He had a handsome, healthy face, which did look vaguely familiar.

'We have met a couple of times before, my lord prince,' Neot said with a smile. 'When you were much younger. My father is a distant cousin of yours. They shared the same name.'

'Ealdorman Aethelwulf of Berkshire,' said Alfred, remembering.

Neot nodded. He had a nice smile. There was a deep-seated happiness in his eyes which Alfred had seen before in religious men.

'But you were a soldier,' Alfred said. He remembered last hearing of Neot as a fighter out east under Blade's command. That had been before his second journey to Rome.

'I was a soldier,' Neot replied. ' But I was wounded and cared for by the monks at Minster Priory. By the time I recovered, I had decided to become one of their number.'

'And now you are a follower of Guernir,' said Alfred wonderingly.

'Indeed I am. And blessed to be one.'

'Was Minster Priory destroyed by the pagans?'

'It was. And so were the next two religious houses we moved to. So now we keep moving. For as long as the Lord God sees fit.'

'Do you miss your priory?'

'Not at all. It is good to be moving amongst the people. We are following Our Saviour's example.'

While Alfred was speaking with Neot, Colman had gone to the hut where Guernir was. He came back with news that Guernir would see them now. They left Neot with the horses and walked over to the hut.

Inside the hut, it took their eyes a few moments to adjust to the dimness. At the far end, where the light was better, a man was seated in a large chair. An opening let in some daylight and in addition a few rushlights were burning on a table before him. They walked up to the man and Colman introduced them.

'My lord Guernir, this is Prince Alfred and his companion, Aethelnoth..'

Seen close to, Guernir was a powerfully-built man of middle age. His hair was still black and his face commanding. He gestured to Alfred, 'Come closer, my lord prince.'

Feeling nervous, Alfred did so. He had a sudden memory of approaching another holy man in very different surroundings, the pope in Rome. He had expected to be struck dead then. He didn't know what to expect here but there was a dark, brooding power in Guernir's smoky eyes as they scrutinised him. And just as the pope had done, Guernir placed a hand on his head. But he did not pronounce any blessing and Alfred felt no influx of the Holy Spirit. Instead, he felt something deep within him rise to the surface, as though summoned by Guernir's hand.

Guernir kept his hand on Alfred's head for several moments, saying nothing but breathing in deeply. Eventually, he lifted his hand and Alfred suddenly felt very tired.

Although Guernir's eyes were upon him, they didn't seem to be observing him. They were withdrawn, focused on some inner vision.

'You are weak, my lord prince,' he said in a soft voice. 'You have been ill many times, and you will continue to suffer illness for the rest of your life. The illness comes from God, and like St Paul, you must learn to accept it. Your spirit is strong and will see you through. And you will be a light for others.' His eyes went to one of the rushlights on the table before him. He lifted it up so that it was close to both their faces. 'This is what you will be,' he continued. 'A weak, flickering light against the darkness. Always at risk of being extinguished but, somehow, surviving. It will be sufficient.'

The audience was at an end. Guernir placed the rushlight back on the table and leaned back in his chair, closing his eyes. Colman ushered them out of the hut. Alfred felt so tired he could hardly stand. He remembered saying goodbye to Colman, and Neot coming up with their horses and helping him up onto his. He remembered nothing of the journey back. Aethelnoth took the lead and his horse was fortunately sure-footed.

*

Easter was late that year and the weather fine. At King Aethelwulf's court, the Holy Week leading up to Easter had been a time of penance and prayer, whatever the weather. At his son's court, established for the present near Winchester, a more relaxed attitude prevailed. There were still church services to attend every day, but between the services, it was not thought a sin to enjoy the spring sunshine, the blossom and flowers, the lambs and stirrings of other new life.

Princess Judith had resumed her habit of riding out with her companions, which she had been forced to abandon at Steyning. Osric was often too busy to accompany her these days, as her husband had entrusted him with ever more military responsibilities.

But other members of the king's guard were available to take his place and protect the queen, as she noted with pleasure she was increasingly being referred to, by the court at least. Blade's refusal to consider her a queen had changed now that she was married to him.

She occasionally asked Alfred and his new friend Aethelnoth to accompany her on her rides, mindful of her husband's desire to ensure his loyalty to them. And Aethelnoth's father was one of Blade's most important supporters. But she would have been happy to have had them along without such considerations. She had always liked Alfred. His intellectual curiosity gave her an opportunity to show off some of the learning she had acquired at her father's court, and his knowledge of that court meant that she was able to share news of it with him, as someone who knew many of the people involved. Her father was now back at Verberie, having resisted his brother's invasion, a sign to Judith that the wheel of fortune was beginning to turn in her favour at last.

It was certainly easier for her to be in the role of elder sister than mother to Alfred. He was about the age of her brother, Louis. She used to tease Louis, and with her brightening mood felt a desire to tease Alfred. He was such a serious boy, and had come back from Mercia with a certain reserve, which intrigued her. She decided, at least for the purpose of teasing him, that he was hiding something important, which it was her duty to find out. When Aethelnoth let slip the fact of their visit to Guernir, it was ideal for her purposes and she compelled him to provide her with all the details.

'So that's it!' she exclaimed, beaming at an embarrassed Alfred. 'You're a man of destiny. You're going to save us all.'

Alfred said nothing. He was still not sure what to make of Guernir's predictions. Part of him was inclined to dismiss them as the sort of cheap fortune-telling which pedlars sometimes engaged in to ease a few coins from the gullible. But why should Guernir feel it worth his while to engage in such trickery? Colman and Neot believed in him, and neither of them were fools. And he had certainly felt something at Guernir's words, although more fear than anything else. He didn't want to suffer from illness for the rest of his life. He thought he was getting stronger.

With such uncertain impressions, it was his habit to leave them be and not try and find explanations for them. He was annoyed with Aethelnoth for mentioning the episode and exposing it to Judith's teasing.

'Would he tell my fortune?' she continued. 'Do you think I could be important, too?'

'He didn't say I was important.'

'A light in the darkness sounds important to me.'

Alfred shrugged. He would never get the better of Judith in debate. She was too quick-witted for him. Sometimes silence was the best response.

But Judith's wish to have her fortune told did find a sort of fulfilment a few days later on Good Friday. It was a solemn day for everyone. Even at Blade's court, the occasion of the Saviour's suffering and death was a time of penance and fasting. A large contingent, headed by the king and queen, with Alfred, Aethelnoth and many others in attendance, rode out from the palace in the morning to attend mass at the cathedral.

The roads were thronged with people making their way to Winchester. Most were on foot and stepped to one side to let the royal party pass with varying shows of deference. Good Friday was a day which could prompt unruly behaviour. Not for the first time, Blade wondered about the social value of Christianity as he rode. Of all Osburh's children, he was the one who had most inherited her feelings for the old religion. Gods could die in the old religion but their deaths were woven into the community's fabric and strengthened it. But the death of this eastern peasant god, who was killed for challenging authority, could lead the poor or weak-minded to believe they had the right, or even a duty, to do the same. And to promise everlasting glory for such behaviour was asking for trouble. A warrior who died in battle fighting for his king deserved glory; a peasant who died preaching rebellion did not.

Not that the Church didn't do some good work. There was a place for the practice of the virtues praised by Christianity. On the whole, Blade approved of monasteries, particularly their caring of the poor and sick. And for those who couldn't fight, the Church was a respectable alternative profession. But the Church had a structure – its bishops and abbots demanded an obedience more absolute than that commanded by any king. So, the potentially rebellious nature of the Christian message was normally kept under control by responsible men. But there were times when it could show itself, particularly at times of heightened emotion. And Good Friday, with its tale of injustice and death, was often such a time.

They entered the town and rode up past the market place. Blade's eyes caught sight of a group gathered around the market cross. A man in a religious habit was standing by the cross. He must have been preaching to the group gathered around him. A wandering preacher, a type particularly disliked by Blade.

'What are you doing here?' he asked roughly. 'Disperse before I make you. If you want to hear religion, then go to church like decent people.'

He could see a dull resistance in the eyes of some of the group. None of them made to move. Blade felt a surge of anger. What had this wretched preacher been saying to them?

'Seize that man,' he said to Osric, pointing to the preacher. 'I will enquire of the bishop what his status is and whether he is authorised to preach to the common people.'

Osric rode forward. The preacher did not move but a few of the group surged around Osric's horse, as though to prevent him.

'Begone, damn you!' shouted Osric, as his horse started at the press of bodies around it. 'Did you not hear your king?'

'He is enchanted by a witch!' a voice cried out suddenly from the group.

Judith's face turned pale. Blade swore.

'Who dares call the queen a witch?' he cried in fury. He turned to other soldiers around him. 'Seize them all! Lock them in the castle. I will have an answer for this treason.'

Easter Sunday and the resurrection of the Lord. A time of rejoicing. But there was no sign of rejoicing in the faces of the two men seated in the bishop's study after the great morning mass. Blade was still incensed at the insult to his queen and Swithun's expression was blank, although his eyes were wary.

'I'm told none of them have confessed to the treason,' Blade said leaning forward and staring into the old bishop's eyes. 'That in itself is a sign of collusion. I shall have them all tortured. And if still no one confesses, they will be executed.'

'You could do that,' Swithun responded carefully. 'What does the queen say?'

'The queen? What concern is it of hers?'

'She was the one called a witch.'

'Yes, but the insult was directed at me. It affects my authority.'

'Even so, it affects her also,' Swithun said. 'You know what our people's view of queens are, don't you, my lord king? They have been opposed to them ever since the days of Queen Eadburh. Because, rightly or wrongly, they associate that queen with a time of cruelty and oppression. If you torture and kill people for insulting your queen, then those who remain will assume that it was done at her bidding. They will see her as another Eadburh. And hate her just as much.'

'I knew you would find a way to defend them!' Blade exclaimed in disgust.

'I am not defending them, my lord king. I am just pointing out that there will be consequences if you punish them as you suggest. And that those consequences will affect the queen most of all.'

Blade glared at Swithun but said nothing.

'What does the queen say?' Swithun repeated gently.

'She wants me to forget it,' Blade admitted. 'But how can I? A woman might forgive an insult, maybe even a churchman might, but how can a king? I'll be seen as weak.'

'No one who knows you would think you weak, my lord king. And I'm not suggesting that you forgive the insult. These men have already been kept in prison for three days, not knowing if they are to live or die. They are poor, uneducated men. If you decide that they have been punished enough, then they will be grateful to you. And to the queen. They will see that she is very different to their grandfathers' account of Queen Eadburh.'

'They are not all uneducated men,' Blade responded. 'There was a preacher among them. One of your profession,' he looked accusingly at Swithun.

'Yes,' Swithun admitted. The preacher, being subject to Church law, had been transferred to the bishop's prison.

'Who is he?' Blade demanded.

'He is a monk, lately of Reculver Abbey. One of the number who have accompanied the hermit Guernir on his travel westward following the sacking of their abbeys by pagans.'

'Then what was he doing preaching at Winchester market cross?'

'The monks have authority to preach repentance of sins. He swears that is all he was doing and that he made no mention of yourself or the queen in his preaching.'

'And you believe him?'

'I see no reason not to. These monks have preached in a number of towns in the course of their journeying with Guernir. I have never heard of any of them preaching other than repentance of sins. Are there witnesses who say differently?'

'No one is saying anything. Yet.'

Swithun said nothing, waiting.

'Why is this Guernir here, anyway?' Blade continued. 'He's a long way from his home.'

'He has no home, my lord king. None of them do.'

'Even so, why has he come into our kingdom? Was there nowhere in the east that he could settle? Or did my brother decide he wasn't going to have him stay there to cause trouble?'

'The lord Wulfstan offered the community land at Cheesefoot on which to settle.'

'The lord Wulfstan should never have made such an offer without my permission.'

'No, my lord king.'

'Why did he?'

'Guernir is reported to have the gift of healing,' Swithun said gently.

Blade grunted. Wulfstan was ill and not expected to survive. It was probably just old age but people at such times tend to think of themselves and their souls before their loyalty to the king. Another example of the pernicious effect of Christianity's emphasis on another world. He had never trusted Wulfstan – he was too close to his father. As was Swithun. Well, it wouldn't be long before the older generation would die out and he could replace them with his own men. He had already decided that Osric would be the new ealdorman of Hampshire. How long before he could appoint a new bishop of Winchester.? Swithun was too powerful and highly regarded to be removed. But his face was lined and his shoulders stooped. It probably wouldn't be that long before he was rid of his father's great friend. In the meantime, he would have to tolerate him for the sake of the kingdom. Winchester had always been lukewarm in its support for Blade, as opposed to further west where Bishop Ealhstan's rule prevailed.

'Any gift of land requires the king's ratification, and I'm not going to ratify Wulfstan's unauthorised gift,' Blade decided. 'I don't want those people at Cheesefoot. It's clear that they will be a source of trouble. They already have been.'

'Where will they go?' Swithun asked.

'Monks should be in a monastery, not under the rule of some wandering hermit. Glastonbury Abbey is looking for more monks. They can go there.' Glastonbury was safely within Ealhstan's domain.

'And Guernir?'

'He can become a monk. And if they won't have him at Glastonbury then he can go and be a hermit somewhere further west. He can live with the Britons, as far as I'm concerned. The name sounds British – I expect that's where he came from originally.'

'The people will be sorry to see him go,' Swithun observed mildly.

'You will tell them not to put their faith in wandering holy men,' Blade responded sharply. 'The Church should not be encouraging such people. They feed on superstitions.'

'And Wulfstan?'

'Wulfstan is fortunate that I do not strip him of his lands for disobedience. If he lives much longer, I may yet do so. You may convey my displeasure to him in what terms you see fit in view of his health. It is well he has not left any sons. His lands will be forfeit after his death.'

Swithun winced inwardly. He had done his best to deflect the king's anger from thoughts of torture and execution but it had found a different outlet. Well, Guernir and Wulfstan would be better able to bear the punishment. As the king said, it was well that Wulfstan had not left any sons. And his daughter was safely married long ago. But he needed to ensure that the punishment was truly deflected while the king was before him.

'The monk I am holding,' he said. 'He may join his brothers in Glastonbury?' A question phrased to invite the answer yes.

'I suppose so,' Blade replied. 'But his authority to preach repentance is withdrawn. And that applies to all of them. They can stay in their camp until we move them to Glastonbury. I don't want them wandering around Winchester stirring up more trouble.'

'And you'll release the others?' It was a risk, but he needed to try.

Blade flushed. 'Why should I negotiate with you?' he snapped. 'It wouldn't surprise me if you were behind what they said.'

'I have the greatest respect for the queen, my lord king.'

'And yet you refused to marry us.'

Yes, that would never be forgiven him. Blade's eyes burned with resentment. But the marriage was clearly uncanonical. He had received a letter form the pope expressly forbidding him to celebrate it. A letter he had never told Blade about.

'I am subject to a higher authority,' he said. He had to say something.

'Higher than your king?'

'In the marriage service, even a king stands before God. A bishop certainly does.'

'So, you condemn my marriage, and therefore the queen.'

'I condemn nothing and no one, my lord king. I am but a poor servant of God.'

'The bishop of Sherborne is a servant of God also. He saw no contradiction between that and presiding over our marriage.'

'I cannot answer for another bishop.'

'No, you're just a poor servant,' Blade responded bitterly. 'How convenient. You can't be held responsible for your actions, even though they encourage the people to think badly of their queen.'

'I have never encouraged the people to think badly of the queen, my lord king.'

'You may not put it into words, but your actions speak, my lord bishop. Why pretend? Do you think I don't know you have always been an enemy of mine?'

Swithun flushed. 'I have never been your enemy, my lord king.'

'You are my father's man; you always were.'

'I was your father's man, yes. While he was alive.'

'And my father did not want me to become king.'

'I was one of those who persuaded him to agree to your inheritance. You will recall that I was present at your meeting with him when he returned from his pilgrimage.'

'He had no option but to agree by then.'

'Even so, he took some persuading, my lord king.'

Blade was silent for a while, considering. 'And the queen?' he said, eventually.

'What's done is done,' Swithun replied. 'You may not believe me, but I have the greatest respect for the queen. And I am confident that in time the people will come to share that respect. But it will take time. The issue of the marriage. . .' he paused for the right words, 'is not so important outside of the Church. There have been greater irregularities in the affairs of some of our most revered kings. It is the memory of Eadburh – the myth of Eadburh I should say – which is what's behind the people's attitude. Our queen can overcome that. And teach this country that it has nothing to fear from a just queen.'

'You are a clever man,' Blade said reluctantly.

Swithun swept the compliment away with a slight gesture of his hand. 'I'm not important,' he said. 'But I would not want you to think that I am your enemy; I have never been that.'

Blade nodded. 'All right. You may have your way. I will tell the captain of the castle to release the others. But their names will be noted, my lord bishop. And if they involve themselves in any more trouble, they can expect no mercy from me.'

'I am grateful to you, my lord king. I will ensure that they are made aware of their position. And of the queen's mercy.'

Blade gave a slight smile. 'Yes,' he agreed. 'It's more her mercy than mine. Very well. That just leaves Guernir and his stray monks. The sooner they are gone from here, the better. I will write to the abbot of Glastonbury to tell him to expect them. And you can tell them to pack up and be ready to leave in a week's time.'

Swithun nodded. 'Will you provide them with guides? I'm not sure if they will know the land between here and Glastonbury.'

'I will do more than that, my lord bishop. I will provide them with an armed escort. Headed by myself.'

'You're leaving Winchester?'

'For the time being. The court is moving to Sherborne. You can educate the people in my absence. Osric will be staying to assist you.'

13. The Flux

Judith had mixed feelings about the court's move to Sherborne. She had become used to Winchester and the people there. Although she knew that Blade resented Swithun, in particular his refusal to officiate at their marriage, she had found the bishop of Winchester a reassuring presence. Unlike her husband, she did not suspect him of plotting against them. He was a holy man, unconcerned with his own personal power. The fact that he had remained loyal to Aethelwulf, even after his effective deposition, showed that.

To her, at least. But not to her husband. She realised that, even though Aethelwulf had been dead for over a year, Blade was still engaged in a bitter struggle with his father. There are certain enmities which death does not end. Just as the father's suspicions of the son had poisoned her life with him and probably hastened his death, so the son's resentment of his father's attitude and attempts to disinherit him still had the power to anger him. In most things, she found her second husband to be cheerful and easy-tempered. But anything which related to his father had the power to arouse a demon within him. She knew enough of the rivalries within her own family not to be surprised by this. She even wondered whether the spark for Blade's love for her, which he had pressed so insistently, was not a desire to possess what had once been his father's. Certainly, Aethelwulf was a continuing presence in their relationship, even though they were both careful to avoid mentioning him as much as possible.

Well, people got married for worse reasons than to score off their fathers. And there was an undoubted warmth and generosity to Blade's love which had nothing to do with resentment. She hoped that with time and increased security the baleful effect of his father's memory would lessen. And for that reason, she welcomed the move to Sherborne. The kings of Wessex travelled around their kingdom more than her father did around his. But even so, they had favourite residences, and Winchester had been Aethelwulf's town. Many of its leading men had been close to him, not just its bishop. Blade's support had always been stronger in the west of the kingdom. He was happier and more confident here. The men who had been first to support him against his father, Bishop Ealhstan of Sherborne and Ealdorman Eanwulf of Somerset, were men of the west.

She had become aware that there was a major division between west and east in the old kingdom of Wessex. A large forest called Selwood separated the two halves of the kingdom. East of Selwood was not so unlike her home in Francia. She recognised similar behaviour and ambitions amongst its people. But west of Selwood felt wilder and more foreign to her. It had been frontier land for centuries. The border with the remaining British lands now lay far to the west of Sherborne, but its people still retained many of the characteristics of their ancestors. They were fierce fighters when roused, self-reliant and suspicious of authority. She soon found that the Church's condemnation of her marriage meant a lot less to the people west of Selwood than it did to those to the east. West of Selwood, people might approve of the Church for some of the functions it performed, but they were less inclined to pay much attention to its strictures, unless they happened to accord with opinions they already held. Old superstitions abounded. Ealhstan was highly popular as their bishop. He was a man everyone respected – a fighter who would defend your home, had done so on many occasions, but who didn't lecture you on how to live your life.

And yet, although Judith felt her marriage was largely accepted west of Selwood, she was less certain of how she was regarded. There was a certain narrowness and self-satisfaction to the ealdormen and thanes of the west. They were less used to having foreigners amongst them and she found their manners to her often harsh and dismissive. The further west a man came from, the worse his manners seemed to be. After a visit to Sherborne from the ealdorman of Devon, a man who belched frequently and paid her no more attention than he would a serving maid, she complained to Blade, only to be told that he was a good man and she would get used to him. It was a long way from her father's court at Verberie.

To begin with after their move west, Blade had been busy travelling around, visiting his supporters. The English expected to see their king. Not just ealdormen but churchmen and even common thanes required visiting.

'Why do you go all that way?' she asked her husband after he had returned, tired and dusty after a long trip to the west of Devon, close to the British border. 'Why don't you send someone to represent you?' That's what her father would have done.

'They need to see me,' he replied. 'Loyalty is personal.'

'Well, tell them to come here.'

'They might not come.'

'You could command them.'

'I could,' Blade acknowledged. 'But it's not a good idea to do that too often. It breeds resentment. Besides, I get a better picture of how things are if I go there. It's important to make sure our borders are secure.'

'Just so long as I'm not expected to go with you.'

'Henlac said he missed you,' Blade replied with a grin. Henlac was the belching ealdorman.

She shuddered. 'I still haven't recovered from his visit.'

Blade took her fondly in his arms. 'What a rare jewel you are for such a rough land as ours.'

'Do you like what I've done here?' she asked hesitantly. She had been spending her time organising improvements to the royal manor, setting builders to work on a large extension to the main building.

'It's a palace,' he replied.

'It's not that yet,' she said. 'But it will be. You need to live somewhere imposing. Then your people will be happy to come to you.'

'Ah, that's the reason, is it?'

'I miss you when you're away,' she said simply. 'I wish you'd stay here more often.'

He kissed her on the lips. 'Build me a palace and I'll stay here the whole time, sitting on a throne and issuing commands, like your father.'

'You don't have to go that far.'

It was a hot summer that year and as the temperature soared, Blade did go travelling less. Hot weather was a mixed blessing; it often brought pestilence in its wake. Outbreaks of the flux were reported from around the country. Many places that the king might have expected to visit were stricken. So, he spent more time in the cool pavilion which Judith had built for him, receiving reports and behaving more as she thought a king should do.

His most frequent visitor was Bishop Ealhstan, whose palace was only a few miles away from the royal manor and, to Judith's irritation, considerably grander. Ealhstan was Blade's earliest supporter and most trusted advisor. He was growing old but was still formidable. While Swithun was shrinking with age, Ealhstan was becoming larger. Always bulky, he was now massive, his great head sunk onto enormous shoulders. He moved ponderously, the heat increasing his normal air of brooding irritation. But his mind was as sharp as ever, and his sources of information as to everything happening west of Selwood unrivalled.

'How are the new monks settling in at Glastonbury?' Blade asked when they were settled in the pavilion and Ealhstan had been provided with a tankard of cooling ale. He had just returned from a visit to the abbey.

'Most of them well enough,' Ealhstan replied, after taking a long draught of ale. 'They're used to the life. A few squabbles but that's normal in the cloistered life. The abbot is impressed by your kinsman, Neot. He's talking about appointing him the next sacristan. Whether that's because of his holiness or his father, I don't know. As we know, the abbot is not immune to worldly considerations.'

'Neot's father doesn't hold land in Somerset,' Blade responded drily.

'I'm sure the abbot would stretch a point and accept land in Berkshire. He could set up a daughter house there.'

'I don't want Guernir going anywhere near Berkshire,' Blade replied. 'He caused enough trouble in Hampshire.'

'And now he's causing it in Somerset.'

'What?'

'Guernir is the one person who hasn't settled into the abbey. It was to be expected. He's not a monk. These hermits have difficulties living with other people. It's why they become hermits.'

'It didn't stop him gathering a lot of people around him in Hampshire.'

'He was in charge, then. That makes a difference. People have to respect your space. Very different if you're just a monk subject to a vow of obedience to the abbot.'

'I sent him to Glastonbury so he would be subject to a vow of obedience to the abbot.'

'Yes, but that depends on the abbot as well. And the abbot doesn't want him.'

'Why not?'

'He says it's because he doesn't have the calling to be a monk. But in truth it's because Guernir is of more use to him outside the abbey.'

'How?'

Ealhstan took another long draught of ale and was silent for a while. 'You know he's meant to have the gift of healing?' he said at length.

'I was told so, yes. Is it true?'

'The people think so. There's a lot of flux in Somerset. Especially in the marshes south of Glastonbury. They're scared. Normally, they would go to the abbey for healing. But the abbot doesn't want them there, spreading the contagion amongst his monks. Much better for him that they go to Guernir for healing.'

'So, where is Guernir now?'

'The abbot's established him in a hermitage on the edge of the marshes. On land belonging to Ealdorman Eanwulf.'

'And Eanwulf has agreed?'

'No, Eanwulf is furious. He has numerous disputes with the abbot over land. You'll recall we ruled in his favour once when your father was on his pilgrimage. The abbot has never forgiven him for that. So, he tries to eat away at his landholdings by various means. This is the latest attempt.'

'But if the land belongs to Eanwulf . . .'

'The abbot disputes his title. This is his way of showing it. And given Guernir's popularity amongst the people, there's nothing Eanwulf can do about it. He'd have a rebellion on his hands if he tried to evict him.'

'This abbot is a nuisance,' said Blade. 'Did we make a mistake in sending Guernir to him?'

'We had to send him somewhere. And the abbot has taken care of all his followers. It's only Guernir that is the problem. And he was likely to be a problem wherever we sent him. He has an inconvenient combination of qualities.'

'So, what should we do? Leave him where he is and hope he dies of the flux?'

'Thereby providing the abbot with a saint for his abbey? No, I don't think we can do that. If the abbot is allowed to get away with this, he'll be looking to establish hermits on all the lands he's disputing with Eanwulf. And Eanwulf is angry enough about this one. He says that the more the abbey encroaches on his lands, the more difficulty he has in raising fighting men. It's not just a question of land; it's a question of allegiance. If Guernir survives and adds to his reputation as a healer, he'll be attracting more followers, just as he did in the east. But they won't be dispossessed monks this time; they'll be Eanwulf's tenants. Which would give the abbot a perfect excuse to claim more of Eanwulf's land.'

'So, we need to move Guernir on again?'

'That's what Eanwulf is asking for. But it won't be easy. He's popular with the people. A number are already calling him a saint.'

'He practised healing in Hampshire. That didn't stop us moving him on from there. And we sent him to become a monk in Glastonbury. If the abbot hasn't accepted him as that, then we have the right to move him again. And the sooner the better, before he becomes too established.'

Ealhstan nodded. 'I think you're right. But where should we move him? He's likely to cause similar problems wherever he goes.'

'As far west as possible. He'd be better on the border. It has less grasping churchmen available to make use of him. These rich abbots tend to be less keen on living close to the border where they might be raided by the British. The land is poorer there also. It supports less men. And if he joins the British, so much the better. They can have the problem of dealing with him.'

'He could take people with him.'

'If we're going to have trouble, I'd rather it was on the border. We're used to keeping an eye on things there. And it will be easier to isolate.'

Ealhstan nodded again. 'Very good. But we will need a lot of men to move him. There could be resistance amongst the people.'

'Should we see the abbot first, do you think? If he orders the move, it might make it easier.'

'Will he order it?'

'We should be able to persuade him, don't you think? If, as you say, we turn up with a lot of men.'

Ealhstan gave a wintry smile. 'I soon won't have any more to teach you, my lord king.'

Elmund, Abbot of Glastonbury, was not fond of visits from his bishop. He had hoped after Ealhstan's last visit that it would be some time before he had to host him again. An ascetic, whose life was devoted to the Church, Elmund found the presence of the old warrior Bishop of Sherborne, who made no secret of his fondness for the pleasures of the table and of women, irksome. Such a man should never have been appointed a bishop. It made a mockery of the Church. That he should be in a position of authority over Elmund's abbey was galling in the extreme. Not only did he set a terrible example for the more impressionable monks, but his conversation teemed with a low, worldly cunning, which he pretended to assume the abbot shared. After a visit from Ealhstan, Elmund felt impelled to submerge himself in ice-cold water to wash away the stain.

And now the man was back again, only a matter of weeks after his last visit. And worse, he had brought with him his protégé, the scandalous king who had married his own step-mother and defiled his father's bed. Elmund had been fond of Aetheluwlf, a man of pious generosity to the Church. He had tried to ensure he had as little as possible to do with his rebellious son. But now the son had descended upon him with a large body of rough soldiers, all of whom needed housing and feeding. And one could hardly turn a king away, however disreputable. He determined, however, to keep the king and his men away from the rest of the abbey as much as possible. Fortunately, neither the king nor Ealhstan showed any interest in inspecting the abbey or dining in the refectory. The abbot hosted them in his private quarters to minimise the contagion of their presence. The only other member of the abbey the abbot invited to this secluded dinner was Neot, who was a kinsman of the king and immune to worldly splendour, having experienced and rejected it.

Blade and Ealhstan drank heavily at the dinner. The abbot kept a good cellar for his guests and Blade felt the need to take away the taste of an oppressive feeling which had possessed him since arriving at the abbey. He had never liked churches or religious buildings. They reminded him too much of his childhood and being forced by his father to sit through long services and listen to frightening sermons about the punishments awaiting sinners in hell. Delivered by churchmen just like this sour-faced abbot sitting opposite, sipping occasionally from his cup of water.

The abbot became even more sour-faced when he learnt the reason for their visit.

'Guernir is doing good work where he is,' he said.

'He is disruptive,' Ealhstan replied. 'He was not sent to you to be set up as a hermit on land belonging to Earl Eanwulf.'

Elmund scowled. 'The abbey has a claim to that land.'

'Then go to court. Bring a case before the king. Don't try and take it by stealth.'

'By stealth?' Elmund looked as though his vow of obedience was being tested to the utmost. 'You judge others too much by yourself, my lord bishop.'

'I am sure he is doing good,' Blade interjected, feeling a little odd playing the peacemaker between churchmen.

'But he can do good elsewhere. On land which is not subject to dispute.'

'I have no other land so suitable for him.'

'The king will provide for him,' Ealhstan said. 'Outside your domain.'

Elmund consented eventually with bad grace. He had no real choice. Blade had expected to find some amusement from the evening in watching Ealhstan confront the abbot and expose his hypocrisy. But he hadn't; it had been rather depressing. Partly due to his feeling of oppression caused by the religious surroundings – the wine had only succeeded in masking that for a while. But more due to the presence of Neot. The young man was about his age – they had played together as children a few times. Back then, he had been lively and mischievous. Now, he was quiet and contained, only speaking when directed by the abbot, and then in a soft, deferential tone. His eyes were what troubled Blade. Mostly, he kept them modestly on the table before him. But when he lifted them to answer a question about Guernir, Blade saw both distress and concern in them. And somehow he knew that the distress and concern were not for Guernir, but for him. Why should Neot look at him like that? Reproach he could understand, but distress and concern?

He slept badly that night. It had been good wine but his stomach seemed intent on retaining it as vinegar. He should not have come here; he could have left the abbot to Ealhstan. He fell into a feverish dream in which a monstrous vision of his father appeared, accompanied by dancing demons such as he had seen in a manuscript illustration of the Last Judgment. He woke suddenly in a sweat, his pulse racing and stomach churning. He forced himself out of bed and walked shakily to the window. There was a flask of water on a low table beside the window. He took a swig to rid himself of the acrid taste in his throat and calm his stomach. But it had the opposite effect, causing him to gag as the fire in his stomach shot upwards. He stuck his head out of the window and vomited onto the ground outside. Afterwards, he felt slightly better and remained with his head outside the window, letting the night air cool his burning face for a few moments. Returning to his bed, he felt weak and feverish. He lay on his back and stared up into the darkness. His stomach was calmer now, but still not right. It was a temporary respite. Something was happening within him. Was it the flux? He pushed the idea aside angrily. It was just this place, and having to deal with sour-faced churchmen. The sooner he got away from them, the better. He would leave Guernir to Ealhstan and return straightaway to Sherborne and Judith. He would feel better there.

He had to get up twice more in the night to go to the latrine. When his servant came to his room in the morning, he saw immediately the look of concern on his face.

'Are you ill, my lord king?'

'No. Yes.' The thought of having breakfast with the abbot decided him. 'I don't feel well. Something I ate, I think.' The abbey's food was plain. 'Send Bishop Ealhstan to me.'

Ealhstan's face when he saw him was grim. He suspects the flux, Blade thought.

'I don't feel well,' Blade said. 'It's this place. I must get away. Can you tell the abbot I had an urgent summons?'

Ealhstan nodded. 'Do you feel able to ride?'

'Yes, I'll be all right when I'm in the open air. It's not serious, but I have to get back to Sherborne. I'll need to leave you to deal with Guernir.'

Ealhstan's eyes lingered on his face. 'I'll move him, my lord king,' he said. 'Do you want your guard to assemble?'

'Yes. At once.' He was conscious of a strained quality to his voice.

Ealhstan hesitated. 'Maybe you should stay here, my lord king? Until you feel better. We can ensure you're not disturbed. It's a long ride to Sherborne.'

'No!' The thought of remaining a moment longer than he had to at the abbey filled him with something approaching panic. 'I must get away. At once, do you hear?'

'Very well. I'll tell your guard to assemble.'

Somehow, with his servant's help, he got dressed. He was conscious of fever again and a pain building in his stomach. He went to the latrine again but it made no difference to the pain in his stomach. He would feel better when he was on a horse and moving. He stumbled outside into the courtyard where his guard was already mounted, waiting for him. He saw they had a wagon converted into a litter also.

His captain, Alden, dismounted and came forward to him. 'My lord, we can take you in the litter.'

'Help me up onto my horse, damn you. I don't need that cart.'

Up on his horse, he felt a wave of nausea pass through him. He gritted his teeth and urged the animal forward, his guard falling into place around him.

He had expected to feel better away from the abbey confines; he didn't. The movement of riding stoked the fire in his bowels and after only a couple of miles, he was forced to dismount and squat down by a bush to relieve himself. He looked down at the liquid discharge his excrement had become. Yes, there was blood there. Alden avoided his eye when helping him back onto his horse.

After that, he remembered little. Fever coursed through him and he was only fitfully aware of his surroundings. The fire in his bowels continued but he no longer had the energy to address it. Let it burn. He was vaguely aware of a moisture in his saddle but amongst all the symptoms afflicting him, it meant little. Flat country this, he thought. Scorched by the summer. Where there was water for most months of the year was now only dust.

At some point, he fell off his horse. Any pain he felt was quickly absorbed into all his other pain. He was aware of being lifted into the litter. Alden must have arranged for it to follow them at a distance. He was too weak to protest any more. Speaking had become difficult. He lay in the litter and stared up at the canvas covering rocking over him. Everything had contracted. The world was now a stabbing pain which pierced him anew with every jolt in the road, and the canvas rocking above him. Is this how death came? He began to see the dancing demons of his dream moving in time with the canvas. Not accompanied by his father this time. One should be grateful for small mercies.

The litter had stopped. They had arrived somewhere. Was it Sherborne? He had no idea how long they had been travelling. If he could see Judith, he would be all right.

The stretcher on which he was lying was being lifted up and out of the litter. No, it wasn't Sherborne. It was somewhere isolated and depressing. A small stone building on a parched stretch of flatland, similar to that they had been riding though when he fell off his horse. Only distinguished by being situated beside a few scrubby birch trees.

He was carried into the building and laid on a large table in its main room. He saw a strong, bearded face looking down at him and recognised Guernir, the hermit and healer. This must be his hermitage, to which Ealhstan would be arriving later in the day in order to evict him. Blade closed his eyes. He no longer felt in control of his destiny.

Alden took Guernir away to a corner of the room. 'Can you save him?' he asked softly.

Guernir looked at him with his dark eyes. 'No,' he replied. 'He is doomed to die.'

Alden felt a spurt of anger at the man's certainty. 'How can you tell? He is the king. You have healed others.'

'Those I have healed were meant to be healed. This man isn't; I have known it for some time.'

Alden wondered if he had put a curse on his master. He felt a sudden chill. This hermit was dangerous. 'He is the king,' he repeated dully.

'He is the king,' Guernir agreed. 'And we can make him more comfortable than he is. I will pray for him, as I have prayed for the others. But I tell you now so you know, I will not be able to save him.'

'How can you if you don't believe you can?' Alden responded angrily.

'I believe what I am told. And I am told that this man will die.'

'And who has told you that?'

'The same power that has healed others.'

'If he dies, you will answer for his death.'

Guernir nodded. 'I thought you would say that at some time,' he said. 'It makes no difference. If I was able to, I would save him. I would not withhold the gift of healing to anyone. But it is not at my command. I am only an instrument. I will pray for him, I will pray over him. But you should send for his confessor. A man should be made ready for death, a king most of all.'

'Do what you can,' Alden said. 'Who knows what faith can achieve?' But he went to the side of the room to where members of the guard were looking on awkwardly and gave them orders to ride back to the abbey at full speed and return with Bishop Ealhstan.

Less than two hours later, Ealhstan's large presence filled the room. In that time, Guernir had arranged for Blade's body to be stripped of its soiled clothing, his body washed and wrapped in linen and blankets. Blade's fevered distress seemed to ease a little as Guernir stretched his large arms out over him and began to pray. But Alden, looking on, felt that was a sign he was growing weaker rather than calmer. His breathing was becoming harsh and impersonal.

On arrival, Ealhstan went over to the table on which Blade's stretcher was lying and stared down at him for a long time. Blade's eyelids flickered open, gave a brief sign of recognition and closed again. When Ealhstan turned away from the table, Alden saw a glitter of moisture on his rough cheek.

'Have you sent for the queen?' Ealhstan asked him abruptly.

'No, I. . .'

'Do so immediately. Send your guard. When the news gets out, she may not be safe.'

'Do you think. . ?' Alden stopped, quelled by the look on Ealhstan's face.

'The rest of you, get out,' said Ealhstan. 'And take that man with you,' he said, indicating Guernir. 'He's doing no good with his incantations.'

'Are you the king's confessor?' Guernir responded, the only person not overawed by Ealhstan.

'What is that to you? Yes, I'm his confessor, and I'm his friend also, which is more than you are. Prepare yourself for a journey. You're not staying here to stir up more trouble.'

Everyone trooped out of the hermitage, leaving Ealhstan alone with the stricken king. Alden positioned himself in the doorway, both as a guard and to observe what was going on within. Ealhstan had drawn up a chair so he could sit beside Blade. He took the crucifix hanging at one end of the room and placed it in Blade's hands, lying on his stomach. Alden, watching on, was surprised by the gentleness of Ealhstan's actions. But then he was no stranger to death. He had seen many men die, and no doubt eased their passing on occasion also. Already, the room seemed more peaceful.

Ealhstan bent his head forward and spoke quietly to Blade. Was he inviting confession? Telling him that he was going to die? If Blade responded, Alden didn't hear anything. It was sacrilege to eavesdrop on confession anyway. He took a step back from the doorway.

Ealhstan's head remained bent forwards for quite some time before he suddenly straightened up and went over to the saddle-bags he had brought in with him. From these he extracted a small golden pyx and flask of wine. The pyx was of the type used by churchmen to transport the communion host to the sick and dying. Ealhstan had come prepared; and now he was preparing the king. Other people crowded around Alden in the doorway to watch the brief ceremony. Guernir was not among them. Alden noticed that he was kneeling on the ground some distance away, oblivious to the soldiers around him.

After administering the bread and wine to the king, Ealhstan remained for a while standing, before turning and noticing the heads peering through the doorway. He didn't seem surprised or angry; just sad.

'Bring that hermit in,' he said. 'He can do no harm now.'

Alden fetched Guernir, who took one look at the body on the stretcher and then knelt down beside it. He started reciting the prayers for the dying. Ealhstan let him continue but did not join him. Instead, he resumed his seat by Blade's head, placed one of his enormous hands over the other's, which still had the crucifix between them, and remained there silent. Alden went back to his station by the doorway.

Towards noon, the abbot arrived with some of his monks, including Neot. Ealhstan allowed them into the room and shortly afterwards stood up, took one last long look at Blade and left the room, leaving the abbot to take his place.

'It could be some time,' he said to Alden once outside. 'With luck, or God's grace,' he corrected himself, 'he'll last until his wife gets here. She can get rid of the monks. Until then,' he shrugged, 'they're more used to praying for souls than I am.'

'There is no hope, then?'

'He's young and strong, but,' Ealhstan shook his head, 'I've never seen anyone recover from the flux when it's as far advanced as that. It's come on very quickly, but it can do that.'

'He looks calm.'

'He's a brave man. He's not scared of death. He will go to it calmly. Especially with a lot of monks watching him.'

'What should we do?'

'Send for his brother. We need a king here. Until Aethelberht is acclaimed and anointed his successor, there's scope for all sorts of mischief. He's a long way away. We can't afford to wait.'

'Anything else?'

'Yes. We should summon Osric from Hampshire. We need more troops here. Osric is loyal to the family. I'm less certain of some of the others.'

Blade died at nightfall. Judith arrived at the hermitage two hours later to find the monks discussing transportation of her husband's dead body back to their abbey. In rage and shock at her sudden bereavement, she drove them all out of the hermitage and remained there alone, weeping beside the body for the rest of the night. At dawn, Ealhstan entered the room to find her collapsed over Blade's head, having lost consciousness. But she revived at the touch of his hand on her shoulder and turned to stare up at him with red-rimmed eyes.

'Did they poison him?' she asked.

'No. If they had, I'd be dead, too. It was the flux. It can kill you if you're unlucky. He was unlucky.'

'He was unlucky,' Judith agreed sadly, her gaze returning to Blade's blank face. She stroked one of his cold cheeks. 'And just when we were beginning to see a way through.'

Her voice tailed off. Ealhstan allowed her a few moments for her thoughts before saying what he had come to say.

'We need to move him. He can't stay here.'

'What?' Judith looked at him in confusion, not understanding.

'He can't stay here,' Ealhstan repeated. 'There's no protection. There's a crowd already outside. He's the king.'

'He was the king,' Judith corrected him. 'And I was the queen. Now no more.'

'Even more reason to move him.'

'I'm not having him go to the abbey for those monks to gloat over.'

'It would be the best place for him at the moment. It's nearby, and they're used to caring for the dead.'

'I will take him back to Sherborne. That is where he should be buried.'

'Sherborne is not safe for you at present.'

'What do you mean?' Judith looked at him in astonishment before realisation began to dawn. 'You think I will be blamed for his death? I was nowhere near him. If anyone killed him, it was the monks.'

'He was unlucky,' Ealhstan repeated. 'And many of our people are superstitious. It will not take much for them to attribute his bad luck to you.'

Remembering the reaction to Aethelwulf's death, Judith knew that he was right. She had been blamed for that. And now another of her husbands had died, less than two years after the previous one. These were primitive people. And she was a foreigner, a stranger, no longer protected by the king. Added to which, was the Church's disapproval of her marriage to Blade. It would indeed not take much to persuade many that his death had been due to a curse, brought down upon him by her. Perhaps it had been? Perhaps she was accursed? She felt a wave of helplessness pass through her.

'What should do?' she asked Ealhstan.

'We must wait for the new king. He will have the authority to provide for your husband's burial and protect you. I have already sent for him. Until he arrives, you should remain here. We have men to protect you here. I can't guarantee your safety in Sherborne.'

'You are bishop of Sherborne.'

'That might not prevent some ambitious ealdorman deciding he could benefit from custody of the late king's widow.'

Judith shuddered. 'I have no choice, then.'

'You have no choice,' Ealhstan agreed.

*

Judith had last seen Berti at Aethelwulf's funeral. He had aged considerably since then. She remembered his lightness of spirit which, together with a certain physical frailty, made him seem young to her. But years of repelling the incursions of pagans into the eastern kingdom had taken their toll and there was a fixed, weary expression in his eyes when he greeted her which had not been there before. And his frailty no longer had anything of the boyish about it. His cheeks were starting to become sunken and his thinness more extreme. But these changes had given an added dignity to his presence. Everyone accepted him as king. He looked like someone who was bearing his people's troubles. The fire of his spirit showed more readily in his wasting body.

With Berti was the other brother, Redi, who had put on a spurt of growth since she had last seen him and now towered over his elder brother. He had yet to fill out and his height gave him a gawky appearance. Not yet a man, but not a boy either. A downy stubble was beginning to show on his cheeks and he wore the rough clothes of a common soldier. He had seen combat out in the east. That would be important to him. She was careful to show him every respect, noting that Berti made a point of including him in conversations and asking his opinion. If Berti was to take over the western kingdom, then the practice of the House of Wessex would be for Redi to succeed him as ruler in the east. He was young for the position but he had been out east for the past few years and the ealdormen and thanes there knew him. If the kingdom in its current form was to survive, then Redi had an important part to play. A part which could prove even more important in the future, given Berti's uncertain health and lack of an heir.

And then there was Alfred. He was still a boy, but a boy who had seen a great deal. His green eyes were watchful, but gave little away. What must he be thinking? Mother, father and now two brothers dead before he had reached the age of independence. Whose charge would he be now? Which surviving brother would assume responsibility for his future? She suspected Alfred might prefer Berti, but Redi might have more need of him. The eastern kingdom had become the blooding ground for princes. That was where the pagan threat was greatest. The House of Wessex could no longer afford to have any of its princes unskilled in fighting. The days when Alfred might have become a priest or scholar were gone forever. She felt a pang of concern for him. He was the one she had known the longest, the one who had known her before she was married. They had shared some experiences which even Blade had not been a party to.

Alfred was not strong. Would he even survive the rigours of combat and command? They looked to be eating Berti from within.

But what could she do? If what Ealhstan had said was right, she was no longer in a position to protect herself, let alone anyone else. Before Berti's arrival, when they had transported Blade's body back to the abbey at Glastonbury, someone had thrown stones at her carriage. After that, she had decided to accept Ealhstan's offer of protection. Soldiers were posted outside the door of her room and even below her window. In the middle of one night, she was woken by the sound of a struggle outside her window. When she asked Ealhstan about it the following day, he simply shrugged, 'Just foolishness. Nothing to be concerned about,' which she did not find reassuring. During the day, she noticed a number of faces staring at her with barely-disguised hostility when they thought she wasn't looking. No one would meet her eye. Glances dropped and heads turned away. Even Ealhstan paid her little attention, except as a burden who needed guarding. He told her to keep to her room and, after experiencing the suspicion and hostility to which she was subject outside it, she decided to take his advice.

Berti's arrival had improved her situation. He did not blame her for his brother's death. He greeted her sympathetically and immediately agreed that Blade's body should be taken to Sherborne for burial. Keeping her by his side, he showed her every attention, forcing the rest of the court to do the same. She rode back to Sherborne with Berti in his carriage and this time no one threw stones.

Even so, she knew that her time at Wessex had come to an end. She had not chosen to come here, or to remain after Aethelwulf's death. Others had decided that for her, just as others had now decided she should leave. When Berti arrived, he told her that he had received a letter from her father. He had not said any more – conversations as to her future should await the burial of her past. But then there was no need to say what was in the letter. Her father would be demanding her return. She had failed in two marriages, the second entered into without his consent and in defiance of Church teachings. She could not be permitted to remain and make another bad, rebellious decision.

Judith knew what awaited her at her father's court – punishment for her disobedience, followed by another marriage to whichever count would have her, if indeed any would after two such ill-fated precursors. Her market value had depreciated considerably. If no one was prepared to take her then she would be locked away in some convent, an embarrassment to be forgotten.

Blade had rescued her from having to return to her father once. If Blade had survived and they had had children, then she might have been accepted in time as his queen. But now? Surely, two deaths in three years were more than a coincidence? In the subdued, helpless mood which had afflicted her since her conversation with Ealhstan, she felt as though she might indeed deserve punishment. Even if Berti invited her to remain, she would refuse. But, for all his politeness, Berti would want her gone. He was a very different character to Blade. She meant little to him. And he would not wish to begin his reign by antagonising the West Frankish king.

They buried Blade at a large ceremony in Sherborne, with many ealdormen and thanes in attendance. Among them, the friendly figure of Osric, now ealdorman of Hampshire. At least he would be on her side.

Two days after the funeral, they held the funeral feast, at which Diarmait sang the great poem of Wessex, with a few extra verses added to record Blade's achievements. It was the second time she had heard the poem, the first being at Aethelwulf's funeral. She felt a similar sense of isolation as she had then. It had not become her country. The list of names meant nothing to her. Except the last two, and they caused pain.

A week after the funeral feast, to allow ealdormen and thanes time to arrive from the eastern kingdom, Berti was acclaimed king over all Wessex. He did not appoint Redi as king in the east. He must think him too young. Or he wanted to show that the division between west and east was a thing of the past. Whatever the reason, it was a lot he was taking on himself. Judith looked at his tired face underneath the crown at his coronation and did not envy him. But then Berti had surprised people before with his resilience. He had not been expected to survive to manhood. And he had learned a great deal about men in his time as ruler of the eastern kingdom.

After his coronation, Berti resolved that he would move the court back to Winchester to better rule his united kingdom. There was no legacy of a rivalry with his father to trouble him in the old capital. But before departing, he made time for a private consultation with Judith to discuss her future.

Without saying anything, he handed over her father's letter for her to read. Yes, as expected, a demand for her immediate return. He would send a guard to collect her.

She handed the letter back to him without saying anything.

'What do you want to do?' he asked.

She gave a wry smile. 'When has that ever been of relevance?'

'There's no need for you to return to Francia. At least, not immediately,' he added, a little awkwardly. 'Not if you don't want to.'

'I do want to,' she replied. 'There's nothing for me in Wessex any more. Except the suspicion of being a witch and of poisoning two kings.'

Berti flushed. 'That's stupid,' he said. 'No one believes that.'

'Whether they do or not, I know that I am unwelcome here. I always have been. When your brother was alive, I was willing to endure that for his sake. For our sake,' she corrected herself. 'But now, there is no reason to do so. I should go home. Immediately. Bishop Ealhstan has warned me that my safety cannot be guaranteed in Sherborne.'

'I will protect you.'

'I am grateful to you for that. I feel safe with you; I always have done. I would like to return with your court to Winchester, and for you to arrange my passage to Francia from there. You can tell my father that there is no need for him to send a gang of soldiers to collect me, although I've no doubt they'll be waiting for me when I land.'

Berti looked at her intently for a moment, and then nodded. 'I think that's wise. It's sad, but all of this is sad. You're still young. You have time to start again, away from bad memories.'

'The memory of your brother will always be sweet to me.'

Berti smiled. 'Thank you. I always looked up to him. I never expected to be taking his place.'

'It seems to me that you are ready to do so. Wessex is fortunate in that, my lord king.'

Another autumnal day. She had arrived in autumn; she would leave in autumn. A certain symmetry to that. It was not as windy as when she had arrived. Slight, misty rain, but calm. It was a longer crossing from Hamwic. But she was in no great rush to reach Francia. If it took an extra day, what of it? She would have plenty of time to do nothing from now on.

Berti, Redi and Alfred all came to see her off. The surviving princes of the House of Wessex. Berti because it was his duty, and possibly also to make sure that she had left. Redi to be with Berti. And Alfred because he did not want her to go. The sorrowful look on his face was the one thing which pierced her heart. As soon as he had heard that she was leaving, he had called on her alone.

'Why are you going?' he asked her directly.

'Because your brother is dead, Alfred. And my father wants me back. To marry me off to someone else.' She shouldn't have added that last sentence. Something made her. He leaped on it immediately.

'You can marry me.'

'No, I can't.'

'Why not? Am I not good enough for you? Am I too young?'

She almost smiled; he looked so disappointed.

'It's not that.'

'Well, what then?'

'The Church would not allow it, Alfred.'

'It says in the Bible that a brother can marry his brother's widow. I read it.'

'But not his father's widow.'

'You married Blade.'

'I know,' Judith cried. This boy had a gift for uncovering her inner feelings. It was as if he felt he had an entitlement to know them. Maybe he did? She had confided in him before. Men don't forget that. 'And many people said that was wrong. Some even say that was why he died. That God was angry with him. They blame me for that. Just as some blame me for your father's death. So, there is no way I could marry anyone else in your family, Alfred. I have brought you enough bad luck already.'

Alfred was silent for a while, frowning to himself. 'It wasn't your fault,' he said. 'My father was old. And Blade died of the flux. Plenty of people have died of the flux.'

'God bless you, Alfred,' Judith said, emotional despite her resolve not to be. 'I'm glad that you don't think ill of me. We've been through a lot, you and I.'

He stayed where he was, looking at her. The look of childish disappointment on his face which had almost made her smile was replaced by something more considered.

'What will you do?' he asked her. 'Will you marry again?'

'I expect so. It is a woman's role.'

'Someone your father chooses?'

There was something in the way he looked at her which made her feel hopeful. He admired her; and his admiration was a gift worth having.

'No.' This time she did allow herself to smile. With gratitude. 'It will be someone I choose.'

He nodded in that stolid way of his, which she suddenly sensed would be a comfort to many others as well as herself. Still a boy, but capable of bearing much. And to be relied upon.

'That's as it should be,' he said. 'Well, I had best say goodbye.'

He held out his hand like a good Englishman. She darted forwards and threw her arms around him, kissing him on the lips and hugging him tight. 'Thank you, Alfred,' she said. 'You make me strong. I'll carry you with me wherever I go. You'll help me resist my father. I won't want to let you down.'

He blushed fiercely but a slow, puzzled smile was forming on his face.

'Now go,' she said softly. 'Go with my love and admiration. Our paths are different, but Wessex will always be close to my heart while you are here.' She took a ring from her little finger. 'This was given me by my mother on my confirmation. When I was about the same age as you are now. A young girl with a head full of dreams. Probably the last time I felt free.'

He looked intently at the tiny ring in his palm. 'I don't think I've ever felt free,' he said.

'Then I give you my freedom,' she replied. 'I know it will be safe with you.'

Available on Amazon by the same author:

Fortuna's Favour

Ravenna 522 AD

Manlius Boethius, Roman philosopher and senator, accepts the important political position of Master of Offices under the Gothic king Theoderic, ruler of Italy after the collapse of the western Roman empire. Immediately thrust into a dangerous court of shifting allegiances and competing ambitions, Boethius must try to straddle two worlds – the ordered, classical past, whose values and learning he champions, and the violent, unpredictable present where old certainties have been swept away. The stakes are high and might include his life.

A towering intellect, whose *Consolation of Philosophy,* written when imprisoned and under sentence of death, has been an inspiration for readers as various as Alfred the Great, Queen Elizabeth I and C.S.Lewis, Boethius was also a man trying to protect his family and friends and live an honourable life in a time and place where all can be lost by an unconsidered word or the caprice of the goddess Fortuna. This novel tells his story.

Printed in Great Britain
by Amazon